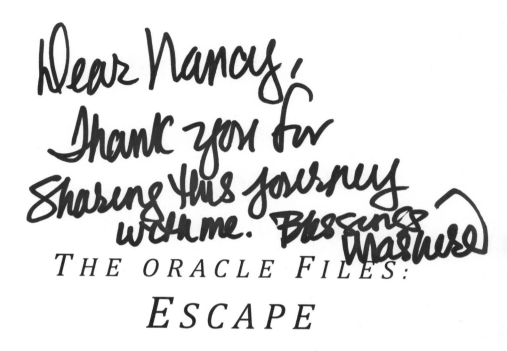

Dear Nancy,
Thank you for
sharing this journey
with me. Blessings
Masheri

THE ORACLE FILES:
ESCAPE

Masheri Chappelle

My Portalstar Publishing

Published in the United States of America
an imprint of
My PortalStar Publishing, LLC
387 Milford Street
Manchester, NH
ISBN: 978-1-7332806-0-0
Cover design by Jeffrey Brown of DPI Graphics

First Edition 2017
Published by Black Rose Writing

Second Edition 2019
Published by My PortalStar Publishing

1 2 3 4 5 6 7 8 9 10

For my daughters Sequoia and Sierra...
and their daughters who have yet to come.

"An eye for an eye will only make the whole world blind."

❧ Mahatma Gandhi ❧

❧THE ROOT❧

1528

THE ORACLE FILES: ESCAPE

He could still see her head. A round dark circle moving through tall green Elephant grasses. The glint of Gambian sun reflecting off of the Portuguese soldier's metal helmet guided him to the direction to which they were running. He prayed his sister, Nyima, would keep her captor in the open grasses.

Like a gazelle he cut through the grasses mined with elephant dung. Tsetse flies joined the chase clinging and pricking his body hungry for his blood. The drum pounding sound of his heart blended with the distant clanging of the armored Portuguese soldiers that chased him. He was thankful their bodies were slowed by the weight of their metal chests and helmeted heads. The laden squad of soldiers moved like a slow herd of water cows. Their heavy armor, tall grasses, and the hot sun allowed him to widen the distance.

His eyes stayed focused on Nyima as she was pulled through the grasses. He gripped his spear. When he got close enough, he would send it into the heart of Nyima's captor. He had no doubt the iron tip of his spear and his perfected throw would be strong enough to go through the soldier's metal chest, but he needed to be closer. He had only one chance to free them both, and escape before the other metal soldiers caught up with them.

Nyima looked back. He caught a glimpse of her eyes. Her head turned back as she continued running forward, faster. Her free arm pointed to the left. She and the soldier disappeared into a dense brush, which immediately slowed them down. He took his last strides through the grasses and then ducked into the dense brush so he could run parallel with them. The coolness of the shade energized him. His eyes quickly adjusted to the shaded darkness, and his ears listened for their movement. In front, to his left, he heard them pushing and fighting their way through the entanglement of thick vegetation.

The pungent stench of lion urine punched his nose. But it wasn't an ordinary lion. It was Jatoo Jinoo, an oversize lion that had terrorized their village since he could remember. Jatoo Jinoo had a distinguishable roar and his urine an unbearable stench. Jatoo Jinoo's spray of urine covered the brush around him forcing him to freeze. His eyes scanned the surrounding brush. He could not see Jatoo Jinoo but he could still hear their movement. Nyima was moving further away.

"Aaaaaeeeeeeeeeiiiiiiiii!" Deemaa! Deemaa!" Nyima's voice cried upward into the canopy of trees. Her voice was punctuated by the grunt, grunt, growling of Jatoo Jinoo. Without thinking he rushed through the jungle with his spear raised in the air. He had only one shot to save Nyima. The grunts of the Jatoo Jinoo grew stronger, which meant it was preparing to attack. As he ran, his foot was pierced by sharp rocks and broken stems and branches.

He saw the silvery chest of the soldier. The soldier's sword was drawn. Nyima was pressed behind the soldier. His eyes spotted a massive bulk of brown fur just feet away. He had only one shot to make, and only one target to choose; Jatoo Jinoo or the soldier. Jatoo Jinoo lowered its body and then pushed off into a leap. His arm drew back and with all of his soul he launched his spear into the air.

Thoomp! Thump! Jatoo Jinoo's speared body fell to the ground within a foot of Nyima and the soldier.

Bang! Craaaaccck!

A single blast from a gun exploded into the air.

"Malachai!" Nyima screamed.

Malachai turned and saw a flash of white light coming at him. It appeared to come from the metal chests of the soldiers. The moment the light reached him his body trembled.

What kind of weapon is this?

Malachai jumped back out of the light and then bolted into the darkness of the jungle to hide until it was safe to come out.

❧ ELIZABETH ❧

CHAPTER 1

The shadow of a large black bird flew over Elizabeth's head and landed on a branch of a bare ash tree. Elizabeth's eyes studied the branch as it bounced gently from the weight of the bird like it was waving goodbye. Black birds always appeared whenever something good happened to her. It was a good omen they would make it to Canada. The wagon jolted making Elizabeth's bottom bang hard against the buckboard seat. Its rear right wheel hit a rock that was camouflaged by a pile of horse manure. Elizabeth gripped the side railing to keep herself on her seat and then twisted her upper body around to eye Belinda and her baby.

"How they doin'?" Simon asked. His eyes did a continuous scan from one side of the road to the other, and then scrutinized the road up ahead.

"Baby sleeping?" Elizabeth softly called back to Belinda.

"He be just fine. Willie is taking to me good," Belinda spoke softly but just loud enough to be heard over the clomping of the horse and the creaking of the buckboard.

It was important for Belinda to get Willie to attach to her breast and keep him quiet like a tick on a dog. The last thing they needed was a crying baby calling attention to their movement. Although Elizabeth wasn't comfortable with the separation, it was a necessary part of their plan.

Elizabeth pulled on the sides of her woolen cape. The cool October night air was scented with the damp fragrance of the surrounding pine trees along Ferry Road. Seeing the vapor of her breath against the moonlit sky warned her that their journey tonight would be a cold one. She wanted to put on her gloves but decided her butter cream skin against her dark grey wool cape needed to be obvious and recognizable.

She wished she had brought the baby's heavier bunting, but Simon said slave babies don't have buntings, just lots of wrappings. Willie needed to play his role like the rest of them.

1846 Bucks County Pennsylvania was crawling with slave bounty hunters who made their living from kidnapping escaped and free Negroes and dragging them down south where they would be returned to their owners for a price or sold into slavery.

Elizabeth's Quaker father, Jonathan Beeson, warned her not to stray from the confines of their community, especially with Simon Carter. Although he was free, Simon was obviously Negro to the eye. But in Elizabeth's eyes, Simon had beautiful dark raisin skin. Seeing sweat glisten on his back or bead up on his forehead was a sensual vision. One she didn't think her Quaker family could ever understand. Simon had rugged good looks and was smart and industrious. He had everything she wanted in a man, and he was everything she was not allowed to be, Negro.

Loving Simon was like loving a part of herself she was forbidden to acknowledge. How could she ever stay away from Simon? She loved raisins. Elizabeth watched Simon's head sway to and fro with the rhythm of the wagon's wheels. In just a few days travel they would reach Canada where she would become Mrs. Simon Carter and then be able to claim Willie officially as her son. There would be no pretending. In Canada she would be able to carry her baby in her own arms.

"Beth, you've got to sit up straight, hold your nose up, and look your part," Simon quietly reminded her. "Remember White women carry themselves in such a way, like they're flowers that grow above the earth."

Elizabeth stiffened her back and lifted her chin. But the jarring banging of the buckboard seat against her tailbone made her hunch slightly to absorb the pits from the rocky and rutted road.

They rounded a bend on Ferry Road as they neared the end of Amos' cornfield. Elizabeth looked over her right shoulder over the tops of the corn stalks to have a final look at plumes of chimney smoke billowing into the night sky. One of those plumes belonged to a place she had called home for the last six and a half years. From across the field, she could see the amber eyes of lit windows glowing back at them. She bolted upright on the board and slapped her hand over her mouth.

"Uh uh, don't look back Beth. That wasn't your home. It was just a stopping station," Simon said softly.

"Simon, there are red lanterns in my windows."

"Red lanterns?" Simon said as his hands gripped the reins. They looked at each other.

"Beth? Who did you tell?" He asked. The whites of his eyes darted back and forth between her and the road.

Guilt pricked at Elizabeth's heart. If it wasn't for Jonathan Beeson, she would have never had the freedom to meet Simon, experience love, and have their son. She owed Jonathan a modicum of respect. The rocking rhythm of the wagon lulled her into a confession.

"I told Emma. I'm sorry. I thought someone should know where I was. But Emma promised not to say a word until five days had passed. I didn't want Poppa to worry...After everything he did for me..." Elizabeth's explanation came to an abrupt halt, as Simon gripped the reins and pulled back.

The silhouette of four men armed with rifles were spread across the road blocking their escape.

"Simon are they real people or am I seeing spirits?"

"I see 'em too," Simon responded with a shaky voice.

"Why we stopping?" Belinda asked in a hushed whisper.

"Belinda hold my baby like you birthed him," Elizabeth warned under her breath.

"Do like we practiced," Simon cautioned through his teeth, and dropped his head. The biggest of the four shadows approached Elizabeth's side of the wagon. Elizabeth sat up, gripped her crocheted linen bag, and smiled nervously.

"Where you headin' Miss?" The large shadow's voice was deep and sounded as though it was loaded with road gravel. The cold vapors of his breath reeked of whiskey.

"I'm going to see my dying father, James Clinton in Clearfield. Why did you stop my wagon?" Elizabeth asked nervously.

"Watcha doin' rollin' through these parts at night with slaves? This is Quaker country. They ain't partial to slave owners."

"I told you I'm en route to see my dying father in Clearfield. These are my father's slaves. I've been travelling since sunup. Perhaps you can tell me if there is an Inn for me and a barn for my slaves along this route. I don't think it's safe for me to stay on the road for much longer."

"Grady, bring the lantern," the large man called over his shoulder.

One of the shadows lowered his rifle and stepped forward. The large man lit the lantern and then swung his finger in the air to direct Grady to examine the back of the wagon.

"I only have two slaves-and their baby," Elizabeth declared.

"It's just like she says boss. There's just a female and her young'un in the back and a couple of satchels. Nothin' else."

"Your slaves got papers?"

"Of course." Her hand shook as she opened her crocheted purse and removed a thick fold of papers. The large man snatched them before she could hand them to him. Simon nonchalantly lifted his chin to signal Elizabeth. She sat up straight and lifted her nose to the night sky. "I think you'll find my papers to your satisfaction," she said with a haughty air.

Grady held the light for the larger man to read through the papers. The light revealed a gun holstered on the large man's right hip. On his waist, on the left, the handle of a smaller pistol was wedged and partially concealed between his pants and belt. Both firearms were easy draws. When the large man was done, he took the lantern and held it up to Elizabeth's face. She thrust her face in his.

"Take that light out of my face and give me my papers back please. I'd like to get to Clearfield before my father dies." Elizabeth hoped her impatient tone would get the large man to obey her. Their horse whinnied and danced for a moment.

"You don't have papers for that baby," The larger man said.

How could she and Simon forget about Willie! Willie was the reason they were making their dangerous escape to Canada. Their own freedom had bewitched them into a false sense of reality. They believed their child was immune to the chains of slavery. Elizabeth's heart pounded in her chest so loud she couldn't hear her own words.

"That's because she had the baby when we got to my Aunt Sally's. When I received word of my father's dire health, I just rushed us out the door. My father's overseer handles all that paperwork. He should have sent the baby's papers the moment I sent word she birthed the baby. I'll have his hide for putting me in this embarrassing inconvenience."

Elizabeth lifted her nose for effect. She felt the grimy man's eyes on her. The cool night air transported the layers of his stench. Stale tobacco, eye-stinging liquor, bitter urine, and possibly weeks of an unwashed body assaulted her nostrils from beneath his long coat. Bile clawed the back of her throat begging to be released. She wanted to slap his face with her vomit, but Willie's whimper reminded her to stay in control. She swallowed hard to push the bitterness of life back down to her stomach.

"Are you going to move your men and let us by, or I shall report you to the law!"

Her mild threat forced him to take a step back. She made him believe she had the upper hand, just like she and Simon practiced. Elizabeth locked eyes with his for extra effect.

"When it comes to slaves, I am the law. No paperwork, no baby. Grady take the baby," the large man ordered and spat over his shoulder.

"No!" She reached for Willie. Without thinking, Simon immediately touched her arm to stop her from breaking character. The moment Simon's hand touched Elizabeth's arm, Grady aimed his rifle at them both.

"Ain't no real White lady worth her breath would ever allow a slave to touch her, not less she be a slave herself," the large man growled. Without warning, he grabbed Elizabeth's right forearm and yanked her down from the wagon.

"Beth!"

"Simon!"

"Grady get the damn baby, and that slave in the back of the wagon. It's pay day!"

"Jimmy, we got us some easy money!" Grady howled.

Bang! Craaaaccck! A shot rang out. Elizabeth's eye caught a fiery flash fly out from the right side of the road. They all froze.

"Let her go!" a man's voice called out. A large group of men stepped out from the cornfield and swarmed onto the road armed with rifles. They quickly surrounded the bounty hunters. "Put down your rifles. Unlike you and your men, we have plenty of bullets to spare." Elizabeth thought she recognized the man's voice, but her ears were still ringing from the first shot.

"You Quakers got no call to be here. These runaways ain't your business," Jimmy growled.

"We're not all peace-loving Quakers," the leader warned. "No fear of using bullets or losing life."

Elizabeth tried to break free, but Jimmy yanked her back like a yo-yo. Jimmy pulled his gun from his holster and placed its cold barrel to her cheek.

"Mister, I'm an especially good shot at night with a full moon. I can see there's just enough space between your eyebrows for one of my bullets. I said put down your rifles and let her go," the voice said menacingly.

Bang - Craaaccccck!

The next shot knocked the hat off Jimmy's head. Elizabeth's eyes focused on the man giving the orders. It was Jonathan Beeson, her father. Her heart pounded wildly in her chest.

"Jimmy, all of them gots revolvers. Best do like he says," Grady whined and then tossed his rifle onto the road.

"It seems Grady is the only one who has received decent schooling and has retained the basic elements of addition and subtraction. The odds of all of you walking away alive are nil. I suggest you all listen to Grady and lay down your guns. You're outnumbered."

The bounty hunters quickly tossed their rifles onto the dirt road. Jimmy lowered his gun with disgust and then tossed it on the road.

"Now let her go."

Jimmy released his grip on Elizabeth.

"Elizabeth, go to your mother," Jonathan calmly instructed as he moved toward Jimmy and kicked Jimmy's gun away from Jimmy's reach. Patricia stepped out onto the road from the cornfield.

Elizabeth would rather endure the harsh cold winters of Canada than run back to Patricia's icy stares and cold heart. Elizabeth broke into a run towards Simon, praying her father would understand. Midway Patricia grabbed her by her wrist.

"Elizabeth let's go! Now!" Patricia gave Elizabeth's right arm another hard tug.

"No, I'm going with Simon."

"Horace, Edmund, and Thomas, ride with Simon, Belinda and the baby in the wagon."

"I'm not leaving without Beth."

"Simon I need you to trust me. Stay on the wagon." Jonathan's voice remained composed. He kept a steady aim on Jimmy.

"Poppa, you're letting them leave without me?" Her father wouldn't look at her. He kept his eye on Jimmy.

"Child, go home with your mother. Simon and your baby will be safe," her father said with the same lilt in his voice he used when he requested her to feed the chickens.

"Poppa, that's my family," Elizabeth cried.

"Difficult times call for selflessness and sacrifices. Save your baby and the man you claim you love and let them go!" Patricia demanded and pulled Elizabeth toward the cornfield.

"You damn abolitionists put on some fine theeeater," Jimmy chuckled. "But I didn't come up North to see no dang show. We all know how the show ends. You peace-loving white worms betray your own kind to protect a bunch of ni..."

The butt of Jonathan's rifle slammed into Jimmy's face, knocking him back. Before Jimmy could spit the blood filling his mouth, Jonathan had the barrel of his rifle pressed against the side of Jimmy's head.

"Your execution is the kind of justice I live for," Jonathan cautioned.

Grady's mouth dropped open.

"I hear tell of only one man who uses those words, and he has a bounty on his head that's worth more than a wagon load of slaves, " Jimmy declared.

"The Black Bird..." Grady gasped.

A night wind rattled the dying leaves on the surrounding trees. Simon's horse snorted. The caw of a crow echoed into the night followed by an eerie stillness. The image of Jimmy's smaller pistol popped in Elizabeth's mind.

"Poppa he has another..."

Jimmy drew his pistol.

Bang craaack!

Something pulled Elizabeth down to the ground. *Pftzzzzz*, a bullet flew over her head. She felt a warm buzzing vibration radiating through her body. She saw an arm pressed against her chest. She wanted to run to Simon and her baby, but she couldn't move. The skin on the arm sparkled and flickered like the golden mica stones she and Emma used to find in the stream just beyond Boynton's farm. Elizabeth's eyes followed the arm up to a shoulder that belonged to a beautiful Native American woman. The light from behind the woman's stunning blue green eyes let Elizabeth know that she was a spirit, a good one.

"You must stay down," she warned.

"Elizabeth, stay down!" her father shouted. Elizabeth looked up to

11

her father and saw him wrestle with Jimmy over his rifle.

Bang! Craaack! Jimmy flew backwards. Thomas Anthony owned the fatal bullet that spared her father from taking human life.

When Elizabeth turned back, the woman was gone. Elizabeth pushed herself up onto her knees to run to Simon. Patricia grabbed her right ankle.

"No! Let them go!"

Elizabeth kicked at Patricia to free herself.

Bang! Bang! Bang! Cracccccck!

"Elizabeth, get down!" Her father screamed.

An explosion of fire from Quaker rifles lit up the road sending Elizabeth back to the ground for cover. Through the blasts of gunfire, she heard her baby wailing, the spastic whinnies of horses, and the quick clacking of their hooves as they did a frantic dance against the rocky road.

Bang! Cracccccck!

Gunfire emerged from a cluster of pine trees, hitting one of her father's men.

"Two more in the pines. Two o'clock!" Thomas Anthony called out.

Bang! Bang! Bang! Bang! Cracccccck!

"They're running! To the pines! To the pines!" Thomas Anthony yelled as he led a charge of men toward the left side of the road.

"Get Simon's wagon out of here!" Jonathan screamed. "Get them out of here!"

Through the midst of the fiery blasts and smoky clouds, Elizabeth felt life leaving her. Horace pulled Simon into the back of the wagon with Belinda and Willie. Edmund climbed up onto the front bench and grabbed the reins. Simon's horse reared up and then the wagon took off.

Bang! Craaaacccck! One final shot echoed from the grove of pine trees, followed by a deathly silence.

"All clear!" Thomas Anthony announced from a distance.

Clouds of smoke and the fiery scent of gunpowder filled the air. Elizabeth clawed the earth as she scrambled up from the ground.

"Simon!" Elizabeth screeched. "Simon!" The air, thick with the smell of pungent sulfur from smoldering guns, cut into her nostrils and raked her throat raw. She tried to run after the wagon, but Patricia restrained her arms.

"They'll be better off without you!" Patricia growled in her ear.

Through the thinning gun smoke Elizabeth saw a fleeting glimpse of her dream. Simon, Belinda, and Willie looked like ghostly shadows floating away. Willie's final wail was trampled into silence by the rumble of Simon's fast-moving wagon that disappeared over the hill on Ferry Road.

"Noooo!" Elizabeth cried. How could you take Simon and Willie away from me? They are my family! They are my life!" Elizabeth screamed in Patricia's face.

"Impudent child, you still have your life!" Patricia blasted in her face. "We can't say the same for these men, who would still be alive if it wasn't for your selfishness. Look at what your so-called love has wrought," Patricia scolded, pointing to the bodies on the road.

Elizabeth saw smoky swirls of gun smoke as it rose from the bullet-riddled bodies of the bounty hunters. Three of her father's men had leg, arm, and shoulder wounds. Their painful moans, the metallic smell of burning flesh, and the nauseating sweet smell of blood heated by fiery bullets grated her emotions and churned her stomach.

"The smoke that you see is nothing more than their hateful spirits rising up to the heavens to ask for forgiveness. God gifts every being with freewill. It was their choice to die today. They chose death over your freedom. We only honored their choice." Her father picked up Jimmy's hat and placed it on Jimmy's bloody chest. His eloquent words offered her a modicum of consolation that was immediately snatched away.

"You cannot release her from her sins!" Patricia protested.

"Mrs. Beeson, love is not a sin. Is that why you fear it so?"

"I fear only the improper love you have for her."

"Wife, you have said enough!" Jonathan's voice shook the leaves on the tree branch above him. The quick burst of vapors from his mouth revealed his labored breathing. In her seven years of living with the Beesons, Elizabeth had never heard her father raise his voice.

"No, I will not be silent! Love is not a romantic potion that makes all the hate in the world go away. The eyes of the world are not ready for Elizabeth and Simon to be husband and wife. Are you so blinded by her wiles you cannot see this massacre? Your gun may be free of their blood, but her selfishness has made us all murderers. This is not our way," Patricia scolded.

"It is the only way. Those men would have killed all of us without taking a breath. Don't worry Mrs. Beeson, these men will receive a proper burial–with scripture."

"Mrs. Beeson, am I not allowed to love or have love because I am the daughter of a slave? Does the color of my skin forbid me the experience of love? Don't you love father? Wouldn't you drive away in the night with him, if there was a law forbidding you to be together?" Elizabeth pleaded through tears.

More men emerged through the cornfield carrying shovels. Two bloodied bodies were carried past Elizabeth and Patricia and were placed respectfully side by side on the edge of the road.

"All I wanted was a child to love," Patricia pushed through her teeth. "She'll kill us all!" Patricia yelled.

Jonathan clutched his heart.

"Poppa!" Elizabeth rushed to him.

"I am fine child." Jonathan replied with winded breath. One of the men stopped to help Jonathan to a nearby tree stump.

"Shall I run for the doctor?" Elizabeth asked. Her fingers pried his neck scarf open to free his throat. His chest wheezed as it filled with air. He pulled Elizabeth in.

"Love is not always easy," he confessed.

The bottom of Patricia's dress flounced in front of them.

"Jonathan Beeson, your weak heart cannot withstand all this turbulence. I'm beg you; send her away, before she kills you."

"Imagine if someone had said the same about you," Jonathan fired back.

The hem of Patricia's dress sprayed his clothes with dirt as she whipped around and disappeared between two rows of corn stalks. Elizabeth heard the snapping of the cornstalks as Patricia angrily plowed her way home. Jonathan pushed himself up off the stump. Elizabeth slipped under his arm to steady him.

"'Hell hath no fury like a woman scorned.' We are about to enter a fire and brimstone that even your devil of a ghost has never seen. Fire and brimstone, fire and brimstone," Jonathan wheezed.

CHAPTER 2

Scrreeep! Scrreeep! Scrreeep!
Malachai pushed the stone along the edge of his spear.
Scrreeep! Scrreeep! Scrreeep!
The soldiers would be looking for him.
Scrreeep! Scrreeep!
He needed to stay prepared.
Scrreeep! Scrreeep!
He ran his finger along the edge of his spear. The edge was razor sharp thin. He put his stone down. Too thin and the edge would crack, rendering his spear ineffective. A good spear sharpened properly, along with a good throw, could send its tip through the belly of a tree.

With one throw his spear went clean through the chest of the Jatoo Jinoo and left its body in a grunting furry heap on the jungle floor before it took its last breath.
Scrreeep! Scrreeep!
He slid the stone over both sides of the tip once more and then touched the point with his finger. The spear's point was sharp enough to go through stone. Malachai stood up and lifted the spear into a launch position. He wished his father could see him, but now he was the only one left. His people and village were gone! The men with the metal chests and hats took everyone away.

He couldn't return to his village. It was bad luck to live in an empty village. Only spirits occupied an empty hut and they would be hungry for his soul. His father would have wanted him to protect the last blood of his people. One day his Mandinka blood would start a new village, but first he had to gather the lost ones

15

and bring them home.

He wasn't quite sure how, but he had seen places in his dreams where his people were traded for gold kodicoroosoos and beaten and whipped like they were wild dogs. He had to stop the killing of his people. His fingers fumbled over his trophy, a necklace he made with Jatoo Jinoo's fangs and claws. He killed Jatoo Jinoo!

Jatoo Jinoo was the lion responsible for killing many of their best warriors. It was an elusive beeyanjo that slipped into their village at night like a ghost and carried off their warriors one by one without a sound. Days, or sometimes weeks later, someone from the village would find remnants of a warrior's adornments strewn amongst his bones.

Right after killing Jatoo Jinoo, Malachai had developed special powers. He was thrust into a mystical world where he could see others living their lives. Malachai believed the lion's breath was still on its teeth and seeped into the pores of his skin empowering him with a magical vision and stealth like prowess that enabled him to enter the world of the pale man and make their earth rumble!

The spirit of Jatoo Jinoo also gave him access to people's minds. He could reach the desperate and weak- minded and bring them to their knees. Or chase away those who would defy him with a blow of his breath. Like Jatoo Jinoo, he marked his victims with his signature scent comprised of his excrement, his urine, and the rotted carcass of Jatoo Jinoo. Malachai found entertainment in smashing dishes, rattling doors, making homes shake with a thunderous stomp of his foot, and breaking into people's minds for absolute domination.

Terrorizing people was his only source of company. The power of Jatoo Jinoo had made him a loner, and he was tired of being alone. He wanted his family, his people, his village, and his life back the way it was. The people of his village were scattered everywhere. He had to reclaim his family first, and then find and rescue the rest of his village one by one. It was an arduous task, but he believed he was born for it. He was a Mandinka warrior who now carried the spirit and the ferocity of Jatoo Jinoo.

Jatoo Jinoo's spiritual powers enabled him to see Mandinka blood running through people's veins. Some wore Mandinka skin while many others hid behind skin that was paler than the metal chest men who took his sister.

The vision of his sister being pulled away evoked a gut-clenching bellow from his mouth.

"Gra gra Graaawwwww!"

He pounded the earth with the butt of his spear. It was time for the next step of his plan. He needed more warriors. He had his eye on a woman in the pale world who seemed more than anxious to do his bidding. Jealousy was an easy emotion to find and control. In the pale world, jealousy was abundant like emotional kindling. He needed only to strike a stone once, and its spark was more than enough to create a fiery conflict.

He was king of his world now and needed to dress his role. He examined the hide of the lion. He had stretched it carefully on a rack he had devised from stiff branches and the sinew from the animal's body. He kept a hot fire going to expedite the drying process. The flesh side that was once dark had dried and lightened considerably, indicating that the hide was almost ready for use.

The hide was to be his robe of accomplishment and would allow him to demand respect from any animal or human that entered his lair. He couldn't wait to try it on. With the edge of his spear he sliced through the sinews that held the hide in place.

Flomp!

The hide fell to the ground. He picked it up and flung it across his back. He quickly tied a few loose sinews together around his neck. The weight of his lion's cape hanging behind him pressed the sinew tie against his throat, strangling him. He quickly retied sinew beneath his left armpit to hold the hide in place.

Malachai lifted his spear and practiced a regal pose. The hide was still heavier than he thought, but a good Mandinka warrior never complained about the weight of his responsibility. He would simply grow into it. However, the weight of the hide on his left shoulder limited his arm movement for battle. He pushed the hide behind him with his elbow and passed his spear back and forth between his hands a few times, and then stopped. He was ready to fight and conquer again. He wanted another fierce animal to add to his totem. One that would add to his powers. With his spear raised

17

in the air, he released a grunting growling challenge to invite competition.

"Gra gra Graaawwwww! Gra gra Graaawwwww!"

A growling snarl answered from a cluster of bushes to his left. A short bark-like growl and then an angry hiss followed. Malachai's eyes scanned the bushes. He recognized that growl and hiss. It belonged to a panther.

The panther was the perfect reflection of a Mandinka warrior. It was dark and handsome. It carried the stealth of an invincible warrior because it couldn't be seen until the last second. Most importantly, it was virile. It possessed powerful sexual energy that could command any female and guarantee her submission.

Another stomach shaking growl rolled out from another section of brush. His eye caught the feral yellow glow of the panther's hungry eyes. He thought of his plan for the pale skinned woman. He could make great use of its sexual power. He pushed his cape behind him and gripped his spear. He was a Mandinka warrior. He commanded the spirit of the Jatoo Jinoo.

"Gra gra Graaawwwww!" Malachai released his roar. He saw a dark blur of black fur rush through a clump of green brush. Malachai raised his spear.

The panther emerged. Its deep yellow eyes seemed to float in the air as its black body slinked towards him. The panther hissed and then bared its sharp dagger-like fangs. Its large right black paw lifted in slow motion and then pressed silently against the ground. Its growl rumbled the earth between them. The panther's rope-thick tail whipped once before it leapt into the air. Malachai anchored the end of his spear into the earth and leaned its razor-sharp point towards the chest of the panther.

"Graaawwwww!"

CHAPTER 3

Elizabeth's eyes popped open. She smelled the cool, sweet scent of pine trees. Someone was standing by her bed. She could feel their eyes on her back. It wasn't Malachai. The spirit of Malachai had haunted her since she was seven. His presence always had a distinct stench.

The murderous scene behind Amos' cornfield from earlier that night flashed in her mind, forcing her to clench her eyes tight. What if the spirits of those bounty hunters were now after her? They all died on Ferry Road that was flanked with fragrant pine trees. What if they wandered through those woods looking for her? As hateful as those bounty hunters were in life, they would certainly be more vengeful from the spirit world.

She opened her left eye to a slit and peeked at her window. With the help of the moonlight, she saw the branches of the buckeye tree just outside of her bedroom window performing its nightly shadow-dance on her adjacent bedroom wall.

She rolled her eye upward and noticed the window frame was still flush with the sill. The pained look in her father's eyes as he nailed her windows shut made it clear he was trying to keep peace. She was certain no one from the outside had gained entry to her room. It was a spirit.

She wanted to call out for her father but knew that by the time he unlocked the lock on her bedroom door, the spirit would be gone. Besides, Patricia would probably forbid him to come to her rescue. She was on her own.

Being a seer of spirits had taken everything from her fourteen-year-old life. Her parents sent Simon and her son away like sacks of laundry, and her best and only friend, Emma, betrayed her. There was no one who could help her. A hot tear rolled down her face and dropped on her

19

pillow. She was tired of crying, and she was tired of spirits entering her life whenever they wanted to taunt and threaten her with their hostile faces and foul stench. She'd had enough!

Her heart thumped hard against her chest. The moonlight through her open curtains provided enough visibility to look around the left side of her bedroom for something she could use as a weapon. Her satchel was still on the floor where Patricia had tossed it. She thought of grabbing one of her shoes to toss at the intruding spirit, but she was still wearing them. She had cried herself to sleep in her clothes. The fireplace! It was at the foot of her bed.

One...two...three... she leapt out of bed and raced to the fireplace to grab the poker. When she turned to swing, she saw the beautiful Native American woman that came to her rescue on Ferry Road. Elizabeth froze. The woman was glowing. Pinholes of light poured through her visible skin, illuminating the woman's face and her vibrant blue-green eyes.

Her beauty was paralyzing. Elizabeth's eyes moved from the woman's startling eyes to her raven black hair, which in the moonlight, was an iridescent silky cascade down the front of her dress. Elizabeth's eyes then jumped to a large pink heart that hung from her neck on a braided gold cord. She looked like a magical creature that only Hans Christian Andersen could create, but she was standing in her bedroom. Elizabeth lowered the fire poker. She found herself being drawn closer to the woman.

"Mitakuye Oyasin," the woman said. Her voice sounded like she was talking under water. "Mitakuye Oyasin," she repeated softly with a smile. "Do you remember me?" the woman asked and then locked her brilliant eyes on Elizabeth's, waiting for recognition.

"You helped me earlier tonight," Elizabeth began.

"Oh..." The glow from her body dimmed with disappointment.

"I am Wakayeja wicahpe, friend of Simon. I brought you his message."

She pointed to a folded piece of paper near the foot of Elizabeth's bed. Elizabeth picked up the note and opened it. Her owl eye marble was inside. The marble was in a pouch Simon made until Willie was old enough to have it. She moved to the window to read the note:

Beth,

Me and wee Willie are waiting at our favorite spot. Hurry! She will help us be together.

With all my love,

Simon

Those were Simon's words. No one else knew that they called their son wee Willie, and no one she knew made the "S" the way Simon did. Wee Willie was their secret code to validate communication. She heard a tap on her window.

"We must go."

Elizabeth heard Wakayeja wicahpe's voice but when she looked where Wakayeja wicahpe was standing just moments ago, she was gone. There was another tap on her window. When she looked out, Wakayeja wicahpe was outside beneath the buckeye tree pointing to Elizabeth's mid-size carpet bag, which was now resting at the base of the tree. Wakayeja wicahpe's hands gestured upward, signaling Elizabeth to lift her window. Elizabeth saw the dull shadows of two bent nails resting on the outside of the windowsill. Her father had nailed her window shut, and after Patricia's inspection, removed them. Love and freedom were waiting for her on Ferry road.

With the marble in her hand, Elizabeth gently lifted her window. A cool blast of crisp October night air slipped beneath her window's frame into her room. As soon as Elizabeth's feet touched down, she snatched her bag and quickly moved to catch up to Wakayeja wicahpe who had proceeded into a wide alley between two houses.

"Wait," Elizabeth whispered loudly. "Genghis Khan." Elizabeth pressed herself against her house and then pointed to a neighboring yard fenced in with chicken wire. The shadow of a large rooster strutting to and fro could be seen patrolling near the fence. "Genghis Khan will chase after us if we try to pass."

"He won't see us." The pink heart around Wakayeja wicahpe's neck

21

released a flash of light that shimmered. It looked like a big wet bubble that was just blown into the air. Elizabeth felt a tickling-type humming in her ears as she passed the rooster's post through the bubble.

"How did you do that?" Elizabeth asked.

"A clear mind. This way!"

They ran through two more backyards which led them to Amos' corn field, which was still filled with its autumn harvest. The thought of the dead men popped in Elizabeth's mind.

"I can't go through Amos' corn field," Elizabeth whimpered.

"Those men are gone. Do not invite them back with your thoughts," Wakayeja wicahpe scolded. "Through the field is quicker." Wakayeja wicahpe disappeared in-between two rows of corn stalks. Elizabeth followed.

The air between the rows of corn held a fragrant, husky sweetness. Elizabeth could taste the corn on her tongue. Initially her elbows brushed and bumped stalks of corn as she passed. Suddenly, she was gliding through the field like Wakayeja wicahpe.

"Catch any corn that falls, it will give you food for your travel."

They plowed through the remainder of the field effortlessly. By the time they exited Elizabeth had stuffed more than a dozen ears in her carpet bag. Elizabeth felt exhilarated as though something was carrying her. She was able to cross the three-acre field in what Poppa would describe as a mouse's minute.

"We must run!"

Wakayeja wicahpe took off down Ferry Road with Elizabeth on her heels. Halfway down the road, the sweet, dewy scent of the corn field faded. A thick night fog rolled in, obscuring Elizabeth's vision. She slowed down to a fast-paced walk. Her heeled shoes pinched her feet. She dropped her corn lumpy carpet bag and leaned on the same stump her father had used hours earlier. She pulled off her left shoe.

"No, don't stop. Keep moving!"

"I can't take another step in these shoes. I want to run to my future husband a free woman. I don't want anything to bind me." Elizabeth quickly removed her right shoe. When she stood up, she felt drained. Something was pulling on her. Her legs felt like heavy sacks of potatoes. A wave of nausea rolled in her stomach. She wanted to retch. "I am not well..."

"You will be well. Simon is waiting for you just up the road, move!"

Elizabeth pushed herself off the stump. She tried to grab her bag, but it felt too heavy. When Elizabeth looked down, she saw a muddy fog rolling around her feet. A stench of rancid meat, manure and what she believed was skunk, attacked her senses-Malachai! Elizabeth's eyes widened with panic.

"Malachai is coming!" Elizabeth shrieked.

"I will make Malachai follow me. Run to Simon!"

Wakayeja wicahpe disappeared into the cornfield. With the help of the moonlit sky, she watched the dank fog pull away from her ankles and roll back into the cornfield after Wakayeja wicahpe.

"Run!" Wakayeja wicahpe's voice rang out from the field.

With the marble in her hand and the clothes on her back, Elizabeth took off down the dirt road in her stocking feet. Elizabeth spotted the dull glow of a lantern a half mile up the road. Hope returned, sparking a burst of energy.

"Simon!" Elizabeth called out. Elizabeth ran with open arms towards love. The soles of her stocking feet absorbed the pain of her rocky road from slavery, to love and freedom. Her lungs were burning and were ready to explode. She focused on Simon's lantern. Simon and Willie gave her purpose for every painful breath she exhaled. She had a family, a real family that wanted her, and loved her. The lantern grew brighter as it moved towards her.

"Beth!" It was Simon's voice. He was close enough that she could see his eyes. He was smiling. Her lungs were on fire as she plodded forward. There was a crack of thunder. A strong wind crossed the cornfield. *Crack crack crunch crack!* Rows of corn stalks were forced down. Something trampled the field.

"It is forbidden!" Malachai's thunderous words rumbled across the cornfield. A gust of his foul, dank, black fog pushed past Elizabeth, knocking her down. His stench left as quickly as it came. Elizabeth opened her eyes. Bits of dirt, husks, and corn silk plastered her face and skin. The light from Simon's lantern had been snuffed out.

Her eyes adjusted quickly and relied upon the light of the moon to find Simon. The silhouette of his body holding a cold lantern moved toward her. She pushed herself up to meet him. Their bodies slammed

23

together as they desperately gripped each other. Their breath mingled for a moment in cold clouds of vapor before vanishing. Simon's lips pecked at her corn silk splattered face and then landed on her lips. She felt the grit of the earth as it pressed between them.

"I love you Simon," Elizabeth said in between gasps of breath.

"We can do this. Beth, we can do this...don't give up on us." Simon begged with his lips pressed against her forehead. "Your father wasn't stopping us. The man who drove my wagon away gave me directions to Canada, with safe houses. Your father came to help us. Willie and Belinda are waiting for us at a safe house. We can still get away and have the life we want-together," Simon pleaded.

Elizabeth rested her face against Simon's chest, eyeing the cornfield. Rows of corn were flattened. The dead bodies of the bounty hunters flashed in her mind.

"Leave Simon and your baby, or we'll be burying them next!"

Tears blurred her vision, but Malachai's attack on the cornfield was painfully clear.

"Look at what all that hate did to Amos' field, flattened it like it was straw."

"I'm not a stalk of corn Beth. I won't let Malachai break me, or us."

"Elizabeth, your selfishness will only get them killed! Is that what you want, a dead baby...a dead baby...a dead baby..."

"Simon, we got to think of Willie," Elizabeth cried into his chest. Simon pulled away and tried to pull her up the road.

"Beth, it's just a little way up the road," Simon coaxed. "We can make it. I'm not going to let you go..." Simon said gripping her hand.

The smoky image of the dead bounty hunters floated towards her.

"Difficult times call for selflessness and sacrifices. Save your baby and the man you love and let them go...let them go...let them go!"

"Give this to Willie," Elizabeth said, extending the marble.

"No. Beth, you give it to him," Simon pleaded.

"Do you want Willie fighting this hatred every day of his life? It's hard enough with the hateful people in this world. You want him to fight Malachai's hateful spirit too? You want to be that selfish?" Elizabeth spat at him.

The snapping of cornstalks and crunching of stone demanded her attention, forcing her to look over her shoulder.

24

"He's coming," Elizabeth cried pointing at the dark fog moving across the flattened cornfield toward them. "Simon, take the marble," Elizabeth demanded slapping the marble in Simon's hand.

"Lord have mercy," Simon muttered. "Beth, we've got to make a run for it." Elizabeth watched Simon grab his stomach and then turn his head to vomit. He spat on the road several times to get the rancid taste from his mouth. Simon grabbed her hand. "I won't let hatred consume you. Run, Beth!"

"No…" Elizabeth said. She dropped on her knees to surrender.

"I'm not leaving you…Our son needs his mother…" Simon grabbed her beneath her arms to drag her up the road. Malachai's, cold, muddy, cloud followed, chilling her bones and heart. The love she felt for Simon and Willie was draining from her. Her arms dangled from her body.

"Stay with me Beth. We need to make that bit of road, and then we're home free. Hatred can't seize you unless you claim it."

Elizabeth looked down and saw the muddy cloud enveloping Simon.

"Difficult times call for selflessness and sacrifices. Save your baby and the man you love and let them go…let them go…let them go!"

"I will always love you Simon. Save our son." Elizabeth leapt from his arms and ran into Malachai's hateful muddy fog. The darkness immediately pricked her skin like porcupine quills. She tried to shriek, but the moment she opened her mouth, Malachai's hate lodged in her throat choking her. She dropped to the ground and surrendered to the hatefulness that had chased her since she was seven.

"Beth!" Simon was over her now. "I'm not going to let you take her. I'm not going to let you take her!" Simon swung frantically at the fog. Simon tried to scoop Elizabeth into his arms. "I love you Beth. Don't you leave me…don't you leave me!"

Elizabeth saw his lips move but couldn't hear Simon's words. She was full of Malachai's hate. Simon pounded her face with his lips. He was trying to kiss her!

"Take your hands off of me!" Elizabeth struggled to break free of his hold.

"Beth, I love you. Don't claim his hatred."

"No!" Elizabeth shouted in his face.

"Don't leave me. Don't leave Willie…We have a son…" Simon cried through tears.

25

"Boy, if you don't let go of me, I'll scream," Elizabeth growled.

"You...nig..."

Simon quickly covered her mouth.

"Don't say it," Simon pleaded.

The sour and bitter taste of hatred puckered the inside of her mouth.

"Beth...I'll let you go...I'll let you go. Just don't kill us," he cried.

His body went limp. They lay on the road their arms and legs still entangled, panting and exhausted from battling the hatred that sought to devour them. Elizabeth looked up at the night sky and saw a blanket of clouds unfurl and obscure the moon. If she had uttered that word, she would have changed them forever to slave and master.

"Simon, you have to let me go, or his hatred will kill us—and Willie. We've got to think of Willie. Take Willie and get far away from me," Elizabeth panted through tears. When she turned to look at Simon, his eyes were aglow with a comforting blue green of Wakayeja wicahpe's loving eyes.

The moon pushed through the clouds. It seemed to be falling from the sky. Wakayeja wicahpe was infusing them both with love. As Simon leaned in to kiss her, a blinding light surged through her body and cleansed her soul of Malachai's hatred. They pulled apart to look into each other's eyes.

"Take Willie and get far away from here, from me," Elizabeth pleaded clutching the marble.

CHAPTER 4

A week later the events of that night were still whispered about. The bodies of the six bounty hunters had been buried in a deep grave where lawmen or animals would never find them. Elizabeth's New Hope Quaker community wanted no trouble. The fallen corn was quickly plucked from Amos' cornfield and the field cleared. Everyone in their community did what they could to preserve peace, but Elizabeth was still seething.

Scraaaaaaaaaape!

The sound of the metal against the wood boards inside the chicken coop reverberated from the scraper to Elizabeth's hand, up her arm, into her shoulder, up her neck and into her head. Every attempt to scrape up chicken poop was a torturous one. Her face still ached from crying.

Sloooomp!

The watered-down hardened poop splattered on top of the slurry pile of excrement in her pail. It was her second pail. A chicken wandered in through the narrow-opened door and looked up at her and then clucked.

"I would think with all of this poop you created; you'd have more eggs to show for it. I'm cleaning. Go outside with the rest of them before I get my roasting pan and turn you into dinner. Go on, shoo!"

The chicken flapped its wings and disappeared through a smaller opening for chickens. Light from the opening flashed the image of Patricia's bony face.

"Witch!"

Elizabeth flung a scraper full of watery poop at the image of Patricia's face, to chase it away.

Scraaaaaaaaaape! Slooomp!

27

Patricia's heart was hard and stubborn like the chicken poop Elizabeth was forced to scrape from the wooden boards. Patricia was the last person she wanted to see. Unfortunately, no matter how hard she tried, she couldn't stop Patricia's cold words from robbing her thoughts.

Scraaaaaaaaaape! Slooomp!

"Fornicating without the blessing of marriage is nothing but a sin before God. Child you are wicked as you are ungrateful!" Patricia declared before she pulled Willie from her arms and placed him in Simon's.

Scraaaaaaaaaaaaaaaaaaape! Slooomp!

Another pasty pile of chicken poop was added to the pail. An October wind blew the narrow wooden door closed, throwing Elizabeth into darkness. She kicked the door open with her foot. The sudden blast of daylight punched her face. Every bone in her body was aching for her family, and it was all Emma's fault. She placed the first pail against the door to hold it open. She was almost done.

Scraaaaaaaaape scrap scrape scrape...

There was only one person she could trust to be in her life, her father. If it wasn't for Jonathan Beeson's kind heart, and Deacon Burrows, she would still be a slave called Eliza. Elizabeth slipped the scraper beneath the slurry of poop to scoop it up, and then dropped it into the large pail. A chuckle rose in her throat as she remembered the last time she saw Master Tobias. Deacon Burrows had Tobias on his knees crawling around in chicken poop, begging for forgiveness.

***

"Deacon, God, please help me! She is the devil incarnate. I can see that now. Her eyes pierce my soul and reflect my sins, and my secrets to the world. I cannot sleep. I cannot eat. The rain falls everywhere but here. My crops are withering in the sun. Worse..." His voice lowered to a whisper. "...I have seen the lion headed devil that watches over her. It follows her and tortures her. Yet, it won't permit me to harm her. The devil in this child is devouring my sanity," Master Tobias cried.

"Your fornication with your slaves has delivered this wrath. I have seen this before. She is the incarnation of your sins against your holy vow of marriage and man. Slavery is the devil of humanity. Look how it

28

has reared its ugly head in your life. Repent! Repent!"

As Deacon Burrows continued his rant, Eliza looked at his bulbous nose with the two tiny red veins which ran from the bridge of his nose to the rounded tip. The veins looked like tiny spiders crawling. "She is your personal devil, born from lusting after her slave mother and fornicating with her to satisfy your own demons. Exorcise this devil from your life and your family right now, and you will be forgiven, and admitted into the kingdom of heaven and all of God's glory!"

Eliza's seven-year-old eyes followed the Deacon's finger as it dramatically lifted to point to the sky. "Save yourself! Save your family! Save your generations to come!"

What on earth did Tobias have to be saved from? He wasn't chased by the lion headed shadow.

Maybe his momma cursed him like mine cursed me and that's why he was so mean. Maybe that's why we all slaves because the White folk be cursed by they mommas.

"God forgive me! Forgive me!" Tobias dropped down on his knees. Eye to eye, she saw how ugly Tobias was. His pale, freckled face looked like a bad, bumpy potato that had been pulled from the ground and peeled. His translucent blue eyes were too big and bulged like boiled eggs when he shook her. Spittle from his mouth landed on her cheek.

"Look what you did to me! Look what evil you brought upon my family!"

Maybe Master Tobias believes I'm a conjurer like my momma. If that be true, then I deserve to be sent away to Hell. It can't be no worse than Master Tobia's house.

Tobias' hands gripped her so hard she felt his thumb would snap the bone in her arm.

She wanted to run to Georgia, the cook, but was too afraid. She heard stories of what happened when a slave ran. The fear of men whipping her and then feeding her to the dogs froze her in place. Before she realized it, her judgment was done. Deacon Burrows scooped her up and plopped her in the back of his wagon.

"I'm going to remove this visible scar of evil from your life and the Tobias name, and pray you sin no more!"

"God forgive my sin and take me back into your arms!" Tobias' knees pounded against small pebbles, dirt, and mashed into the chicken poop as

29

he cried out to the heavens.

Deacon Burrow's wagon lurched forward. She feared a greater doom awaited her down the road. Her body bounced against the wagon's buckboards as she held on for dear life. At the last second, she saw Georgia run out and raise her hand to say goodbye as the road dust blurred her last vision of the place she had called home.

Deacon Burrows cracked the whip and the horses barreled the buggy around the oak tree entrance. Her head whipped back as the horses picked up speed. Bits of earth kicked up by the horses' hooves pelted her skin as she tried to peer over the side of the wagon to see where they were headed. Her knees banged hard against the wagon's floor, and her fingers gripped its rough boards. Out of nowhere, a large black bird swooped over her and made Eliza duck down into the wagon. When Eliza lifted her head, she saw it was flying above their wagon. It lifted into the sky and disappeared off to the left of the road.

As they came to a narrow road, Deacon Burrows reined in the horses and came to an abrupt stop. Elizabeth rolled backward like a pumpkin. The dust from the road sprayed up and then showered down bits of dried earth. The Deacon jumped off the wagon, parted the bushes with his arm, and led the horses onto a narrow path.

"Keep down, just keep down." His hand waved her down below the side boards of the wagon.

Was he stealing her? Were the dogs coming after them? The tree limbs swung and smacked the top of the wagon. Branches from an overgrown bush clawed and scraped her arms like fingers unwilling to let go. After several turns of the wagon wheel, the Deacon appeared at the rear.

"Move quickly, child. Your life depends on it," He extended his hand. She stared at his hand, afraid to take it. Where had this devil taken her? Would the dogs find her? Frightened, she crouched down into the corner of the wagon.

"Come on, come on. Move fast!"

Elizabeth scrambled quickly to the edge of the wagon. She was prepared to jump, but Deacon Burrows' large hands grabbed her around her waist and lifted her down. The large black bird made one more pass over her head and then lifted high into the sky. The wind from its wings lifted the tendrils of hair from the nape of her neck. She watched as it floated upward into the sky and then disappeared into the blazing sun. She blinked a few times to adjust her eyes from the blinding sun and saw a couple standing before her. It was as though they appeared out of nowhere. With pale skin and dressed in black with bits of white around their neck and wrists, they looked ghostly. They appeared to have no lips.

"Did you bring a change of clothes?" Deacon Burrows asked.

The woman unfurled a ball of burlap with a black dress, stockings, and black shoes tucked inside.

"Child, come." The woman's voice was soft, quiet, but firm.

"Go with them. Do exactly what they tell you, and you'll be safe," Deacon Burrows instructed.

Eliza was so confused. She couldn't tell if the Deacon was doing something good or bad. The way the couple looked, she couldn't tell if they were going to help her or hurt her.

"May God bless you and keep you." He patted the top of her head the same way Master Tobias petted his dog and led his horse quickly back through the bushes. When she heard the crack of Deacon Burrows' whip and the creak of his wagon wheels, Eliza knew she was alone with two tight-lipped strangers, and the deafening sound of a thousand cicadas.

The thin-lipped woman quickly stripped Eliza's tattered clothing. A worn strip of bed sheet that held her prized possession in place was bound around her waist. The woman's head recoiled at her finding.

"What is this?" The woman asked fingering the worn strip of bed sheet. "Child, is this covering a wound?"

Eliza's heart pounded in her ears. She never thought anyone would ever undress her. Eliza's fingers wrestled with something beneath the worn strip. Her finger lifted an owl eye marble. Eliza placed the marble between two fingers to present it to the woman. The woman's narrow face lowered to get a closer look.

"It's only a marble," the woman said with disappointment.

"If you roll it like this in your hand it looks like an owl's eye blinking at you," Eliza explained proudly as her fingers moved the marble back and forth in her palm. "The mouse done give it to me. I ain't steal it," Eliza defended.

The woman opened her palm demanding Eliza's marble. Eliza quickly surrendered it. Hot tears filled her eyes. It was Eliza's only possession.

"Lift your arms up to the sky," the woman instructed. Eliza quickly

31

obliged and the woman slipped a long-sleeved black dress over her head. "As long as you live, you must never tell anyone that you were a slave. No one must ever know that you have dark roots, or that you come from Tobias' place. Tobias' men will find you and make you a slave again. You will lose your marble, your freedom and your life," the woman said coldly and thrust the marble back into Eliza's hand. It was the first time a White person ever gave her something. She thought of putting it in her mouth and swallowing it, so it would never be taken again, but the woman redirected her attention to her legs.

The woman's cold hands gripped Eliza's right foot and pushed it into a black band of material. Stockings! Eliza never wore a pair of stockings in her life. May Tobias had drawers filled with them. The thought of having her own stockings excited her until the woman pushed her road-dusty legs into them. Yanked up just below her knees, the black band of material wound tightly around her legs, like a snake.

Shoes! They were giving her new shoes. She never wore a shoe without someone else wearing them first. The moment the woman crammed her dirty feet into her right shoe, Eliza's toes throbbed with pain from lack of freedom. Her feet were in total bondage. It felt like she had a plank of wood strapped to the bottom of her feet No wonder why White folk are mean. They can't move their feet. She didn't care about her throbbing feet. She got to keep her marble.

"Your civilized name from now on will be Elizabeth. Remember that," the woman said coldly without even looking at her, and then pulled Elizabeth toward their wagon, which was hidden on the other side of a group of trees.

The pale-faced man scooped up Elizabeth and plopped her down in the front of the wagon. She stood waiting instruction. She had never been in the front of a wagon. The single horse harnessed to the wagon looked small compared to the horses on Tobias' plantation. The man helped the woman up, and she quickly sat down and pulled Elizabeth down onto the hard plank seat next to her. When the man climbed into the wagon on the other side, the wagon didn't creek or tilt. He reminded her of an owl that could drop down from a tree and take a rabbit without a sound. With his brown eyes forward, he spoke to her.

"From here on, your name is Elizabeth Beeson. This is your mother, Patricia Beeson, and I am your father, Jonathan Beeson. Your home is up

32

north in New Hope, Bucks County Pennsylvania. We have a goods store that sells food, supplies, and fabrics to make dresses. You understand me, Elizabeth?" He turned to look her directly in the eye.

"Yes, suh."

"We've got a long journey home, so mind your tongue, and speak only when I tell you to. You're safe now." He offered her a small smile. The warmth of his smile reached all the way down to her throbbing toes.

"Child just do like we tell you," the woman added coldly. "What is your new name?" the woman demanded.

"Elizabeth...Elizabeth..."

***

Somebody was calling her name. When Elizabeth looked up from the pail of chicken poop, she saw Emma Butler.

CHAPTER 5

Emma held her hand over her nose to block the fowls' stench. She was dressed in a new frock with matching cape and hair ribbons. Emma was beautiful. Soft brown doe-like eyes, elegant cheek bones, whipped cream skin, porcelain doll lips, and the perfect nose, which was slightly pointed and softly rounded at the tip. Elizabeth wanted to punch Emma's perfect nose.

"What do you want?" Elizabeth snapped.

"That's a fine way to speak to your only friend," Emma shot back with a pout.

"I don't have any friends," Elizabeth fired back. Emma's hand dropped away from her nose.

"Elizabeth Beeson, what a horrible thing to say to your best and only friend. I came over to share my chocolate with you," Emma whined. Elizabeth carried the pail of poop and headed toward the door. She hoped Emma wouldn't move so she could bump into her and slop some poop on Emma's dress.

"Emma Butler, you're not my best friend anymore. You told my parents about me and Simon. I told you our plans in the strictest of confidences and you couldn't even wait till we were past Amos' field. You promised to wait five days," Elizabeth growled as she collected the second bucket of poop and crossed the yard to the manure pile.

"I did it for you. If I hadn't told your father, those bounty hunters would have made slaves of you all," Emma shot back. Elizabeth could feel Emma's breath on her neck. When Elizabeth dropped the pail next to the manure pile and turned, they were nose to nose.

"You did nothing for me. You did it for yourself. You're nothing but a selfish cow. You wished you had a man like Simon to love you. You wished you had a baby to love. You wished you had your own family. You wanted what I had, and when you couldn't get it you made sure I couldn't have it. Nobody wants your friendship, least of all me. Now git," Elizabeth threatened.

"Listen to you and your plantation talk, 'now git'. You may be off the plantation, but you're still nothing but a White man's slave. You took to Simon like dirt to water, and the two of you made a muddy little baby."

"You shut your filthy mouth Emma Butler!"

"Don't you forget missy I was your friend when nobody wanted to be around you with all your evil ways. The White world doesn't want you and neither did your own slave mammy. You've got no one, but me. Humph-you think Simon loved you? All he saw was a pretend White woman that he could make his slave. You don't even match your own baby. The closest you'll ever get to having brown skin is by eating chocolate," Emma said. With a flourish she unraveled the paper from the chocolate square and took a bite. "Hmmm mmm mmm—I just took me a bite of Simon, and he tastes so good..."

Elizabeth shoved Emma onto the manure pile.

"My dress! Look what you did to my new dress. I'll have your mother horse whip you for this."

"They're Quakers. They don't whip. But I do. Have some poop with your chocolate!" Elizabeth hurled a pail of chicken poop into Emma's face. Emma's blood-curdling screams brought Patricia to the yard.

"Elizabeth Beeson! What have you done? What have you done?" Patricia stomped across the yard towards them. "Have you not shamed us enough?"

Craccck! Patricia brought the palm of her hand across Elizabeth's face.

The sting of Patricia's slap made her lip bleed. Her finger touched her bottom lip and withdrew bright red with her blood. All her years as a slave on Tobias' plantation, she had never been hit. Seven years in the free world and she gets hit–by a Quaker! Patricia helped a crying Emma up from the manure pile.

"I will make Elizabeth pay for your dress. She'll work it off with chores," Patricia consoled.

"Woman, I am not your damn slave!" Elizabeth screeched. Elizabeth's booming voice sent the chickens scurrying into the coop. The milking cows stopped chewing and lumbered quickly to the other side of

35

their small paddock.

"You ungrateful, impudent child ..."

Elizabeth hurled the second bucket of chicken poop into Patricia's face and dropped the bucket with a clunk. As Elizabeth stormed back to the house, she heard Patricia choking on all the shit she had put Elizabeth through for the last seven years.

***

Hours later, Elizabeth sat on her bed waiting for father to administer her punishment. All she could think of was her real mother and the first time Georgia took her to the rear of the three slave cabins and pointed to a chocolate-skinned woman, whose dark arms were elbow deep in a white, soapy washtub.

"See that slave there? She's your mammy. Stay away from her." The memory of those words rubbed a painful callus on her heart. She remembered wanting to run to her mother, touch her, but that yearning was remedied when her mother walked right past them with a basket of wet laundry, without so much as a glance.

Slavery had forbidden her from loving her mother and her mother from loving her. She couldn't understand why May Tobias could have a mother while she was forced to stay away from hers. The abandonment left her with a hunger that wanted any crumbs her mother would offer.

It was desperation that made her trust her mother that fateful October night during hog slaughtering season. When Eliza was seven years old, and too big to be May Tobias' play toy, she was made to work in the kitchen with Georgia. Georgia made her help with the curing of the hams. One night, Elizabeth emerged from the curing shed and her birth mother was standing there. Up close her mother was hauntingly beautiful with round eyes and face, and full lips. Her hand held a corn cob pipe to her lips. As the smoke billowed upward, her mother glared at her.

"What name they give you?" her mother asked. Her mother's voice was husky as though she had screamed all her life.

"Eliza." Eliza took a step backwards toward the main house. Georgia would beat the skin off her if she knew she was talking to her mother. Her mother reeked of pungent lye soap, tobacco, and cold earth. Her feet were bare, and her hair was tucked beneath a spiral mound of fabric.

"What's your name?" If she couldn't be with her mother, she wanted to know her name.

"Jambia."

"What kind of name is that?" Eliza asked as she shifted the wooden bowl of rock salt to her right hip.

"It's a name of my people."

"Do I have a name like yours?"

The whites of her mother's glaring eyes chilled her. The chirping of the crickets filled the silence between them. Her mother's eyes narrowed and then she spoke through the smoke of her pipe.

"Come. I give you a name like mine." Her mother walked towards a slave cabin. Eliza placed her feet in the dirt stamp of her mother's footprints and followed.

"Cassie, what you doing wit that girl? Georgia will have you skinned alive if you mess with that child," another slave called out from a neighboring cabin.

"Mind your own pot. She's my blood. I can do what I want." Jambia disappeared between a slit of burlap that hung in her doorway. Eliza quickly followed her mother inside.

"You got two names?" Eliza asked.

Before the burlap curtain dropped down, Jambia turned and handed Eliza a tin cup with steam rising from it.

"You drink this and I'll give you a name like mine." Eliza reached for the tin cup. From the small oil lamp in the corner she could see little leaves floating on top.

"What this be?" Eliza asked innocently. Jambia snatched the cup out of Eliza's hands.

"You be no daughter of mine. Go!" Jambia shoved Eliza into the burlap door opening.

"No, I want it. I'll drink it," Eliza cried as she brought the cup to her lips and took a gulp. The strange bitterness made her tongue slippery and the sides of her cheeks pucker. After the third sip, Georgia emerged from behind and slapped the tin cup from her hand.

"Eliza, I told you to stay away from her! Cassie, what kind of mother is you, poisoning your own child?"

"Now master's little pet carries my hate. The hate of my people now

37

runs through his house." Jambia smiled with satisfaction.

Her mother's hateful words sent Eliza running out of the shack and into a hell that would haunt her life forever. It was shortly after that night Eliza saw shadows in the dark and during the day. One particular phantom shadow, who called himself Malachai, wouldn't leave her alone. His identifiable stench was worse than the gut-wrenching bloodied stench of slaughter season. It was even worse than the eye-stinging chicken coop poop on the hottest day in summer.

***

Sitting on bed waiting for her father to make his appearance, Elizabeth couldn't decide who was worse, Emma or her mother. They both betrayed her without provocation. At least with Emma, she had an opportunity to retaliate. She wiped a hot tear from her face and then crossed her arms and decided there will be no more betrayals in her life.

She heard the soft release of the gate hook lock from outside her bedroom door; she knew it was her father. When their eyes met, she saw the pain she had caused him. She dropped her head. His six-foot frame filled her door. He held his Meerschaum pipe, his prize possession, in his right hand. She had determined the pipe's bowl, the head of a man, was that of a bearded sea captain. The pipe bowl, still a plaster white, had never been smoked. She had come to believe it wasn't the activity of pipe smoking he enjoyed, but the feel of something in his hands when he talked. He pressed the pipe bit in his mouth for a moment, reflecting on the words he was about to speak, and then released a big sigh.

"I don't think Mrs. Beeson will ever ask you to clean the chicken coop again. It gives you too much ammunition," Jonathan said fighting back a smirk. Elizabeth craned her neck expecting to see Patricia.

"Mrs. Beeson is minding the store," he announced.

"Is she clean?" Elizabeth mumbled.

"As clean as she can be," Jonathan said concealing his smile by pressing his lips on his pipe bit. "Elizabeth, you do understand that what you did wasn't acceptable."

"Poppa, I'm so sorry."

"I know you are, child."

"But I'm not a child."

"I know that too." He removed his pipe from his lips and pointed its mouth bit at her. "You have experienced more life than four adults."

"Why does Mrs. Beeson hate me so much?"

"You mustn't go down that rocky road of self-pity. You'll find no comfort there," he said, sliding the bit of the pipe back in his mouth.

"I can never do enough to free a smile from her."

"Neither can I," Jonathan replied and then released another big sigh. He removed the pipe from his mouth and aimed its bit at her. "Though I suppose, if you knew the truth about Mrs. Beeson, you might be more inclined to show a bit of restraint with her." His head did a quick nod as he returned the pipe to his lips.

"What truth?"

Jonathan's lips pulled on the pipe bit as he squinted his eyes to collect his words. During her father's thoughtful silence, Elizabeth listened to an October wind as it blew and swirled leaves into piles outside her window.

"Mrs. Beeson is just like you," Jonathan said softly pointing his pipe bit at her on his last word for emphasis. "She was rescued just like you were, only she didn't fare as well. She still carries hate for herself. So, my dear Elizabeth, if you could oblige me a little patience and restraint when you address her, I would greatly appreciate it," Jonathan said with a weary voice and returned his pipe to his lips.

Elizabeth noticed his brown hair had a crown of gray. She wondered when did her Poppa get so old? The pain of his loveless marriage was etched deep in the lines of his leathery face. His soft brown eyes were a bit sunken. Life had worn him out.

Her Poppa made the ultimate sacrifice that night behind Amos' cornfield. He saved Simon and their baby and made it possible for Simon to come back for her, but she didn't go. She didn't want to bury her baby. It was her choice to stay behind. She had no right to continue to blame Patricia.

"I'm sorry for Mrs. Beeson's pain, and I'm most sorry that you don't have the loving marriage you deserve." Her throat tightened from the emotion she fought to contain.

She noticed her father's eyes soften from tears forming. He removed his pipe and focused his eyes on its bowl as his thumb gently massaged the face of the sea captain while he spoke.

"Elizabeth, what I love most about being a Quaker is the tolerance and acceptance we are taught to give because we don't always know why people do the things they do. I don't understand slavery. Never have, never will. I have a hard time eating meat because I don't want to eat from another being's suffering. I guess I'm like you, caught in between God and some other place that is in need of love and compassion. There is one thing I do know, and that is you need somebody to love you, just like Mrs. Beeson needed someone to love her. Do you understand what I'm saying?" He slipped the pipe in his mouth and lifted his head. His watery eyes exposed his sorrow.

"Poppa, I'm never leaving you."

"Well now Elizabeth, that's just not reasonable. You've got to go off into the world and make your own family, your own life, and your own legacy. The day will come when you'll finally see you are a courageous loving woman who turned a hateful curse into a gift. It takes a mighty soul to do that," he lauded her lifting his chin. "I know it's probably hard for you to see it now, because your heart is raw from pain, but I suspect there was a greater reason why you stayed behind," he emphasized, pointing his pipe bit at her.

"Now staying behind doesn't mean that you're supposed to stay here. Besides if you stay here, it'll drive Mrs. Beeson crazy. I'd like to have a little peace on this green earth before I die," Jonathan snorted with smile. "That's enough sermon for today. I have to administer your penance," he said flatly. He slipped his pipe in his shirt pocket and stood with his hands locked behind him.

"It's all right. I know I have to be punished, Poppa."

"Elizabeth, you ruined Emma's new frock. Lucky for you we own a goods store. Emma's new dress will only cost you some yards of fabric and some ribbon. You'll work in the store until the material for her dress is paid off."

"Oh, Poppa, I would love to work at the store," Elizabeth said brightly.

"Wait there's more. Since you're handy with a needle, thread, and pattern, you will make Emma a new dress with whatever fabric and ribbon she selects."

"You want me to make Emma a new dress? That hardly seems like punishment. You know I love to sew."

"There's more...As for your punishment for Mrs. Beeson's

40

humiliation, I've decided that you will not cook for two weeks."

"But Poppa if I don't cook that means we have to eat Mrs. Beeson's cooking."

"And that is your penance…and mine. I feel that I am, in some roundabout way, responsible for your standing up to Mrs. Beeson. I've always taught you to never back down from your convictions, if they're righteous. This is my fault as much as it is yours," Jonathan said removing his pipe from his shirt pocket. He aimed the bit at her and squinted his eyes. "Chucking that chicken slop in her face —Was it worth it?"

"Yes."

"Feel better?"

"Much better," Elizabeth said.

He slipped the bit of his pipe between his lips, and then removed it.

"Now don't go telling your mother I said this, because I'll deny it. Between you and me, a good soul shaking laugh is hard to come by," he said with a wink and disappeared from her doorway.

CHAPTER 6

"Emma, that Beeson girl is nothing but trouble," Gwendolyn Butler said as she emptied another kettle of hot water into the wash tub that sat in the middle of the kitchen. Her mother wouldn't let Emma go any farther into their cozy colonial. The moment she stepped through the back door, her mother made her strip and forced her into a wash tub used for sheets. She was treated like a barn animal that had wandered inside. For once Emma was grateful for her petite size. Had she been any taller she would have looked like a giant sitting in a teacup.

Steam floated in the air as the last of the hot water disappeared into the tub. Emma didn't need any more hot water; she could easily boil the water with her rage.

"Mother, you don't understand..."

"Elizabeth is a lunatic. Imagine, hurling excrement at you because you offered her a piece of chocolate. If Jonathan Beeson wasn't such a generous man, I'd....I'd...I forbid you from seeing her ever gain," Gwendolyn commanded. She brought forth a small bottle and emptied its contents into the tub.

"What's that?"

"My good lavender water. I fear if we don't get that stench off your skin, you will never marry."

"Aarrrrrgh!" Emma's hand slapped the water. "I want to claw her eyes out."

"Aggression is not becoming of a proper lady or a Quaker," Gwendolyn admonished. She palmed a bar of soap from the nearby chair, and fiercely rubbed Emma's hair with it. "I'm sure Mrs. Beeson will punish her in the most painful way. I'd rather be barren than bring a cursed child into my home. Desperation I tell you, Mrs. Beeson was

42

soaked in desperation."

Gwendolyn took a scoop of water and poured it over Emma's hair. Gwendolyn leaned over the tub and sniffed the air.

"There still isn't enough lavender. I'm going to the garden to get the last of the roses and mint. That should do the trick. I expect you to smell like a field of fresh flowers when you get out of this tub. Stay put," her mother ordered with a pointed finger. Gwendolyn took the kettle and disappeared through the back door.

"I hate you; I hate you, I hate you Elizabeth Beeson!" Emma slapped the water. "Arrrrrrrrgggghhh!" Emma's head disappeared beneath the water and then emerged. She dried her face with the small towel on the chair next to the tub, then brought her hair forward to smell it.

"Your hate is good..."

Emma bolted up in the tub and then stood up. Her body glistened from the film of soap that slid down her body like melted wax. She snatched a towel from a nearby chair to cover herself.

"I stopped her like you asked. Show yourself. You promised me you would give me the same powers Elizabeth has. I want to see what she sees. I want to know people's secrets. Give me the power you promised." Emma stepped out of the tub.

"You want to see?"

"Yes, I want to see. Give me my power."

"Emma what are doing out of the -Aeeeeeeeeeeeeiiiii!"

A force pushed her mother out of the back doorway.

Bang! The back door slammed shut.

"You want power!!!"

"The bathwater was lifted above the tub. The murky soapy water floated in the air.

"Witness my power!!!"

Splash! The water cascaded to the floor. The room went silent.

"Emma! Emma! Open the door!" She heard her mother's screams from outside.

"Mother, all is well!" Emma yelled. "Your trickery does not impress me. Show yourself," Emma demanded. "Show yourself!"

Thump-Bang! The dishes rattled on the shelves.

Thump-Bang! The glass in the kitchen window shattered.

Thump-Bang! A crack travelled across the kitchen ceiling.

Silence. The water on the floor began to vibrate. Emma could see ripples on its surface. The water disappeared between the kitchen floorboards leaving only dirt behind. A cold wind pushed through the broken window and swirled the dirt upward into a funnel that did a slow dance around the kitchen. A dark figure began to take shape within the cyclone of dirt.

"Show yourself!" Emma demanded.

The whites of eyes flickered between the flurry of darkness. A rancid stench seized her senses and sent her into a convulsion of coughs. Naked, Emma tried to make it to the back door, but something stopped her, held her. She clawed along the cupboards to get to the window to breathe fresh air and met her mother's horror stricken face.

"Mother!"

"You will know my power!!!"

The dark dirty funnel enveloped her. As Emma tried to breathe, she inhaled Malachai's hateful dust. Something slammed her body to the floor. She couldn't scream. She couldn't breathe. A dark figure stood over her. It had the head of a lion, fangs bared, eyes frozen with rage. Her naked body paralyzed and vulnerable could only receive his hateful intentions. She tried to crawl away. It was too late! He pummeled her with his hatred. It exploded in her body. Her body went limp.

"Now, you be my slave."

Crash!

The crockery and plates which lined a wall shelf exploded with his departure. Shards of glass rained down upon Emma's body.

***

"Emma?...Emma?...are you in there?"

Emma heard Mr. Dayton, the blacksmith, calling her. Mr. Dayton was banging against their back door. She wanted to move but couldn't. The floor was cold, damp. Her left eye opened. Daylight pained her vision. Her left hand twitched and flopped in a small puddle like a fish taking its last breath. Emma heard three hard bangs at the back door and then it flew open. Cold air blew across her damp body. Heavy footsteps approached.

"Mr. Dayton, is my daughter alive?" her mother's voice called out.

"Help...meee..." Emma uttered. "Hel...lp..."

"Mrs. Butler, you better come in." When Emma's mother entered, her hand clamped over her mouth. Her quaint and cozy kitchen was in shambles. Muddy water and dirt covered everything. Emma's creamy skin was covered in dirt as though she had been dragged by a plow horse through a muddy field.

"Mom..ma..." Emma whimpered. "Momma..."

Mr. Dayton quickly turned away to avoid looking at Emma's naked body.

"Mrs. Butler, I better go find the doctor, and ring the bell. This looks like witch..." Mrs. Butler covered his mouth with her hand.

"No, don't say it!"

"Mrs. Butler, someone came in your house and attacked your daughter. We have to ring the bell," Mr. Dayton urged.

"No! My daughter is not bewitched like that... that... Beeson girl. Mr. Dayton once that bell is rung, we'll have eyes on my house, and everything we hold dear will be lost. *Everything* will be over," Mrs. Butler pleaded with teary eyes.

"Mom...ma?..."

"Don't ring that bell. Please, Mr. Dayton, don't ring that bell," Mrs. Butler's fingers dug into his arm through his shirt. Tears rushed from her eyes. "

"Let me go find the doctor and maybe Mr. Butler?"

"Yes...yes...but quietly-please."

Mr. Dayton disappeared out the back door and closed it behind him.

"Momma?" Emma whispered. Her face felt glued to the floor. She lifted her head and was able to see her mother's shoes.

"Emma, don't move."

"Momma..." Emma lifted her left hand for her mother to take. Her mother refused to touch her.

"Emma, did Elizabeth do this? Tell me, did Elizabeth Beeson do this to you?"

"Feel my power. Rise!"

Emma sat up slowly. Bits of dirt dropped off her body onto the kitchen floorboards. Emma's eyes scanned the kitchen. Her mother's once scrubbed kitchen looked like it was ravaged by a flood.

"Stand. Feel my power."

Emma stood up and raised her arms to examine them. Other than a thick caking of dirt here and there, her nubile body appeared unscathed. She looked down and noticed her pubescent breasts looked larger, and she now had nipples, rosy and erect. Beneath her navel her once downy forest of pubic hair had become dense and thick.

"Emma, child, cover yourself. Mr. Dayton went for the doctor."

"I don't need the doctor. I am well, mother."

Mr. Dayton burst through the back door and stopped in his tracks when he saw Emma's naked body. Emma's eyes met his. She heard his thoughts.

"What a fine pair of tits!"

"Mr. Dayton turn away! "Emma! Make yourself decent!" Gwendolyn scolded and flung a damp towel at her.

When Emma looked up at her mother, she saw a blurry vision of her mother and Mr. Dayton in a stall of his Blacksmith shop. Her mother's dress was up around her waist and Mr. Dayton was pressing against her mother's body with his mouth devouring her mother's face and her bare breasts.

"I'm done with my bath. May I go to my room now?" Emma asked wrapping the damp towel around her body.

"Yes...yes...go to your room, go," her mother pleaded.

Emma stepped on broken glass and debris as she made her way towards Mr. Dayton. Emma adjusted her wet, dirty towel to offer him a peek of her left breast.

"Mr. Dayton, you can look now. My 'fine tits' are covered," Emma murmured and sashayed out of the kitchen savoring her new power.

~June 1849~

CHAPTER 7

"Savannah, Georgia, December 1848. The General Clinch steamboat blasts a rage of steam as Mr. Johnson, a White man with his right arm in a sling, approaches the steamboat ramp. Although distinguished, Mr. Johnson is feeble and sickly in appearance and walks stiffly with a cane. A bandage wraps the frame of his face, and eyeglasses sit on the end of his nose. He is followed by his slave, who carries two pieces of luggage. As they proceed up the ramp, the White man looks nonchalantly over his shoulder at his slave, who follows him closely.

"At the entrance of the steamboat, they are stopped by the steward who demands their tickets. Mr. Johnson's slave presents two tickets. The steward looks briefly at the tickets as Mr. Johnson slowly hooks his cane on his left forearm so he can dab beads of perspiration on his upper lip. The steward stares at Mr. Johnson and asks if he is well.

"Mr. Johnson explains he's traveling to seek special medical attention for his rheumatoid arthritis, and infected teeth. The steward requests that Mr. Johnson sign the registry. Mr. Johnson motions to his sling and explains his writing hand is incapacitated and requests the steward to sign for him.

"The steward pauses and then leaves. He quickly returns with the captain, who requests proof that Mr. Johnson owns the slave accompanying him. The captain explains there have been many thefts of slaves and that if a slave is a runaway or is reported as stolen property and is traced to their boat, their company could be challenged legally to pay the true owner for his lost property.

"Mr. Johnson calmly states he was never questioned before nor had he had problems with his other travels. The captain asks them again to produce proof of ownership or leave the boat. Without further

49

argument, Mr. Johnson turns to leave the boat.

"Outraged at feeble Mr. Johnson's treatment by the captain, another White passenger, Mr. Beauchamp, who is a frequent traveler on the General Clinch, claims he was on the train with Mr. Johnson from Macon, Georgia. Mr. Beauchamp verifies that Mr. Johnson did board the train with his slave. Mr. Beauchamp also offers to sign a note to guarantee the cost of the slave if they should find any misrepresentation.

"Embarrassed by Mr. Beauchamp's offer, the captain instructs the steward to sign the registry for Mr. Johnson. Mr. Johnson thanks Mr. Beauchamp and the captain and then boards the boat with his slave. As the steamboat pulls away, Mr. Johnson and his slave stand on the deck and watch as the harbor of Savannah, Georgia grows distant and disappears into an early morning fog.

"Days later, a train pulls into Philadelphia station. Mr. Johnson and his slave get off the train and quietly but quickly secure a coach to take them to a boarding house, where Mr. Johnson checks in. Exhausted from his journey, Mr. Johnson enters the bedroom and sits on the bed. There is a knock at his door. When he opens it, he finds his slave in the doorway who asks if he would like his boots shined. Mr. Johnson nods silently and points to his boots.

"The slave enters to retrieve the boots and Mr. Johnson closes the door. They stare at each other for a moment. Mr. Johnson bursts into muffled cries and buries himself in his slave's chest. The slave holds him and releases his own tears. The slave helps Mr. Johnson remove his sling and the bandage from around his head. The slave then removes Mr. Johnson's glasses, folds them and places them gingerly on the bureau. Last, the slave removes his master's hat and run his fingers through his master's hair. They kiss. A white slave, Ellen Craft, age twenty-two, and her husband William Craft, age twenty-four, have escaped slavery.

"Poppa, what do you think?"

"I think it's a miraculous story every time you read it." A loud rumbling of wagon wheels poured into their store. Jonathan rushed to the door. "When will these people slow down and learn they can't run their horses through town like they're in a race. How old is that issue of *The Liberator*?" Jonathan asked.

"The story was published in April's issue," Elizabeth answered. "Poppa what do you think?"

"I think you should stop punishing yourself. Your situation was completely different from Ellen Craft's."

"We both can pretend to be White," Elizabeth said.

"But there was no possible way you could pretend to be a man," he said with a sigh. "No matter what you think now, it won't change what happened. Let it go," Jonathan said, touching her shoulder.

The bell jingled on the store's door announcing the entrance of Mrs. Chadwick.

"Now Mrs. Chadwick can easily pass for a man," Jonathan said softly in Elizabeth's ear. Elizabeth turned and saw trouble coming. Mrs. Chadwick reminded her of an old hen that would probably rule over Genghis Khan if he didn't own a formidable pair of spurs.

"Good Lord let this twister pass over my farmstead quickly," her father prayed under his breath as he conjured a smile. "Good morning Mrs. Chadwick, how can I help you today?"

"I need a few supplies. I wrote everything down so you can't confuse my order." Mrs. Chadwick groused as she handed her paper to Jonathan. She raised her spectacles to her face and then looked over Elizabeth. "You're still here."

"She's my daughter. She runs the store with me. Why shouldn't she be here?"

"I'm accustomed to seeing your wife. It's the more appropriate and acceptable partnership," she admonished with a heaving bosom shaped like an old farm hen that extended beyond her small feet. Two tight finger curls dangled on either side of her small face.

"Poppa, I'll fill her order," Elizabeth offered.

"You will not!"

"Elizabeth, go take inventory while I fill Mrs. Chadwick's order."

"But Poppa, I did inventory last week."

"This is a new week," he replied.

Elizabeth placed the inventory list on top of her copy of *The Liberator*, and headed toward the back of the store to the stockroom behind the curtain. Guilt washed over her. She knew the moment she got behind the curtain her father would have to contend with an old biddy who would only aggravate his heart condition. She didn't want to leave him. She turned around to go back into battle.

"Poppa…"

"I'll take care of the customer, Elizabeth. Go to the supply room," Jonathan said firmly. As soon as Elizabeth dropped the stockroom curtain, she burst into tears. She hated that her father had to defend her presence to the women in town. It was all Patricia's fault. Patricia was blinded by jealousy. Knowing that Patricia was once a slave like her didn't seem to help the situation between them. No matter how much compassion Elizabeth offered, Patricia would find a way to verbally slap her face.

Elizabeth's eyes landed on the engraved photograph of Ellen Craft dressed as a man. She gripped her mouth to muffle her cries, and wished it was her story. If only she and Simon thought out their plan a little more. Her travelling as a woman with slaves was not an acceptable mode of travel. No wonder the bounty hunters stopped them.

She got a new handkerchief from a box on the shelf, dried her tears, removed a handkerchief from the inventory list, and then blew her nose. She didn't want her tears to bubble the ink and make a mess of the inventory sheet. As she dabbed the corner of her eyes, she perused *The Liberator* to see if there was any announcement of Mrs. Craft at another venue, but the paper was too old. She would have to ask about town or go to the meeting house. Surely someone knew where she could go to meet the Crafts. Her father would support that trip.

She positioned a stool against the back wall to begin inventory. She looked at the shelves that held sacks of cornmeal and flour. The large sacks made it the easiest starting point. She counted nineteen sacks of flour when her father lifted the curtain.

"Are you done with the inventory?"

"I just started."

Jonathan looked at Elizabeth's eyes.

"Your eyes are dry, you're done. The store is busy. I need your assistance with a customer. Right now, please."

"Yes, Poppa." Elizabeth shoved her papers on top of a shelf of canned goods and rushed to the front of the store expecting to see a modest crowd of customers. Instead there was a man standing at the counter. He was the most perfect looking man she had ever seen. He was tall, but not towering, broad shoulders, that didn't make him look like an ox, and his presence radiated a captivating peace she had been searching for her entire life. When he turned to look at her, she caught a fiery golden glint of his hazel eyes which set her bosom on fire. She quickly turned her back to him.

"Poppa? Where are all the customers?" Elizabeth's face felt hotter than a Blacksmith's face in July.

"Mr. Samuel Chase, my daughter Elizabeth Beeson will help you with your special order. I have some inventory that needs to be done," Jonathan announced.

"Poppa?" Elizabeth scurried after him.

"Why can't you help him?" Elizabeth whispered under her breath.

"Because I'm not the one from whom he needs the help. Go tend to your customer."

Panic seized her. The nearest mirror was in the ladies' section. She smoothed her store apron and pressed her lace collar with her fingers, and then pinched her cheeks to bring a little pink to them. When she turned around her eyes immediately locked onto his. Her heart danced in her chest. She felt her nipples harden and her face flushed from embarrassment. Who was this man who was awakening parts of her she had declared dead?

"You are beautiful..."

She heard his thoughts in her mind. Was he another spirit? She wanted to run. It had been three years since Simon's departure. No man had ever been able to reach her. She looked at the entrance to the stock room. Her father appeared from behind the curtain with a smile and clip board. He lifted his chin to her; his signal for "get to work." He would not allow her an easy escape. He lifted his chin once more and then disappeared back behind the curtain.

Perspiration dotted her upper lip as she made her way back to the counter. She felt a smile growing on her face and surreptitiously pinched herself to remove it.

"Mr. Chase, how can I help you today?" Elizabeth asked, keeping her eyes focused on a small display of beeswax candles on the counter.

"I'd like to buy a gift for a very special woman in my life," Samuel said.

Her knees weakened from his words. He was taken.

"Did you have something in mind?" Elizabeth asked coldly. Her throat constricted with disappointment.

"Your father thought you could make a few recommendations."

"Perfume or handkerchiefs?" Elizabeth offered with a dismissive tone. "If you're interested in the handkerchiefs, they can be embroidered for a small charge—that's if I have time."

"Which would you prefer?"

"It doesn't matter what I prefer. What would your 'special woman' want?"

"I think she would prefer an elegant handkerchief. How long does the embroidering take?"

Elizabeth felt his eyes on her. She turned her head and pretended to sneeze into her handkerchief so she could blot the corners of eyes and catch tears that were demanding their freedom.

"Gesundheit."

"Thank you."

"The embroidering will take only an afternoon," Jonathan called out as he approached the counter carrying a velvet covered box. "Elizabeth is fast with the needle and talented too."

"Actually Mr. Chase, it depends on how much you would like embroidered. If it's just your lady's initials, I can do that in an hour and be done with it," Elizabeth said flatly.

"Er...That means you'll have to come back to pick up the handkerchiefs," her father interjected and placed the velvet box on the counter. "If these aren't fancy enough Elizabeth can show you our lace handkerchiefs. I have a selection that came all the way from Spain."

"Spain? They sound very fancy and expensive," Mr. Chase replied.

"The right woman is worth the expense," Jonathan added with a big smile and then opened the lid to the velvet box.

"I'm sure Mr. Chase is capable of deciding which kind of handkerchief his lady friend will appreciate. Mr. Chase, if cost is a concern, we do have a simpler, but lovely, cotton ladies' handkerchief, that would please any woman."

"Actually, I'd like to see the lace ones. I believe she is worth the expense."

"There will be the added cost of the embroidering, not to mention the time to do it. I'm sure my father wouldn't mind delivering them himself—for a small delivery fee, or course."

"That will be acceptable. I'd like to have handkerchiefs embroidered- and I'll come back for them."

"Oh..." Elizabeth offered a teeth-clenching smile.

"Looks like everything is under control out here. I'll be in the stock room if there are any further questions."

Elizabeth opened the velvet box. She felt his eyes burning her skin. She was torn between flattery and rage that he would flirt with her while buying a gift for another woman.

"Mr. Chase, in this box we have several styles of gift handkerchiefs; Irish crocheted and linen," she explained coldly.

"I'm afraid they're not special enough for my mother."

"Your mother? These are for your mother? "

"Yes, she is a very special woman."

Elizabeth's chest heaved from emotion. She cupped her hand over her mouth to suppress a cry of relief.

"How wonderful!" she exclaimed with a bright smile. "In that case, I'll show you the Spanish lace, but I don't know if that particular handkerchief would be an appropriate gift for your mother, being that she's already married."

"My mother is not a conventional woman, so she won't mind. My father is an import dealer. He has taken my mother on many trips abroad. I'm afraid she's accustomed to being in the presence of all that is beautiful and unique, such as yourself."

His words set her face on fire. She opened her mouth to contest his comment, but nothing came out. Her chest heaved. The top button on the back of her dress popped opened. His eyes groped her body. Perspiration moistened her upper lip.

"The special handkerchiefs are in the stockroom. Excuse me," Elizabeth said bolting toward the curtain. She planned on hiding out there until he left. Her heels clacked against the wood floorboards. Her eyes focused on the split in the curtain. A few more steps and she would be safe from the frightening passion that was claiming her body. Before she could part the curtain, her father thrust another velvet lined box of wedding handkerchiefs into her hands.

"Show him these. I'm sure he'll find something he likes," Jonathan said quickly and then closed the drapes.

Elizabeth's body was on fire. Her head was ready to explode. She blotted her lip and brow with her handkerchief and returned to the counter. Emotion gripped her heart.

"My father seems to think you'll find what you're looking for in this box. These handkerchiefs are for a bride-to-be, for her special day. I don't think your mother, or any woman would think it appropriate to be given a bridal handkerchief for a gift if she's not getting married, or if she's already married - conventional or not." Elizabeth said as she arranged the handkerchiefs for him to peruse.

"My mother is rather unique and outspoken. I dare say a bit like you. Would you care about convention if a gentleman caller presented you with a set of these beautiful Spanish lace handkerchiefs, or would you care more about the gesture of his love for you?"

"I...I..."

The bell on the front door chimed. Emma was dressed for shopping. Her soft curls framed her face. Her royal blue sateen dress made her look like one of May Tobias' fancy dolls. Emma was a treat for any man's eyes, but it was rumored Mr. Dayton slyly warned Emma's lookers that she was a treacherous beauty. Emma approached the far end of the counter and headed towards them. Elizabeth hoped Mr. Dayton warned Samuel.

"I suppose that your mother's unique character would find these handkerchiefs to be quite suitable. She would appreciate the effort and care you expended to select them for her." While Samuel examined the handkerchiefs, Elizabeth quickly glanced at Emma and narrowed her eyes to angry slits to chase her away.

"Shop girl, I'd need help filling my order..." Emma announced with a haughty air as she approached the counter with a sneer.

"What do you think of this one?" Samuel asked.

"That's the Spanish lace. It's our most elegant handkerchief. Your mother will love this. Any woman would."

"Shop girl... "

"Miss Beeson, would you love this handkerchief?"

His words seized her heart and made it beat like a fife's drum, drowning out Emma's demands.

"Yes, I would fancy this handkerchief."

"That settles it! I'll take all three. Three is a good number, isn't it?"

"Three handkerchiefs make a wonderful set," Elizabeth declared.

"I am a paying customer. Are you going to fill my order or not!"

"Miss Butler, what brings you in on this fine day?" Jonathan's voice boomed as he burst through the curtain and scurried to the counter.

"Your wife always took charge of the customers. She is most professional. Perhaps your profits will pick up again if she returns," Emma said snidely.

"I'm sorry Miss Butler. Elizabeth is helping a customer, and I was in the stock room. I didn't hear you come in. I'd be more than happy to fill your order. Will this be going on your account?" Jonathan ushered Emma to the other end of the counter away from Elizabeth and Samuel.

Samuel's eyes had drawn Elizabeth in. She didn't notice that her father had rescued her from Emma.

"What are you mother's initials?" Elizabeth asked Samuel.

"E.C. Eugenia Chase."

"Since I will need to embroider three handkerchiefs, I won't have them ready until closing. I'm sorry for the inconvenience, but I don't want to rush through my sewing."

"End of the day will be fine. Shall I pay you now?"

"Yes, please. I'll write up your bill. Excuse me." Elizabeth did three sidesteps towards her father. "Father, are you using the receipt book? Mr. Chase has selected his mother's gift." Elizabeth felt Emma's cold stares on her. She locked her eyes on her father to avoid any unpleasant confrontation in front of Samuel.

"Is that Mr. Samuel Chase?"

"I don't know," Jonathan volleyed back.

"I hear he's back from a very long stay abroad; India I hear," Emma announced with a drooling smile. "I've read that India has the most delectable spices—curry I believe. Are you sure that's not, Mr. Samuel Chase?" Emma persisted.

"All I know is that he is a paying customer. Elizabeth, why don't you go take care of your customer and I'll handle Miss Butler," Jonathan suggested sliding the receipt tablet to her. Elizabeth dismissed Emma with one final cut of her eyes, took the tablet, and returned to Samuel.

"I'm sorry for the delay. Three ladies' wedding handkerchiefs...with the embroidery...that will be...one dollar and twenty-five cents."

"And worth every penny to see you smile," Samuel said.

"I'll have them ready for you by close of business today," Elizabeth replied with a nervous smile.

"Thank you, Miss Beeson. I look forward to seeing you again." Samuel peeled away from the counter and headed towards the door.

Emma broke away from her conversation with Jonathan and rushed across two aisles to catch Samuel.

"I don't believe I had the pleasure of meeting you," Emma said extending a gloved hand. "You're Horace Chase's son, aren't you?"

"Yes, I am," Samuel said, bowing his head politely.

"I'm Miss Butler. Emma to you...I don't suppose you'd mind getting that parasol down from that display. It's so important for a true lady to protect her skin from the ravaging heat of the sun, don't you agree?"

"I'm sure Mr. Beeson will be happy to tend to your needs. Good day," Samuel bolted out the door like a wild horse freed from captivity. Elizabeth pulled her lips inward and clamped down on them with her teeth to keep from bursting into laughter. She looked to her father who shot her a quick wink, and then rushed over to Emma.

"Miss Butler, that parasol is for display only. I have two more like it in the holder if you would like to examine one up close."

"No thank you. Put my order on my father's bill, and have your little shop girl deliver it," Emma ordered with a snarl. Emma gave Elizabeth one last glare and stormed out the door, banging it closed behind her.

"There's no need for you to enter into a competition with that one. There's no competition," Jonathan said.

A loud rumbling of wagon wheels poured into their store.

Crash!

A woman's screams echoed in the street.

"My dress! My dress!"

Jonathan rushed to the door, and Elizabeth rushed to peer out of the storefront window.

From each of their positions they saw the same thing. Emma Butler clawing her way out of a pile of horse manure that spilled out of an overturned wagon. Elizabeth rushed to the front door to join her father. They stepped out onto the top step together.

"Is she hurt?" Jonathan called out.

"Take your filthy hands off me! Look what you did to my dress! You'll pay for this!"

"It sounds like Emma is just fine," Elizabeth said with a big grin. "Poppa, I think the manure matches the color of her eyes."

"Elizabeth, it's not proper to laugh at someone's misfortune," Jonathan chided, fighting back his smile. "Back to work." They went back inside and closed the door. "That was a terrible thing that just happened," Jonathan said.

"Yes, it was." Elizabeth said. "But a good soul-shaking laugh is hard to come by," Elizabeth added and then sprayed her laughter into the store until tears ran down her face.

CHAPTER 8

Elizabeth returned the feather duster to its hook. The store was always quiet just before closing.

"Poppa, what time is it?"

"It's 5:20. Only one minute later than the last time you asked me. Don't worry, he'll be here."

"There is only ten minutes left. How rude to keep me-us waiting," she said with a pout. "I finished the embroidery in record time, the least he could do is show up, so I could present the finished handkerchiefs to him properly." Elizabeth slammed the receipt tablet down on the counter.

"You'll see him again," her father said with a smug smile.

"I don't want to see him. I just want to show him the work and go home."

The bell on the front door chimed. Elizabeth turned and saw his face, smiled and then replaced her smile with a scowl to show her displeasure.

"We were just about to lock up," she said.

"My deepest apologies. I would never keep you waiting, but we received a shipment that took five men to unload. You have my sincerest apologies. Is it too late for me to collect my mother's gift?"

"Of course not. Elizabeth, show him your handiwork and then lock up. I'm afraid I had a very long day." He placed a large key on the counter next to the package of handkerchiefs.

"Father, surely you can wait just a moment for Mr. Chase to look at the handkerchiefs."

"No, afraid I can't. Samuel, would you be so kind as to see my daughter home after she locks up?"

"It would be my pleasure, Mr. Beeson. Again, my apologies for holding you up."

"It's no problem at all. Goodnight Samuel. See you at home Elizabeth." Jonathan dipped his head and slipped on his tall soft felt hat. The bell jingled as the door closed. Elizabeth and Samuel stood staring into each other eyes for almost a full minute before Samuel broke their trance.

"Is that the gift for my mother?"

"Yes, yes, it is. I have it all set to be wrapped." Elizabeth gently lifted the tissue paper to reveal a three-tier arrangement of the laced wedding handkerchiefs. She had delicately arranged them so the embroidered monogram on each handkerchief was rested above the other, leaving the lace on the bottom handkerchief exposed to show the handkerchief's elegance.

"Exquisite. Your work is simply exquisite. And you displayed them in such a lovely way. My mother will be pleased."

"The arrangement is part of the giving of the gift. Great care should go into preparing a gift. Every aspect should reflect that the gift came from the heart."

"If that was your intention, you have a lovely heart," Samuel smiled.

"I have two gift wrapping papers from which to choose," Elizabeth replied.

"Wrapping paper?"

"Yes."

"No, this is a real special gift. I like to wrap it in the most beautiful fabric you have in the store."

"Using fabric like wrapping paper? I never heard of such a thing."

"In my business travels with my father I have learned about so many different customs. In Japan..."

"You have been to Japan?"

"Yes, once. I was taught the most interesting Japanese custom called furoshiki. In Japan giving a gift is like wrapping one's heart, so they use square pieces of cloth to wrap and tie their gifts. It's a very special technique. I will show you if you like."

"Yes, please."

"First we must select the fabric and cut it into squares that, when tied, will create a bundle furoshiki. What fabric do you think will go best with this gift?"

Samuel excited her. He was taking her on a tour of another country without leaving the store. She rolled in her bottom lip as she thought of the perfect fabric. Her face lit up.

"I know the perfect fabric for the furo...sheekee?"

"Yes, very good."

Elizabeth ran to the fabric section of the store and removed a bolt of ivory silk, and a bolt of Spanish lace.

"I'm afraid I'll have to charge you for the fabric."

"I'm fully prepared to pay whatever it costs to be in your presence," Samuel responded, looking into her eyes.

"Silk...is very expensive...and will make the most luxurious and elegant presentation. I'll need you to measure and cut what you need."

"Delightful!" Samuel quickly removed his jacket, folded it and laid it across the counter. She handed him a pair of shears.

"Silk is a dollar a yard," Elizabeth warned.

Samuel laid the handkerchief box on the silk and made one cut into the fabric and then sailed the shears across it like it was water.

"That cut was magical. I would love for you to teach me...I mean learning how to handle the shears with fabric will save my father money. There'll be no ragged edges to cut off...no waste."

"It will probably take a minimum of five lessons," Samuel said with a sly smile. "Lace is so delicate. You have to mind how far down you close the shears otherwise the edges can become jagged." His hand moved the shears quickly through the Spanish lace. "See, no rough edges."

Samuel quickly placed the package on top of the layers of fabric, and then began making a series of folds over the package. A narrow creek of perspiration rolled down her spine. She brought her handkerchief to her lips and focused on the elegantly tied bundle of lace and silk to keep herself from kissing him.

"That is the most beautiful gift wrapping I have ever seen," Elizabeth sighed. "I'll have to marry you so I can create this beauty every..." She pressed her handkerchief against her lips wishing she could cram her words back into her mouth.

"I am happy you agree. You will marry me," Samuel said firmly. "You are more precious and beautiful than any gift that could ever be unwrapped in my eyes."

"Please go." She thrust the silky bundled into his hands.

"Forgive me for corrupting your virtue with my words. But the love I feel when I am in your presence requires I speak from my heart. Elizabeth..."

"It's Miss Beeson. I hope in the future you are more careful not to mistake my curiosity for an open door to your advances," Elizabeth shot back.

Her words riddled his body, wounding him. The vibrancy in his vibrant hazel eyes faded.

"Allow me to pay for the fabric," he said without looking at her. He fumbled in his coat pocket for his billfold.

"That won't be necessary. You can come back tomorrow when my father is here." Elizabeth marched to the door and opened it. Samuel stepped through the door onto the landing outside.

"Your attempt to defraud yourself of love is obvious. I meant every word. You will marry me, because we are twin flames joined at the heart. I loved you Elizabeth Beeson the moment I heard your name."

His words pulled her from her body. She could hear his heart beat in rhythm with hers. He was a complete stranger to her eyes, but a familiar soul to her heart. She wanted to leap into his arms.

"Leave Simon and your baby be, or we'll be burying them next!"

"I can't... I can't..." Elizabeth said softly and then gently closed the door. "I don't deserve your love," she murmured through the glass and then pulled down the door's window shade before she burst into tears.

CHAPTER 9

Elizabeth opened her window. The scent of manure-fertilized fields was a reminder of her earlier run in with Emma. The sight of Emma clawing her way out of a pile of manure was still delightfully etched in her mind, and so was the face of Samuel Chase. She closed her eyes and yanked the bed covers over her face to make the vision of him disappear. Her tears plastered the sheet to her cheeks.

Stupid, stupid, stupid, stupid! She punched her mattress with her fists. She couldn't believe she declared out loud that she needed to marry him. More importantly, she couldn't believe that he quickly agreed.

No! I don't deserve love; I don't deserve love...I don't deserve happiness...

"Do you believe that you are here to love only one man?"

The sweet scent of pine permeating through her sheet meant she had company, Wakayeja wicahpe. Elizabeth sprang up in bed.

"How would you like it if I followed you around and spied on you during your most intimate moments?"

"You are welcome to. Maybe then you will remember me."

"Go away. I don't want to play your silly memory game," Elizabeth whined and then dove under her covers. "No man will ever want to marry me. I've been touched, spoiled...I had a child out of wedlock. My soul will undoubtedly drop through the floor and carry me straight to Hell," Elizabeth cried from beneath her covers.

"Why get out of bed? Sounds to me, you're already in hell,"

"My life is over."

"With Samuel, your life is just beginning."

"Do you keep coming back so you can haunt me with unattainable dreams?"

"Samuel is your truth to claim when you are ready." Wakayeja
wicahpe faded into the night.

"How can anyone love me, when my own mother hated me, cursed
me?"

"That's because she saw your evil ways."

Elizabeth emerged from beneath her sheets. Patricia was standing in
her doorway. Even in the darkened room, Elizabeth could see the scowl
that scratched across Patricia's face.

"What evil did you conjure to bewitch another man. How many souls
will it take to satisfy your devil's hunger?" Patricia demanded with
crossed arms. The visible outline of Patricia's body through her
nightgown made her appear ghostly.

"Leave my room please," Elizabeth said firmly. In three angry strides,
Patricia was at the side of her bed looming over her.

"Your room? And just who do you think gave you this room?"

"Poppa gave me this room." Patricia's hand withdrew in preparation
of a slap. "I have already warned you, I am not your slave to beat on,"
Elizabeth countered as she scrambled to her knees. Patricia dropped her
hand.

"They should put you in the public square with your neck in a block
and let your body wither in the hot sun, so your wretched soul will turn
to dust and blow far away. You're nothing but an evil witch," Patricia
snapped in Elizabeth's face.

"Poppa loves me, what do I care what you think?" Her words hit
Patricia right between her eyes. Patricia's fingers curled like an angry bird
ready to snatch its prey. "Touch me and I'll call on the spirits to render
you senseless," Elizabeth threatened as she jumped out of bed ready to
fight.

"You may have bewitched Mr. Beeson's mind with your nubile body
and evil thoughts, but I see you for what you are-fornicator. You're the
only reason why Mr. Beeson doesn't have to make a trip out to the barn!"

A warm light flooded the room when Jonathan appeared in the
doorway. The light washed away the lines of their bodies. They looked
like lost souls converging in a dense forest.

"Mrs. Beeson, you will hold your tongue. Delirium has filled your
mind with the vile visions and vulgarity. Apologize to Elizabeth!" His
right index finger, crooked with arthritis, pointed to the floor like he was

scolding a dog.

"I will not! Ever since she arrived you have done nothing but dote on her like she was your wife, your queen. I am your wife!"

"Then act like it. Your jealousy over a child is barbaric!" Jonathan's voice rattled Elizabeth's window.

"She's not a child; she gave birth to a baby without the benefit of a marriage! Everyone sees how she bewitches you; the way the two of you carry on in our store–in broad daylight. People don't come to shop, they come to gawk like you're two dogs in an alley. Jonathan Beeson, I will not have you shame me one more day. You must choose who you will have in your life, me or her."

"I will not choose! You cannot make me cut off my limb for you! What kind of love is that?"

"It would be an easy choice for any husband."

"Yes, it would be an easy choice for a weak man, a man of no stamina, of no compassion. I have given you love for twenty years. With or without a child under our roof, you still screech at me everyday like a fisher cat. When will you show me, your husband, a modicum of tenderness, gratitude? You refused to allow me to touch you. You refuse to give me a child of my own seed. And yet you have the audacity to demand I remove what little peace and joy I have cultivated so you can continue to torment me with loneliness and your sour existence. God has not made a saint who can bear your grueling penance. You despise life, despise it! And I have loved you despite it. Return the love you owe me Mrs. Beeson or be damned to solitude!"

Her father's face glistened with tears. Patricia's face became like stone.

"Poppa, we have to show her compassion..."

"I don't need your compassion; I need you gone!"

"Elizabeth, it's time Mrs. Beeson chooses to be a part of love."

Elizabeth watched Patricia's bottom lip quiver and eyes water. Her lips parted. Elizabeth looked for the presence of Patricia's tongue, a sign of surrender but then her lips closed- tight.

"I will pray for you, Mr. Beeson," Patricia said with narrowed eyes.. "Sleep in the barn with the rest of the animals. You will no longer share my bed."

"Thank you, Mrs. Beeson. A pile of hay will be a welcome relief."

"The two of you will burn in hell for your carnal sins," Patricia spat.

As Patricia blew past Jonathan, the wind from her fury snuffed out his light and opened a dark door to Malachai's world.

"Burn her...burn her..."

***

Jonathan coughed and turned over. His hay bed, although bountiful, was still prickly through the blanket. He coughed again. He smelled a thin scent of a distant fire and thought Patricia got up before the roosters to light the fireplace in the kitchen.

The kitchen faced their small back yard of their little farmstead. Their property was only an acre, enough to raise chickens for eggs, a few milking cows, a little paddock for their two horses, and a small four-stall barn, which was now his sleeping quarters. He coughed and then sniffed the air. The scent of burning wood in the kitchen didn't carry its usual sweet scent.

The cows thumped and bumped against their stall while the horses snorted and danced in theirs. Something wasn't right. His eyes opened from underneath his blanket and noticed the barn was glowing. He yanked the cover off and bolted up and saw Wakayeja wicahpe.

"Run to the well!"

"Fire! Poppa, fire!" Elizabeth's voice screeched into the darkness. He looked at the opened barn door and saw the reflection of a wavering orange glow. He heard breaking glass!

"Poppa! Fire!" Elizabeth's voice was louder.

The horse whinnied, the cows wailed, and the chickens squawked and clucked frantically inside their coops. Jonathan scrambled to his stocking feet, dragging his blanket behind him. When he shoved opened the barn door, he saw the right corner of the back of the house, Elizabeth's room, was on fire.

"Oh my God! Elizabeth! Elizabeth!" He called into the darkness. There was no moon to shed any light. There was only the glow of the fire. He retrieved the two milking pails and scooped up water from the horses' trough and raced towards the fire splashing life-saving fluids onto the dirt.

"Elizabeth!"

"Poppa!" Elizabeth ran to him in her bare feet and took one of the water pails.

"Poppa, look!" Elizabeth pointed to a dark figure holding a flaming torch. Jonathan saw Patricia's face aglow with delight as she watched the fire spread towards the kitchen.

"Go ring the bell, and then get more pails!" Jonathan ordered. Elizabeth darted off to the side of the house and he raced up to the house and threw the two pails of water onto the corner of the house. When he turned to get more water, he saw Patricia move towards the kitchen door with the torch.

"Patricia, no! No!"

Patricia touched the torch to the pile of kindling at the back door and it ignited a small fire. The frantic clanging of the fire bell erupted in the darkness. There was a pause, and then more fire bells rang!

"They're coming Poppa! They're coming!" Elizabeth shouted as she struggled to carry two buckets of water. Jonathan took one of the pails, tossed it onto the blazing basket of kindling, and threw it to the ground

"More water! More water!" Jonathan yelled. When he tried to grab the second pail from Elizabeth, she jerked away.

"No!" Elizabeth cried and darted around him. She ran with the bucket towards another fire. Patricia's nightgown was on fire. Patricia was running across the yard towards the barn with Elizabeth chasing after her. Jonathan ran towards the barn scooping up his blanket along the way. The fire began to engulf Patricia's body and her hair, slowing her pace. Elizabeth was able to catch up to her and partially douse the fire with water. Part of Patricia's gown still flickered until Jonathan tackled her to the ground with a blanket.

"Retched evil must burn to preserve the good...the retched must burn to preserve...the good...let me burn...let me burn..." Patricia mumbled through her delirium. "Let me burn..."

Jonathan gripped the embers of his wife. The stench of her smoking flesh churned his stomach. As he gripped Patricia, he saw his neighbors in nightshirts filling his yard. The flames at the right corner of the house were now licking the roof's eaves. A bucket brigade had formed. The screams of his neighbors, the splashing of water, the wailing of the animals was not enough to drown out Patricia's words of self-hatred.

"Let me burn...Jonathan...let me burn..."

Jonathan recognized the familiar rancid stench that oozed from her body. It belonged to Malachai. He looked at Elizabeth.

"Is everyone safe?" A voice called out in the darkness. Jonathan looked up and strained his eyes to focus. It was Samuel Chase standing over him covering his nose to block the scent of her burning flesh. "Are you hurt, Miss Beeson?" Samuel asked Elizabeth.

"No, but Mrs. Beeson...I fear..." Elizabeth didn't dare finish her words.

"I'll get the doctor," Samuel ran off disappearing into the neighboring crowd of rescuers and onlookers.

Jonathan tried to arranged Patricia's body gently on the grass. She moaned with his every move.

"It's all my fault," Elizabeth cried through tears.

"No, it wasn't your fault, or Mrs. Beeson's fault. She wasn't in her right mind when she did this. She reeks of Malachai," Jonathan declared. You and I are the only ones who know the hateful things Malachai is capable of. We must never say a word to anyone about this. This must be our secret. Understand?"

Elizabeth nodded in agreement.

CHAPTER 10

The next morning Elizabeth surveyed the debris that was once her bedroom. The hole in her floor, and the hole through her back wall, reminded her of Simon and Willie, the other two holes in her life. She was too exhausted to cry. She looked at her hands and saw soot had turned them charcoal black. She wiped her hands on her damp bedding. Her butter cream skin emerged. She was safe until somebody decided to peel her skin back and examine her blood.

A bright June sun poured through a two-foot hole in Elizabeth's horsehair plastered bedroom wall. The wall looked like it had been punched. Patricia had landed the final blow.

Elizabeth's foot pushed against her pillow, mattress, and bedding which had been overturned onto the floor. They were a wet and soggy mess of soot, feathers, and batting. Nothing was salvageable. She didn't know what it meant to lose her possessions because she never had any-except her marble!

Her eyes widened with panic as she looked down at the section of floor the fire ravaged. The men had chopped and hacked up the floor where her lamp exploded and sprayed the floor with its fiery oil, so they could stop the fire from spreading. The corner floorboard, under which she hid her marble from Patricia, was now somewhere in that five-foot wide hole. When she looked down into darkness, all she saw was May Tobias' face looking back at her.

***

"Fetch my marble Eliza," May demanded. Eliza looked at May's face as it peered at her from beneath the other side of the chifferobe. "Don't look at me. Fetch my marble out from under the chifforobe before the mice get it," May ordered.

The last thing Eliza wanted to do was stick her hand where mice live. She heard stories about rats eating toes clean off the foot overnight.

"There's nothing to worry about. Papa made Winsome stuff the hole. Now fetch my marble. It's my favorite. It's my owl eye," May said. Her lip rolled into an angry pout and then her face disappeared.

Eliza lay flat on her stomach and moved her hand cautiously under the chifforobe. Her bare arm felt the coolness of the oak floorboards. May's shoes were now next to her head.

"Can you feel it?"

"It's too far."

"Go at it some more. Stick your face in there so you can get a good look," May ordered with a snicker and prodded Eliza's shoulder with her foot. Eliza pushed her shoulder against the chifforobe as her fingers clawed outward to reach the marble.

"It's just too far," Eliza whined.

"I didn't want it anyway. I just wanted to see if the mouse was going to bite you," May announced and skipped out of the room.

That night as May slept, Eliza was awakened by small squeaks. She bolted up on her pallet and blinked several times to adjust her eyes to the darkness in the room. Using the light of the half moon, she scanned the oak floor for the vicious rodent. There was nothing she could grab to protect herself. She heard something moving.

She caught the glimmer of the owl eye marble as it rolled out from beneath the chifforobe towards her pallet. It rolled right to her. She stared at it and then stared at the chifforobe waiting for the mouse to appear. It never did. She quickly scooped up the marble and stuck it between the hay of her makeshift mattress.

The next morning Eliza went to the kitchen and asked Georgia for a strip of an old bed sheet used for bandaging. That night when she went to bed, she retrieved the marble from her mattress and pressed it into her navel. She tied the strip around her waist to hold the marble in place. She reasoned it wasn't stealing if no one wanted it. Besides she could honestly say the mouse gave it to her if anyone ever found out.

***

Elizabeth blinked and saw the pile of debris sticking up from the hole. She dropped to her knees, reached into the hole and began pulling up pieces of wood. Her hands groped the earth fearless of bugs and rodents, or anything that lay in wait for her desperate fingers.

She broke off edges of floorboards to enlarge the hole and invite light into the darkness of the pit. With pieces of the floorboards piled next to her, her fingers began stumbling on soft pebbles and little jagged rocks. After ten minutes she had scooped up every rounded pebble her fingers touched and still no marble. Desperation bubbled up within her.

"I can't lose you...I can't lose you...Where are you?" she called out with her face pressed to the edge of the pit's opening.

"I'm right here," a voice answered back.

Her head popped up. Samuel Chase was standing outside the hole in her wall.

"Is something wrong?" he asked.

"I can't find my...something very important to me. I had it hidden beneath a floorboard in this area where the fire was, and now it's gone."

"Sounds pretty serious."

"If you're looking for my father, he has taken Mrs. Beeson to the Pennsylvania Hospital."

"Actually, I was looking for you. Your father asked me to look after you and the shop while he was gone."

"My father told me no such thing."

"Maybe because he knew you'd say no."

"I am not a child that needs tending to."

"That's where we agree. You are not a child. You are a woman, a very independent, headstrong woman, who is refusing help during her time of need. I made a promise to your father, which I intend to keep. The shop must open. People depend on it. I will help you run the shop."

"It seems I'm not the only one who is mule-headed."

"That's why we are the perfect match Miss Beeson," Samuel said with a smile. "With your father's permission, I contacted a framer, a plasterer and other tradesmen who will be arriving shortly to start rebuilding what was damaged by the fire."

"I suppose I should say thank you."

"Only if you want to."

"Thank you."

"You are most welcome. It must feel strange to be on the other end of the candle."

"What do you mean?"

"You're normally the one with the ability to see through everybody, now with this opening, everybody can see you," he said with a soft smile.

Elizabeth forgot she was in her robe. She turned her back to him and pulled her soot-covered robe together.

"Turn your head, Mr. Chase. It's inappropriate for you to see me in this state of undress."

"Undress? You have enough garments on to clothe a village in India. Miss Beeson, in my travels through cultures, I have come to understand that clothing was made not to cover our bodies but the truth in our hearts. It is not your body you fear I will see, but your feelings...about me."

"Clothing or not, they are my feelings to share, and I'll do so when I am good and ready. A hole in my wall does not give you the right to peek into my private space..."

A warm blinding June sun filled the space where he was standing and then poured into her heart.

***

Samuel waited until Elizabeth opened the shop before he returned to her house. He had only a few minutes before the tradesmen were to arrive to assess the damage. He had to act quickly. Jonathan told him exactly where to look. He wanted no witnesses.

He entered through the kitchen and went straight to a set of built-in cupboards to the right of the dry sink. He opened the cupboard as Jonathan instructed him and removed its contents. He removed the shelf so he could get a clear view of the cupboard's floor. He saw the finger-sized notch on the edge of the cupboard floorboard, slipped his index finger inside, and pulled. The board popped up without a struggle. Lying in the well of darkness were three small black leather journals. Without looking at them, he quickly stuffed his coat pockets with them, and returned everything back to their place inside the cupboard.

He was about to go outside and wait for the workers, but he was drawn to Elizabeth's bedroom. He felt guilty sneaking into her space, but he couldn't help himself. Her mattress and bedding were in a soggy heap on the floor next to the door. He couldn't resist touching where she slept, where her body left its imprint. He laid his right palm flat on a section of mattress. What came back at him, made him weep. Her mattress was like an overripe tomato left on the vine too long. It was heavy, weighted, and ready to explode with her sorrow and sadness.

He withdrew his hand and wiped his tears. He knew her feelings like they were his own. He wanted to put an end to her sadness, her isolation, her solitude. He looked down in the hole. Except for a few splinters of wood, he saw nothing but dirt. He lowered to one knee, lowered his hand inside the hole and scratched the earth's floor. He found nothing.

Elizabeth believed something was there or was supposed to be there and that was good enough of a reason for him to use his ability to excavate. He stood up and opened his palms over the hole. After a minute, bits of rock and dirt began to hit the underside of the floorboards.

"Come on...come on...show me what she needs...bring it up...come on... bring... it...up!" The hole burped up a small cloud of dirt. The dirt dropped to the floor.

Clack...

A small marble rolled away from the edge of the hole and stopped at his feet. He picked it up with two fingers and then examined it in the sunlight.

Why would a marble make Elizabeth so frantic?

He slipped it into his pants pocket and then looked over the hole.

"Find any gold?" Thomas Anthony asked as he tossed his shovel to the ground with a clang. Thomas poked his head through the outside wall hole to peer inside. Folks always say Jonathan has more money than he lets on. I heard he has a stash in his house somewhere. Did you find anything?"

"I was checking the floor joists. I don't think this one was affected by the fire. What are you doing here? Edmund is supposed to do the plastering."

"He changed his mind. I think folks are beginning to find all this hocus pocus stuff a bit too much. People are talking about how Mrs. Beeson was lit up like a human torch last night. Not a pleasant thought."

"No, it isn't."

"Any news on Mrs. Beeson?"

"No."

"I don't imagine that when there is news, that it will be any good…Heard she was burned pretty badly. I also heard and that maybe their daughter was the one to set her on fire."

"Seems like you heard a lot," Samuel shot back. He gritted his teeth. He was ready to rip Thomas' head off.

"Women are clucking louder than a coop full of chickens. How long is Jonathan planning to be at the hospital in Pennsylvania?"

"Why? Are you looking for another opportunity to clean someone else's house of their valuables?"

"It looks like you've made yourself right at home, haven't you Sam? It's right off the boat and back to business for you."

"You shut your mouth. By the grace of God and my father, that reckless life is behind me."

"Just because your father took you all over the world to heal your wretched soul doesn't make you a prince that can lord over me. You're no better than that Black witch. Lucky for you, I'm a forgiving and accepting Quaker, otherwise, someone would pay top dollar for you."

"Jonathan knows it was you who brought those bounty hunters here to grab Elizabeth, Simon, and her son. You're the last person he'd want working on his house."

Jonathan looked at Thomas' shovel. He wasn't here to work; he was looking for those journals to give to the bounty hunters.

"Be on your way," Samuel warned.

"He knows no such thing because it's not true," Thomas defended. "I'm as good a friend to Jonathan as anyone."

"The only friend you have is the devil, and even he doesn't want to be seen in public with you. I know why you came here, and it's gone. Jonathan took it before you could get your grubby hands on it, but I'll tell Jonathan you came by."

"Speak one libelous word about me, Sam Chase, and I will take great pleasure in creating a coffin of plaster for you."

"Your services are not needed here."

"We'll let Jonathan decide that."

"He just did. Jonathan left me in charge. Leave!"

"Turning over his daughter and the keys to his store to you, a common thief, are not the actions of a charitable man, but a fool," Thomas said snidely. "Perhaps it is Jonathan who needs to be committed to the asylum, not Mrs. Beeson."

Rage coursed through Samuel's body and he needed to redirect it. The last three years on sailing ships to study with a yogi in India, and a Buddhist monk in China, and a Master teacher in Japan were all about this moment of control. He could not lose it. He had to channel his energy elsewhere. The pile of boards began to tremble from the force of his burgeoning anger. Samuel closed his eyes and inhaled deeply. A metal spade flashed in his mind's eye—his answer.

"It's time for you to shove off," Samuel said.

Thomas saw Samuel's right hand swipe the air. Thomas had no idea that Samuel had created an intention, or that he was about to receive the blow of a shovel to the back of his head.

CHAPTER 11

Elizabeth entered the front room of her house. Her makeshift bed: pallets, hay, and a pile of quilts greeted her. Ten days sleeping on pallets made her think back to her bed in May Tobias' room. She closed her eyes to forget that part of her life. She could have slept in Poppa and Patricia's bedroom, but she wasn't that desperate.

She entered the hallway that led to her bedroom and then closed her eyes. She wanted to be surprised by her new bed. Samuel told her it was going to be delivered today. The house was finally repaired. Her room was whole again. The hole in her floor had fresh pine boards and her bedroom wall no longer bore an opening for birds to enter.

Her hands groped along the hall walls as she made her way to her bedroom door. When her hand hit her door frame, she stopped.

One...two...three...

Her eyes opened and all that she saw was her old braided rug, a chair, and her bureau. No bed. Her shoulders dropped. She really wanted to sleep in a bed, her bed. It was only noon. Perhaps it was arriving on the three o'clock freight wagon. Samuel had orchestrated the parade of tradesmen to quickly fill the visible holes in her life. His efficient restoration of her home filled her with hope, which she was willing to embrace—cautiously.

Elizabeth touched the newly plastered wall. It was cold to the touch, still drying. The cold, clammy, sweet scent of the horsehair plaster lingered in the air. She opened her new window to bring in warm June air to help dry the plaster, and noticed the windowsill had no nail holes. The sill was smooth and freshly painted with two coats of white paint. Evidence of Patricia's venomous containment was gone.

She immediately went to check her bedroom door. She pulled it to her to check the outer frame and saw that Samuel had replaced the door and the door frame and painted them the same color, slate blue. She had not noticed until now, that there were no outside locks on her door.

However, when she looked down at the new doorknob, she saw a key sticking out of it. The only lock on the door was the one she now controlled. She turned the key and watched a bolt of metal extend outward from the side of the door into the air. She twisted the key again and the bolt disappeared back into the door. She removed the key and gripped it in the palm of her hand. She had never held so much power before. The concept of being able to stop someone from entering her space was one she'd never fathomed. Samuel empowered her.

She was grateful he had entered her life. Over the last ten days, she discovered how well they worked together at the store. Samuel didn't follow convention. He made it clear to everyone who entered that she was the boss, and he worked for her. He didn't mind the stares and grimaces from men. Nor did he surrender to the flirtatious flashes of lashes with which he was bombarded.

Each day Samuel made it easier for her to take a step forward toward a new life. Additionally, the absence of Patricia's scowling face and hateful words provided her with a profound sense of peace. Elizabeth loved running the store, and the house that she now felt she could call home. She wished her father was there to enjoy the peace with her, but she understood he would never abandon Patricia.

The last letter she received from her father conveyed Patricia's condition was worsening each day. Between Patricia's fog from the medicine the doctors gave her to fight the infection from her burns, and her crazed hateful obsession with Elizabeth, the doctors weren't sure in which hospital Patricia should be placed. Her father begged them to keep Patricia at the main hospital and not transfer her to Pennsylvania Hospital for the mentally ill in West Pennsylvania. Thankfully her deteriorating physical condition required she remain at the main hospital.

While Elizabeth wanted to go to Pennsylvania to be by her father's side, she was relieved that he needed her to stay behind. For once, being left behind was a good thing. The awkwardness between her and Samuel had worn off by the third day. She was finally comfortable with him. She even caught herself smiling several times in his presence.

The clock in the front room chimed half past noon. She needed to get back to the store. She slipped her key in the little silk and velvet purse she made for herself and pulled the drawstrings taut. She had no intention of losing her first key. She would thank Samuel for her new door as soon as she returned to the store.

Once she left the house, she found herself scurrying to the store. With a smile on her face, she darted around people and scooted across cobblestone streets until she saw something that stopped her in her tracks. Emma was heading towards her store. Samuel was there alone. She watched as Emma approached the front door. When Emma disappeared inside, panic set in.

Emma had been campaigning for Samuel since that day she tried to get him to get a parasol from a display. The countless times Emma made flirtatious appearances to gain Samuel's attention infuriated Elizabeth. Elizabeth refused to let Emma steal from her again. She wished she had another pail of chicken poop for Emma, but she didn't want to look petty and vulgar in front of Samuel.

She lifted her chin and decided to let Samuel decide whom he preferred and then bolted to the back door that was used to receive deliveries. Once inside, Elizabeth eased her way toward the front of the store to listen. True to form, Emma was already demanding Samuel's attention.

"Mr. Chase, I need your help, your undivided attention," Emma announced.

"How can I help you today?" Samuel replied courteously.

"Where's your little shop girl, in the back—counting beans?" Emma asked snidely.

"Elizabeth is running an errand. How can I help you, Miss Butler? I'm the only one here so my time is limited. There will be other customers."

"But none like me," Emma responded coyly.

"No, and I thank the heavens for that," Samuel shot back firmly with a smile. "How can I help you?"

"Actually, it's more what I can do to help you," Emma taunted.

"I'm a capable man, Miss Butler."

"Yes, anyone can see that you are..."

"What do you want?" Samuel asked with growing annoyance.

"I have an invitation for you," Emma began.

"I'm sorry Miss Butler, I don't have time for invitations. If there is nothing you need to buy, I have crates to unload. Excuse me…" Samuel moved away from the counter and headed toward the curtained doorway leading to the back door.

"I am hosting a small rally for two special abolitionists. You may have heard of them, Mr. and Mrs. Craft?" Emma blurted. Her words stopped him. "It's a little rally to support and celebrate their incredible and miraculous journey to freedom. I've arranged for food, a music quartet, and then the Crafts will speak of their harrowing journey. I thought you would want to come and support the cause. Only people of importance and means are invited," Emma said, spreading her pleated fan with a taunting smile. "I came all the way over to deliver your invitation in person."

Samuel moved toward her. Emma smiled and extended his invitation. When he reached for it, she withdrew it behind her back and smiled seductively.

"If you want to come, you'll have to take it from me."

"No," Samuel said coldly.

"What do you mean, no?" Emma demanded.

"There is no party. You've created this charade to amuse yourself at Elizabeth's expense. You're a carney, a barker without a show. You just want me to pay the price of the admission-to hurt Elizabeth. I won't let you hurt her," Samuel announced flatly.

"Your precious Elizabeth is a nothing more than a slave's whore. She's already borne a child out of wedlock. Is that what you want for a wife, a slave's whore?"

"My God, you're a poisonous tarantula. You come up from the earth to grab at any poor victim that passes your hole. You don't want a mate. All you want is a prey so you can devour them from the inside out.

"What kind of woman are you? You look to poison a man's heart against life and love. I don't want you to come into this store or near Elizabeth ever again. Take your little tarantula trap and get out or I'll squash you!" Samuel threatened.

Elizabeth emerged from behind the curtain and saw a petrified Emma. Her mouth slackened, jaw dropped, eyes wide with tears, and her creamy face redden with humiliation. Emma's chest was heaving with emotion.

"Samuel..." Elizabeth said his name softly.

"Miss Butler was just leaving. She just closed her account," Samuel said coldly, and walked over to the counter. He furiously flipped through the pages of a large ledger. Emma shot Elizabeth a seething look. Samuel ripped a page from the ledger and balled it up. "Your account is officially closed, Miss Butler." In three hard heeled strides, Samuel was at the front door. He yanked it opened. "Good day, Miss Butler. I said good day!"

Angry tears blurred Emma's vision. Humiliated, she twisted left and then right, making her bell-shape dress swoosh at her waist. Her arms flapped like a skittish bird trying to take off. Her eyes locked Elizabeth's one last time and fired departing daggers of rage. A June breeze pulled her attention to the door held open by Samuel. Her heels clacked furiously against the wood floor as she made her way through the door.

"I promise you I will be the one doing the squashing!" Emma declared.

Samuel raised his hand and swiped at the air slamming the door in Emma's face. Elizabeth gasped.

"It was the wind," Samuel blurted.

Samuel's secret was out. Elizabeth closed her eyes to keep from prying, but it was too late. Balls of light exploded in her mind's eye flashing visions from Samuel's life.

Samuel lay crying on a floor mat, while an Asian man sat quietly across from him...Samuel standing with his right hand outstretched as a bowl of rice floated in front of him... Samuel sitting with a man wearing a swath of bright white fabric wrapped with great ingenuity around his head—Poppa had shown her pictures of men like this, He called them men of India. The frail looking man had his hands together in prayer.

She saw his lips move silently and quickly. From the view of the frail man, she saw Samuel floating a foot above the earth.

"I pray what you have seen hasn't changed your feelings for me," Samuel pleaded softly. His voice brought her back. Elizabeth's heart pounded against her chest, shaking her body like thunder striking the earth; the tips of her ears felt on fire and perspiration beaded on her upper lip. She ran to Samuel and kissed him passionately the way Jane Austen's Elizabeth Bennet would have kissed Mr. Darcy. She would absolutely allow him to walk her home tonight!

CHAPTER 12

After a very solemn and quiet dinner at the Logan Inn, they walked back to her home side by side. Elizabeth could tell that Samuel was still troubled by the incident with Emma, and she knew he felt exposed and uncomfortable. She thought her kiss would have made it clear she wanted him even more. But he said nothing of her kiss and became distant.

Right after she kissed him, Samuel made an excuse and left her alone in the store for almost three hours. He returned shortly before closing with an apology and an invitation to dinner, but he wouldn't allow her to discuss what happened or acknowledge her kiss. During dinner he sat on his hands unless he picked up a fork and knife to feed himself.

Elizabeth couldn't understand why he was so distant. Perhaps the growing chasm between them was because Emma blurted out information about Simon and her illegitimate child. He knew the worst about her, except he didn't know that she was really Negro and a former slave. Or maybe he did know and that's why he was so quiet. Maybe Emma had done more damage than Elizabeth realized. The last thing she wanted him to think was that she was a promiscuous woman.

But if he felt any less of her, why did he want to take her to dinner? They normally went their separate ways after she locked the door to the store. She closed her eyes out of frustration.

"Are you not well?" Samuel asked.

"I think I have a slight head pounding."

"Yes, there was a little too much excitement this afternoon," he replied solemnly.

Was he ready to talk about what happened with Emma, what she saw, their kiss?

"The best thing to do is just wipe it from your mind, the way one washes a dirty window," Samuel suggested.

"A dirty window?"

"I'm sorry. That didn't come out the way I wanted. I think my tongue has retired for the night," Samuel said. "If you don't mind, I'd rather just enjoy the peace and quiet with you," he concluded as he gave her a quick smile.

Tonight, the short distance to her home was the longest walk in her life. She had hoped that Samuel would become her Mr. Darcy, now it seemed another dream vanished before she had the chance to ponder it. One house away and she was ready to bolt to her door, unlock it, and slip inside without an awkward goodnight, but the taste of his lips made her linger.

"I want to thank you for all the work you did to restore our home. I appreciate everything and I'm certain my father does, too."

"You're quite welcome Miss Beeson."

Miss Beeson?

"Did your bed arrive?"

"I'm afraid not. I checked at noon and there was nothing. With all the commotion at the store this afternoon, I forgot to check with the freight depot to see if it arrived on the last freight wagon. One more night on a pallet and hay won't hurt me."

"You sound like you're enjoying camping out in the front room."

"Actually, I would prefer any bed at this point," Elizabeth confessed. Samuel had stopped walking. She had walked past her front door.

"Would you like me to check your home before you enter?"

"Yes, please." Elizabeth handed him the key. She was letting him into her life.

He unlocked the door. They stepped inside together. Her upper lip began to perspire as she lit the oil lamp. The faint scent of lilacs hung in the air inside the house, which Elizabeth thought strange. The moment Patricia found out Elizabeth loved the lilac bushes that adorned the left side of the house, Patricia made Jonathan cut them down. When she came home at noon, all she smelled was the fresh scent of the new pine floorboards, the acrid odor of paint, and the cold damp sweet clay scent of the plaster.

Samuel lit a second lamp and then disappeared from the front room into the short hall to the bedrooms. There was a pause. She took a step toward the hall and the scent of lilacs grew stronger.

"Samuel, is the house safe?"

"Elizabeth, I think you should come see this."

Elizabeth's feet couldn't move fast enough. In five quick strides she was at the doorway to her bedroom. What she saw paralyzed her. Samuel had lit her room so she could see her new poster bed with its soft elegant curtains billowing softly in the June night air. Her braided rug was replaced with a beautiful oriental one. To the left of her bed she saw a beautiful wood nightstand, a gleaming brass hurricane oil lamp. Its white globe was painted with vibrant purple lilacs. When she turned her head, her bureau with the lopsided top drawer had been replaced with a bureau and wall mirror that matched the nightstand. On top of the bureau was the biggest vase of lilacs she had ever seen.

Tears blurred her vision. She had to go touch everything to make sure it was real. When she lowered herself onto her bed, her knees were barely bent before she was sitting. The poster bed lifted the mattress high off the floor. She fell back onto her bed and felt like she was lying on a cloud. The fluffy comforter on top of the feathered mattress was divine.

"I presume it meets your satisfaction," Samuel said.

Elizabeth bolted upward. She forgot she was in her bedroom and that Samuel was only feet away. She jumped up and moved away from the bed.

"You did all this?"

"Yes," he said with a smile. She was never so happy to see his smile.

"But when?"

"This afternoon, after…Emma."

"You were here at my house, in my bedroom?"

"Yes. And I guess when you say it like that, it doesn't sound very good."

"No, no this is good, this is very good. Why would you do this?"

"Because I love you Elizabeth Beeson, and you deserve the finest life has to offer. I want to marry you. I want you to be my wife," Samuel said softly as he approached her.

"You still want to marry me?"

"Yes. You would make me the happiest man in the world if you would become my wife."

"But Poppa…"

"I've already asked him. He gave me his blessing before he left for the hospital."

"All this time the two of you..."

"Yes, please don't be angry. I am a man who knows what he wants, and I want you."

Elizabeth's mind began swimming. She felt like she was drowning in an old fear. Samuel was offering her what she couldn't have with Simon.

"I had a son out of wedlock," she reminded him.

"I know," Samuel said and stepped closer.

"I see spirits," Elizabeth confessed.

"And I can move things with my mind. You saw me do it at the store today...when I closed the door without touching it. This invisible force is a part of me Elizabeth. I'm afraid I can't make it go away. We're not evil Elizabeth, just different," Samuel explained.

"I know," Elizabeth said and took a step towards him.

Samuel opened his right hand. Her marble sat in his palm.

"You found it!" She grabbed her marble and clutched it to her heart. "God Bless you! I never thought I would see Willie, my son, again-I was saving this for Willie in case I should have the fortune of being in his life again—Thank you, thank you so much... I know you may not understand, but this is...so important to me."

"If you allow me, I promise you these hands will only love and protect you. I will never raise a hand to you or...any of our children—and that includes Willie, if he were to miraculously return." His voice cracked. "Elizabeth, we're two of a kind, birds of the same feather. No one else understands what it feels like to be us," Samuel said as a tear made its way down his cheek.

"My mother was a slave," Elizabeth said and took a step closer. She felt completely naked. The love and passion from his eyes seared her soul. She imagined so many reactions, none of them good. She looked down at his feet. They were moving towards her. Before she could speak Samuel had her in an embrace. His face was in hers.

"Mine, too," he whispered back into her ear. The heat of his breath on her ear felt like fire. His words melted her soul. "Can you forgive me?"

"Forgive you? Samuel Chase, I have fallen in love with you, and I don't care who your real parents are, or what you can do. Can you forgive me?" Elizabeth blurted through tears.

"How can I ever fault you for being who you truly are..."

In the warm glow from her lilac hurricane lamp, Mr. Darcy kissed Elizabeth Bennet with all the passion in his soul, and she kissed him back clutching her marble. Feeling the warmth and peace of his love surge through her body, she vowed she would find a safe place for her marble, so that she would never lose this feeling again.

***

Elizabeth heard the familiar sound of her father's boots as he made his way down the hall. Her eyes opened and she was in her new bed with the scent of lilacs still swirling in the air. She couldn't wait to share her good news of her upcoming marriage to Samuel. She knew he would be happy for her. She turned over and saw her father standing by her window. He was looking at the lilacs in the vase on her bureau.

"Poppa?"

"Hello Elizabeth."

"Poppa when did you come home? I didn't hear the wagon... "

"Ssssh sssh sssh ssh ssh...Now don't be upset."

"Why would I be upset, when I'm so happy. Samuel proposed marriage. He wants to marry me, me."

"Did you accept?"

"Yes of course, Poppa."

"That's wonderful news. That makes me very happy. Now everything is all set for you. I had a long talk with Samuel, and he knows what needs to be done. It's time for you to go off into the world and make your own family, your own life, your own legacy."

"Poppa? Nooo... "

"Elizabeth, I need you to listen to me. Everyone is where they are supposed to be. There's no going back. Simon and Willie are safe and doing just fine. Samuel is going to make you a very happy woman. The two of you will have to head north because you've got to use your gift... Use your gift to find the secret to end all this hate and make a difference."

"Poppa...nooo..."

"You can't stay here. Mrs. Beeson will never leave you alone. Besides,

I'd like to have a little peace..." Jonathan said with a smile.

"Noooo..."

"Elizabeth, I love you and I'm proud of you. What made my life bearable was knowing I wasn't alone. I had you, and now you have Samuel. He understands you and loves you the way you deserve to be loved. You can't stay here. She'll never let you have any peace. Sell everything and leave as soon as you can..." Jonathan pleaded. "Elizabeth...Mr. Lincoln will make things better...all will be righted...all will be righted..." Jonathan said with a smile that lit up her room like a sunrise and then disappeared with the crow of the rooster.

CHAPTER 13

Days later Elizabeth looked in her mirror, and saw her eyes were swollen from tears. Saying goodbye to her father was harder than watching Simon and Willie disappear over the hill. She looked down at the large vase of lilacs Samuel gave her. She had moved them to the floor next to her bureau to make room for the pitcher and basin she took from her father's bureau. It was the one he used to wash his face in the morning and his hands before dinner.

She lifted the pitcher and filled the basin part way with water. She took Jonathan's cloth and dipped it in the cool water. The moment her hands touched the water, tears flowed and rippled the water's surface. She wrung out the cloth, returned to her bed. Although she was fully dressed for father's memorial services, she wasn't ready to go, or let him go. She climbed onto her bed, stretched out and placed the cool cloth on her eyes. She didn't want to see any spirits good or bad. She just wanted peace.

Resting on her cloud of a mattress she heard the clucking of the chickens, a bark of a dog. The usual chatter from her neighbors was gone. Where was everyone? More importantly, where was God and why did God take so much from her? Perhaps there was merit in Patricia's animosity toward her. Perhaps Patricia did the right thing in locking her in her room. Perhaps Patricia was right to call her wicked. After one afternoon of complete freedom, her father died. The light scent of Samuel's lilac blooms mixed with the sweet pungent scent of pine. Company.

"I don't want to talk today," Elizabeth said quietly without removing her cloth.

"You can't blind yourself to life," Wakayeja wicahpe said softly.

88

It was as though she was speaking right into Elizabeth's ear. Elizabeth slapped her hands over her ears. Elizabeth's hot tears warmed her cool cloth.

"Death, like spring, offers a new beginning and a chance for the things we love to...come back,"

Elizabeth bolted up in bed and removed her compress.

"Simon is coming back?" Elizabeth asked. She heard the heavy clacking of a man's boots as they made their way down the hall to her room. She swung her legs over the side of her bed. Her eyes focused on the doorway. It never occurred to her Simon could return. Her father already surprised her once with a reunion with Simon that night on Ferry Road, but she turned him away. Did Poppa bring Simon home again? She stood up and pressed her fingers across the bodice of her dress. A nervous smile crawled across her face. When Samuel emerged in her bedroom doorway her smile vanished.

"It's time to go," Samuel announced.

"Samuel..." The wells of Elizabeth's eyes swelled with tears. "...I thought you were...my father."

"My darling, I'm so sorry." He embraced her. "I know this is difficult, but I will help you get through this day, through this time. I will never leave you," Samuel murmured in her ear. The warmth of his breath lightly brushed her neck.

"Don't make promises you can't keep," Elizabeth said, fighting back tears.

"Forgive me. That was very insensitive of me."

"No, I'm the one who's sorry. You did nothing wrong. I'm...I'm overwhelmed with grief. Please, forgive me."

"Of course, my darling, you are forgiven. Your pain must be indescribable. I found something that I hope will offer you solace on this day. He reached inside his coat pocket and removed a piece of red Asian fabric with little goldfish embroidered on it. It was tied in the furoshiki manner. She looked at him.

"Samuel, I don't think this is the appropriate time for receiving any gifts."

"I think you father would want you to have this," he urged, lifting his palm for her to take the gift.

When she untied the fabric, she saw her father's Meerschaum pipe.

Its white face sea captain had been scorched on one side. Tears flooded her eyes and spilled onto the fabric.

"I'm so sorry if this has upset you. I thought having his pipe would ease your pain," Samuel lamented.

"It does." Gripping the pipe, she threw her arms around Samuel's neck. "This is the most thoughtful and loving thing you could ever do for me," she cried in his ear. "Thank you...thank you..." Her eyes studied the sea captain's face as she moved her index finger across his face. She thought it looked a bit like her father. She pressed the pipe to her chest and reminded herself that all of the talks they shared were still in his pipe.

"Elizabeth, I'm sorry, but we have to go," Samuel stepped aside for Elizabeth to go through her bedroom door.

She collected her draw string silk purse and handkerchief and led Samuel to the front door where Samuel's wagon and horse awaited.

"Why do we need the wagon? Aren't we walking to the meeting house?" she asked.

"Not today," Samuel answered.

Samuel kissed the air and slapped the horse's back with the reins. The wagon eased forward. Sitting in front with Samuel made her think of the first time her father lifted her up onto a wagon, and how she stood waiting for permission to sit. As they ambled forward, she looked over her shoulder. The image of Belinda holding her baby flashed before her eyes. Samuel freed his right hand from the reins to grab hers.

"Look forward, your new life has much to offer you. I can't bring him back, but I promise I will make this sadness go away."

Bring who back? Willie or Poppa?

Elizabeth dared not ask her question out loud. She tightened her grip on his hand to signal her appreciation.

Samuel turned the wagon on to Ferry Road heading towards the Delaware River and Amos' Cornfield. Her heart skipped a beat. Her nails dug into his hand. Tears mounted in her eyes.

"Elizabeth, what's wrong?"

"Ferry Road..." Elizabeth said. "This is where Simon and Willie..."

"I'm so sorry. I didn't think..." He tugged the reins to the left and pulled the wagon off Ferry Road through a canopy of pear trees whose sweet scent filled their noses. "When the minister suggested we move your father's memorial to the field by the river, it never occurred to me...I'm so sorry."

Tears cascaded down her face. Just being in the same area where she was forced to say goodbye to Simon and her baby was like digging up the dead.

"Why couldn't we do my father's memorial at the meeting house?" she asked, dabbing her tears.

"Because there wouldn't have been enough room at the meeting house to hold all these people," he replied.

The wagon came to a stop. When Elizabeth looked up, she saw the field was packed with wagons and people. Elizabeth couldn't count how many people she saw, but she thought it was at least three hundred, if not more.

"All these people came for Poppa?" Her mouth was agape.

"I thought it would comfort you to see how many people loved your father," Samuel added as he secured the reins and then jumped down. More wagons slowly pulled in behind them. "This was the only place that was big enough to hold all of your father's friends," Samuel concluded with a smile.

Elizabeth scanned the field. She had never seen so many Negro and White people in one place. Samuel extended his hand to help her down. She took her eyes off the crowd long enough to secure her footing on the wagon step. Once she was down, Samuel drew her in with a gentle hug.

"Your father lived a good life, one that everyone here came to celebrate. Jonathan Beeson is still here in every one of these people. He didn't leave you alone."

Elizabeth couldn't take her eyes off of the crowd. She saw her father's coffin in the distance, which was surrounded by handpicked flowers and boughs made from branches of flowering trees. The field became silent. The crowd parted as Samuel escorted her to her father's coffin. On either side of the crowd, Negro men, women, and children two to three rows deep lined the path.

The minister of their meeting house, John Barton, greeted her with a smile.

"These are some of the people your father helped free. They wanted to come and pay their respect...in song," he said softly.

91

Elizabeth's eyes scrolled across both sides of the path glimpsing all the faces and thought she should be standing in that crowd.

"Your place will be at the helm, Miss Beeson. Your father would have wanted you to have a front row seat to see what is possible with God and the good heart of man. Come with me." When Mr. Barton turned to lead the way to the coffin, he nodded his head and the free Negro voices erupted into the Spiritual, "*Roll Jordan Roll.*"

Their united voices made the earth shake beneath her feet. When she got to her father's coffin they were still singing. She thought after she reached her father's coffin it would bring an end to the singing, but then one person called out the first line of another spiritual, "*No More*", launching them into another earth-shaking song.

When that song ended, the sound of the rushing Delaware River filled the gap for a moment, but quickly disappeared when their voices merged to sing "*Hold On*". When the voices reached the crescendo chorus, Elizabeth let go. Her tears flowed like the river that ran beside her. Clutching her father's pipe, she cried. She cried for her father. She cried for Simon and the life they would never share. She cried for the son she would never raise. As she continued to cry, Samuel held her and never let her go.

CHAPTER 14

"When we bury those we love, the most comforting thing is knowing that they are always in our heart," Horace Chase said as he gripped Elizabeth's hands.

Two weeks later, Elizabeth's first meeting with Samuel's parents wasn't as frightening as she imagined. Samuel's father was a very gentle and compassionate man, and a true gentleman.

"My darling Elizabeth, my son has said the most beautiful things about you. Now I know why, because you are beautiful inside and out," Horace said as he lifted her hand and kissed it.

Horace Chase was shorter than Samuel, balding, and with a potbelly. His blue eyes carried a twinkle that lit his round face. On the end of his pointed nose sat his spectacles which required him to tilt his chin downward whenever he wanted to examine something closely.

"Mr. Chase, I certainly see where Samuel gets his charm."

"Agreed. My men are nothing short of spectacular," Mrs. Chase injected with a warm smile. She stepped forward with open arms. "We are so delighted to finally be with you dear Elizabeth...under more pleasant circumstances."

"And I you."

"Please, come join us in the sitting room," Mrs. Chase said and moved through a doorway.

Samuel was all smiles and bursting with pride. He was sharing his little family with her. He extended his arm, which Elizabeth latched onto, and they followed Mrs. Chase into a luxurious yet cozy sitting room. Upon entering, Elizabeth saw the most beautiful crystal bowl on a red silk Asian table runner that adorned a circular table. The sparkling crystal bowl was displayed like it was a piece of art along with the all the wood carvings, paintings, and furniture pieces that obviously came from Horace and Samuel's trips abroad. She didn't know which piece she should examine first.

Forgetting her manners, she pulled Samuel over to a Chinese silk triptych painting that hung on the far wall. The center panel had a large fortress-type structure that expanded onto a portion of the other two panels. Just behind the fortress were the ornate rooftops of other smaller buildings. Beautifully painted white horses and their elegantly jewel-toned robed riders guarded the entrance. The detail of the artistry shocked her. She clearly saw the individual hairs of the riders' mustaches and the whites of their eyes.

"She has an eye for fine art. Samuel, you have selected well," his mother said.

"This is a silk painting of the gate to the Forbidden City where the emperor's palace is located. In Peking, China it is called *Zijin Cheng*. Our translator told us it meant Purple Forbidden City or Palace."

"It is the most elegant thing I have ever seen. Forgive me, I didn't mean to be rude. Your collection is a treat for the daughter of a shop keeper."

"Elizabeth, you mustn't sell yourself short. Your father has bolts of Chinese silk in his store. I know because I sold them to him," Horace added.

"Yes, and I've always thought the silks lovely, but seeing this painting helps to justify their beauty even more so. Samuel, the fact that you got to see this Forbidden City must have been thrilling."

"Every place has things that are beautiful about it as well as things that are not," Samuel's mother said rather firmly. We must talk Elizabeth, please sit down. My apologies if I am rather abrupt, but I feel we have a great deal to discuss and resolve."

"Mrs. Chase…"

"Horace, don't shush me. He is as much my son as he is yours."

"Mother, please, bullying father won't change my mind."

"I'm no longer counting on your father. I'm counting on Elizabeth to change your mind. It's one thing to go abroad for business. It's another thing to move to New York to marry, and start a family without the support of your family—your father and I."

Elizabeth's eyes widened.

"From the look on Elizabeth's face, she had no idea you were planning to uproot her," Mrs. Chase added.

"Mother–Elizabeth, I was planning on discussing it with you."

"New York?" Elizabeth muttered. She had heard New York was a bustling and somewhat dirty city filled with gangs.

"See, Elizabeth agrees with me. I'm grateful you selected a woman with a good head on her shoulders. She'll talk some sense into you. Go ahead Elizabeth dear, the floor is all yours."

"Samuel..."

"Elizabeth, darling, given all that you've been through, I thought it prudent that we should start our lives together in a new place. I thought if we were in a new place, we could create new memories."

"New York?"

"I know it's a city, but it does have sections that are just like here."

"Samuel, I don't know. I have the shop. What am I going to do with the shop?"

"My thoughts exactly," Mrs. Chase interrupted. "The shop will provide you both with financial stability and an outlet to sell imports, I wish to add."

"I love that idea..." Elizabeth declared.

"Mother, please..."

"Mrs. Chase, you are meddling," Horace interjected.

"As well I should, and you, Mr. Chase, should be helping me. Elizabeth is about to make a decision that will determine the rest of her life. It's only fair that she is forewarned..."

"Mrs. Chase, why don't we go see how dinner is progressing in the kitchen," Horace urged as he jumped up. He stood over her and extended his hand. "Thanks to you Mrs. Chase, they will need to have this conversation now instead of after dinner as we agreed. Your hand please."

"I can stand up on my own. Thank you very much." She stood up and locked eyes with her husband. "I'm not one to be pushed about."

"My dear Mrs. Chase, a herd of Burmese elephants couldn't move you."

"Elizabeth, I shall have to leave it to you to make sense of this ridiculous plan. Don't let Samuel leave this room until he agrees to let go of this foolish talk. Samuel, if you emerge from this room without a

95

different plan I shall…I shall…" she swatted him several times with her handkerchief and then dabbed at her eyes. "Elizabeth, use everything in your power to change Samuel's mind, and I mean everything," Mrs. Chase urged with a raised eyebrow. "We women must show solidarity during a crisis. It's so good to have you join our little family," she kissed Elizabeth on each cheek gently. "Horace let's go. Elizabeth has work to do," Mrs. Chase ordered as she passed Mr. Chase who scurried behind her like a puppy.

"This room seems to be filled with surprises," Elizabeth started.

"Elizabeth, I'm so sorry. I was planning to discuss it with you."

"Before or after we sold the shop?"

"Well before, obviously."

"Samuel, why didn't you speak with me first before speaking with your parents?"

"I wanted to ease you into the idea of moving to New York. Besides, you suffered so many difficulties. I didn't want to toss another one onto the wagon. Would it have helped if I discussed it with you first?"

"No, I would still have agreed with your mother. New York… Samuel… New York! It is a beast of a city."

"It is a fresh start."

"You'd like me to trade one beast for another?"

"New York would be nothing like Malachai…I'm sorry I said that. That's not what I meant."

"What did you mean?"

"New York will have more opportunities for us…for people who sit on the fence."

"People who sit on the fence?"

"People like us, who have roots in the soil of slavery. No one will know us there. We can make a fresh start and get further away from the bounty hunters and never have to worry about anyone pointing at our children…"

"Our children?"

"You do want to have children, don't you?"

Elizabeth's mind jumped to Willie.

"I already have a son."

"Of course, you do. I'm so sorry. Forgive me."

"Samuel, don't expect me to forget about Willie, because I won't."

"Of course, you won't, nor should you. I know what Willie and Simon meant to you. I can only pray that there is room left in your heart for me."

"I'm sorry. Forgive me. I'm being selfish. It's just the thought of moving to a new place where I know no one is like starting all over again."

"Exactly."

"Where would we get married?"

"In New York. We'd find a justice of the peace to marry us. Getting married in New York means we don't have to go through all the rigmarole with our Quaker traditions. There'll be no series of meetings, letter writing, and the best part, we'll need no one's approval. My parents have already given their blessings, and your father already gave his blessing. You see, we're free to do what we want. You don't have to give me an answer today. Just promise me, you'll think about it. And you'll have plenty of time. We still would have to deal with all the details of selling the store and the house..."

"Samuel, I can't sell the store and the house."

"Why not?"

"It's not mine to sell. Mrs. Beeson still owns everything."

"You're right. I forgot that Mrs. Beeson is still alive."

That thought made Elizabeth want to move far, far away.

***

Later that night Elizabeth lay in her bed wide awake. On top of her cloud of thick mattress and down feather topper, her body was heavy with conflict. She didn't know how to move forward. The awkward dinner with Samuel's parents only added to her insomnia. She and Samuel tried to come up with a plan, but the only thing they agreed about was using a justice of the peace to get married. There was a great deal to do to get married in a Quaker-style wedding. With all of the complexities of her life, she longed for simplicity. If the marriage process were to drag on for too long, she feared she would get too comfortable and want to stay with her life just as it was.

Her routine with the shop and the house was a comfortable one, especially with Samuel. Without Samuel, she didn't think it would offer the same joy. She wished Poppa was alive. He'd know what to do, and then she wouldn't have to deal with the shop or the house.

The irony of her present situation was almost ludicrous. When she wanted to escape with Simon, they made a plan, and she got on the wagon. Now that she had the freedom to leave, escape, with Samuel, coming up with a plan seemed daunting. Perhaps the fear of being stopped again by slave bounty hunters was preventing her from taking action, or maybe it was the fear of experiencing failure and loss all over again.

"Get out!"

Elizabeth heard a snarling voice in her ear. She bolted up in bed. She recognized that snarl.

"This is my life. Thief!"

Elizabeth peeled back the linen curtain on her poster bed and saw Patricia whose bandages appeared soaked with dark blood. It was official, Patricia Beeson was dead, and now another threatening spirit.

"This is my house. Get out!" Patricia growled.

"You don't belong here anymore," Elizabeth responded firmly. She was almost relieved to see Patricia in the spirit world. At that moment her father's words replayed in her mind:

"You can't stay here. She'll never leave you alone."

"Fornicator! Get out of my house! Get out of my house!" Patricia screeched in her face and then disappeared. Patricia's threatening screeches rang in her ears. Elizabeth yanked her canopy curtain shut. In her new bed with her canopy curtains drawn, Elizabeth felt like a prisoner. Her father's warning was real.

Elizabeth wondered if she moved to New York with Samuel, would Malachai, Patricia, and other spirits follow her, or would they be happy enough to know she was gone. The chance for peace without the taunts and jeers from spirits was a welcome thought.

Patricia's head thrust through her curtains startling her.

"Get out! Get out! Get out!"

It was time to go!

***

Samuel walked slowly and quietly through the jungle. All he had to do was follow the stomach-churning stench, and he would find him. His eyes scanned the jungle ahead and he noticed what looked like a lion moving about. It was too small to be a real lion. Based on the retched odor it had to be Malachai.

Malachai danced around his little fire, and then crawled on his knees like an animal.

"Graaawwwww, graaawwwww," he shouted lifting his head. This was the beast that wreaked havoc in Elizabeth's life!

"I suppose not knowing what one's adversary really looks like is part of the mystery of the fear," Samuel said announcing his presence.

Malachai tried to jump up but the weight of his lion's hide made him stumble back and fall on his butt.

"Who are you? No one enters my kingdom without my permission," Malachai proclaimed.

"This is what it feels like when you come after Elizabeth. You enter her world; you torment her with your stench and your weak magic to make her believe you're bigger than you are."

"I am Mal-"

"I don't care who you are!" Samuel yelled as he rushed toward Malachai.

"This is what it feels like when someone invades your space and disrupts your little world."

Samuel looked like a tall white tree standing in the blinding sun. Malachai shielded his eyes to get a better look, but the glaring light around Samuel forced Malachai to close his eyes to slits.

"Who are you and what do you want from King Malachai?"

"Stay away from Elizabeth."

"She has stolen from a Mandinka warrior," Malachai yelled up to Samuel from the ground.

"I don't care what you feel she took from you, stay out of her life," Samuel threatened with his bright face looming over Malachai's.

"When you cause suffering to a Mandinka warrior, we will find you and punish you throughout eternity. It is the Mandinka way," Malachai turned quickly, clutched his spear and stood up. With a wave of his hand Samuel snatched the spear from Malachai's hand and tossed it into the brush.

"I'm not like the others. I can and will hurt you."

"Your bit of magic does not frighten me. I can flatten fields with my breath," Malachai threatened.

"I'm not a field. The door to your world works both ways. I can come into your world as easily as you can come in mine. Come near Elizabeth or any of our children, and I'll come back and slit your throat with your own spear while you sleep! I mean it. Stay away from her!" Samuel growled and then quickly faded into Malachai's fire.

Malachai couldn't believe his eyes. The White spirit disappeared in his fire. He quickly kicked dirt on his fire to extinguish it, and then ran to get his spear. He sat on the ground staring at the embers of his fire, rocking his body beneath his lion's hide.

The thought that someone could enter his kingdom unnerved him. Now he would have to guard the very fire that was supposed to give him warmth. Hot angry tears slid down his face onto his knees.

"Graaawwwww!"

He released a body-shaking growl and then panted and grunted. It was the first time he was haunted by life, and it was truly frightening.

***

When Samuel opened his eyes, he was on the floor in the corner of his bedroom. The sweet smoke of the Buddhist incense greeted his nose. His body felt like a boulder, heavy and dense. His yogi in India warned him that returning the consciousness to the body after astral travel was like placing packing straw inside a cold thick metal box. He would have to let the straw settle. Samuel sat for several minutes before he uncrossed his legs. He leaned over to stretch and touch his toes. He hoped that his visit ended a battle instead of starting another war. A sudden burst of sweet pine filled his nose. He could see her taking shape. He jumped up. Little needles pricked his toes with pain for moving before his blood was fully circulating.

"Next time, we will go together," Wakayeja wicahpe said and faded into the smoke of his incense.

❦PART TWO❧

CHAPTER 15

New York City was bigger and more crowded than Elizabeth could ever have imagined. She had been to a big city before. Her father had taken her on several trips to Philadelphia when he had to pick up delicate shipments that he didn't want to entrust to freight wagons. Compared to New York, the city of Philadelphia with its town green and cobblestone streets, had more open space. She was already missing home.

When she and Samuel arrived on December 27, 1849, her first view of New York, although cold and cramped, was somewhat picturesque with its smoky chimneys, snow-covered rooftops, steps, and windowsills, and smoky gas lit streets. But as their carriage slowed in front of the Astor House Hotel, Elizabeth felt like a true country bumpkin. The Astor House Hotel exuded elegance beyond her wildest imagination. It looked like a golden mountain of brick and glass.

"Samuel, did the driver bring us to the right place?"

"I promised you I would give you the best life had to offer. This is what you deserve. This is where we will get married and honeymoon," he whispered in her ear.

"Samuel, do we have the money?"

"We will always have money. I will see to that," Samuel whispered and kissed her gently on the lips. The door to the carriage opened. Bright light from the gaslight posts on either side of the entrance blinded them. A shadow stepped in the carriage doorway.

"Welcome to Astor House Hotel," the hotel footman said as he placed a step stool for them to disembark. Samuel descended quickly to the sidewalk and then turned for her with an outstretched hand. Elizabeth felt like royalty. As she emerged from the carriage, she saw two men scurry up to the carriage to unload their luggage. Everything seemed to be happening too fast. Elizabeth feared the footmen would scoop her up if she didn't move quickly. She turned to reach for her small carpet bag, and a footman whisked it from her grasp.

"No dear," Samuel said softly. "Everything is taken care of. Mr. and Mrs. Samuel Chase," Samuel announced to the footman. Elizabeth released an awkward smile, and then took Samuel's hand. The irony of her predicament would be amusing if it weren't so painful.

Years ago, she and Simon wanted to be husband and wife and weren't allowed to be seen together on the same buckboard seat. Now Samuel was presenting her to the world as though they were husband and wife without the benefit of marriage, and it was so readily accepted. They had to offer a marital camouflage. Without a chaperone, she would attract suspicious eyes and be viewed as a prostitute. The Astor House Hotel would never allow her to cross their threshold unless she was properly titled or chaperoned. Samuel did his best to protect what was left of her virtue.

Nothing Samuel told her about the fancy New York hotel prepared her for the luxury that greeted her once she entered the grand foyer. Her eyes danced about the luxurious reception area trying to take it all in. There were beautiful wall murals of trees, elegant country sides, and royal courtyards, seas of sumptuous seating groups, and the most intricate carpet designs her eyes ever had the fortune to see. When her eyes lifted up overhead, she saw stylish lighting décor that warmed and brightened the museum quality ceiling artwork of celestial blue skies and angelic beings.

"Mr. and Mrs. Samuel Chase," another footman announced to the tall man behind the front desk.

Elizabeth removed her left glove and fingered the thin gold band on her ring finger. She wanted to make sure the man behind the desk saw they were married. Samuel gripped her hand and pulled her gently to the front desk.

"Mr. and Mrs. Chase, welcome to The Astor House Hotel, the grandest hotel in the east!" The tall man greeted them with a courteous toothy smile. His mustache was groomed and lightly waxed, his black hair was oiled and slicked down onto his white head, and his black tail attire was adorned with a white carnation boutonnière.

"I'm Mr. Harrison, your host and concierge. Anything you need, ring

104

for your floor footman and we will get it for you," he said with a hard grin. His movements were precise and minimal. He dipped the nib of a pen into an ink well, and then presented it along with a stylish short form. It had the art rendering of the hotel in the top corner and its print was done in a clean Garamond font. Elizabeth couldn't remember a bill or receipt done with such artistry. "We have received your full payment for your two week stay. Just your signature is needed Mr. Chase. I took the liberty of completing the rest of the form myself using the information from your telegraph. You're more than welcome to review the form to see that it is to your satisfaction."

"That won't be necessary," Samuel said.

"May I read it?" Elizabeth asked.

Mr. Harrison's eyes widened ever so slightly.

"But of course, Madam." He presented the bill to her with a slight flourish and a forced smile.

"I just wanted to examine the beautiful artwork in the top corner," Elizabeth said and quickly handed him the bill. She was grateful she found a way to rebound from the obvious insult she levied against his integrity.

"If madam would like, I can give you a few sheets as a souvenir," Mr. Harris offered with a slightly raised eyebrow.

"Oh no thank you, one bill will suffice," Elizabeth volleyed back.

"Perhaps we should get to our rooms so we can freshen up for dinner," Samuel said placing his hand at the small of her back. Elizabeth smiled. Her husband knew to get her away from Mr. Harrison's condescending behavior. Her tongue could be as sharp as her mind. She was Jonathan Beeson's daughter, a shop girl. She would never sign anything without reading it first.

"Would you like me to make dining arrangements for you?"

"Thank you, no. We have plans to dine with friends this evening," Samuel answered. He gave Elizabeth a wink.

"Yes, of course. If there is anything you need, your floor footman will be happy to retrieve it for you or find you the person who can. Would Mrs. Chase care to visit the Ladies' Salon? After a long travel, a visit to the Ladies' Salon is always refreshing."

"How much does it cost?" Elizabeth asked.

Mr. Harrison rolled his eyes and pursed his lips.

"I beg your pardon?"

"My dear, you don't have to worry about anything. You don't need money. You can have anything you want, and it will be billed to our room."

Money is a valued luxury, spend it wisely, Poppa always said. Even though they sold the shop and her home to Charles Beckwith, a wealthy textile manufacturer, and had a surplus of money, she didn't want to waste it on frivolity.

"Thank you, Mr. Harrison. I'd like to freshen up in *our* room and unpack."

"But Mrs. Chase, you have a maid to do your unpacking. You have a lovely suite on the second floor."

"A suite?" Elizabeth turned to Samuel. Mr. Harrison gently tapped the bell on his desk. A young uniformed man swooped to their side. She felt a whoosh of wind when the bellman stopped and lifted his chin, awaiting his orders.

"Albert, please take Mr. and Mrs. Chase to room twenty, the honeymoon suite," Mr. Harrison instructed and handed the bellman a set of keys. "Mr. and Mrs. Chase, I wish you a joyful stay," Mr. Harrison concluded with a slight bow of his head.

"Right this way please," Albert said and then clicked his heels together before he took a step to lead them to the stairs. Following Albert's quick pace left Elizabeth little opportunity to peruse the hotel's patrons who were well dressed and coiffed like royalty. From the twinkling crystal chandeliers, gold-framed wall mirrors, velvet settees, lavish oriental carpets, to the tuxes and tails, sateen and chiffon dresses, and sparkling hair combs, Elizabeth had never seen so much opulence in one place in her life.

The stairs to the second floor were wide, carpeted, and curved like grand staircases she had seen in art renderings of European palaces. Elizabeth looked up and saw a swirl of vanilla railings and banisters that spiraled upward to the fifth floor. At the very top of the spiral she saw a beautiful stained-glass sky light. She felt completely out of her element.

She climbed the steps to the second floor and noticed the hem of her dress was caked with bits of dirt frozen from the snowy streets. Compared to the other guests she looked like an orphan. She couldn't wait to change into her wedding dress. It was the fanciest dress she had ever owned.

As they moved down the hall, their heels were absorbed by a beautiful burgundy runner with a gold-braided pattern that ran along its edges. She saw the remnants of the hotel's Christmas Holiday decor: elegant side tables stationed along the corridor filled with vases of sweetly scented pines, white sugar-coated fruits, and small shiny brass bells.

Just a few doors down the hall, Albert stopped, and with a flourish, inserted the key inside the room door, and then pushed it open. Samuel bowed slightly and waved his arm across the threshold to allow her to enter first. Their honeymoon suite was grander than the foyer. The gaslights, the candles, and the fireplace, created a magical glow. It was like she was entering her own private heaven.

The poster bed had steps that led to the thickest mattress she had ever seen. The white satin bedding reflected the glow of all the lights. When she touched it, her hand slid across the fabric.

"I hope that you are pleased with your accommodations," Albert said with a smile.

"Are you pleased Mrs. Chase?"

"Very pleased," Elizabeth said. Her mouth was dry from holding it open.

"When you're ready, just pull that cord by the fireplace and your maid will come and assist you with whatever you need. Will there be anything else Mr. Chase?"

"No Albert, that will be all," Samuel placed two quarters in Albert's palm. Albert did a military turn on his heels and disappeared into the hotel hall, closing the door gently behind him.

"It makes me happy to see you happy Mrs. Samuel Chase."

"Samuel, this is too much."

"No, Elizabeth. Don't ever say that. Don't send your fortune away. Embrace it. This is how we're meant to live. One day I will buy you an entire brownstone and you'll have three floors as lavish as this."

"Samuel, we can't afford to live like this…"

"Bup bup bup," He said putting a finger on her lips. "Darling, open your mind to the possibilities and they will fall into your lap. I have a plan, a grand one. All I ask is that you open your mind and keep it open," he murmured and then kissed her long and softly on her lips.

She felt drunk from the surrounding luxury. She was almost ready to forgo their little visit to the justice of the peace. When he kissed her again, she felt the part of the lady, and pulled away completely. "Mr. Chase, please wait downstairs while I change into my wedding dress," Elizabeth requested.

"Your wish is my command. I will wait for you downstairs in the gentlemen's lounge where I shall receive a shave, have them brush me off, and find a bootblack. But before I go, a small wedding gift," he announced and opened a large satchel. When he removed the package, she recognized it immediately. It was the furoshiki gift he wrapped in her store. Mounting tears blurred her vision.

"Samuel Chase, you lied to me," she said, choking on her words.

"No, I didn't. I said these handkerchiefs were for the special woman in my life. I know it's not as special as it could be because you did the embroidery work, but I thought we could think of it as a gift of love we worked on together. You adorned the inside with your love, and I adorned the outside with mine."

She looked in his eyes and saw them glossy from clinging tears.

"I can't wait to marry you and make love to you," he whispered in her ear.

Elizabeth's ears flashed red and perspiration immediately dotted her upper lip. He dotted her neck with a few kisses, then gave her one soft peck on the lips and vanished through the door to the hotel's hallway.

Elizabeth rested against the door as her eyes absorbed the decor of her honeymoon suite. A bowl of fresh fruit sat on a small table that was adorned with a white linen tablecloth. Two chairs were positioned inviting the patron to sit. She slid onto a chair and pulled herself up to the table. She pretended to lift a teacup and have an imaginary conversation. She touched the fruit. It was real.

Her eyes roamed over to the bed. She jumped up from the table to run towards the bed and then stopped. She climbed the stairs to the bed seductively and then lowered herself down. Her body sank into the pile of down feathers beneath the satin duvet. She lifted her right arm over her head and looked at the foot of the bed where Samuel would stand before he joined her later tonight.

She practiced releasing sensual sighs. Simon's face appeared and floated above hers. She slapped her hands over her watering eyes. This should have been her life with Simon and their son. But the world would have never allowed them to come here, stay in this beautiful hotel. Tears escaped through a crack of her pinky and slid down her cheek. Her head popped up. She didn't want to stain the satin bedding. She pressed her furoshiki wrapped gift to her heart.

Perhaps the best thing happened that night. Poppa said Simon and Willie were alive somewhere in the world and that was better than having them six feet under. Alive meant there was a chance they would meet again. If it wasn't for Emma...She covered her eyes, but Emma's face still found her. However, when she saw Emma, she was sitting in another pile of manure back in New Hope, Bucks County, Pennsylvania, screaming her head off. Elizabeth erupted into a fit of giggles. Poppa was right; everyone was where they were supposed to be.

CHAPTER 16

The front parlor at the Justice of the Peace was anything but peaceful. Unlike the mural walls of The Astor House Hotel, the parlor walls were dark and streaked with the plumes of black fumes from the oil lamps. There were two old chairs, and a desk for signing the wedding license. The room was clearly set up to marry quickly, move bodies, and make money.

A small woman sat behind the desk with a sprig of holly in the crown of her hair which looked more like a rat's nest Elizabeth had seen in the barn back home. From the glow of the oil lamps, Elizabeth could feel the woman's beady eyes fixed on her. She was staring at her wedding dress, which was a deep shimmering emerald green, with a piping of black velvet along the waist of her bodice.

Elizabeth quickly pulled her black wool and velvet hooded cape closed. She was obviously overdressed and out of place. Initially she chose the green dress from a catalogue to blend in with the holiday season and not call attention to their clandestine matrimony. But it was clear she had failed. She took a step back toward the door.

"Don't worry, the rest of our wedding will be beautiful and special as you my love," Samuel consoled as he gripped her hand and moved her forward.

"...You may kiss your bride," the Justice of the peace said with disinterest. "Go to the desk to pay and sign for your certificate." He dismissed the newlyweds with a flick of his right hand and then pointed to the next couple who quickly stepped forward.

"Samuel, I don't want to get married here," Elizabeth whispered under her breath.

"This is the only place I could find that wouldn't question our roots,"

Samuel whispered softly.

Elizabeth felt her smile slip off her face. If anyone found out they weren't White, they would get thrown out of the hotel and someone would alert slave bounty hunters to their whereabouts. It felt like Ferry Road all over again. She turned ready to bolt out of the door. Samuel pulled her in for a hug.

"We are safe. I will never let anything ever happen to you," Samuel whispered in her ear.

"Step over to the desk to pay and sign your certificate," the Justice of the Peace instructed. "Next. Step forward please."

Samuel slipped her arm through his and moved them forward. Tears welled in Elizabeth's eyes. When they stood before the Justice of the Peace, he barely looked at them.

"Rings and registration please," he demanded with an opened hand. With their registration and rings in his hands, his eyes focused on their names.

"Do you, Elizabeth Beeson, take Samuel Chase to be your lawfully wedded husband?

"I do."

Do you, Samuel Chase, take Elizabeth Beeson to be your lawfully wedded wife?"

"I do."

"Exchange rings," he said flatly.

"I pronounce you man and wife. Kiss your bride and go to the desk to pay and sign your certificate," the Justice of the Peace instructed.

"Elizabeth, you're mine now, and I'm yours," Samuel said and then kissed her passionately on the lips. She felt completely awkward kissing her husband in the dingy room with the straggly strangers. She was too afraid to close her eyes and kept her eyes on the man who married them. Samuel, however, showed no fear whatsoever. He slipped his tongue inside her mouth briefly. Her eyes widened from embarrassment. She would have enjoyed it more had they been in their hotel suite. She pulled back.

"Let's get back to our hotel and celebrate properly," Samuel said in her ear. The breath of his words caressed her neck. She nodded.

As Samuel paid the woman, she watched the Justice of the Peace remove a flask from inside his coat and take a swig. Samuel redirected her attention to the certificate which she quickly signed. The woman blew several breaths over the ink and then handed it to Samuel.

"Good luck," the woman said and then shot a hard look at her husband as he took a longer swig.

***

The walk back to the hotel took them through a dark section of New York she never wanted to see again. Elizabeth couldn't understand how a luxury hotel could be surrounded by crowded tenements and squalor. Perhaps all of New York was dirty and derelict like the neighborhood of the Justice of the Peace, and the hotel was an oasis for the wealthy.

Although she couldn't see the neighborhood they were moving through, she could smell it. Her ankles were cold and wet from the snow-covered dirty streets. From the dim glow of the gas streetlights, she noticed a band of black growing on the hem of her wedding dress. The filth of New York was grabbing at her ankles. She tried lifting her dress, but it slowed her down. It was more important that they get out of the dark and dangerous streets, and back into the light of the hotel.

They moved quickly along Chamber Street heading towards Broadway, the main thoroughfare. Samuel promised to find a carriage once they were on Broadway. Finding a carriage on Broadway was easy and would never draw any questions as to why guests of the Astor House Hotel would be slumming so close to The Points. Samuel warned her that there would always be eyes watching them in New York City, and tonight he wanted no one to know that they had traveled to get married without a chaperone for her.

As they crossed Church Street, the stench of horse manure, urine, garbage, and poverty was clawing at the back of her throat. She had never seen so many poor people. New York seemed to be more struggle than success, but Samuel told her that in New York, success was just around the corner. However, every time they turned a corner, she was met with the same stench. At least it wasn't Malachai's. She expected Malachai to make a threatening appearance, but perhaps New York was even too scary for Malachai, and for that she was grateful.

"Noooo! Noooo! Bethany, run! Run!" A woman's voice shrieked into the night.

Elizabeth looked across the street. She saw a group of shadows struggling in a huddle. Elizabeth adjusted her eyes and saw two women struggling with a burly man.

"Leave us be! Leave us! Nooo!" A second woman's voice cried out.

"Help us! Somebody help meeee! Bethany, run!"

"Elizabeth stay here," Samuel ordered and rushed to their aid.

"Samuel!" Before she could blink, Samuel was across the street and fighting with a man twice his size. Jimmy, the slave bounty hunter, popped in her mind. Panic seized her. She saw Samuel's shadow, his hands flailing at the large man. The man fell back in the doorway of a tenement. Samuel turned to the two women. Elizabeth's eyes were drawn back to the man. He was moving again. He removed something from behind his back. Her eyes only saw its shadow, but the moment he raised it she knew it was a gun.

"Samuel!" Elizabeth's voice careened off the buildings and blasted into the night sky.

Samuel's hand reached out in front of him and then swiped at the air. A flash of light exploded into the night. A horse whinnied. The fast clacking and pounding of hooves on icy and dirty streets warned her to look before she stepped off the sidewalk. Her vision was blocked by two wagons that rumbled past her in a race to escape more gunfire.

Elizabeth sucked in the air she couldn't breathe. The moment the wagons were gone, she saw Samuel fist fighting with the man.

"Samuel!" As Elizabeth approached, she saw one of the two women run and grab the man's gun from the ground. The woman picked it up and aimed at the two fighting men. "Don't! You'll shoot my husband."

The man drew back his fist. Just as he was about to swing, Samuel became a blur as he leapt into the air and connected his foot with the man's face. The man's head twisted to the left from the kick and then his body dropped into a heap onto the sidewalk.

Samuel stood with his feet wide apart in a fighting stance. His fists were clenched. He waited for the man to move. When he didn't, Samuel rushed to Elizabeth and the women.

"Are you hurt?" Samuel asked, embracing her. She buried her face in his coat. Hot tears froze on her face. "It's all over, darling. Ladies, are you hurt?"

"No, sir. By the grace of your chivalry we are alive and well. Thank you so much." Elizabeth lifted her head and got a better look at the two women. The woman who held the gun was White, and the other woman was Negro. The Negro woman clutched a bundle of fabric—it was a 'get away bundle.' Runaway slaves used them.

"My name is Cassandra Dennings. You just save Bethany's life. That man is a slave bounty hunter. He was trying to kidnap her and take her south. I don't know how I could ever repay you. What is your name?"

"Mr. Samuel Chase. And this is my wife, Elizabeth–Mrs.Chase"

"Mr. Chase, where do you live?"

"We just arrived in New York. We're staying at the Astor House—"

"The Astor House Hotel? What on earth are you doing here?"

"We got lost," Samuel answered quickly. "We're on our honeymoon. We thought we'd take a walk and got lost. Perhaps we should all leave before he wakes up?" Samuel herded the women away from the unconscious bounty hunter.

"But I have to repay you. Are you planning to stay in New York?" Cassandra asked.

"Yes…"

"You'll need work. I shall speak with my father and request he give you employment. He's a businessman and can always use an honest man, and a man with your unique skills. I'll arrangement the meeting for you and send word to the hotel. I'm sorry, but we have to go, or she'll miss her train to Boston." Cassandra slipped the man's gun into her satchel and scurried down the street and disappeared around a corner into the darkness.

"Samuel," Elizabeth murmured as she pointed. The man was struggling to sit up. Samuel grabbed Elizabeth's hand and broke into a run. As they ran towards the bright lights of Herald Square, all Elizabeth could think about was that night on Ferry Road behind Amos' Cornfield and how dangerous it was to be Negro in America.

CHAPTER 17

After everything Elizabeth had witnessed an hour ago, the last thing she was interested in was a fancy dinner, and what was going to come afterward. She was afraid of her Mr. Darcy. Between his dodging bullets and taking down a man with his feet, she didn't know who she had married. Was he some type of assassin? Or was he Malachai in another form, which would explain why Malachai disappeared shortly after Samuel entered her life.

"Are you still upset?" Samuel asked. "I'm sorry you had to witness that violence, but I had to save those poor women." His eyes were heavy with concern. "Obviously neither of us is hungry. Why don't I get the bill so we can go upstairs?"

The last place Elizabeth wanted to be was alone with him in a room. Elizabeth wanted to run. Her eye scanned the expansive dining room for an exit.

"I promise you, I will explain everything. You don't have to be frightened of me," Samuel pleaded as he touched her hand to reassure her. Elizabeth felt a jolt of electricity shoot up her arm from his touch. The tips of her breasts came to life. Perspiration dotted her upper lip. She thought she was too afraid to be aroused by his touch, but something inside him reached her heart. Overwhelmed with emotion, she failed to notice the waiter as he presented the bill for their meal, or the waiter's disappointment at her untouched food.

"Was there anything wrong with your meal?" the waiter asked with a furrowed brow.

"No, it was wonderful. We had a long day of travelling. I'm afraid my wife is exhausted. Thank you so much," Samuel concluded and gave the man a whole extra dollar. The waiter's eyes widened and then a big smile rolled across his face.

"Thank you, sir. It was my pleasure to serve you," the waiter said and lifted their plates from the table with a flourish.

As he pulled out her seat, Samuel's fingers brushed her right shoulder sending a chill down her spine. She inhaled and released a big breath when he took her hand to lead her to the grand staircase. With each step she kept her eye on the main door. Her heart jumped about in her chest.

"You're trembling. Are you cold?"

"I'm tired," she lied.

When he slipped the key in the door to their suite, she looked down the hall to see if anyone was in the hall in case she had to cry out for help. The door to their suite swung open. Samuel stepped aside to allow her entry. Her mouth dropped open. Their bed had been turned down, a hot fire danced in the fireplace, and a bottle of champagne sat in a silver bucket of ice with two crystal flutes arranged on the little table with the two chairs. It would have been truly romantic had she not been overwhelmed by Samuel's fight.

Two more steps inside and she saw their luggage had been unpacked and her beautiful ivory nightgown was resting across the gold brocade recamier. New white candles had replaced the ones that were burning earlier. Samuel closed the door to their suite and locked it. There was no escaping unless she was prepared to jump out the window

"Is it too much?" Samuel asked. His eyes penetrated hers, which were welling with tears. "Or am I too much?"

The room grew so silent, Elizabeth could hear the candles flicker.

"I don't know who you are or what you're capable of," Elizabeth began. Samuel dropped his head. "Of all people, I should be the last person to question anyone's special abilities. You have accepted who I am and what I can do without a question...You're my husband, and I should trust you implicitly...But I don't understand how you could take down a man who is a foot taller and twice your width with only a kick that did not look it could knock down a chair. Can you explain it to me please...Husband? Is that deadly kick a part of that 'invisible force' you mentioned?"

"It's called Kung Fu."

"Kung Fu?"

"It is a form of hand-to-hand combat. I learned it when I was in

116

Peking," Samuel said brusquely and then threw the room key on the bureau. "When I was twelve, that invisible force frightened me too. In America, no one was equipped to explain what it was, why I had it, or where it came from. Because of my father's travels for imports, he knew of people and places where he could get answers about what was wrong with me."

To hear Samuel speak of his abilities as an illness was something she knew all too well. She knew what it was like to believe her abilities were a curse of the devil. She knew what it felt like not to fit in or be accepted, and worse to have your only parent abandon you. They were so much alike in that regard. Besides her Poppa and Simon, Samuel was the only other man who understood and accepted her as she was. Guilt scraped at her heart for making Samuel explain his actions. After all, he was protecting a woman, a free Negro woman.

"Samuel, I…"

"It's better that you know everything now…I want you to trust me," he said softly.

Elizabeth wanted to surrender. She moved to the bed and sat. She tapped the bed for him to sit next to her. He remained standing.

"When my father first left me in Peking, I was so angry. I was in a foreign land. I didn't speak the language. I didn't like the food. I didn't understand their customs. I didn't even look remotely like any of them. I was an outsider all over again. But it was worse. It was obvious I didn't belong there.

"The first year was horrible, the second year, bearable because I finally agreed to listen. Ten years later, I found a new home and a deep form of acceptance that surpassed any form of love and acceptance I could find in America—until I met you. Elizabeth, you are my reflection. When I look in a mirror, I see you," he said as he sat on the bed next to her.

Elizabeth and Samuel sat side by side in silence for a few moments. His hand crept slowly towards hers. She moved her hand to meet his.

"The world and customs of the Far East are vastly different from the customs here. They have a great respect and reverence for the simplest things. They also have tremendous knowledge about that which we cannot see. Did you know there is a life force that flows through everything? They call it chi. We're all connected to it. We're not demons

117

or in cahoots with the devil. You and I just happen to be more connected to that energy than others. One day I'd like to take you there so you can see just how powerful we truly are. Until then, we're going to have to create our own world so we can be safe."

"I have one more confession," Samuel said quietly.

His words carried a heaviness. Elizabeth did her best to sit up straight on the plush bedding that made her sink into its cloud of down feathers.

"I am listening..."

"I did something. I hope you will approve," Samuel began.

"What is it?"

"I confronted Malachai," he blurted out.

"I don't understand."

"He won't be bothering you anymore. I let him know that he is to never come near you."

"How can you confront him? He is a spirit."

"...There are ways to travel outside of your body and return. I learned how to do it while I was abroad. You should know that Malachai is only a ... "

"I don't want to know anything about him," Elizabeth blurted through tears. He has taken so much from me without the slightest provocation."

She pushed herself up from the bed and walked to the fireplace. Her eyes focused on the flames in the fireplace. She was furious. She wished she had been able to confront the monster who had terrorized her. She touched her face. It was hot. She didn't know if it was from the heat of the fire, or her own rage.

"Did you kill him?"

"I don't think you can kill a ghost," Samuel answered. "But I am certain he will never come near you again," Samuel said firmly.

Samuel's news should have made her happy, instead it dredged up all her old pain, her losses, her regrets sending chills through her body. Her teeth began to chatter. Samuel joined her at the fireplace and covered her trembling body with a hotel robe.

"I'm sorry, I thought you'd welcome this as good news. Had I known it would upset you I would have kept it..."

"A secret? "

"But I don't want to have any secrets between us. I want you to know you can start your new life with me without fear, and that I will do everything in my power to keep you safe," he pleaded softly.

Having Malachai removed from her life was a dream she never thought was possible. She should be elated, but for some reason she felt numb with disbelief. Samuel stood behind her with his arms wrapped around the front of her body. She felt his groin emerge beneath his pants and press against her. His erection was thawing her, reminding her of his love.

"From this day forward, let's never think of that evil being again," she declared. Elizabeth turned to face him. The glow of their candlelit room reflected in his eyes. He rested his forehead against hers.

"Let us take a vow never to keep secrets from each other," Samuel said softly. "My secrets are safe with you, and yours with me. This is the one part of us we keep between us, and not share with the world."

"I love that."

Samuel lifted her chin and kissed her gently. She wrapped her arms around him to return his kiss. Her robe slipped from her shoulders and dropped to the floor at her feet. Her wedding dress quickly followed. Once in bed, they sunk into a pile of down that cradled them from the outside world. That night when Elizabeth cried out, it was from passion, and not fear.

CHAPTER 18

Elizabeth smiled politely at Cassandra Dennings and took another sip of tea. She had no idea what to say to Cassandra, but evidently Cassandra had plenty to say to her. Unfortunately, based on the stares and glares from the other women, the Lady's Salon at the Astor House Hotel wasn't the appropriate place to discuss an abolitionist's agenda. Cassandra's loud and unapologetic voice intentionally broadcast the subject of their conversation. Elizabeth was certain Cassandra's voice reached the glass rafters of the conservatory-like room.

"I thought while your husband met with my father, you and I could get acquainted. You don't look like the normal high society women in New York. Where are you from?"

"New Hope, Pennsylvania," Elizabeth responded in a hushed voice hoping that Cassandra would heed her vocal volume.

"New Hope...New Hope...I've heard of it, but never visited. It must be nice to live in a place where there is hope."

"We're Quakers," Elizabeth offered softly over her cup and then sipped her tea.

"Quakers—that means you're abolitionists!" Cassandra answered with bright eyes.

"Please, lower your voice," Elizabeth warned. "Although we are up north, in New York City, I cannot imagine that everyone has my view on slavery. As you have experienced firsthand, bounty hunters are skulking about everywhere. My husband said they can be anyone, male...or female," Elizabeth whispered as she leaned in. "I am most certain their sentiment toward slaves applies to abolitionists. I do not think it wise we call attention to our position on slavery."

"Then why are you here? This isn't a hotel for Quakers. Quakers don't care for all this superficiality," Cassandra countered, as she leaned in with narrowing eyes. "This hotel is for materialistic people who don't care about the poor and down trodden. My step-mother would love this place: butlers, maids, and luxury oozing from every cornice and corner. All she cares about is money. But I can tell you're nothing like her. Why wouldn't you take the money you paid to stay here and put it toward... 'the cause'?"

"This is our honeymoon, not our way of life."

"Point, well taken," Cassandra said. "But I say, if you have money you should do good with it. I help free Negroes keep their freedom."

Cassandra leaned in. "And when I can, I help slaves, but I can't talk about...the rail...road," Cassandra mouthed and put a finger to her lips. She leaned back and sat up. She slathered a piece of scone with butter and popped it into her mouth. A glistening dollop of butter rested in the right corner of her smile.

As Cassandra bantered on, she failed to remove the butter from her mouth with her napkin or notice Elizabeth's signals. Out of frustration, Elizabeth reached across the table and took a loving swiped at Cassandra's face to remove it. Cassandra caught Elizabeth's hand.

"You did that just like my mother used to." She pressed Elizabeth's hand against her cheek, but quickly released Elizabeth's hand when she noticed others staring. "We must be careful. New York City, while progressive is still antiquated when it comes to forms of love. But I dare say, I feel as though you and I are going to become the best of friends."

"I shall welcome your friendship."

"No."

"No?"

"We will be more like sisters. I will watch over you and you will watch over me, and together we will watch over the Negroes. I think everyone here will agree that slavery is a barbaric act of inhumanity. Every able bodied—man, woman and child— must take action to stop it," Cassandra announced, so everyone could hear her. "If we don't, we shall all be without souls."

Cassandra's words dug at her heart. Elizabeth brought her teacup to her lips and allowed it to linger to prevent her from telling Cassandra how Jonathan Beeson saved her.

"I feel we're like kindred souls traveling along the road of life. We're meant to do good things you and I." Cassandra said placing her hand on Elizabeth's.

A quick flash of light entered Elizabeth's mind to reveal a moment of intimacy. Cassandra shared a kiss. When Elizabeth saw the other party with Cassandra, she quickly pulled her hand away and pretended to sneeze.

"Gesundheit!" Cassandra said. "Now that your husband will be employed by my father, we'll have to find the two of you a suitable place."

"But Samuel already paid for two weeks at the hotel. It's our honeymoon," Elizabeth asserted. While she was grateful for Cassandra's assistance, she would rather spend her first day, as Mrs. Samuel Chase, with her husband. Besides, the last person who claimed to be her sister betrayed her. Like New York, Cassandra was moving too fast.

"Well then, we'll find you a place after your honeymoon. You can't live here. You're one of us, and it would be safer to be with your own kind," Cassandra instructed. New York City is filled with gangs, you must find yours and form a fast and strong alliance if you wish to survive. Which leads me to believe it was fate and not luck, that brought us together. You were meant to meet me. Birds of a feather will always flock together," Cassandra added and discreetly pulled up the sleeve of her dress, and gently tapped the area of her arm just above her wrist to direct Elizabeth's eyes.

Elizabeth looked down at Cassandra's beautiful pea-size pearl bracelet, which pressed into the ivory skin of her wrist. Cassandra pressed her index finger on a wide blue vein that traveled from the pulse of her wrist to the well of her elbow. Elizabeth didn't own a pearl bracelet, and everyone had veins. Perhaps Cassandra was referring to an affluent club where women wore pearl bracelets.

"I'm sorry, I don't understand. What are you showing me?" Elizabeth asked with a furrowed brow.

Cassandra quickly withdrew her arm and pulled down the sleeve of her dress. Her face flashed red as though she had been slapped.

"Aren't you a 'Blue Vein?'" Cassandra murmured over her sip of tea. "We normally are very good at spotting each other in a crowd."

"Are the Blue Veins a fancy organization for ladies? Or are the Blue Veins a charitable organization that help abolitionists?" Elizabeth hated to sound ignorant, but New York was a big city and she felt like an immigrant moving to a new country. "Perhaps if you explained it to me…"

"It's not something that is ever explained. It's something you would already know," Cassandra said firmly. "You really don't know, do you?" Cassandra leaned over the table. Four fingers beckoned Elizabeth to join her. "Just know you're not alone."

Apparently, Elizabeth wasn't the only one who could see people's dark secrets. Cassandra Dennings was more like her than she realized.

***

Samuel's eyes scanned the library. Its grandeur was beyond his imagination. Dark oak shelves filled with beautiful leather-bound books that covered the walls from floor to ceiling. A beautiful brass rail that wrapped around the library's upper shelves held an oak ladder. The buzzing of electricity pouring into the large brass chandelier overhead made Samuel look upward. The chandelier, like the library, like the home, was massive.

The Barclay, named after the abundance of birch trees, that had inhabited the property before they were cleared for building. Even after the death of its previous owner, Elise Dennings, it was still considered to be a symbol of wealth and grandeur. It stood alone and separate from a row of sophisticated and elegant row houses. A beautiful wrought iron fence covered by lush emerald green arborvitaes defined its territory, which included a six-stall stable, courtyard, and carriage house. Everything Mr. Henry Dennings did was big, and so was Mr. Dennings.

"Mr. Samuel Chase—it's a pleasure to shake the hand of the man who saved my daughter. I don't know how I can repay you, but I promise you, I will find a way. Please, sit, sit," Mr. Dennings said.

Mr. Dennings was a tall muscular White man, with black hair, brown eyes, strong chin and a wide smile. He had a relatively soft voice for a man of his stature. Samuel thought Elizabeth would probably describe him as dashing. When Samuel shook his hand, Samuel observed his large hands were clean, and his nails, shiny. But it was the gold ring with what looked like a stamp of a black bird on it that grabbed his attention. Before he could a good look at the ring, Mr. Dennings released his grip and moved behind his massive oak desk.

Mr. Dennings' tongue rolled across his bottom lip like he was savoring a tasty thought, and then reached for a leather-bound book on his desk. He flipped opened the cover and revealed the book was a camouflage for a cigar box. Inside were one neat row of six gold banded cigars.

"El Rey del Mundo," Mr. Dennings announced as he lifted one from the box, sniffed it, and slipped off its gold band. "I'm told it's a sample of a new cigar that came all the way from a place called Cuba. I had one last week, and I can say this is the finest tasting cigar I ever had.

"My wife would have a fit if she knew I had cigars in the library. She can't stand the smell of them. But hell, this cigar is for a very worthy cause. It isn't every day that a stranger in this big bustling, dog eating city, will come to the rescue of a White woman—and a Negro woman. It's a very special day indeed.

"It was suggested I ration myself until the cigar is readily available here in America, but I say let's both have a fine cigar to celebrate your good deed and figure out how I can repay your chivalry."

"Thank you but I don't smoke," Samuel replied. He detected a slight southern drawl in his words.

"You don't smoke? Well then, that's two good deeds you've provided me. I will have six instead of five of these fine tobacco specimens to carry me to my next delivery. I've never met a man who didn't smoke. I'm sure your wife appreciates that, indeed."

"It's a bit early, but since you don't smoke, may I offer you a drink?" Mr. Dennings asked and nonchalantly tugged on a servant's cord.

"No, thank you. Forgive me, but I'm afraid I can't stay long. My wife and I are on our honeymoon. We just arrived last night," Samuel explained.

"Arrived? Where are you from?"

"New Hope, Pennsylvania—and what part of the south are you from?"

"You have a good ear, Mr. Chase. I left the south a good twenty years ago, but my southern tongue followed me. Can't seem to get the taste and the sound of the south out of my mouth."

A soft knock on the door and it was quickly opened.

"Yes, Mr. Dennings."

"Sorry Mr. Twitterly, I called for you prematurely. Our guest is not a drinker. That will be all," Mr. Dennings said lighting his cigar.

Mr. Twitterly bowed his head slightly, took one step back and closed the door.

"You, Mr. Chase, are a good and rare man for keeping your wife needs in the forefront of your thoughts. Most men don't carry thoughts of their wives unless it concerns the boudoir. Do you have a brother? My Cassandra burns through men faster than kerosene and a good strike of a match on a pile of kindling. I'm starting to believe having a grandson will remain a dream."

"I'm an only child."

"Gee, that's too bad," Mr. Dennings said with a sigh and blew a stream of thick white smoke across his desk. "Well, in the interest of time and your honeymoon, why don't we get down to business? I asked around this morning, and the man you knocked down is a very dangerous man."

"Cassandra told us that man is a bounty hunter."

"Yes, he is a bounty hunter, but he probably is working with one of the gangs. Which one, I'm not sure. Unfortunately, you have your pick of vicious gangs to choose from. Have you heard of the Bowery Boys?"

"The Bowery Boys? No, I haven't."

"They're one of the many gangs that are trying to run New York from the Five Points. You have heard of the Five Points, The Bowery, and Hell's Kitchen?"

"I heard to stay clear of those places."

"Well, that's easier said than done. I've heard a few of the gangs are expanding their business to include slave bounty hunters. They provide tips about the whereabouts of free Black men, women, and children, so they can get a cut of the bounty.

"Now take the Daybreak Boys. They're river pirates. They rob ships docked at the port. Anything that isn't nailed down on the ship's deck is up for grabs".

"Am I in danger?"

"If you're staying, yes. If you're leaving town today, no."

"We're paid for two weeks at the Astor House Hotel."

"There's no doubt in my mind they'll try to find you. You'll need protection. I wouldn't be able to put my head to pillow, knowing that you were out and about without a pair of eyes on you and your wife."

"I'll go to the police."

"The police won't be able to help you or protect you. They're afraid too. That damn Tammany. You'd think a political structure is created and put in place for the good of the people. But it seems democracy and fairness is for a select few. Some of the police officers are gang members. You'd do better to trust me— but that's up to you. At least allow me to provide you with a few talented men to ensure that the remainder of your stay is enjoyable."

"I humbly accept your offer," Samuel said.

"Which one?"

"For one talented man. I could use a man who knows his way around the city. A newcomer can also use a good friend in high places."

"People in high places can also use a good man like you. I'd like to hire you," Mr. Dennings said as he rolled his cigar in his mouth.

"Hire me?" Samuel asked. His right leg bounced gently. There was more to Henry Dennings than he could immediately see. He wished he had Elizabeth by his side to get a read.

"I would like to hire you to teach my men to do what you do. My daughter said you took down that big bounty hunter without landing a punch, and from a distance. How did you do that?"

"It is a form of hand- to-hand combat. It requires a lot of time and a lot of training to learn, not to mention disciplining the mind."

"What is it called?"

"Kung Fu. I learned it at a monastery in China."

"You learned how to fight in a Chinese monastery? All the way in China, huh?"

"Yes, but it was worth the trip," Samuel added with a smile.

"Learning to fight in a monastery seems quite the contradiction."

"That's the irony of human nature. Sometimes you've got to fight to maintain peace," Samuel added.

"Touché, Mr. Chase, touché. I'll pay you good money and give you a grand place to stay if you can train my men in some of the rudimentary skills of Kung Fu," Mr. Dennings offered with a blast of cigar smoke.

Samuel waited for the smoke to clear. He didn't want to be ungrateful. A well-paying job and nice accommodations are two miraculous things to find in New York. It would mean he wouldn't have

126

to touch Elizabeth's dowry they created when they sold the store and house. He looked at Mr. Dennings, whose pleasant poker face offered no additional information about his real intentions.

"Mr. Chase, Elise, my first wife—God rest her soul—always said, *'Don't look a gift horse in the mouth, take him for the ride of your life',"* Mr. Dennings said with a hard grin. He tapped the ashes of his cigar into a floor standing ashtray he removed from beneath his desk. "I'm offering you a good horse. I hope you take it for a ride."

"May I speak to my wife? I would like to consider her feelings." Samuel wanted Elizabeth's feelings and insight into any secrets she could find about Mr. Dennings.

"That's a fair request," Mr. Dennings said and gently pushed out his leather chair to stand. He shoved his cigar into the side of his mouth. "I'll have my driver take you back to the hotel, so you and the missus can have your discussion and give me an answer." Mr. Dennings escorted Samuel to the library's oak paneled door. Each step of Mr. Dennings' boots on the carpeted floor reverberated in Samuel's body. Mr. Dennings was weighed down with burdens; burdens that transcended running a big house and a business—whatever that was.

When the library door opened, Samuel saw a woman primping herself in a gilded mirror as she donned her velvet gloves in the elegant foyer. With her raven hair and alabaster skin, ermine cape, blue velvet dress, and heeled black boots she looked like an expensive porcelain doll.

"Henry, I'm going shopping," she announced coldly and then pinched her cheeks as she peered into the mirror.

"Mr. Chase, this is my lovely wife Charlotte Dennings."

Charlotte's head whipped around to face them. As they approached her, she looked Samuel over from head to toe and then her mouth twisted with disdain.

"I supposed you're just another one of my husband's 'Blue Vein' minions?" Charlotte scowled. The air in their foyer turned colder than the December air outside.

"'Blue Vein' minion? I'm sorry I don't understand..."

"*Dear,* Mr. Chase is a potential employee, unless you decide to run him off with your charms," Mr. Dennings softly admonished.

"Mr. Chase, you'll have to excuse my husband's droll sense of humor. Truthfully speaking, the very charms he speaks of are the ones that made

127

him fall head over heels in love with me and propose marriage to me on the spot. He just loves my alabaster skin, it's so valuable," she said smoothing her cheeks with her velvet gloved hand. "By the way *dear*, I will be opening a new account at the Dress Emporium, so when the bill comes please pay it. I wish to avoid any further embarrassment for us both. I'm taking the good carriage," Charlotte announced.

The footman jumped to open the door as Mr. Dennings' burden flounced out through the front door. Henry and Samuel stood awkwardly in the foyer breathing in the last of Charlotte's frosty air. All Samuel could think of was 'Blue Vein' minions.

***

"Clack!" The lock on the hotel door alerted Elizabeth someone was about to enter her suite. Elizabeth watched the doorknob turn and then quickly jumped up from the bed. The maid had already frightened her when she entered her room with a key and without knocking. She didn't dare report her out of fear she'd lose her job. If it was the maid again, she would politely request that she knock before using her key. When the door swung open, Elizabeth was relieved to see Samuel crossing the threshold. She ran to him.

"My goodness, I swear I don't believe I'm cut out for big city living. Did you know the maid has a key to our room?"

"Yes, but she has keys to all of the rooms she is assigned to clean."

"I don't like it Samuel. Let's go home. We'll buy a new house. We'll start a new business. It's not safe here."

"My darling Elizabeth, you're in one of the finest hotels in New York. You're safe. And don't worry about that bounty hunter coming after us." Samuel opened their door. The right side of the door frame held a broad shoulder of a large man. "Franz, our bodyguard, is courtesy of Mr. Dennings."

"Bodyguard?" Elizabeth quickly closed the door and locked it. "Samuel, get rid of him right now. We don't know who this Mr. Dennings is. He could very well be a gang leader himself and his men would make us a target of other gangs. Get rid of that man or take me back home to New Hope right now. I don't care if we have to sleep in a barn. I would rather be with four-legged animals than the two-legged rats in this city," Elizabeth begged.

"Elizabeth, there's nothing back in New Hope for us."

"Samuel, you still have family we can stay with until we find housing. We have more than enough money from my dowry to build a house and start a new business of some kind..."

"Elizabeth, I've Mr. Dennings offered me a job and to provide housing for us."

"Did you say, yes?"

"I told him I wanted to discuss it with you first. A job and a place to stay is a strong start in New York City. I think we should seize the opportunity. If we don't like it here after six months, we can return to New Hope."

She didn't want to disappoint him, but she didn't want to say yes. She attributed his ease to laying down roots in New York to his years of travel to exotic and new countries with different customs.

"May, I have a little time to think about it. This is only the second day of our honeymoon and..."

"Of course, of course. Take all the time you need. I am grateful that you are being so generous and understanding to even consider his offer," he said pulling her in for an embrace. "I promise you, I will keep you safe. I need you to trust that," Samuel said. He kissed the top of her head. Standing in the middle of their extravagant hotel suite Elizabeth decided she would rather deal with the hateful spirits of Malachai and Patricia than the threats of New York gangs and bounty hunters. 1850 New York was not a safe place for anyone: Negro, White, or 'Blue Veins', whoever they are.

CHAPTER 19

Sitting on her red velvet chair, in a private mezzanine box, in *Tripler Hall Theater* made Elizabeth very uncomfortable. She wore her wedding dress, the fanciest dressed she owned. It felt snug around her waist, and its bodice bones cut into her torso making her feel like a sausage ready to pop. She squirmed in her seat to find a more pleasing sitting position.

The clamor of the individual orchestra instruments warming up did little to excite her. It was live music, but her guilty conscious was louder. All she could think of was how Simon and Willie would never be allowed to have such pleasures.

She looked down into the orchestra section and saw swarms of elegantly dressed people moving to their seats, while others chatted in the aisles. The beautiful arrangement of men in black tails and white ties paired with women dressed in richly colored tulle, lace, chiffon, velvet, and satin was a symphony of stylish fashion. Normally her love of fashion would have her salivating, but she had too much on her mind.

Four weeks ago, they arrived in New York with luggage and a possibility of a dream of marriage. With that dream fulfilled, Mr. Dennings offered Samuel another dream, gainful employment, for which Samuel has relentlessly campaigned. At the end of their two-week stay at the *Astor House Hotel*, Samuel was supposed to give Mr. Dennings an answer. His only mistake was telling her she could take all the time she needed to make her decision, which she reminded him every time he asked for her answer.

Evidently Samuel not only learned Kung-Fu from his trip to the Far East, but also tremendous patience. He had not shown one ounce of frustration about her inability to give him an answer. Soon, she was the one who was frustrated and convinced herself Samuel's patience was really a facade for being stubborn. Again, he proved her wrong.

To her surprise, he lovingly created three options from which she could select a plan for their future: to stay in New York, move back to Bucks County, or move to Philadelphia. Philadelphia evoked memories of her father and offered the chance to start fresh—No Malachai, no Emma, and no Patricia. She liked that choice best but still withheld her decision. She began to realize she was the stubborn one. It was the first time she felt selfish. That was when she knew she needed help. She prayed her father would come to her in a dream and guide her, but he didn't.

Their relocation from their honeymoon suite to a regular hotel room, was pulling her into reality and pushing her to decide. Cassandra was right, hotel living was expensive. Elizabeth hated using any of her dowry to cover their hotel expenses, but she had only herself to blame. It was time she made a decision.

During their five-course French dinner at *The Parisian*, a French restaurant owned by the Marquis DeMontier, and on the way to the theater, all she thought about was the turnout at her father's funeral. She was overwhelmed by the sea of slaves he helped to free, and how those Negroes were able to create a life for themselves. She had decided, in honor of her father's legacy, she would choose the place where she felt she could do the most good.

Sitting in the gilded elegance of the *Tripler Hall Theater*, hardly seemed like the ideal place to make that decision. The theater's opulence was so far removed from the real-life struggles that existed in the outside world. She found it difficult to relax and be entertained, and thus, did what she was accustomed to doing as a "shopkeeper's daughter", she took inventory.

Her box was identical to the one across the theater. Its front had intricately patterned gilded wrought iron. The theater boxes floated above the orchestra seats and stage. The large stage was elevated for a clear view required that one climb ten stairs to get to the stage.

Beneath her box, which was to the right of the stage, she counted the heads of twelve musicians, who were dressed in their finery of tails and starched white shirts and collars. They were huddled in a pocket of space on the side of the stage's stairs, so they couldn't obstruct the patron's view.

Onstage, she counted three doors with ornate frames and cornices for the actor's entrances and exits. Near the ceiling, on the walls, she counted five large, circular, portraits of different White women, which made them appear to float above the theater like angels.

Sitting in the theater's grandeur she still felt like a shopkeeper's daughter. *Tripler Hall's* extravagant interior made her want to strip it down to a more accepting reality. She removed her glove and used her thumbnail to surreptitiously scrape at the gold paint on the wrought iron at her knees to see if the gold was real or only paint. Her father taught her, if it was gold it would flake off. If it was paint, it would curl from her scrapping. Just before she could get a good sample, Samuel reached for her hand and placed a pair of theater glasses into it.

When she turned to look at him, his lips were moving, and then his chin lifted to the right of their box. He was directing her attention towards a mezzanine box that was closer to the stage. She had no idea what she was looking at because she couldn't hear what he said.

"I don't know what you want me to see," Elizabeth spoke loudly above the tuning of instruments.

"Mr. Dennings is in that mezzanine box," Samuel said leaning in to speak directly into her ear.

Elizabeth nonchalantly lifted her theater binoculars to get a better look at the man she believed was holding them hostage with a promise of employment. He was a handsome, debonair White man. She could see from where Cassandra got her stunning looks. He sat erect, but silent, almost solemn. However, the porcelain skin woman seated next to him felt like a cold stone—*Cassandra's stepmother?*

Mrs. Dennings sat upright with her nose in the air, fanning herself, which Elizabeth found strange. *Tripler Hall Theater* had a cool cavernous interior temperature. The wintry weather outside only added to the chill. Elizabeth and quite a few female patrons opted to keep their capes on their shoulders. It was clear Mr. Dennings' wife wanted to show off her jewels, her dress, and her wealth. With bare shoulders, she fanned herself as though she was in a July heat wave.

Elizabeth studied the woman's alabaster skin, her perfectly selected jewelry, the elegant draping of the garnet colored tulle fabric that caressed her shoulders, and the way the garnet velvet expertly draped her body, there was no doubt her dress was handmade by a dress designer.

The color of Mrs. Dennings' dress suddenly changed to a dark brown. Elizabeth lowered the binoculars to look at Mrs. Dennings and caught the vision of shadow as it appeared. It hovered for a moment and then faded. The rich garnet color of her dress had returned.

Was that a spirit? Did Mrs. Dennings have a ghost haunting her?

Perhaps she and Mrs. Dennings had something in common? Elizabeth looked through the binoculars again to see if she could find the shadow, but found only empty seats behind them. She wanted to meet her, but how?

"What do you think?" Samuel asked.

"Of what?"

"Mr. and Mrs. Dennings?" Samuel said hiding behind his program.

"They are obviously wealthy," Elizabeth said scanning the theater through binoculars. Elizabeth didn't want to say a word about Mrs. Dennings and her possible ghost. Until she could get a better look, it was best to say nothing. Elizabeth did a quick scan of the theater. Every seat was now filled. She looked at the back wall of the theater and saw at least two dozen people standing. They were not as elegantly dressed as the rest of the audience, but she saw that those people made a valiant effort to be a part of a lavish cultural evening.

She directed her binoculars back to the Dennings' box and counted four empty chairs. She lowered her binoculars, turned around, and saw four empty seats behind her and Samuel.

"How come there are empty seats, yet people are standing in the back of the theater? Mr. Dennings has four empty seats behind him as do we. That hardly seems fair."

"He owns his theater box."

"What do you mean? Does he own the theater?"

"No, he doesn't own the theater, but you can buy a box of seats, so you can sit there every time you come to the theater. It's what patrons of the arts do."

"Samuel, look at all the people standing in the back of the theater who would love to sit down. Why doesn't Mr. Dennings allow them to sit in the empty seats behind him, and why aren't people sitting in the four empty chairs behind us?" Elizabeth demanded.

"Because Mr. Dennings gave us this box tonight," Samuel admitted sheepishly.

"Why didn't you tell me?" Elizabeth said. Her face flushed hot with embarrassment and anger.

"I wanted you to see what it would be like to live in New York."

"Samuel, there are people standing who should be sitting. Go get two couples and have them join us immediately."

"I can't. Those empty seats behind us are not mine to give away. They belong to Mr. Dennings."

"Samuel, this is hoarding. We were not raised like this."

"No, we weren't. But this is New York, if you buy something it's yours to do with as you please."

"I'm not sure I want you working for a man who refuses to acknowledge the less fortunate," Elizabeth said crossing her arms with a pout.

"My darling wife, this is how the rich live," he said with a chuckle.

"Then I don't want to be rich. Samuel Chase, you are not the man I married if you find any of this acceptable. We have empty seats to offer, while others are made to stand."

"It's called the haves and the have-nots."

"No, it's called greed."

"And that's why I love you," Samuel said warmly and then kissed her gloved hand.

Perhaps we need to stay in New York to balance the scales," he taunted.

"Samuel, you tricked me," Elizabeth hissed under her breath.

"My dear, you are too smart to be tricked by anyone. If you want to change things about New York you don't like, you have to be here to do it."

"I will make a deal with you. I will get information about Mr. Dennings, and in return, I get to fill these empty chairs," Elizabeth countered. She was a shopkeeper's daughter who was taught the importance of bargaining. A grin stretched across Samuel's face.

"If there wasn't an audience, I would have you naked in a heartbeat," Samuel whispered in her ear.

"Samuel Chase, that kind of talk in public certainly won't get you what you want. You must agree to my terms: I'll give you information on Mr. Dennings in exchange for filling the empty seats behind us with the people who are standing," Elizabeth volleyed back with a droll smile.

"You do drive a hard bargain, Mrs. Chase. I'll agree to your terms—only, we'll not only fill our empty seats, but we'll also fill Mr. Dennings' empty seats."

"Samuel that's wonderful…"

"Buh buh buh—When we fill Mr. Dennings' seats, you will have to introduce yourself and inform him that I have accepted the job."

"That hardly seems fair."

"Darling that's my offer. Eight free seats for information and a job."

"Agreed. Now let's fill these empty seats before the curtain goes up," Elizabeth said with determination. She dropped her cape on the back of her chair and put her binoculars and program down on the seat. "Follow me."

The usher could barely open the door before Elizabeth pushed past him. Elizabeth moved quickly through the narrow-carpeted hall down two sets of short stairs.

"Tickets, please," the next usher asked guarding the door that led to the orchestra section.

"My husband works for Mr. Dennings. We are sitting in one of Mr. Dennings' mezzanine boxes with extra chairs that we'd like to fill with some of your patrons that are standing in the rear of the theater. Would you be so kind to get eight people and bring them to us? Thank you very much."

"I beg your pardon, Miss, but Mr. Dennings is a very private man. He has strict instructions that no one is allowed in his seats."

"Samuel, he doesn't believe that you work for Mr. Dennings," Elizabeth said.

"I would hate for you to lose your job over a little misunderstanding. Please do as my wife asked. We will escort everyone to our box and Mr. Dennings' box," Samuel instructed.

The usher's marble size eyes rolled back and forth between the two of them.

"Young man, the show is going to start. I would hate to interrupt Mr. Dennings' enjoyment by seating people after the curtain has gone up," Samuel added.

"Stay right here," the usher ordered and disappeared through the door.

"My darling, I hope you don't get me fired before I am officially

135

hired."

"Not possible. Mr. Dennings needs you," Elizabeth said firmly.

Within a minute the usher returned with eight perplexed theatergoers. They were simply dressed: men in wool jackets, clean shirts, ties and wool caps; while the ladies wore their best dresses with bibs of lace trailing down the front. The women's faces were clean and shiny and they wore their hair pulled upward or twisted in small buns.

"Thank you. We'll take it from here," Elizabeth said. "Everyone, please follow me," Elizabeth announced with a smile as she led them down the narrow hallway, up the first short flight of stairs to Mr. Dennings' box. Two large men greeted them on the landing. Getting to Mr. Dennings wasn't going to be as easy as she thought.

"Mr. Dennings is expecting us," Elizabeth said calmly. "Would you be so kind to let him know that Mr. and Mrs. Samuel Chase are here."

"And who are all those people?"

"Guests," Elizabeth replied with a smile.

"Mr. Dennings didn't tell us he was expecting guests. Shove off." The larger of the two men said and pushed Samuel back. The small crowd behind Elizabeth and Samuel began to back away.

"No, don't leave," Elizabeth begged. "Please stay. I promised you we will get you seats. Sir, I don't think this is the appropriate time or place for my husband to show you what he'll be teaching you. We are Mr. Dennings' guests. Please tell him that Mr. and Mrs. Chase are here."

"I said shove off," the guard said through his teeth.

"May I speak to you over here?" Samuel asked.

"A punch-up before the show—jolly good! I'll bid a shilling on the little guy!" A tweed capped Englishman called out from the group.

Samuel stepped to the side. The bodyguard moved towards him. Samuel motioned the bodyguard to lean in as though he was going to whisper in his ear. As the bodyguard did so, Elizabeth watched as Samuel placed his right hand on the man's shoulder near the man's neck. Within seconds the bodyguard's eyes rolled into the back of his head and he dropped to his knees. The other bodyguard moved quickly to his aid.

"What did you do to him?" the second bodyguard demanded.

"Nothing. We were talking, and all I did was touch him here, like this, and he..." The second bodyguard eyes closed and then he dropped to his knees. Samuel quickly propped the second bodyguard against the wall alongside the first.

"Samuel, what did you do?" Elizabeth asked in a hushed whisper.

"Put him to sleep. I'll explain later, darling. Let's get these people seated. We won't have much time."

"See here, we don't want any trouble with Mr. Dennings. We're happy to go back to our standing room places," a man's voice called out from the group.

"Everybody, you're going to be seated. Follow me!" Elizabeth called out over the intro music. Elizabeth quickly stepped over the men and parted the velvet curtain that led to Mr. Dennings mezzanine. "Mr. Dennings, I'm Mrs. Samuel Chase. It's a pleasure to meet you," Elizabeth called out over the music.

"Mrs. Chase? How did you get by my bodyguards?" Mr. Dennings said as he jumped up.

"Your new employee cleared the way for us," Elizabeth said pointing to Samuel.

"He took the two big blokes out with just a touch of his hand. I won a nice little wager for myself tonight. Jolly good show!" the tweed capped Englishman said, flashing a small hand full of coins.

Mr. Dennings gave Elizabeth a smile. He seemed amused by her take-charge attitude; a good sign.

"Samuel, you could have waited till tomorrow to tell me you accepted the position."

"But how else could he demonstrate that he is worth every penny you're going to pay him? You had two rather large men blocking your entrance and he took them down without wrinkling his shirt," Elizabeth said with pride. "You need a man like my husband in your company, for the right price."

"Elizabeth, we can't negotiate the terms of my employment here..."

"Of course, we can. Mr. Dennings, is the job offer still available?"

"It is. Let's talk during intermission to select a meeting time to discuss your terms, if that is agreeable with you, Mrs. Chase?"

"That will be splendid, Mr. Dennings. Now I'd like to discuss another matter. You see, I promised my husband he could work for you if you agreed to allow us to fill the empty seats in your box and the box you were so gracious to give us."

"Oh, an addendum."

"If an addendum means filling the empty seats in your box, then yes, I would like an addendum to close this business deal."

"Your business acumen is impressive Mrs. Chase," Mr. Dennings said with a grin.

"Henry, the show is starting. Make them go away," Charlotte demanded without looking over shoulder.

"Mrs. Chase, this is my wife Mrs. Dennings. Charlotte, would you please say hello to Mrs. Chase."

Charlotte glanced over her shoulder and glared at Elizabeth's opened hand and then spoke without looking at her.

"A woman of class would realize that it is highly inappropriate to barge into someone's private box to discuss business and to foist unwanted guests. Now turn around and take your little band of merry men and go."

"I'm sorry, Mrs. Chase. Unlike you, my wife is a creature of social ceremony."

"Mrs. Dennings, I do apologize. I realize my manners at this moment can be compared to a stampede of wild horses. But sometimes, it's the only way to usher in civility. There are many people standing in the back of the theater who could make use of the extra seats you and your husband have in your box, and the extra four seats Samuel has in the box you and your husband so generously gave to us this evening. I thought we could fill those seats as a gesture of goodwill."

"Henry, the show is starting. We don't know these people," Charlotte demanded without turning her head.

"Mrs. Chase, your idea sounds like a very charitable and gracious thing to do. We have room for four people. Samuel, show them in."

"Henry!" Charlotte scolded. Her voice was like an out of tune viola. She stood and turned to face her husband. Her collapsed fan twisted in the grip of her hands.

"This is inappropriate. We don't know these people, and the VanCleefs are staring."

"Let them stare," Henry said grinning. "Everyone, wave to the VanCleefs."

"You are humiliating us. I suppose this breach of my social boundaries is another bitter pill you'd like me to swallow... for your cause. Thankfully I have a strong resistance to your form of apothecary."

"Mr. Dennings, we don't want to cause any trouble with you and the missus, we'll leave. We don't mind standing," the young woman said. She was dressed in a simple dress, with a large clunky garish brooch that pinned the lace bib of her blouse down to her chest.

"No, please stay. We're civilized people. There is room for everyone," Mr. Dennings offered with a forced smile.

"You're a real good egg Henry." The Englishman said as he sat down.

"Goodness, it's like sitting in the Royal Box with the King and Queen of England," a young woman said.

"Henry, if those people stay, I'm leaving," Charlotte growled through her teeth.

Elizabeth's cheeks flashed a cherry red from witnessing their private fight. Now she wished she hadn't barged in. She only wanted to help the less fortunate.

"Don't worry Mrs. Dennings, the only thing I think we will ever have in common, is that neither one of us will ever forget this moment," a man said. He was seated in the back row. In contrast to the tweed capped Englishman, he was taller with a broad chest and partially bald. His eyes were a simple brown and contained a silent sorrow. He reminded Elizabeth of a sad clown she had once seen in a traveling circus.

Elizabeth saw Charlotte's bottom lip quiver as she fought back mounting tears. She glared at Henry, and then looked away.

"For God's sakes, keep your voices down," Charlotte muttered. She dropped into her seat, snapped her fan open, and lifted her chin to contain her tears.

"Samuel looks like we got ourselves a deal…Welcome aboard," Mr. Dennings said.

"Thank you, Mr. Dennings," Samuel said shaking his hand.

"Call me Henry. We can dispense with all the formality. Now I see why you refused a good cigar. You have a wonderful, beautiful, and smart wife. She's also a fine negotiator," Mr. Dennings added.

The two bodyguards appeared in the doorway.

"Peter, Jake, we're fine. These people are my guests," Henry said with a wave of his hand. Peter and Jake grumbled silently as they eyed Samuel. "Samuel, I think you better get your wife and guests back to your seats before the curtain goes up. We'll talk during intermission. I'd like to buy everyone refreshments."

"Oyyy! Me lucky night!" The Englishman exclaimed.

"I look forward to intermission. Thank you, Mr. Dennings you are an angel in disguise," Elizabeth said and then reached up on her toes to give him a hug.

The moment she embraced him; her mind opened with a flash of light. A pubescent Henry Dennings stood in a vast field of cotton. His brow was covered with earth and sweat. When he turned his back to pull cotton from the bolls, she saw more evidence of his life. His back had been sliced up from a overseer's whip. Another flash and she saw a black bird fly over an adult Henry Dennings. She wanted to burst into tears for judging him so harshly earlier. A twinge of light headedness followed by nausea made her release her hold and stumble back. Mr. Dennings' left hand pressed against her back to steady her.

"Mrs. Chase, are you in need of a doctor?"

"I'm fine, fine. All the excitement made me a little woozy."

"Darling, do you want to go back to the hotel?" Samuel asked.

"Miss, take my seat. I don't mind holding up the wall," the sad clown-like man offered.

"I'm fine, really. Enjoy the show everyone. Samuel, we must get our guests seated," Elizabeth said with a weak smile.

"Are you sure you don't want to go back to the hotel?"

"No, I want to stay," she whispered and gripped Samuel's hand for him to lead her back to their seats.

When the lights lit the stage, Elizabeth had no idea what she was about to see. Four men with dark painted faces and bright white lips and eyes sat on the stage on what look like the front porch of a rundown cabin. When they spoke she could barely understand them. But there was one word she understood, "massa". While she couldn't understand what they were saying, every word stabbed at her heart, and brought tears to her eyes.

A man entered the stage carrying a whip. He waved it into the air.
Crack!'

The four male slaves broke into song and dance. The audience erupted in howling laughter. She looked at Mr. Dennings, who sat silently. Charlotte tittered along with the audience and then dropped her hand to release an opened mouth laugh. The people Elizabeth brought to sit in the empty seats were also laughing. Elizabeth lifted her chin to direct

Samuel's attention to Henry Dennings whose head was bowed like a hung man.

"He's just like us," Elizabeth said. "He's one of us."

Samuel shifted uncomfortably in his seat. The flash of Cassandra's pearl bracelet formed in Elizabeth's mind. Her mind's eye followed the blue vein from Cassandra's wrist up to the elbow. That's what Cassandra meant when she said they were all the same, "Blue Veins". Free Negroes passing for White.

Sitting in luxury and watching White men with the black faces as they were terrorized by the White slave owner's whip, Elizabeth didn't feel privileged or free. No place was safe or guaranteed their freedom. If she and Samuel and other "Blue Veins" wanted to survive, they would have to create a safe place to exist or face the wrath of humanity's merciless whip of racism.

A wave of nausea forced a burp that tasted like mustard, and then churned up a throat-burning acid. The performance was gut wrenching. She watched the White actors in blackface shuffle across the stage, scratch their heads, and dance about like buffoons. Tonight, she would blame the show for making her sick. She didn't have the courage to tell Samuel they were going to be bringing a baby into their hateful world.

CHAPTER 20

There was a soft knock at their hotel suite door. Elizabeth opened her eyes and through the canopy sheers she saw a soft blur moving. It was Samuel. He gently opened the door and raised a finger to his lips to silence the footman before he spoke. She watched as Samuel pointed to the small table by the window. The footman moved to the table and swiftly deposited the contents of the tray. Samuel tipped him, the footman bowed and then left easing the door behind him.

"Samuel," Elizabeth said softly. Her mouth held the bitter taste of soap and mustard.

The canopy sheers parted, and Samuel's smiling face emerged. He knelt by the side of the bed.

"How are you?"

"Better. I think all I needed was a good night's sleep."

"I ordered some coffee and toast if you think you can handle it."

The moment he spoke she remembered last night and what happened during intermission. She closed her eyes shut, but the scene still unfolded in her mind.

***

"What did you think of the show Mrs. Chase?" Charlotte asked with a droll smile. "Don't you just love the humor? They say theater is a slice of life. I say it's high time that entertainment shows the way the world should be, don't you? Keep the darkies where they belong—on the plantation." Charlotte's eyes rolled to her husband and then her lips formed into a condescending smirk.

Elizabeth's stomach jerked, and before she could turn away, the overly rich bechamel sauce splattered Charlotte's garnet velvet dress and the delicate nest of tulle that swathed her alabaster shoulders.

Charlotte's mouth dropped open and her eyes popped like a frightened horse. The gasps and shrieks from theatergoers filled Elizabeth's ears. Charlotte's eyes targeted Elizabeth.

"You did this on purpose!" Charlotte screeched.

Charlotte's face was speckled with bits of herbs and chicken. Elizabeth immediately tried to offer Charlotte her handkerchief, but when Elizabeth opened her mouth to apologize another wave of her dinner from The Parisian gushed outward and did a slow creamy cascade down the front of Charlotte's garnet velvet dress. The twisted and disgusted look on Charlotte's face would remain etched in her mind.

***

"Did I get sick on Mrs. Dennings last night or was that a horrible dream?" Elizabeth asked through her hands.

"Yes, but you mustn't worry…"

Elizabeth covered her face with a pillow.

"How did we get home?"

"Mr. Dennings' carriage brought us back last night. He sent his doctor to examine you, but you fell asleep. I had to extricate you from your clothing and that horrible corseted thing. I wonder if that's what made you sick. It was so tight. How could you eat anything with a corset choking your body?"

"Samuel, women have been bound by corsets for centuries."

"Those female contraptions should be abolished."

"Don't be silly. Without my corset I'll look like a badly stuffed mattress. Besides, the corset isn't what made me sick. That show last night was despicable. How can anyone find that entertaining?" she said pushing herself up on her elbows. "Samuel, they turned slavery into a joke. We can't allow that." She sat up and closed her eyes.

"Are you sick again?"

"I'm just a little lightheaded," Elizabeth said, fanning her face with her hands.

"I'm going to send for Mr. Dennings' doctor to examine you."

"Samuel, I don't need a doctor. I need to go home. That show was

143

beyond upsetting. It's not safe here. We're safer in our own community, with our own people."

"Our people are stuck on plantations."

"Then we have to help them. We have to continue what my father has started."

"Darling, this is New York. The Quaker rescue in Bucks County is a very detailed and secretive operation. They worked with abolitionists who kept their identity a secret. We don't know anyone who can help us."

"But we do," Elizabeth said with her eyes popping.

"Who?"

"Mr. Dennings, the Blue Veins. Cassandra said I was one of them. She said *them*—that means there are others like us." Her excitement forced her from her bed. Her bare feet padded the Aubusson rug in a circle as she spoke. "The first time we met Cassandra she was helping a free Negro woman keep her freedom. Why can't we do the same? And who's to say that Cassandra isn't already a part of a secret network? Samuel, it would give us a real purpose for settling in New York. You can work for Mr. Dennings, and I can work with Cassandra helping to protect free Negroes, and maybe help free slaves from the south," she declared.

The thought of the throngs of thankful people at her father's service, and the opportunity to carry on her father's work excited her. It was becoming clear why her father told her to go to north. He had seen a glimpse of her future. Perhaps this was the legacy he spoke of. She looked at Samuel. He looked like she had just splashed his face with cold water.

"Samuel, what's wrong?"

"Elizabeth, darling, slavery is not a little goods shop in a Quaker community. You're acting as though you can abolish slavery by changing the window display."

He was talking to her like she was a simple-minded child. She shoved her hands into his chest knocking him back onto the bed. He sprung back up. His eyes wide with shock.

"Samuel Chase, don't you dare speak down to me." she reprimanded. "It is inhumane and sacrilegious for us to stand by and do nothing while others suffer. We were spared. We are surrounded by luxury and can have whatever we want, and you mean to tell me you wouldn't lift a finger to help a slave? We were once slaves."

"Lower your voice," Samuel said through his teeth.

Samuel was right. Her eyes roamed their luxurious room. Even in the luxury of a New York Hotel suite, freedom still eluded them. Tears clung to her eyes.

"Imagine if our parents had lowered their voices," she said with a hushed voice. "Where do you think we would be right now? Not in this fancy hotel. Nor would we be married. I would be a mistress to a slave master, and you'd be nothing but a buck for breeding. We cannot let our hearts become numb to this indecency. We cannot fall victim to comfort and luxury. I am your wife and the mother of your child..."

The words fell out of her mouth and onto the carpeted floor between them. His mouth dropped open. He jumped up.

"You're carrying my child?"

Before Elizabeth could answer, a wave of nausea twisted her stomach and rolled up into the back of her throat.

"Oh no," she uttered. She slapped her hands over her mouth, dashed to the bathroom and released the last of her French dinner into the basin. With her face over the sink, she turned on the water to clear the sink of the tawny slurry of acidic cream. She never wanted to hear the word bechamel again. The acid from her regurgitation stung and scraped the back of her throat.

"When did you know?" Simon asked.

Elizabeth saw Samuel's navy-blue slippers. She was afraid to look at his face and see his disappointment. Elizabeth patted her mouth with a hand towel on the settee next to the sink.

"Three days ago," Elizabeth replied. Her eyes met his. Worry washed his faced. He looked as though he was ready to cry.

"Are you not happy that you are carrying my child?'

"I was afraid..."

"Afraid? What could you have possibly been afraid of? I love you."

"Simon loved me too, yet he and Willie are gone...I was afraid of losing everything."

"I do understand."

"You do?"

"Elizabeth, I would never do anything that would jeopardize your safety or happiness, or the safety and happiness of our children."

145

"Children?"

"I'd like to think we'd have more than one. We both know what it feels like to be an only child," Samuel said with a soft smile. "We can do this."

Those were the same words Simon had said to her. The fancy marble sink bathroom began to fade. She was on Ferry Road behind Amos' cornfield again.

"Don't go back to that horrible night, stay with me," Samuel's face was in hers. Stay right here, with me," Samuel pleaded.

"I'm here," she said nestling her face into his chest. Samuel was a man of many worlds, but she was thankful he chose to be in hers.

CHAPTER 21

"Enter! Enter! My home is your home, for the right price that eeez!" taunted the Marquis DeMontier. From what Elizabeth could tell he wasn't any older than twenty. He looked like a young French King. His appearance was as flamboyant as his accent. He reminded her of a garish French puppet. All that was missing were the strings. Or were there strings she couldn't see?

Dressed in a white fur-trimmed gold brocade robe, waves of lace ruffles cascaded from beneath his chin like ripples of waterfalls and poured out of his robe's sleeves. A midnight blue jeweled brooch floated in the flood of ruffles at his breastbone. His hair, high above his head, was clearly a wig. He wore it like he was playing a role in a theatrical stage play. She pulled her lip inward and bit down on it to stop from laughing. She couldn't figure out why Mr. Dennings brought them here.

However, the moment Elizabeth stepped across DeMontier's threshold onto the marble foyer floor, she was transported to a magical fairytale castle. Music erupted to announce their arrival. Startled, she stumbled back into Samuel, who quickly steadied her.

"You must have a very, very, sensitive heart, *mon cherie* for the music to touch you with just one draw of a violin's bow. *Oui?* If you are touched by my music, you'll be touched by my beautiful home. Welcome! Welcome to zee Versailles in America, Chateau Elysian." DeMontier said with a smile and a flourished wave of a lace handkerchief which released a delicate scent of gardenias.

Elizabeth's eyes didn't know where to look first. Her father once showed her a picture of a beautiful French castle. It was bigger than Chateau Elysian, but somehow, not as grand. The thought of living in such grandeur when she was surrounded by so many people, who have so little, made her feel selfish. But then again, the thought of having money to live in the Chateau Elysian would mean she could help others and make a difference.

Her father always said, 'There was no reason to feel guilty about having wealth. Money is a welcomed gift that should be used to help others.' As humble as her father was, he managed to save a small fortune. She felt another flutter in her stomach, a reminder that her decision was not just for her and Simon, but also for their child.

"Let's start in the reception room," DeMontier said leading them to the right.

Start? If this is where she and Samuel are starting, where are they going to end up? There's no place left to go, but down.

"Samuel, this is too much," Elizabeth heard the words escape her mouth before she could take her next step.

"Elysian eez supposed to be too much. Elysian eez zee resting place for heroes and zee virtuous when they arrive in zee afterlife," DeMontier announced with a dark-penciled raised eyebrow. "This eez my heaven on earth. Only those worthy of such a place cross my threshold," he declared with a dramatic point to his front door. "This sanctuary within zee bowels of this pedestrian city offers zee most discerning an indulgence of all the senses. It eez only natural one would feel overwhelmed with emotion as they set foot in heaven! This way pleeze." DeMontier waved his laced handkerchief in the air to direct their eyes.

"Zee Salon to your right offers its host zee perfect size space for intimate gatherings of thirty guests. As you can see, zee salon can hold a musical quartet or a small orchestra of twenty. It eeze zee perfect space for, as you Americans say, 'mingling'. *Cherie*, you are meant for a grand life. What better place to start than here? *Oui?*"

Elizabeth's eyes looked around the salon. It was extravagant beyond her wildest dreams. Her stomach fluttered again. There was something about this place that didn't agree with her. As vibrant and elegant as it looked, there was something sinister about it. She wanted to run. She looked at Samuel and offered her objection with several slight shakes of her head. Samuel offered her no resistance.

"Marquis DeMontier," Elizabeth began. "Your home is beautiful beyond my imagination, but I feel it is too grand for us. We're very simple people. We don't have elegant parties, and the two of us together don't know thirty people to invite to sit in this beautiful salon."

DeMontier snorted his disappointment and then forced a smile.

"But of course. I do understand. You are as you say, country folk," he tossed back with a droll smile.

"Yes, we're very country," Elizabeth shot back. Her stomach rumbled.

"Now ladies," Mr. Dennings said stepping between them. DeMontier rolled his eyes at her and then lifted his nose in the air. Elizabeth wanted to smack it down.

"Marquis DeMontier, there is no reason to be rude, country folk and all, we are still your guests."

"Darling, perhaps we should say our goodbyes and look at another house," Samuel urged as he pulled her arm towards the door.

"I think that will be a good idea," Mr. Dennings inserted. "I have another home that I think will be perfect for you."

"Yes, run along country folk, run along. Tra la la..." DeMontier taunted with a flutter of his handkerchief.

"Tra la la? Tra la la?" Before Elizabeth could stop herself, she was nose to nose with DeMontier.

"I don't care if you are the King of France, you are in America. We are hardworking, honest, and decent people. No one will ever want to buy your precious Elysian. It may be beautiful with all the fancy artwork and rugs, but your snobbery makes everything about this place ugly!" The music stopped.

"Little woman..." DeMontier tossed back in her face. His antagonizing words brought out only one response from Elizabeth as she hurled what little breakfast she had earlier onto his robe, hair, and waves of ruffles. DeMontier stood motionless with his mouth agape. Mr. Dennings exploded in laughter.

"Bru haaahaaahaaahaahaahaahaa!"

"Despite your lowly view of French people, we are passionate and a compassionate people, even when we are before sickening Americans. There is a water closet just around zee corner on zee right. Refresh yourself Madame," DeMontier said as he offered his lace handkerchief to Elizabeth. He then turned to his small orchestra.

"Jouer sur, jouer sur," DeMontier instructed. "Imbeciles, play!" The small orchestra erupted into melody. The Marquis DeMontier lifted his

nose in the air and twirled on his heels. His fur-trimmed robe flounced behind him dragging a wet streak of Elizabeth's morning sickness along the marble foyer. His polished heels clacked against his marble floor in time with the music as he retreated. Mr. Dennings sucked in air to catch his breath and then wiped the tears of laughter from the corner on his eyes.

"Mrs. Chase, I think you just prevented another war with the French. The Marquis surrendered his handkerchief. He despises American women—they're too much competition. But he has definitely made you the exception.

***

Five hours, seven thresholds, and twenty-eight flights of stairs later, everyone's feet and hands were numb, and darkness had set in. Mr. Dennings sighed with a polite frustration.

"Mrs. Chase, you have outdone my wife. I thought she was the toughest woman to please. The Chateau Elysian is like the castle of Versailles in these parts. The only place left to look at is my little carriage house and..."

"May we see it?" Elizabeth asked quickly.

"My carriage house?"

"His carriage house?" Samuel echoed in disbelief.

"Yes. It sounds cozy," Elizabeth defended.

"Mrs. Chase, don't you think a carriage house is a little small for the mark you and your husband are capable of making in this world? I mean, after all, this is New York. Some of the finest families come here to stake their claim. Don't you want your address to be more...grand?

"Mr. Dennings, I can't imagine anything you have created not being grand, even your carriage house. With your and Mrs. Dennings' permission I would really like to look at it."

"Elizabeth, Mr. Dennings is not a landlord. His carriage house isn't for rent," Samuel interjected with a nervous smile. "Mr. Dennings, I'm sure my wife and I can find suitable housing..."

"Now wait a minute. Your wife is trying to construct a deal. I like a woman with initiative. I'm interested to hear what kind of deal she is going to offer me. So, what kind of deal are you offering?"

"Truthfully Mr. Dennings, New York is a big and dangerous city. I want a clean, safe home for my family. Living in your carriage house would provide us a sense of peace and security."

"Mrs. Chase, you never cease to amaze me," Mr. Dennings said and then slapped the palm of his right hand with his gloves. "Samuel, I'm going to have to find a position for your wife. I don't like to waste a smart mind."

CHAPTER 22

The light of the half moon was enough for Elizabeth to see that Mr. Dennings' carriage house would make the perfect home for her little family. As the carriage driver carried them to the back of Barclay, they were immediately greeted by a good-sized courtyard which was landscaped with shrubs and trees. Elizabeth looked at the shadowy, wiry, drooping branches and knew they were cherry blossom trees. They would flower in the spring and not only provide a burst of springtime color, but also a much-desired buffer of privacy from prying eyes of the main house. So far so good.

Although the inside of the house was dark, her eyes could make out that there was a second floor. She also noticed a large dark opening that took up the right front side of the carriage house. In the dark it looked like an arched opening of a cave.

"Wait here a moment please," Mr. Dennings instructed. Under the night sky his body moved like a wraith wandering the earth seeking shelter. Elizabeth saw a pall of sadness cloaked him, slowing his movement. Something burdened his soul. Ice and stones crunched beneath his feet as he made his way down the path to the front door. The mouth of the house moaned as he opened the door. His shadow vanished into the darkness of the carriage house.

Frozen fingernails of icy wind flicked and clicked the willowy branches of the trees, and then clawed at Elizabeth's face and ankles. She shuddered. Samuel quickly stepped into the wind to shield her with his body. The cave-like opening suddenly glowed with light. It was the largest window she had ever seen. She could not remember any storefront window in New Hope being this big. She counted fifteen panes across at the bottom and at least thirteen panes tall, which meant a lot of cleaning.

However when her eyes looked past the window panes and into the carriage house she couldn't wait for an invitation.

The moment she crossed the stone threshold she entered an enchanting cozy cottage. The gleaming, wide floorboards, along with the large rustic wrought iron candle chandelier, white plaster walls, and overstuffed furnishings made Elizabeth want to take off her pinching shoes and roam about in her stocking feet like a child.

Elizabeth didn't know where to look first. The snap of a match across the scratch square on the mantle made her turn to the fireplace just as Mr. Dennings tossed the match onto a bundle of wood. The fire smoked for a moment, crackled, and then flames began hungrily licking the wood. The pungent smoky sweet smell of burning wood began filling the cottage.

Her eyes did a quick scan of the main floor. It was like one big open room with designated areas. There was a dining table with four chairs on a small rug to the left. To the right, in front of the large cave window, there was an overstuffed divan with end tables and two Hitchcock chairs arranged for intimate conversation. Amateur oil paintings, which hung on the walls struggled to fit in with the quaint decor.

"There is a small kitchen through that doorway, and a good-sized room for sleeping upstairs. While not in keeping with your luxurious bath at the Astor House Hotel, there is a serviceable bath off the kitchen," Mr. Dennings explained. He raised an oil lamp to his face and led the way to the kitchen. In the lamp's glow the kitchen was obviously not large, but it did have a small working table to prepare meals. There was a sink and a small stove with two burners, and ample cupboards.

"I believe there are dishes and cutlery for your use. The bath is through that door." Mr. Dennings extended the oil lamp into the dark doorway.

Elizabeth saw the indoor commode: a luxury, with a marble sink and a small claw foot tub. When they returned to the main room the fire had engulfed the wood. She removed her gloves to feel the heat and noticed that the fireplace mantle was made of carved wood, adding a rustic elegance to the room. Mr. Dennings' carriage house was perfect!

"Your guest home is lovely. May we sit down and discuss the terms of our lease?" Elizabeth asked.

"Why don't you and your husband stay on as my guests until such time you find a place you think is suitable?"

"Mr. Dennings, we could never take advantage of your hospitality. We insist on making a monthly payment, sir," Samuel said firmly.

Elizabeth watched Mr. Dennings unbutton his street coat. Samuel followed. Both men stood eyeing each other with their chests puffed like roosters.

"Mr. Chase, it wouldn't be proper for me to take your money. A man of my social standing cannot become a landlord. That would be unseemly. I have a reputation to uphold. Landlords are people who rent cold-water rooms to poor families. My guest home is far from a cold-water box. Hence the phrase, guest house. You don't charge your guest to stay with you. It is uncouth."

"I do understand, Mr. Dennings. My wife and I will have to continue our search. Thank you so much for your time. We'll continue to stay at the Astor House Hotel."

"Gentlemen, please. I'm sure we can come up with a solution that would make everyone happy."

"Mrs. Chase, in all due respect, there are some social conventions that cannot be tampered with. Someone in my position does not rent out his guest home. People will think I am experiencing financial difficulties."

Elizabeth looked at Samuel, who quickly locked his arms across his chest and planted his feet shoulders width apart to convey his stance on the matter. Their standoff reminded her of the time Genghis Kahn got into their chicken coop and battled with their rooster for domination. With all the squawking, the flapping of feathers, and scratching up of dirt, she was terrified to come between them. Her father, however, walked right in and threw down two biscuits. Both roosters immediately shifted their focus long enough for her father to walk in and remove Genghis Kahn.

"Only one rooster can rule a chicken coop, but every rooster likes a good biscuit," her father would say as he carried Genghis Kahn back to his yard.

Something made her look up over the fireplace. Hanging in a wooden frame just above the mantel was a phrase done in needlepoint, "Charity begins at home." It was done in a simple half cross stitch. She found her biscuit.

"Mr. Dennings, if you don't wish to be a landlord, and we certainly don't wish to be viewed as a charity case, why don't we give the money to rent your guest home to a charity, like an orphanage? Samuel, we'll get to pay our way, and Mr. Dennings, you will get to maintain your social standing as a benefactor."

The fire popped igniting more wood melting the cold air between the two men.

"Mrs. Chase, you are an incredible negotiator," Mr. Dennings offered with a slight bow of his head. "You've got yourself a deal, if your husband is amenable," Mr. Dennings said extending his hand. Elizabeth watched Samuel's face warm into an uncomfortable smile as he extended his hand.

"My wife is always right when it comes to these matters. I trust her judgment implicitly," Samuel said with a forced smile letting her know one rooster was not happy with his biscuit.

CHAPTER 23

Barclay Manor, although majestic for New York life, would have been considered a nice cottage in 1850 Charlestown, South Carolina. In Charlotte's mind, Twin Magnolia Plantation, owned by Charlotte's father, Miles Cooley, was by comparison a grand estate with two hundred thirty-five West African slaves, lush floral and vegetable gardens, and a very prosperous rice field.

With seven hundred acres, Magnolia was considered a substantial plantation in Charlestown. For most southerners it wasn't the size of the land as much as it was the number of slaves that made you appear prosperous and significant in the eyes of fellow planters. Slaves cost more than land in the south, especially slaves from rice growing region of West Africa such as Gambia, Sierra Leone, and the Windward Coast.

Southern planters were not only buying labor, when they bought West African Slaves, but also the slaves' technical knowledge and labor skills that had been perfected in their native rice-growing African country. Charlotte heard stories about her father's slaves being stolen, and distinctly remembered how he hired armed guards to protect his valuable property from theft. The southern gentleman's code of conduct was often breached by the slave traders themselves who wanted to make money by stealing back the very slave they had sold. Or in very rare instances, slaves were kidnapped by small farmers from the "Upcountry" looking to cultivate a cash crop so they could buy more land and slaves to work it.

Charlotte missed Twin Magnolia and her southern life. She longed for a house slave that could make a good sweet tea, or the perfect lemonade that sweetened her tongue and made her cheeks pucker. She missed walking along the tree-lined path of live oaks dripping with

Spanish moss. She missed the sweet blending scents of her favorite honeysuckle bush and the dewy scent of the Ashley River that filled her bedroom each morning.

Seated in their living room with a dying fire, the memory warmed her. Charlotte brought her teacup to her lips. Her tea was cold again. The tea's bitter flavor grated against her tongue. The tea up north was cold and bitter like its weather. She quickly swiped her napkin from her lap to catch the tea as it dribbled from her lips and then spat the remainder back into her cup. The tea sloshed onto its saucer as she pushed it away from her. She slapped the tabletop with her damp napkin and then dug her heels into the carpet as she stomped across her sitting room. She pulled the tapestry servant's cord.

Seething, she paced her carpet in a circle. Ava, a petite, fifteen-year-old housemaid, and immigrant from London appeared with wide eyes that remained cast on her shoes.

"Yes, mum."

"How many times do I have to tell you not to call me mum? I am the lady of the house, not some doddering old biddy!"

"Yes, mum—my lady," Ava apologized with a curtsey.

"The fire has died, and my tea is cold," Charlotte sniped.

"Yes, mu—my lady." Ava said and rushed to the table to collect the small tray with teacup, tea pot, cream, and sugar bowl.

"Ava, don't let cook send me another pot of cold tea, do you hear me? And send Mr. Twit in to stoke the fire before it goes out."

"Yes, my lady."

"If we were in the south, you'd be horse whipped with the slaves for your insolence. Now go!"

"Ava, please leave Mrs. Dennings and me alone."

Charlotte turned and saw Henry standing in the doorway. His thick brows looked like check marks above his eyes. He was angry. She didn't care. All of it was his fault. Charlotte bit her lip and crossed her arms ready to do battle. Ava scooped up the tea service and scurried out of the sitting room. Charlotte shoved the door behind Ava, banging it closed.

"How dare you chastise me in front of the help," Charlotte growled between her teeth.

Henry's chest heaved. He moved to a library table. His index finger tapped the surface before he spoke.

"I'm not going to argue with you. It is pointless. I will respectfully ask you to show a modicum of control in front of the people who work hard to maintain this   home and take care of our family."

"Control? You act like they are the masters and I am the slave."

"Mrs. Dennings, there are no slaves in this house. Every man and woman who works for us does so because it is their right to earn a living. When you give respect, you will receive respect."

"Are you saying cook is deliberately sending me cold tea because she doesn't respect me?"

"Perhaps if you were kind..."

"I don't have to be kind! I am the mistress of this plantation, and they should do whatever I want without a fly's thought to how I convey my wishes."

"And therein lies the problem. This is not a plantation. You're not in the south, they're not slaves, and you're not—"

"Don't you say it! I am your wife and that should mean something in this house. Heaven knows the Dennings name is the laughingstock of New York."

"I don't see the store owners laughing when you charge hundreds of dollars of fancy dresses, shoes, and jewelry to my account."

"You owe me. Until you pay for what you took from me, I'm keeping the tab open."

"Maybe I took the wrong one," Henry spat back at her.

The vicious sting of Henry's words brought angry tears to her eyes.

"You wouldn't dare speak to me like that if the illustrious Mrs. Chase wasn't in our back yard," Charlotte hissed back.

"What does that mean?"

"You desire her. Everyone sees it. Including her husband."

"If you weren't a woman, I'd give you a good thrashing. Mrs. Chase is married. I have nothing but the utmost respect for her and her husband."

"Where is my respect? How could you let them move into the guest house without so much as a word to me? How could you let her discard furnishings I selected?"

"The furniture was not discarded. It is in our attic. The Chases are renting the carriage house until more suitable accommodations become available. They couldn't stay just anywhere. You seem to have forgotten; Mrs. Chase is with child."

"Forget? How can I? I'm reminded every time I see her pass in front of that window. I wished you boarded up that window like I asked you to do months ago. It's too big."

"Then stop looking at it!" Henry yelled.

Charlotte wanted to cry, but she didn't want to admit defeat.

"You are bringing disgrace upon your name," she countered. "What respectable man caters to the needs of another man's wife while abandoning the needs of his own?"

"You have made it abundantly clear what your needs are. I have followed your list of demands to the letter," Henry volleyed back.

"If that is true, why is the east wing still cordoned off?" Charlotte countered.

"If you're allowed to have boundaries, I am allowed to have boundaries," Henry fired back.

Charlotte's eyes locked on his throat. She was going in for the kill.

"You're nothing but a hypocrite. You will deny me love and freedom, but you'll look the other way when your daughter..."

"Don't you dare put her name on your lips, or I shall be forced to rip out your tongue!" Henry was in her face his fist drawn, and in the air, ready to land a blow.

"You would strike a woman? You're no better than the gangs that run the Five Points. Until you return what you have stolen from me, you will remain without a male heir!" Charlotte blasted his face and flounced out of the room slamming the door behind her.

She stormed across her grand foyer and stopped at the circular table adorned with a large vase of flowers. She never expected to have competition. She was certain her refusal to give him a male heir, would break him down and force him to return what he stole.

However, the added competition right in her backyard, meant she would lose control of Henry. Charlotte had to go to the source of her problem. No respectful woman, married or single, should want to be the object of affection by another woman's husband. Any gossip would make her a social outcast.

Charlotte snatched a handful of flowers from the vase splattering water on the marble floor and table. It was high time she called on Mrs. Samuel Chase. As she turned to head to the kitchen, a stomach-churning stench assaulted her senses and stopped her dead in her tracks. She slapped her hand over her nose and dropped the flowers in a heap onto the floor. Since when do flowers smell like excrement?

"Ava...Ava...Ava!" Charlotte called out.

Ava scurried into the foyer.

"Yes, mum–my lady?"

"These flowers need to be changed. Take them to the kitchen. They smell absolutely disgusting! Tell Mr. Twit to contact the florist and have them send over a fresh arrangement.".

Ava approached the table and lifted the large vase of flowers, and then disappeared behind it. She wobbled quickly to the kitchen struggling to hold the heavy arrangement.

"Wait!" Charlotte approached her. "Don't they smell to you?" Charlotte asked.

Ava's arm began to tremble from the weight of the arrangement.

"No, my lady. They smell as fresh as a daisy."

Charlotte put her nose on the flowers in the vase and sniffed. The flowers smelled fine. She sniffed again, and the odor was gone. Charlotte folded her arms.

"Do you still want me to have Mr. Twitterly order you fresh flowers?" Ava asked.

"You didn't smell anything when you came into the foyer?"

"No, my lady. May I go to the kitchen now?"

"Yes, yes, go." Charlotte waved her away. "Ava."

"Yes, my lady," Ava said from behind the arrangement.

"I want you to pick up these flowers and wrap them in a bow for me."

"The flowers on the floor?"

"Yes."

Ava lowered the large vase to the flower and collected the flowers off the floor and added them back into the vase.

"I want you to remove the flowers from the water and wrap them with a bow immediately. I want them to be delivered."

"Delivered, my lady?"

"Yes."

"Shall I get the footman for your delivery? Ava asked as she strained to lift the vase.

"No, I'll be delivering them myself."

"Yes, my lady," Ava bent her knees for a feeble curtsey and wobbled off with the large vase of flowers.

As Charlotte turned to head toward the stairs, the odor punched her senses again causing her to gag. Charlotte bolted to the main floor water closet just in time to release the bile that surged upward from her stomach into the sink.

Malachai had found a new way into Elizabeth's life.

CHAPTER 24

Dearest Madame Chase,

I wish to extend my congratulations on your new abode. Although a carriage house, Barclay, or any mansion, for that matter, could never compare to the Elysian, I admire a woman with conviction.

Nonetheless, I have selected a present to christen your home that will insure your home, wherever you make it, will always have the bold and incomparable Parisian flare lacking in American design.

I shall expect an invitation soon.

Your new friend for life,

The Marquis DeMontier

Elizabeth placed his note next to the large ceramic peacock figurine DeMontier had delivered. She had never seen anything like it. From a distance, it was almost lifelike, except it was larger than a real peacock. The ceramic tail of the bird had, what appeared to be, real peacock feathers extending from it. The note, the envelope it came in, and the peacock were as flamboyant as the Marquis DeMontier. DeMontier, as her father would say, was 'quite the character'. She covered her mouth like a pubescent girl and giggled. She couldn't wait to see Samuel's face when he came home.

She looked at the main living area. She still had one small crate, and a barrel in the kitchen to unpack. As she stood in front of the large window, which she learned was originally the arch opening for horses and carriages, she was grateful she had a view of the courtyard and the rear of the main house. The beautifully treed courtyard made her feel she was back in New Hope and not in the dirty city.

The large window also provided her with much needed company, or at least the illusion of company. From time to time, she was able to see Cassandra bounding her way through the courtyard for a loquacious visit of gossip and political fare. It also provided Elizabeth with an excellent view of how the other half lived.

At night the east side of Barclay always remained dark. She couldn't recall ever seeing any life in that corner. However, the west side of the house, that held the library, was always lit up at night by the huge gas chandelier. The library looked grand with its leather-bound books and wood-paneled walls. Elizabeth imagined the long drapes that hung in the library cathedral windows used more fabric than her goods store would have stocked at one time. The library window, in the far-left corner, is where she always noticed Charlotte lurking.

The first few days she saw a figure standing in the window, Elizabeth believed it to be some sort of statue because it was motionless for long periods of time. But one day when she caught the statue move away from the window in a distinctive huffy way, she knew Charlotte was keeping a close eye on them.

Charlotte's disdain didn't end with distant cold stares. She also voiced her protests at least a half dozen times. From the clarity of her voice, it sounded like Charlotte had opened the windows or stood in the courtyard to make her feelings known. Elizabeth was embarrassed for Mr. Dennings, whose kind heart was being routinely trampled upon by Charlotte's satin-heeled shoes. Elizabeth was grateful she and Samuel left behind what she hoped would be their only disagreement in their hotel suite.

It started right after they agreed to lease the carriage house. On the way back to the hotel, Samuel was silent and pouted like a little boy. When she placed her hand on his lap to take it, he refused to acknowledge it. He wouldn't speak to her until they got back to the suite, and he closed the door.

"Samuel, what on earth is wrong?" Elizabeth asked.

"I am displeased with our lease arrangement," he said.

"Why would you be displeased? Mr. Dennings was happy with my resolution."

"And that's just it. It was your resolution when it should have been mine," Samuel countered.

It was the first time she saw him angry at her. She watched him move to the other side of their room and cross his arms.

"Samuel..."

"I felt like a little boy whose mother had to come and intervene as to who was going to have the ball first." He balled his shirt and threw it on the floor.

"I didn't mean to make you feel that way."

"Well, you did," he said putting his hands on his hips. "I should be the one who makes the deals for us. He's my employer Elizabeth. It's degrading to have my wife negotiate a deal for me."

"Correction: I negotiated a deal for our family," Elizabeth argued. "It's what I always did when we worked in the store together."

"And it was fine when you negotiated for your store, because it was your store. This is different. This is my employer. A man's wife should never negotiate a deal for her husband."

"The two of you were acting like a pair of proud roosters. I had to do something."

"All I wanted you to do was trust me to take care of you, to take care of us," Samuel lamented.

"I do trust you. I left everything I know and came here with you. I agreed to your working for Mr. Dennings, and our staying in New York. That is a lot of trust for me...Samuel, we're a team. We both have a voice. If you had said that you didn't like my suggestion, I would have respectfully told Mr. Dennings we needed to keep looking."

Samuel's puffed chest deflated. He dropped his arms to his side.

"I'm being a complete idiot, aren't I?"

"Not completely. You made a valid point. I did step on your toes a bit, and for that, I'm sorry. I could have pulled you aside first to discuss it, and let you do the talking."

"No, no, you did the right thing. I should be counting my lucky stars that I have a smart woman instead of punishing her."

"Well, that's true," Elizabeth said with a smile.

"Say you'll forgive me?"

"Of course, if you will forgive me," Elizabeth volleyed back.

"Of course." Samuel wrapped his arms around her. "You are my wife, the mother of my child, a very good businesswoman, and my business partner. I will happily defer to you in these matters," Samuel submitted with a kiss.

The next day Elizabeth showed him her calculations, and all the money they would save renting the carriage house. When Samuel saw that renting the carriage house would allow them to purchase their own home within a year's time, which would be shortly after their first child was born, he was excited and had not questioned her again.

Even though Elizabeth knew she was right about renting the carriage house, she also knew it was not a suitable place to raise a family. With only one bedroom, she and Simon would feel cramped once the baby was born. They would need to investigate areas of New York that would meet her needs for a little country, convenience to shopping, and easy travel for Samuel's work. For now, the carriage house was their home and she planned on putting her touch on it.

Thankfully, Mr. Dennings gave them permission to make any changes they wanted, but she didn't wish to insult him. She asked Samuel to have his parents send only a few items she felt would make the carriage house their home. Her mother-in-law, however, felt it was important that they have more than what was on their short list and sent extra crates and barrels she felt were necessary to properly start their new life together. Consequently, some of the furnishings in the carriage house were moved back into the main house's storage area, which only added more ice to Charlotte's cold stares.

As Elizabeth removed a wedding gift from a small crate, the satisfaction of setting up house for her new little family made her smile. Family. She was finally going to have her own family, and soon her own home. Her moment of joy was quickly chased away by guilty thoughts of Simon and Willie. She still grieved for them. She was grateful Samuel not only understood her pain, but also accepted her loss as his loss. She was grateful he taught her a trick he learned in the monastery to her help deal with her pain. Elizabeth took a deep breath and held it for a moment just as Samuel taught her.

When I release this breath, I release my guilt about Willie and Simon from my conscience but hold onto my love for them in my heart.

Puuuuuuhhhh, her breath blew out from her mouth, rattling the straw inside the small crate. She quickly wiped a burgeoning tear, shifted her focus, and then dug her hands deep into the straw. Once her hands had a grip on the object, she lifted it out of the box to reveal a large crystal bowl filled with two envelopes. It was the beautiful Waterford crystal bowl from Ireland she had admired when she had dinner at their home.

Because of Samuel's father's import business, he had connections with many interesting and enterprising people. The first envelope she opened was from her father-in-law. Horace, the eternal collector, penned an informative historical note on the piece describing how the Penrose family started their Waterford Crystal business in the late 1700s. At the end of the note, he intimated instructions for its use:

My dear children,

I want you to treasure this bowl. Remember, it's one of the original Waterford glass bowls, which means that one day it will be a valuable collector's piece, especially if the Waterford company is shattered financially.

Your faithful father,
Mr. Horace Chase

Elizabeth loved that Horace was such a doting father to them both. She missed her father and was grateful for any paternal conveyance Horace offered. Although his wife was officially her mother-in-law, Eugenia insisted on maintaining formality, which Elizabeth didn't mind. She thought her in-laws made a very interesting couple. He was a free spirit, while his wife was faithful to formality and convention. Elizabeth saw them as a pair of lovesick swans entwined at the neck. They accepted each other's differences without judgment. Thus, it was no surprise when Elizabeth found a separate note from Mrs. Horace Chase.

My Dearest Samuel and Elizabeth,

I hope the two of you enjoy this gift from your father and I. I selected it because I thought the bowl is large enough for you to fill it with all of your love! Additionally, it

THE ORACLE FILES: ESCAPE

will also function as a good hostess service piece for a lovely holiday punch for you and your guests, and not to mention a wonderful family heirloom to pass down to my grandchildren.

Please remember this is not only a work of art, as your father has so emphatically stated, but it is also a functioning piece of service ware for when you entertain in good company. Take note that that you are in New York where your tableware and quality of your service as a host is scrutinized as much as your reputation. Therefore, I have added a few extras to insure you both remain above reproach.

Lastly, Waterford crystal is one of the finest glass pieces to own, so do beware of nefarious art collectors. I have heard from many of your father's clients who have traveled to New York that lying beneath many a gloved hand can be a set of sticky fingers.
Enjoy it and use it in good health and in good company!

Much love and happiness,
Mrs. Horace Chase

Elizabeth committed both notes to memory, and then returned them to their respective envelopes. No doubt her in-laws would interrogate her upon their first visit to insure she read their notes, which she didn't mind at all. They were now her family, and better parents than her birth mother could ever be.

Elizabeth approached the window with her crystal bowl and hoisted it into the morning light. As the light struck the bowl it dispersed little dancing diamonds of prism like colors onto the carriage house's white plaster walls. She wrapped her arms around the bowl, brought it to her stomach, and clutched it like a baby.

Her eyes scanned the main floor for a display area and came to a stop at the dining area. The oriental rosewood dining table and chairs, another wedding present her in-laws included on the freight train, was perfectly proportioned for the bowl. When she placed the Crystal bowl on top of the table's rich dark gleaming rose wood surface, it looked like one large diamond. The mother of pearl inlay on the table's border added a reflective ring of light around the bowl. It looked like a museum display. It was as though her in-laws raided their import business of their finest pieces for them. She was loved. How could she have all of this without Simon and Willie? She closed her eyes and inhaled.

Puuuuuuhhhh She released her breath.

A rap at the door made her jump. She had not noticed anyone approaching their door. Cassandra was the only person she knew, and she was in Boston Massachusetts attending an abolitionist's rally. Who could possibly be knocking on their door unannounced? Elizabeth removed her shop apron, smoothed her dress, pinched her cheeks and pushed a smile onto her face. When she opened the door, her smile fell onto the stone threshold.

"Mrs. Chase, I have recovered from our last unfortunate meeting at the theater. I thought it was high time I came by to pay my respect and welcome you to your new home. These are for you," Charlotte announced thrusting a bouquet of hastily wrapped slightly wilted flowers into Elizabeth's hands. The satin ribbon that held them together was barely tied, and the stems were brown as though they had been sitting in water for a week. "May I come in?"

"Of course, it's still your home."

"Of course it is," Charlotte replied with a sneer.

CHAPTER 25

"I'm afraid the place is in no state to receive visitors. I'm still unpacking" Elizabeth explained apologetically.

"But, Mrs. Chase, I'm not a visitor. I am the owner." Charlotte turned and came face to face with DeMontier's peacock. "Is that peacock real?"

"No, it's a gift from a new friend we made here in New York."

"The Marquis?" Charlotte asked with a raised eyebrow.

"Why, yes."

"Naturally it is from the Marquis. It is obscene and gaudy. Who else would have sent it. He probably gave it to you just to make my skin crawl."

"I would move it, but it's rather heavy. I'll have to wait until my husband returns."

"Nonsense, I'll send one of my footmen to have it removed immediately."

"That's not necessary. I rather like it. I suppose it grows on you," Elizabeth said touching its feathers.

"Let's hope it doesn't grow any bigger than it is. It's like having an oversize rooster running about. This is not a country farm. Whatever you do don't leave it in front of the window. I don't want to see that thing every time I look out into my courtyard," Charlotte ordered, as she made her way around the peacock.

"I'm sure when my husband returns, we'll find an appropriate place for it."

"I've noticed you've had quite a few deliveries," Charlotte said. She stood in place and did a slow turn taking inventory. "How on earth are you managing all those deliveries, unpacking, cooking and cleaning without any help?"

"There haven't been that many deliveries, so it's manageable," Elizabeth responded.

"Even though the carriage house is small, you should have help. I wanted to stop by and assess just how many maids I should send over to help put this place back together so you can receive guests," Charlotte announced. Elizabeth couldn't tell if Charlotte was admonishing her or offering her help.

"Oh, Samuel and I have no guests to receive."

"I am a guest. From the looks of things, I've arrived just in time." Charlotte tugged at her black leather gloved fingers as she looked around. As usual, Charlotte was impeccably dressed in a sapphire blue velvet dress with black fur collar and cuffs, and a piping of fur that ran down the center of her bodice and wrapped perfectly around her tiny waist. On her ears, Charlotte wore the most delicate sapphire tear drop earrings Elizabeth had ever seen.

Charlotte gasped. "You removed my paintings."

"Those are your paintings?" Elizabeth asked. "I'm so sorry. They just didn't go with our decor. But they're not quite removed," Elizabeth said pointing to a small stack of canvases resting against the wall near the kitchen doorway.

With her brows knitted together, Charlotte marched over to the paintings and picked up one.

"Mrs. Chase, I know you are not as fortunate to have the benefit of a good appreciation for fine art, but my paintings have been requested by some of New York's finest museum curators," Charlotte declared.

"Really? I had no idea. Well I certainly don't want to be the one who suppresses your artistic fame. Why don't you tell me the name of the museum and its curator and I'll have Samuel deliver your artwork so it can be displayed in the proper environment." Elizabeth pressed her lips together to keep from bursting into laughter.

"Don't be ridiculous, I'm Mrs. Dennings. I could never humiliate my husband and have my work hung in a gallery of struggling artists. Everyone knows painters remain paupers until their death, and I have no intention of dying anytime soon. I'll send my footman over to collect them," Charlotte concluded and returned the painting to the stack. "Perhaps I should send over a couple of my maids to help you clean," Charlotte suggested with a sudden sharp southern drawl. "If we were

170

back in Charlestown, you'd have a slave for your every need. It's been my unfortunate discovery that Northern men don't fuss over their women."

"Mrs. Dennings, one look at you and anyone would see that you are a fussy woman."

"I'm a Southern Belle, a very rare and desired commodity in these Northern parts, which is why I came over to help you."

"Help me?"

"Why, yes. Believe it or not, you are now an extension of the Dennings name. Before you moved in, I had the carriage house decorated perfectly. Now I fear we will have to start all over again," Charlotte added with a sigh. "But once we're done, you'll be able to host your first formal dinner. It'll be small, but perfect. Of course, I'll offer my suggestions on decor, hostess etiquette, and all the best butchers, florist, and the agencies who supply the best footmen and cooks. But right now, be a dear and *fetch* the celery vase for me and I'll arrange the flowers for you and bring back a bit of Southern Charm."

Elizabeth shoulders hunched up around her ears. Charlotte Dennings had waltzed into her living room tracking the dirt of the south with all its hateful implications. Her face heated as though she was stoking a blazing fire. Charlotte's words had transported her back to May Tobias' bedroom. Charlotte sat regally on the loveseat as though she was posing for a portrait.

"You're staring at me. Is there something wrong?"

"I was just thinking a celery vase would be too small," Elizabeth said politely.

"Well if that's all you've got, you'll just have to make do," Charlotte said with a snide smile. "Why are you still standing there? The flowers are dripping on the carpet."

"I was wondering, would you like some tea?"

"No, thank you. I have suffered through many cups of cold tea. I don't know if it's always cold because of the dreadful northern weather, or if that's how tea is served here," Charlotte added arranging the seam of her dress.

As Elizabeth walked away, she noticed Charlotte's reflection in the small mirror hanging on the back wall by the kitchen doorway. Charlotte's green eyes were narrowed like a hunter who was looking down his rifle at his prey. Elizabeth slipped into the kitchen with the wilted flowers and shook them angrily and then tossed them into the dry sink.

She wanted to handle the prissy and prickly Mrs. Dennings like she handled Emma, but too much was at stake. Not only could her sharp tongue cost Samuel his job, but also their home. She had a baby to think of. She couldn't complain to Samuel after she convinced him to stay for a year to save money for their own home. She would have to suffer in silence.

Elizabeth snatched the wilted bouquet and recoiled when a thorn pricked her index finger. It drew blood.

"Elizabeth, the rose's thorn is not the problem. Roses will always have thorns. It is their nature. The problem lies in how you handle the rose."

Her father's wisdom always brought calm when her emotions were swept up in someone else's storm. Like a thorny rose, Mrs. Dennings would require great care in handling. She would have to prune Charlotte, without Charlotte knowing she was being cut down. Elizabeth opened the cupboard and saw the glass celery vase. It was obviously too small for the wilted bouquet Charlotte brought, and Charlotte knew it. Charlotte wanted her to feel inadequate and unprepared. From the corner of her right eye, Elizabeth saw the perfect solution.

"God bless you Mrs. Horace Chase," Elizabeth whispered. Peeking out from beneath a nest of straw from on the top of the barrel of dishes was a vase. Elizabeth combed the straw away and quickly filled it with water. She used a paring knife to quickly cut down the stems. She added the pruned flowers to the vase, along with two splashes of vinegar to liven the flowers. She carried the vase of flowers to Charlotte like she was carrying a crown for a royal coronation.

"Mrs. Dennings, I'm afraid the celery vase your cupboard offered was far too small, but I think the flowers look absolutely lovely in this Limoges vase," Elizabeth announced with a Cheshire smile.

"Limoges?"

"Yes, it was a wedding gift from Samuel's parents. Samuel and I are so fortunate that his father is an importer of fine pieces. This piece came all the way from France," Elizabeth added and placed it on the side table next to Charlotte. "Are you familiar with Limoges? It's French. As an artist, I'm sure you'll appreciate the delicate brush application used to paint the tea roses. Perhaps you can educate me about the painting style of this vase," Elizabeth baited.

The Limoges vase was an elegant watercolor painting of pink, deep mauve, and cream-colored tea roses in full bloom. The tea roses with their soft watery edges flowed up and down and around the vase in fluid strokes. Elizabeth wished it was summer, so a fly could enter Charlotte's open mouth.

"A true Southerner knows it's unpatriotic to buy things not made on your own soil. I don't patronize foreign goods."

"But your dress is the latest fashion from Paris, isn't it?" Elizabeth countered.

"How do you know that?" Charlotte demanded with her lips pressed together.

"Before I was married, I helped my father operate our family goods store. The catalogues we would get from French dressmakers were always a treat."

"You have dresses from France?"

"Oh heavens, no," Elizabeth said. "A dress from France would have been impractical for working in a goods store. Besides our customers would have thought I was putting on airs," Elizabeth said under her breath as though she was sharing a secret.

Charlotte's lips formed an angry pout.

"Oh my goodness. Please forgive me. Mrs. Dennings, I didn't mean to imply you were snooty. Your dress suits you just fine," Elizabeth added with a cunning smile.

"Refined clothing and manners are a sign of good southern breeding. Twin Magnolias, that's my family's plantation, is the epitome of Southern refinement. We grow rice, which is more expensive to grow than cotton, and we have two hundred and thirty-five slaves—the expensive ones," Charlotte countered.

"Twin Magnolias is rich with southern tradition that has been handed down generation after generation—like this divan and those two Hitchcock chairs. They're family heirlooms. They were handmade for my grandparents by the best southern carpenters. My father used eight different wagons to deliver all the furniture for this carriage house. He didn't trust the railroad to deliver such fine, handmade pieces. My father said the north is filled with thieves. Speaking of which, where did you say your people are from?"

"We're Quakers."

"Quakers? That means you don't believe in slavery," Charlotte said.

"No, we don't."

"Surely you have something interesting about you. How about your little shop? Where is it?"

"New Hope Pennsylvania, but I've sold the shop."

"Sold it? What will your father do?"

"My father died."

"Oh—Well I'm sure you and your mother must be very close. Is she back in New Hope all by her lonesome?"

"No, she died in a fire."

"A fire? How horrible. Siblings?"

"No."

"Aunts, uncles?"

"No."

"Is the town still standing?" Charlotte asked as her face puckered with frustration.

"Oh yes, and I do miss it. I'm afraid big city life is not what I expected," Elizabeth added. "I'm so grateful for your courtyard. I imagine in the spring it will deliver much needed nature that is missing with city life. Enough about me. I would love to hear about you. How did you and Mr. Dennings meet?" Elizabeth asked.

Tears rolled from Charlotte's eyes before she could blink to stop them.

"My goodness. I think the smoke from your fire is affecting my eyes," Charlotte said quickly dabbing her moist cheek and eyes with the back of her hand. I'll have one of my footmen come over and make sure all of your wood is good and dry. We don't want smoke seeping into the upholstery." Charlotte stood up and pushed her fingers into her leather gloves and then used a gloved finger to swipe the surface of a side table and revealed her grey dusty finger to Elizabeth. "Well, I've taken up enough of your time, and you still have a lot of tidying to do."

"Mrs. Dennings, thank you for the flowers," Elizabeth did a slight curtsey.

"Of course," Charlotte replied and bolted through the door.

Elizabeth watched Charlotte move quickly through the shoveled path back to the rear of the main house. Just as Charlotte approached the

174

French doors, the shadow Elizabeth saw at the theater appeared again. Charlotte reached for the door. For a moment, Elizabeth saw a darker, shadowy, version of Charlotte as it scurried behind her. It moved like it was afraid of being left behind. A flash of blinding light reflected from the glass of the opened French door forced Elizabeth to turn away. When she looked back both had vanished, and the door to Charlotte's secret was closed—for now.

***

Inside Barclay, Charlotte hid in the one place Henry would never think to look for her, the east wing. She needed to scream. She felt she had been murdered all over again. She looked around the salon for a place to sit. Every piece of furniture was covered in a white sheet to protect it from the dust of life. She was surrounded by ghosts. The memorial room for Henry's late wife was the last place she wanted be.

"Aaaaaaeeeeeiiiii!" Charlotte released a scream from the soles of her feet, and then collapsed on a chair to sob. Her tears blended with the dust and made a grey splotch on the white sheet.

"Henry stay away, stay away. Give me this one moment of solace to mourn for my loss of love," she prayed.

Her chest tightened with pain. She felt like her heart was about to burst. She was dying all over again. Henry killed a part of her the day he took her away, and there was no getting it back. Eight years of marriage and denying him her body, yielded no results. Henry wasn't going to change his mind, or his heart for her.

"What are you doing in here?" Henry asked.

"Trying to get away from you," Charlotte said into the damp sheet. "Go away," she cried.

"You can't be here," Henry said coldly.

Charlotte's head popped up. She saw the silhouette of her husband in the doorway.

"Murderer," Charlotte growled.

Henry's head dropped.

"The day you took me away from Twin Magnolias was the day you murdered any love that I could ever have for you. Until you do right by me, your heart will never have a moment of peace," Charlotte threatened.

175

Every word she uttered stung her tongue and fired her heart with rage.

"You cannot be here. Please..." Henry countered coldly.

"Fine! Warn your banker, I'm going shopping," Charlotte shot back, and stormed out.

Charlotte's rage ignited her sapphire dress into a hot blue flame that lit up the hall as she blew her way to the main sitting room. Charlotte wanted to torch any semblance of love Henry had left in his life. With Cassandra gone, that left Elizabeth.

"Ava! Ava!" Charlotte bellowed into the foyer.

Ava rushed towards her and did a quick curtsey.

"Yes, my lady?"

"I have been calling, where have you been?"

"I..."

"Never mind. I don't care. I need you to pack my trunks." "Are we traveling? Mum—my lady?"

"No, *we* are not. I am. You will stay here, keep your ears open, and report to me when I get back."

"Back from where my lady–In case Mr. Dennings should inquire."

"Mr. Dennings won't be inquiring, and if he does, he need not know."

"Yes, my lady. How shall I pack for you? Evening dresses, ball gowns?"

"Ava don't be ridiculous, I'm going shopping in New Hope, Pennsylvania—and don't you dare tell a soul, or you'll be on the next ship back to England with a lump of coal for your pay."

"No, Missus, not a word."

"As a matter of fact Ava, don't pack anything fancy. The simpler the better," Charlotte said as she ascended the stairs. "Ava, you're not following me."

"Coming my lady."

CHAPTER 26

"Elizabeth...Elizabeth..."

Elizabeth recognized that voice. She opened her eyes.

"Poppa?" Elizabeth's eyes popped open. Jonathan Beeson stood beside her bed. His appearance was different than before. He looked like he was under water. His whole body seemed wavy. A soft radiant light surrounded him and emanated from his smile.

"Elizabeth, I don't have much time, so you'll have to listen."

"Poppa, where are you? How come you look like you're standing in Honey Hollow Pond?" Honey Hollow Pond was one of the clearest ponds in New Hope. When she was a little girl she used to escape Patricia's tirades by laying down in the shallow area of the pond. With just a few inches of water above her body, the world above water looked wavy and peaceful, like her father did at that moment. "Poppa, are you back home? Are you back in New Hope? I can't go back. I sold the store..."

"Elizabeth."

Jonathan's voice was stern. It was his no shenanigans voice he used when he had to be firm with a customer. He had her attention. His eyes cast downward in slow motion. As long as she had known him, he had never spoken harshly to her. She was so grateful to see her father she, didn't care.

"What's wrong, Poppa?"

"I know what you saw today."

"What do you mean?"

"You saw her secret."

"Mrs. Dennings has a ghost?"

"It was no ghost. Look again. You were meant to see it Elizabeth.

You needed to see it."

"But Poppa, I don't know what I'm looking at."

"Her secret reflects a truth for us all...bring it to light..."

"Poppa, why can't you just tell me what I'm supposed to know?"

"Because that would be cheating," he answered with a soft smile. "You and I are not cheaters."

"Poppa, where are you?"

"In another part of life. It's what happens when you decide to move on."

"Move on? I don't understand."

"It was so good to see you Elizabeth." His smile radiated a soft light as he stepped back. "Stay out of the south Elizabeth. Stay out of the south."

The light of his smile faded into the watery shimmery essence.

"Poppa...don't leave me...no...no."

"Elizabeth...Elizabeth..."

Elizabeth opened her eyes. Samuel's shadowy face was above hers.

"You were crying out in your sleep. Are you all right? Is the baby?"

"I saw Poppa."

"Your father? What did he say?"

"Stay out of the south." Elizabeth nuzzled into Samuel's chest. She heard the thump-thump, thump-thump of his heart and was so grateful he was alive and in her world.

CHAPTER 27

One ghastly long train ride, and one dusty rocky coach ride later, Charlotte found herself standing in front of the telegraph station of New Hope, Pennsylvania. Although New Hope was a lot bigger than she imagined, it didn't have a station. But fortunately for her, it did have a little hotel, The Logan Inn.

She was exhausted and dusty from her trip, and thankful the Logan Inn was directly across the road. She had so much luggage, and no one to carry it. Perhaps she should have brought Ava. At least she would have someone she could send to the Logan Inn for help. The thought of lugging her bags and dragging them across the road to the inn unnerved her. Her feet, although numb from the cold railcar ride, were quite swollen, and were ready to pop the buttons on her expensive boots.

She wanted to cry, but she was too tired and cold. Besides she was on a mission. She wanted to find Elizabeth's little "shop" before it turned dark. Charlotte's green eyes did a quick scan of what she believed was the center of town. She was going to check into the inn, find the store, go speak with the store's present owners, get some damning information on Elizabeth before dinner, and then get on the next stage back to New York. However, Elizabeth's little goods shop was nowhere to be seen.

Directly across the road from the telegraph office, down an alley was a wooden sign for a tavern. To the right of the Inn, she saw an apothecary. Behind her, to the left of the telegraph office on the same side of the street, there were signs for a dressmaker's shop, a bakery, and a candle shop. To the right of the telegraph office, was a newspaper office, next to that was a small grassy green and a brick building with a sign defining the building as the TOWN HALL.

The rumble of a fast-moving wagon demanded her attention and made her look up the street to the right of the Hotel. That section of the street was wide and heavy with wagon and horse traffic. A wagon with two horses plowed around the corner. When the wagon disappeared, she saw a two-story small department store on the corner. She took two steps forward and read: BECKWITH EMPORIUM AND FINE APPAREL. The words were elegantly painted on a large wooden sign. Each letter, outlined in gold, reflected the last of the winter's late afternoon sun.

Charlotte's face heated with anger, thawing her frozen cheeks. Elizabeth had lied to her. From Elizabeth's description, Charlotte was made to believe Elizabeth's *goods store* was some old dusty store with wood floors covered in sawdust. The EMPORIUM was almost as big and stylish as a store back in New York.

Charlotte's eyes narrowed to the size of pumpkin seeds as her nails clawed the back of her hands inside of her muff. She didn't need all the clothing she brought. She was ready to go home. Now she was stuck in an unfamiliar town, on a street corner, without help, unable to move.

"Miss are you staying at the Logan Inn?" a man's voice called out from behind.

When Charlotte turned around, she saw the face of a man with the most unusual amber colored eyes. His chestnut brown hair beneath his hat was tousled and pulled back into a short ponytail. His shoulders were broad and comforting, and his large hands looked like he could handle her without effort. Carnal thoughts flushed her face a bright cranberry red.

"Why, yes. Yes. I didn't know how I was going to get there from here," Charlotte said with a sigh of relief. "Can you get the footman from the inn and have him come to retrieve my luggage?"

A big grin rolled across his face.

"Did I say something funny?"

"Sorry, ma'am, but there is no footman."

"Well, then alert the innkeeper that I need help with my luggage."

"He already knows. That's why he sent me."

"Why didn't you just say that you were from the inn?"

"I think I was thrown by the lady's request for a footman. I'm no footman, but I am a man who can carry all of your luggage, and you, if need be," he replied with a taunting smile.

"Who are you?"

"I'm Robert Kincaide with an 'e'. I'll carry you safe and sound to the Logan Inn."

"I don't need carrying. I'm perfectly capable of walking on my own."

"Ma'am, it was a figure of speech. Any man can see you're capable...of a lot of things," Robert volleyed back. "And what is your name?"

"Why do you need to know my name?"

"So, I can present you, like royalty, to the innkeeper," Robert said snidely.

"Mr. Kincaide with an 'e', I find your manners to be repugnant."

"Good, that means you'll love the rest of me even more," he shot back with a smile.

He has good teeth, Charlotte said to herself, taking inventory. His deep voice was virile like his body. His accent was one she had never heard before. Charlotte found his confrontational behavior alluring. It was the first time any man brought beads of perspiration to the curve in her lower back. He was exciting her.

"It's Mrs. ...Miss...Miss Greene, with an 'e'," Charlotte replied lifting her chin in the air.

"Well, Miss Green, with an 'e', is there anyone else traveling with you?"

"No, I'm perfectly capable of traveling on my own. Not all women are fragile and helpless."

"My question was not directed at your capability, but the amount of luggage you brought. This is a lot of luggage for one person."

"Oh."

"And it's not normal for a beautiful woman to travel by herself without an escort, or chaperone."

"Well that's because I'm not a normal woman. I'm...I'm a businesswoman looking to open my own...dress shop," Charlotte defended. "This luggage holds some of the dresses, I've made...I'm a dress designer.... I'm here to sell my dresses to...to...The Beckwith Emporium and Fine Apparel."

Robert's smile left his face. He quickly reached down and lifted the larger of her two trunks onto his shoulders.

"Did my words offend you?"

"Look, Miss Greene. It's none of my business what you do with your

181

dresses, but I can think of better places to sell them," Robert warned and slipped his large fingers around the leather handle of her smaller trunk.

"Is there another goods store in town?"

"No, it's the only one. It was sold to the Beckwith family, who turned it into a fancy department store. It doesn't cater to the people around here. Most people now travel across the river to Lambertville to shop. You'd be better off opening your trunks right here on this corner and selling them than going to that place." His left pinky hooked the handle of her remaining satchel. "Let's go get you settled in. Follow me, but mind stepping out into the streets. People drive their horses like they're in a race to beat the devil," he added.

"That is the second time you said devil. Do I need to be concerned for my safety?" Charlotte asked, scurrying behind him.

"I hate to see a pretty lady get herself into trouble over a dress," Robert said without looking back.

"Thank you, Mr. Kincaide. I shall take your warning under advisement." Charlotte deliberately kept a few paces behind him. She didn't want him to catch her staring at him. From behind, he reminded her of a big live oak tree from the south and she wanted to climb him. Her gloved hand pressed against her lips as she studied his lumbering gait. She began to imagine his body against hers in bed. She stared at his pants leg and imagined his muscular hard calves touching her legs.

The vision of them in bed together distracted her. She didn't realize she was inside the inn, and he had already deposited her luggage.

"Miss Greene...Miss Greene?" Robert said.

"I'm sorry, I was looking at what a lovely inn this is," Charlotte said. His eyes met hers. She quickly looked away. "This is very charming,"

"This is Miss Greene, with an 'e.' She'll be needing lodging," Robert announced and placed her satchel on top of her trunk.

"Thank you, Robert," the innkeeper said.

Charlotte looked around to take in the interior. It was a very nice and serviceable inn. The front desk, although not large, was welcoming with its rich dark wood panel. The brass chandeliers added a bit of elegance to the rustic interior. A small brick fireplace, filled with a well-stoked fire, heated the reception area. In front of the fireplace were four chairs and a table.

"Good afternoon, Miss Greene. Welcome to the Logan Inn. I'm Mr.

Bailey, your innkeeper, and host." Mr. Bailey was much shorter than Robert Kincaide, stout, slightly bald, and he balanced a pair of spectacles on his nose.

"Thank you." The heat from the lobby fire wasn't the only thing warming her face. Charlotte could feel Mr. Kincaide's fiery amber eyes searing her skin. When Mr. Bailey presented her with a pen to sign the registry, she found it hard to focus. She smiled at Mr. Bailey and signed her name next to room number six. She was about to spin the registry back around to Mr. Bailey when she noticed she signed in as Mrs. Dennings. She quickly tried to scratch it out before anyone could see it.

"Miss Greene, I'll personally see to it that your stay at the Logan Inn is a peaceful and joyous one. We have a nice little dining tavern through that doorway. We serve breakfast, lunch, and dinner, and I dare say our cook rivals some of the fancier restaurants in Philadelphia," the innkeeper boasted with a wink. If you're tired, I can have a meal sent up to your room."

"No thank you, Mr. Bailey. I prefer to eat in the dining room with the other guests."

Mr. Bailey's hand lifted a small brass bell and shook it once. Another man quickly appeared. He was not dressed in the formal uniformed look she was accustomed to seeing. She looked him over. His appearance was neat, his face scrubbed, and his hair combed.

"Is Mr. Dale to your satisfaction Miss Green? He is very trustworthy. But if you prefer, Mr. Kincaide will show you to your room."

She looked at Mr. Kincaide's fiery eyes and then turned away. She was in the little town for one reason only.

"I'm sure Mr. Dale will be quite suitable. Mr. Bailey, I was wondering if you have a little goods shop in town? I'm a dressmaker. Mind you, they're nothing fancy, but I'm sure the women in this town would find them quite serviceable. I thought a nice *goods* store might be interested in buying some of my dresses. Perhaps you can make a recommendation."

"We used to have a nice little goods store. But the Beckwith Family bought it and expanded it into a full-size department store—finer than any store you'll find in the city of Philadelphia," Mr. Bailey added with a lifted chin. "I'm afraid it's closed for the day, but it will open at eight am tomorrow if you would like to pop in. They have a delightful gift section. Mrs. Bailey always says a bit of shopping does wonders to lift one's spirits. I believe they still have their holiday decorations up, too. Seeing them might provide you with a bit of joy. Yes, it's quite the store, quite the store."

"Why Mr. Bailey, your words are most encouraging. I was counting on my visit to New Hope to bring me a bit of joy."

"If you do go, mention that Mr. Bailey from the Logan Inn sent you."

"I shall."

"Mr. Dale, escort Miss Greene to room number six please. Enjoy your stay."

Robert waited until Charlotte disappeared.

"I'm sure Miss Greene has better things to do than to go that horror shop," Robert said angrily.

"I'll thank you, Mr. Kincaide, to mind the luggage and not the itinerary of our clientele."

"Why would you send her there?"

"Because it's good for business. If Mrs. Beckwith knows that I send her business, she'll leave us alone. That's how we keep our doors open and our beds full."

"You mean that's how you keep your pockets full."

"I don't see you complaining when I give you a decent wage at the end of every week. Keep your thoughts about Mrs. Beckwith to yourself. If the ladies didn't take a fancy to you, you'd be out plowing fields with the other oxen. Now go make yourself useful," Mr. Bailey snapped.

CHAPTER 28

The bell over the Emporium's door announced Charlotte's entry.

"Hello and welcome to Beckwith Emporium and Fine Apparel. Is madam shopping for a gift or pleasure?" the greeter asked her.

The young woman was dressed elegantly in a rich burgundy crepe de chine silk dress that had piping of black velvet along the waist of her bodice, collar and cuffs of her sleeves. Charlotte recognized great fashion when she saw it. The woman's face had a very soft dusting of rouge to give her cheeks a rosy glow and her lips were a pale pink.

The greeter was a walking advertisement for sophistication and elegance. Charlotte felt underdressed standing next to her. If this was indeed Elizabeth's little shop, she couldn't see finding any joy in her archeological dig. Expansion or not, the bones of the main floor were impressive. The floors were polished dark oak wood, the three bay windows let in ample light. This was not a sawdust floor, crate and barrel, and canned goods store. Elizabeth Chase was already above reproach.

"Actually, I am here to inquire about the owner. Is the owner on the premises?"

"Mrs. Beckwith is here. Is there a problem with a product you bought from our Emporium?"

"No, not at all."

"Are you a dress designer or salesperson for a dress manufacturer?"

"Yes! I am a dressmaker and seamstress. May I please speak with Mrs. Beckwith?"

"Who shall I say is inquiring?"

"Miss Greene," Charlotte replied.

"Miss Greene, please excuse me," the greeter did a slight bow of her head and floated away up the store's grand staircase and disappeared at the top.

Hanging in the center of the store was the biggest chandelier Charlotte had ever seen. It looked like there were hundreds of fine teardrop crystals dangling above the store. She wanted to cry. Everything about the Beckwith Emporium was upscale and expensive looking. It was the kind of store in which she would love to leave a lot of Henry's money behind, but not on this trip unless she wanted to reveal her true identity. Charlotte regretted not having Ava pack a few of her designer dresses.

Charlotte rolled her bottom lip into a pout as she crossed her arms and turned to her left. It wasn't fair Elizabeth came from such luxury. Her nose detected the delicate sweet scent of talcum powder, French lavender soaps, and parfums. When her eyes focused, she saw the most tantalizing array of sparkling parfum bottles, and oval, round, and square decorative powder boxes. On the same counter to the right of the display, was a vibrant holiday arrangement that still sparkled with sugar-coated fruit, pine boughs, and sprigs of waxy green holly perfectly dotted with bright red berries.

A counter for beautiful hats was to the right of the parfums. These weren't the country bonnets she expected to find in rural New Hope, Pennsylvania. These were elegantly designed hats for ladies of sophistication. No country daisies or gaudy chrysanthemums sticking up in the air as though they were ready to be plucked. These hats had sprigs of lavender and delicate flowers she did not know by name. There were also hats that were trimmed in the most luxurious fur she had ever seen.

The hats had to be imported. They were better than the hats she had purchased in New York. Elizabeth did say her husband's family had an import-export business. Elizabeth came from all this luxury and grandeur. There was nothing she would find here that she could use against Elizabeth, but there was something she found for herself.

In the back right corner of the main floor, positioned on a slow-moving carousel was her dress! It was the garnet duchess satin and French silk dress with the delicate emerald teardrop crystals that circled the scoop shoulder. She saw it in the Paris Couture Catalogue before Christmas. It was designed by Charles Frederick Worth, an emerging fashion designer. She demanded Henry buy it for her, but he refused. Afterwards, he publicly humiliated her when he visited her dressmaker and dress shops to informed them, he would not pay for any couture dresses.

She turned away. The humiliation of that day infuriated her still. This was obviously a wasted trip. She snorted a blast of air through her nose and bolted toward the door. It was time to leave before she embarrassed herself or worse, said something that would reveal her identity.

"Miss Greene," the greeter called.

Charlotte watched her glide down the stairs. "I'm afraid Mrs. Beckwith has a busy schedule today."

"I do understand. I arrived without an appointment. Please give her my deepest apologies."

"Miss Greene," a woman's voice called out from a distance.

At the top of the grand staircase stood a dainty young woman stylishly dressed. The woman had to be none other than Mrs. Beckwith. She descended the staircase gracefully. In a stylized duchess satin dress, Mrs. Beckwith looked as grand and luxurious as her store. Charlotte clenched her teeth so hard she thought they would break inside of her mouth.

"I am Mrs. Beckwith. I understand you wished to speak with me."

Charlotte's heart began to pound. Something was wrong. She wanted to run all the way back to New York, but something was paralyzing her. Mrs. Beckwith's eyes remained locked on her as she made her way down the stairs.

"Miss Greene, I hear you're a dressmaker and seamstress?"

Mrs. Beckwith was a petite and doll-like woman, yet there was something ominous about her. Charlotte took a step back.

"I'm sorry. This was a mistake. Your store is so extravagant. I have over-estimated my abilities. You have a Charles Frederick Worth dress. I cannot compete with that."

"But you've traveled so far," Mrs. Beckwith said. "Miss Christy, please prepare a pot of tea for us, and bring it to my office."

Before Charlotte knew it, she was inside Mrs. Beckwith's office which was strategically placed in the front of the department store on the second floor. Inside the office were two windowed walls. One set of windows overlooked the outside of the storefront. The other wall of windows overlooked the grand staircase and most of the second floor which held departments of women's clothing, special dishware, linens, and furnishings. It was clear Mrs. Beckwith liked to keep her eye on the comings and goings in her store.

"Please sit down." Mrs. Beckwith pointed to a pair of beautiful Queen Anne high back chairs with a small marble top table between them. Beneath Charlotte's feet was the most luxurious Oriental rug her feet had ever felt.

"You have the loveliest store," Charlotte began.

"I detect a southern accent."

"Yes, the Carolinas."

"It's so rare to find a young southern woman roaming the country without a chaperone, who is a dressmaker and seamstress. The values of the south must be changing."

"The south hasn't changed one iota. Woman are still treated like children. I'm an independent woman who does not want to marry and have children. I would rather have my own business. That's why I moved up north, so I can open my own dress business. I thought I would stop here, in this quaint little town, and see if there was a store that could use my talents and that's when I saw your signage...It was so enticing I had to come by and see what kind of goods you offer, and perhaps find out if you had room for a seamstress," Charlotte explained and punctuated her prattle of lies with a nervous smile.

"As you can see, I don't have *goods,* but I do offer only the finest products money can buy. People come from the city to shop in my store. Normally it would be the other way around, but I have seen to it that my store has what everyone wants," Mrs. Beckwith said with a taunting smile. "You're not a dressmaker or a seamstress, are you?"

"I..."

"Miss Greene, you do not have the battered calloused fingers of a seamstress, and you certainly aren't a dressmaker. If you were, you'd be wearing one of your own unique creations."

"I..."

"Something tells me you're here for something very special. I do have some specialty items that are not on the floor for public viewing," she added with a raised eyebrow. "Collect your thoughts Miss Greene, our tea has arrived. Come in Elizabeth," Mrs. Beckwith said without waiting for a knock.

Hearing Elizabeth's name made Charlotte's heart pump hard. When

Charlotte laid eyes on the woman carrying the tea service, her corset suddenly compressed her lungs, making it difficult to breathe. The woman bore an uncanny resemblance to Elizabeth Chase, except the woman was heavier and lacked that magical air Elizabeth Chase always exuded. The woman was dressed in a drab black uniform, with a simple maid's cap attached to her head and a pained expression on her face. She reminded Charlotte of a child that was being punished.

The maid moved swiftly without eye contact. She set a sterling silver Tiffany tea service, complete with matching tray, on top the marble table between them and commenced pouring tea. To avoid staring at the woman, Charlotte forced herself to look inside the Crown Staffordshire teacup and focused on the blossomed petals of a pink rose until the hot dark brown tea made them disappear.

"That will be all, Elizabeth," Mrs. Beckwith said and then gave Charlotte another taunting smile.

The maid did a quick curtsey and then closed the door quietly behind her.

"What a lovely Tiffany tea service," Charlotte said nervously.

"Sugar?"

"Yes, please."

"Cream?"

"No thank you," Charlotte replied.

"Chocolate?" Mrs. Beckwith offered, lifting the lid of a second Tiffany covered sugar bowl.

"No thank you," Charlotte refused with a smile.

Mrs. Beckwith dropped a small piece of chocolate into her hot tea and stirred it slowly.

"Like life, mint can be bitter, but I find that adding chocolate sweetens things and makes everything more palatable. Perhaps you'll find the courage to try a little chocolate before you leave. I promise you, chocolate has its rewards," Mrs. Beckwith added with a raised eyebrow as she sipped her tea.

Charlotte quickly moved her spoon in a circular motion through the hot liquid until the sugar cubes vanished. She felt Mrs. Beckwith gaze on her every move.

"Oh my, that's quite a desk," Charlotte remarked.

"It came all the way from England."

"And what exactly are those winged creatures on each leg?"

"Gargoyles. Aren't they fascinating? Imagine the carving expertise of the man who created them. He had to create four identical gargoyles. I had a Chippendale desk, but when I saw this, I told my husband I had to have it."

"Oh, so this is your husband's store?"

"No, it is mine. It is sort of a wedding present from my husband. This used to be a simple little mercantile country shop. My husband bought it before we were married. I convinced him to allow me to turn it into the magical emporium you see today. So, why are you really here?" Mrs. Beckwith asked.

"I don't know if I can explain..." Charlotte said and then brought her teacup to her lips.

"Then allow me to explain. The people I allow in my life are either here to help me or hurt me. We shall find out to which category you fall. What do you think of my desk?"

"Your desk? It certainly is unique," Charlotte remarked with a half-smile. Charlotte added unwanted cream to her tea and stirred it slowly. She desperately wanted to avoid looking at the desk out of fear the creatures would come to life and tear her to pieces. Indeed, there was something magical about Mrs. Beckwith's Emporium. But her need to hurt Elizabeth was overriding her conscience and common sense, which told her to run.

"The gargoyles are supposed to ward off evil spirits," Mrs. Beckwith added with a sip of her tea. "I find them to be very useful. In business, as in life, there is always evil looking for a home. Miss Greene, do they frighten you?"

"Frighten me? No... no. I find them to be most unusual, albeit pitiful, creatures. I can't imagine them receiving much interest or a loving pat on their head like a dog," Charlotte responded with a shrug of her shoulder.

"Miss Greene, even the lowest beast deserves recognition and love. Pet it."

"I beg your pardon?"

"I invite you to show the poor creature compassion...Pet it."

Charlotte stared at Mrs. Beckwith. Her soft brown eyes were now dark like a sky before a storm.

"Thank you for the tea, but I'm afraid I made a terrible mistake by coming here." Charlotte stood up, offered Mrs. Beckwith a slight curtsey and quickly made her way to the door.

"It's a shame. I had you pegged as a formidable competitor against Elizabeth Chase," Mrs. Beckwith teased. "You're just like all the others who wither and crumble to dust at her feet."

Charlotte's heart pounded so hard her hand rattled the doorknob she was holding.

"You know Mrs. Chase?" Charlotte asked staring at the doorknob.

"Yes. This used to be her little *shop,*" Mrs. Beckwith goaded.

Charlotte turned around. Her eyes locked on the hideous gargoyle leg on the right. She went to it and placed her hand on its head and then looked at Mrs. Beckwith who released a devilish smile.

"The information I can provide requires devotion," Mrs. Beckwith said with narrowed eyes.

Charlotte bent over and kissed the head of the gargoyle.

"Bring it to life and I shall feed it for you. How's that for devotion?" Charlotte asked.

"My, my. You are devoted to bringing down Mrs. Chase. Clearly Mrs. Chase has brought some strife into your life. Why don't you sit down, and finish your tea while it's still hot?" Mrs. Beckwith offered.

Charlotte felt something cold moving through her body.

What had she done?

Charlotte lowered herself back into the Queen Anne chair, placed her tea napkin in her lap, and picked up her teacup to take a few sips to warm her body. When she looked into Mrs. Beckwith's eyes, she noticed her soft brown eyes had returned. She looked satisfied.

What had she done?

"Now that we have an understanding and a mutual enemy, I can tell you everything you need to know about Elizabeth Chase."

"How do you know her?" Charlotte asked.

"We were once friends until she betrayed me."

"If that's true, how do I know you're telling the truth?" Beads of perspiration collected on Charlotte's upper lip. Her trembling hand reached for her tea napkin. She felt nauseous.

"Trust me, I'm not the witch, she is."

"Witch?"

"Yes. When Elizabeth was seven-years-old, her mother cursed her.

She was nothing but a nightmare to the Beeson family. Burned their house down to the ground with her witchcraft."

"She said her parents died."

"Those weren't her real parents. The Beesons were her adoptive parents."

"I don't understand. She said she was a Quaker."

Mrs. Beckwith snorted and then released a throaty chuckle.

"She was a slave, rescued by the Beesons."

"A slave!" Charlotte jumped up from her seat bumping the table and sloshing her tea into its saucer.

"I thought you'd be excited to hear that," Mrs. Beckwith said and then calmly sipped her tea. "If you want to get her out of your life, just repeat what I have told you, and she'll be gone before the sun sets."

"How do I know this is the truth, and you're not sending me to do your dirty work?"

Mrs. Beckwith tittered and took a sip of tea. "My dear, I am perfectly capable of doing my own dirty work. Trust me, I certainly have no need for the hands of an amateur," she replied drolly. "Having nigra blood isn't the worst of her secrets. Everyone you meet these days seem to have a bit of nigra in them."

"I don't." Charlotte moved to the window that overlooked the main street. Mrs. Beckwith followed her. Charlotte could feel Mrs. Beckwith's breath over her shoulder when she spoke.

"Miss Greene, I assure you no matter how much we protest, our truth lives on waiting to be discovered— unless you find a way to kill it. Once the truth is dead, you will never have to suffer that painful horror in silence again," Mrs. Beckwith cajoled. "I have more condemning information about her. She bore a child out of wedlock."

"She has a bastard child?"

"Yes, a son. There's even more," Mrs. Beckwith taunted in Charlotte's ear.

Mrs. Beckwith's breath revealed a hint of their mint tea and the sweetness of chocolate.

"More?"

"My dear Miss Greene, I have so much dirt on Elizabeth Chase that if used properly, we could cultivate a most satisfying garden of revenge."

Charlotte looked down the street. She saw the corner of the Logan

Inn. It seemed miles away, and so was her conscience. If Henry ever found out what she was doing, he would probably divorce her.

"What has she done to you?" Charlotte asked.

"Let's just say, she took something of mine that I can never get back." Mrs. Beckwith said and returned to her seat.

When Charlotte turned around, all she could see was the back of Mrs. Beckwith's carefully coiffed head. Her beautiful pearl lacquered comb fanned across the top of her head like she was a Spanish Queen. Her back was erect and unyielding. The outside rumble of horses and carriages pulled Charlotte's attention to the world below. Charlotte wished there was a ladder she could climb down to escape the pull of desperation.

"If you're not careful she'll take it from you too," Mrs. Beckwith added without turning around. "She'll turn everything you love against you and leave you with nothing."

Henry's endless compliments of Mrs. Chase washed over Charlotte's mind like relentless waves. Before Elizabeth's arrival, she was getting so close to breaking Henry and getting back the one thing he took from her. She needed another month, or two, and he would have acquiesced. But then Elizabeth Chase showed up on her theater balcony and humiliated her into filling her balcony box with low life squatters! Throwing up on her during intermission in front of the VanCleefs only added to her humiliation. The last straw was moving into their carriage house and making them appear desperate for income. The longer Elizabeth stayed in their carriage house;, the more distant Henry would become.

"Tell me. Tell me everything about our little nigra," Charlotte said with a drawl and a cackle as she returned to her seat.

Charlotte smiled at the thought of throwing Elizabeth's dirty secrets in her face. The information about Elizabeth's slave past and bastard child was more than enough to remove the Chases from her backyard, Henry's approval, or any social acceptance. As she raised her teacup to her lips, she realized it was the first time in a long time she'd had the perfect cup of tea.

"Chocolate?" Mrs. Beckwith offered raising the Tiffany Silver bowl to Charlotte's face.

"Yes. I believe I will. Thank you." Charlotte selected the smallest piece from the bowl. She was about to drop it into her teacup, but instead popped it directly in her mouth. The moment she bit down, she was ready to retch. The rancid smell she first smelled in her foyer the day she visited Elizabeth exploded in her mouth. She didn't dare spit it out. Mrs. Beckwith was watching. She swallowed the chocolate like a bitter pill and washed it down with tea, and then forced a smile.

"I never saw so many lovely things under one roof. It's like going to the finest New York Department store," Charlotte said as she got up to take in the view of the departments on the second floor. Her eyes roamed each department. She was ready to do some shopping to celebrate.

"Isn't it lovely?" Mrs. Beckwith joined her at the observation window.

"You have outdone yourself with your store Mrs. Beckwith."

"Miss Greene, I feel the budding of a new friendship," Mrs. Beckwith said with a sigh.

"Mrs. Beckwith, may I dare say I feel the same," Charlotte said with delight.

"Miss Greene, please feel free to go and shop to your heart's content. Let's dispense with social formalities, shall we? You may call me Emma...and what is your real name?"

"And you may call me Charlotte."

"Charlotte, you're my very special customer. You may go pick out whatever you want and it's yours."

"Oh my. I can't. Please, let me pay..."

"Pay? So, you are a woman of means," Emma declared. "There are some lovely one of a kind crepe de chine dresses I ordered straight from Paris, or maybe you'd like a pair of new boots, or parfum? Pick out whatever your heart desires."

To turn down Emma Beckwith's offer would be a social slight she didn't think she could afford.

"There was a dress I saw while I was waiting for you. It was displayed on the moving table..."

"The garnet gown with the emerald teardrop crystals circling the shoulders. It's our showstopper."

"It's was made by Charles Frederick Worth. He's a new Paris designer," Charlotte announced.

"Charlotte, you do have exquisite taste. It's the most expensive dress in the store."

"Well, then I insist on paying for it," Charlotte replied.

"If that's the dress you've chosen, it is yours. Miss Christy will take you down so you can try it on, and then she'll make any necessary alterations."

"Alterations. Oh dear, I didn't think about that. Alterations will take quite a bit of time. May I take the dress with me, and take care of the alterations myself? You see, I'm on a bit of a tight travel schedule..."

"Whatever you would like my dear Charlotte. After you're done dress shopping, Miss Christy will bring you back and I'll tell you more about Elizabeth's bastard child that she bore with a Negro," Emma teased as she opened the door.

"A Negro? It sounds absolutely salacious."

"Shop first," Emma urged as she opened the door. Miss Christy was floating toward them with a welcoming smile. "Miss Christy, please show Miss Greene, our very special customer, the exquisite Worth gown on the carousel."

"How can I ever repay you?"

"We're friends now. I'm sure I'll come up with something," Emma said and then gently pressed her hand against Charlotte's back to guide her toward Miss Christy.

"I shan't be long. I'm dying to know more," Charlotte.

"I know you are," Emma replied with a satisfied smile, and then closed the door.

"This way, Miss Greene."

"You have the most wonderful occupation. Is she as generous with you?" Charlotte asked.

"Once, but everything has a cost, Miss Greene," Miss Christy said without turning around.

As they descended the stairs. Charlotte looked up and saw Emma's eyes as they followed her every step. She waved to her. Emma nodded and offered a soft smile of acknowledgment.

Once downstairs, Charlotte noticed the store was stone cold quiet. Her eyes roamed the main floor as Miss Christy led her to the dress of her dreams. As they drew closer, the eerie silence became overwhelming. Charlotte looked around. Not only were there no customers, but there were no other salespeople. She could feel the lump of rancid chocolate in her stomach.

"Here is Worth's creation. It's called temptation," Miss Christy commented.

Charlotte looked up at the dress that spun on a mirrored carousel table. The whirring of the carousel motor grew louder upon their approach. Charlotte watch the dress spin around and around. The details of the dress began to blur. Miss Christy pressed a large button on the side of the table. The carousel came to a stop. Charlotte felt a pressure on top of her head. She looked up and saw Emma staring down at them. Emma wasn't smiling. Miss Christy took the first step to climb up to the mirrored platform to retrieve the dress.

"Wait!" Charlotte felt a wave of nausea seized her and began to pull her out to into a dizzying sea.

"Is there another dress that has caught your eye?" Miss Christy asked.

Charlotte looked up and saw Emma's stare was now a menacing glare. Charlotte looked around the empty store again.

"Where are the other customers?"

"I don't understand," Miss Christy replied.

"This store has been open for hours. Where are the customers and salespeople?"

"The Beckwith Emporium is designed for that special clientele," Miss Christy recited.

Charlotte watched Miss Christy's eyes glance upward. Charlotte looked at the barren store again, and then the garnet dress. The image of the gargoyles perched under Emma's desk flashed in her mind.

What had she done?

When Charlotte looked up at Emma again, her scowling face and hands were pressed against her office window. Emma looked like a child locked in her bedroom unable to come out to play.

"I've changed my mind. I don't want the dress. Please tell Mrs. Beckwith that I am sorry," Charlotte blurted making her way to the front door. Glancing up, she noticed Emma's face was gone. She wanted to run but didn't want Emma to see her escape.

What had she done?

Outside into the numbing January air, Charlotte struggled to breathe. The air stung her nostril and scraped her lungs. Charlotte looked up over her shoulder. Emma's face was now pressed against the office window to the outside. Her mouth was moving, her face contorted from her silent screams. Charlotte bolted into the street without looking. A fast-moving horse and carriage barreled toward her. She was paralyzed. The world around her seemed to slow to a crawl. She heard the muffled sounds of a woman shrieking and men shouting. A flash of bright light, and then something jerked her right arm.

"Miss Greene!" Robert screamed. Her body slammed into his. "I've got you," Robert said gripping her in his arms. His breath warmed her face and brought her back to life. "You're safe now. I've got you."

CHAPTER 29

It was a time like this Elizabeth wished her carriage house would magically expand to accommodate surprise guests. Her in-laws, who arrived in New York a few days ago on business, were staying with friends because the carriage house was too small to accommodate them. Elizabeth felt guilty and a bit selfish about her choice of living accommodations, but her mother-in-law reminded her they were a newly married couple starting out and no one expected them to be living like the Rensselaers or the VanCleefs.

She was grateful to visit with her in-laws but wasn't too sure about hosting a dinner party for six. Initially, Elizabeth thought the wedding gift of the rosewood dining table with its six chairs was too much. She never dreamed of using all six chairs for dining because she and Samuel didn't know anyone in New York to warrant the extra four. But tonight, the extra four chairs were sorely needed. She had to remove two of the dining chairs from the table to use for extra seating in their little sitting area.

Truthfully, she had no reason to complain. Her mother-in-law had seen to every detail of their first formal dinner. Eugenia hired a cook, a server, a footman, the florist, and rented a complete hostess setting of dishes, silverware, and glasses for the evening. The only thing Elizabeth was instructed to do was rest and dress.

Samuel was equally stressed about their hosting responsibilities. He hovered over the hired help until the server discreetly inquired if there was anything they could do for him. Samuel finally exiled himself to their bedroom. He released enough sighs to ignite a good fire. It was the first time Elizabeth saw him so insecure.

"Darling, my tie. I can't seem to finagle this blasted material into a recognizable tie. It might as well be a noose. Can you manage a proper formal bow?" Samuel pleaded. "I do apologize for my parents bursting in on us this way."

"Don't apologize. We have nothing to do but smile. Although you'd think the Queen of England was coming with all the hired staff. Whoever heard of hiring so many people to serve dinner for six people? Samuel, you have to admit it's a bit comical."

"As is my mother at times. But these are her dearest and oldest friends. She wants us to meet them so we can have 'proper' connections here. They buy a lot of artwork and imports from my father. I guess he feels he owes them a meal."

"But why here Samuel? Our place is too small for a formal dinner party."

"Because mother thought we should bring the party to you, seeing that you are with child. We have plenty of room."

"For six people to dine?"

"It will be cozy," Samuel said and gave her a kiss on the forehead. He checked his tie in a floor mirror. "It's perfect. Thank you." He pulled Elizabeth inward to join him in front of the mirror. "We're quite the couple. What lovely babies we will make."

Elizabeth's hand smoothed a few wrinkles of her new dress. It had a relaxed corset to give her belly ample room to expand. While only two months along she noticed that her tiny waistline was already disappearing. Elizabeth was thrilled about starting a family with Samuel, but not so thrilled about all the changes her body was to undergo.

It was different when she was fourteen. She was so deeply in love, and so excited about having something that was her own, she completely overlooked her pubescent and maternal hormones. Now that she was stable and for all appearances, proper, she noticed every little change to her body.

"The waist is the first to go," she said with a small frown.

"I should hope so. Otherwise, there would be no room in there for our child." Samuel wrapped his arms around her stomach and rested his chin on top of her head.

"I feel like I belong in a barn, and any minute you're going to bring in a pail to milk me."

"Moooove over please," Samuel mimicked a cow.

She swatted him with the hand towel from their wash basin.

"My darling, you look marvelous. You are glowing with motherhood."

"Remember that, Mr. Samuel Chase, when I grow bigger than this carriage house," Elizabeth said angling her body in the mirror for a side view. She noticed the relaxed corset bowed out near her stomach and frowned.

"Our child is inside there somewhere. Thank you," Samuel said and lifted her chin for a kiss.

The bell on the inside of the door jingled announcing the arrival of their guests. They jumped to attention and then spun each other around to give the other a once over. The bell jingled again.

"I'll get it.".

"No, I'll get it." Samuel protested. They smiled at each other like children and broke into a short dash to the stairs. They bounded down the stairs together laughing trying to beat the other to the door. A formally dress footman approached the door.

"I've got it! I've got it!" Samuel called out arriving at the door before the footman. He slid into the door with a bang. Elizabeth caught her laughter with the cup of her hand. The footman rolled his eyes. "Perhaps, what is your name again?"

"Gerald, sir."

"Perhaps, Gerald, you should wait in the kitchen until I call for you."

"Oh Samuel, I don't think that's where he belongs."

"Sir, I am being paid to open the door and greet your guests."

"But it's my door."

"As you wish," the footman said. He lifted his nose in the air and returned to the kitchen doorway.

"Oh Samuel, I don't think you were supposed to do that."

Samuel pulled her in for a kiss, but the watchful eye of their hired footman, forced her to keep a proper public distance between them. The doorbell jingled impatiently. The footman took a step forward but was halted by Samuel's hand. Three firm knocks followed.

"I suppose we have to let them in," Samuel whispered in her ear.

"If we don't, who's going to eat all this food the cook prepared?"

"You will. How else will you become bigger than this carriage house?"

"Pardon me Mr. and Mrs. Chase, but I think it's impolite and indecent to keep your guest standing on the other side of the door. It is February sir," the footman urged. "I can answer the door. That would be the proper thing."

"I think stuffy would be more like it," Samuel shot back with a smirk and then opened the door. A blast of cold air entered and parted the flames in the fireplace. Standing in their doorway where four red-nose dinner guests.

"Samuel, where are your manners, making your guests wait in the cold? Where is the footman I hired?" Eugenia scolded.

"Sorry mother, we were busy," Samuel replied with a smirk.

"Mrs. Chase, I do apologize, but I'm moving slowly these days."

"That's what the footman was for." Eugenia summoned the footman with a wave of her hand. She turned for him to remove her cape.

"Hello my dear!" Horace announced with a frosty peck on her cheek and a gentle squeeze of her hands. "Elizabeth, you should know we saw you two running down the stairs like children on Christmas morning. Your little carriage house is like a human terrarium. Mind what you do downstairs, I guarantee there are eyes everywhere," Horace warned with lifted eyebrows.

"Running down the stairs in your condition? Really Elizabeth, I think you're allowing Samuel to corrupt your good sense of judgment," Eugenia surreptitiously turned and whispered to Elizabeth. "You're being tested tonight. Just smile and play along."

"Eugenia, they're newlyweds. They still have the mischief of little mice. Let them enjoy their privacy," a woman spoke as she entered behind the Chases.

"Horace, you said this would be informal, no fuss and no footmen. We were so looking forward to a departure from the normal dining pomp and circumstance. Footman, don't stand there making a wall of yourself, come get our coats," the woman ordered.

The woman was clearly of Eugenia's generation. Elegantly coiffed, with soft blonde hair smooth down the middle and curled and pinned tightly around her head. The woman had a body like a city pigeon. She was top heavy, no waist, and looked as though she was stuffed like a sausage into her dress. The woman's feet emerged from beneath the bell shape of her dress. They were so tiny Elizabeth expected her to topple over.

"You mustn't listen to your mother-in-law, she'll take all the fun out of being a newlywed," the woman added as she relinquished her coat to the footman. The woman looked very familiar. Elizabeth couldn't quite place the woman's face, but she knew she had seen her before.

"Doesn't my daughter-in-law look ravishing?" Horace announced.

"Of course, she looks ravishing, she is having our grandchild. She can't be anything but ravishing," Eugenia countered. "Oh my, a peacock. Horace, look, a peacock."

"Yes, and it's a rather big peacock."

"It was a gift from the Marquis DeMontier," Elizabeth explained.

Elizabeth felt like she was in a carnival. There were no introductions, people were milling into their home as though they paid an admission. Her in-laws were acting rather strangely. They didn't bother to introduce their guest, and they were calling each other by the first names. What on earth did Mrs. Chase mean when she instructed her to 'play along?

"My that is a big peacock!" an older man announced as he entered. He was of average height, and slender. Draped in a cape and top hat, he looked like a magician ready to perform. "DeMontier is quite the eccentric. Fortunately for you, he didn't send the real thing. Mind you, don't fall victim to DeMontier's debauchery. He's a caterpillar hoping to turn into a butterfly. Oh look, brandy. My favorite!" The older man clapped his gloved hands and made a beeline towards the rented cart filled with decanters of wine, scotch, and brandy.

"A great hot toddy would make up for keeping us at the door like village dogs," he said and flipped his cape behind his back to prepare a drink.

"Julius, you're being horribly uncivilized. One would think you've been raised by wolves, demanding a hot toddy without even an introduction, or the benefit of a meal."

Elizabeth rolled her lips inward to fight her burgeoning smile. Her guests' bizarre behavior was refreshing. She had no idea what to expect. Julius clapped his hands together.

"Eureka!" he exclaimed as he raised the decanter of whiskey into the air. "My dear, perhaps we should get ourselves a little carriage house. We have only just arrived, and I can't remember when I had so much fun," Julius said. He removed his cape and gloves with a flourish and dropped them into the waiting arms of the footman.

"Honestly Mr. ..."

"Uh uh uh, no formalities tonight my dear. Tonight, we are normal people, without any responsibilities. Please don't take away my joy. It's so rare we get to really kick up our heels, as they say."

"Julius, they are newlyweds and new to New York. It is paramount that we set an example," his wife chided.

"My dear Clara, we'll have plenty of dinners to set an example. Tonight, we are Clara and Julius, your delightful and fun dinner guests," Julius said to Elizabeth with a bow of his head.

"It is a pleasure to meet you, Julius and Clara," Elizabeth said stepping forward with a slight curtsey. "Welcome to our humble home." Elizabeth extended her hand.

Elizabeth recognized the eccentric couple. She had seen them at the theater the night she got sick. She wanted to hide.

"Horace, I love your new daughter-in-law. She embodies the true spirit of life!" Julius approached Elizabeth. His slender body waltzed over to her. Donned in tails, vest, necktie, and pants, he looked like an average New Yorker. He allowed her to believe that they were all the same. Elizabeth looked nervously at Mrs. Chase for a cue on what to do; she offered Elizabeth a hard smile and a nod of her head.

No White man other than her father had ever touched her. In New Hope, everyone knew she was a slave. While there was acceptance of her presence, she always felt there was some sort of proper distance from her. She couldn't decide if the distance was because of her Negro roots or her reputation to know people's secrets. Julius didn't seem to care about any convention. He crossed the boundary of impropriety without hesitation.

"My dear lady, may I have this dance?" Julius asked with a slight bow of his head.

"There is no music," Elizabeth replied with a nervous smile.

"If it's music the lady wants, music is what she shall have," Julius said with a clap of his hands. A violinist emerged from the kitchen doorway and launched into a Vienna Waltz.

"Where did he come from?" Elizabeth asked bewildered.

"I believe the musician fell out of my cape," Julius said presenting an opened hand. Elizabeth gingerly placed her hand in his.

"Clear the floor Horace, we're breaking in the rug!"

Julius' silvery pompadour fluffed forward as his head lowered to kiss her hand. The moment his lips touched her hand, Elizabeth's familiar bubble of light appeared in her mind's eye. Inside of it was an image of Julius as a young boy talking to a man who wore a little black skull cap.

Was Julius Jewis?

Not wanting to intrude any further, she quickly withdrew her hand. The shocked look on Julius' face made it clear she offended him. Elizabeth caught Eugenia's gaze. She looked to Samuel. Samuel approached them and placed Elizabeth's hand in Julius'.

"We're newlyweds. I'm afraid my wife is not accustomed to the lips of another man, especially a married man, touching her skin," Samuel explained.

"Forgive me?"

"Of course, I will forgive you anything," Julius responded and bowed. Elizabeth curtseyed. When his hands embraced hers, Elizabeth couldn't help but stare at the union of their fingers. While physically, their skin bore no difference, Elizabeth knew that through her blue vein flowed the blood of a former slave. She wondered if Julius knew she was really a slave, would he touch her without gloves?

His hand led her to the open floor space in front of the large window. Images of Julius' life floated to her. She struggled to stay present. She focused her eyes on the DeMontier's peacock.

"I'm afraid I don't know how to dance a waltz, Julius," Elizabeth confessed.

"You will be dancing the waltz when we are done, my dear lady. Am I competing with a peacock?" Julius asked with a pout.

"You have my full attention," Elizabeth replied.

"Now eyes on me," Julius instructed.

"One...two...three...one...two...three..." Julius began moving her slowly around the living room. "Chin up and show the world how accomplished and graceful you are," Julius added.

Elizabeth felt the gentle push of his hand against the middle of her back. After a few stumbles, she was following in his footsteps. Gliding about the room from the fireplace to the window to the door, they waltzed. When she could, she locked her eyes on the peacock.

"Now keep your eyes on your dance partner," Julius coached.

As Elizabeth danced, she looked at the smiling faces in her living area. It appeared that a bit of New York was already embracing her. Could the color of one's skin allow one to waltz through life without scrutiny? Julius' hand tightened slightly on hers as he moved her back toward the window.

"I believe you've got the hang of it, my dear. Splendid! Splendid!"

"We can't let them show us up, Clara," Horace said with a grin. He bowed and opened his hand to receive Clara's.

"Mother?" Samuel said.

As the three couples waltzed, the music and their laughter carried out into the courtyard through the windows of Barclay. When Elizabeth and Julius waltzed by the large window again, she thought she saw a shadow standing in front of the library window. It wasn't Charlotte's.

***

The stillness of the February night air carried the sound of music from the carriage house into the courtyard. Henry watched Elizabeth, Samuel, and their guests spin like toy tops in front of the window for at least fifteen minutes before they disappeared. It was the first time in a long-time joy and life were on his property.

When he was married to Elise, the sole heir to a button factory, they hosted many parties and dinners that he joked he should sleep in his formal dinner attire. There was always chatter, wonderful food, and smiles. Elise was always brought an abundance of life into his lonely world. She made him acceptable to New York's aristocracy. The moment she was laid in her casket, he was tongue stamped a gold digger because the origin of his social pedigree always remained a mystery.

His marriage to Charlotte only isolated him more. He thought he found someone who was poised and beautiful help him reopen doors. Instead, the only doors she opened was to expensive shops. Perhaps if he had given in and granted Charlotte's request, maybe Cassandra would have never moved out. Maybe Charlotte would have given him an heir. It seemed what he denied Charlotte mirrored back into his own life. His loneliness was his penance.

Thus, Charlotte's sudden departure three days ago had been difficult. Henry couldn't decide if he hated the silence or missed the company of

205

Charlotte's animosity. According to Ava, Charlotte was scheduled to return tomorrow, but the arrival of Charlotte's coach was still unknown. He pushed the drape aside to peer out his library window one more time. Another couple twirled past the carriage window. Solitude clawed at his heart. He needed to escape. His painful loneliness was overriding all social etiquette. He hoped they would forgive his intrusion and offer him a morsel of life.

He opened the door to the courtyard. It was pitch black. No moon or stars to guide him. The dark shadows of the cherry trees looked like headless ghosts of slaves he refused to help. He moved quickly through the courtyard slipping and sliding on patches of invisible ice keeping his eyes on the light of life in the carriage house.

CHAPTER 30

What had she done?

Traveling by coach in the dead of winter stretched a day of traveling into one and a half days. The Good Intent Stagecoach was advertised to offer speed and comfort, neither of which they delivered. Charlotte's feet were numb from the cold and her bottom was stiff from sitting in a full coach. The driver picked up two more passengers, a young couple, just outside of the Philadelphia station. She would have been happy to exchange the chatty couple with the braggart beast, who boarded the coach with her in Philadelphia. His constant leers were more objectionable than the smell of his disgusting cigar. Unfortunately, everyone was riding all the way to the New York Station.

Because of the icy roads, the driver warned them they would be arriving one hour later than originally scheduled. Her coach was now two hours behind schedule. The drivers suggested they stop and stay a night at an inn along the route and leave early the next morning so they can travel more safely in daylight, but the beast decided their fate to be otherwise.

"Get me to New York tonight, and there will be an extra one hundred dollars in each of your pockets." The man's voice was deep and arrogant. Dressed in what looked to be a very expensive handmade woolen suit and fur coat, it was easy to see he cared only about himself.

"I will see to it that my husband will give you each two hundred dollars to let us stay at the inn tonight so we can travel in the daylight as you suggested," Charlotte countered.

"I have two hundred dollars right here in my pocket," the man quickly countered. He removed a wad of bills and unfolded them. "Fifty dollars now, and fifty dollars when you get me to the New York station.

"My husband will pay more," Charlotte countered.

"Your husband is not here," he jabbed back.

"Sir, your ego is so big, I'm surprised there is room inside the coach for the rest of us," Charlotte volleyed back. "If anything happens to me, my husband will hunt you down."

The man rolled the wet end of his cigar between his lips and grinned.

"Sit next to me, little lady and nothing will happen to you. I'll keep you safe," he added with a wink.

"I'd rather ride the horse bareback into New York than sit next to the likes of you," Charlotte shot back and returned to the stagecoach.

As the coach ambled down the icy rutted roads, it pitched its passengers side to side. Charlotte placed herself against the far window. Not the best seat. If the coach slipped and fell on its left side, she'd be crushed. However, she didn't want to risk sitting next to that man. The only good thing about her seat was that she had a strap to grab hold of every time the coach slipped on ice. Charlotte's left hand was exhausted and ached from white knuckling the hanging strap, and she was too afraid to fall asleep.

Her thoughts shifted to her last night in New Hope. If it wasn't for Robert Kincaide she wouldn't be on this coach. He saved her three times. Once when she arrived. The second time was after her horrible visit with Emma Beckwith. The last time, the last time...

What had she done?

Tears escaped her eyes. She quickly blotted them with the back of her gloved hand. She had no explanation for what took place in her room. She was only grateful Robert Kincaide heard her screams when she was attacked. She bit her lip to stop the flow of tears and to erase the events of her last night from her mind, but the memory of her attacker's odor punctured her senses. She cupped her mouth to prevent from vomiting.

"Miss Greene, are you sick?" Mrs. Dunham asked. She was the female part of the chatty couple. Mrs. Dunham's chatter reminded Charlotte of a yard of crickets on a hot night. Mrs. Dunham leaned forward, crossing the boundary of Charlotte's side of the coach. "If your stomach can't handle the ride, this should help," she said extending a piece of peppermint stick wrapped in a twist of wax paper. "Peppermint works wonders on an upset stomach. You can have it. I have plenty."

"Go on take it," Mr. Dunham chimed in. "You should listen to my wife, she's like a bonafide miracle worker. Anything that ails you, she'll find the remedy and then it's gone by sunset. I'm thinking she should go to one of them fancy medical schools and become a doctor."

"She's a woman," the beast said.

"That should make no difference, as long as she makes you feel better."

"You obviously come from a small tumbleweed town," the beast admonished. "First time in a real city?

"Yes, but she's got a gift we know a city hospital can make use of," Mr. Dunham defended.

The beast rolled his cigar in his mouth and chuckled. Charlotte felt sorry for the couple.

"Thank you, for the peppermint. I'm sure your wife will be a great addition to any hospital." Charlotte placed the peppermint stick between her fingers and broke it in half. She quickly popped the smaller piece into her mouth. Its sweet flavor coated her tongue and released a vapor of peppermint into her throat. When she parted her lips, the scent reached her nose. "I'm feeling better already," she said addressing the beast. She wanted to stick her tongue out at him.

"Are you from New York?" the young woman asked.

"Yes."

"This is our first time to the big city. It's nice to meet someone from New York. It helps to know a kind face."

"What does your husband do?" the young woman's husband asked.

Charlotte regretted taking the peppermint and defending them. They were obviously looking for a pocket to fleece once they arrived in New York. She wasn't about to have another regret.

"My husband is a farmer."

"In New York?" Mr. Dunham said incredulously.

"He must be doing really well if he can afford to pay each driver two hundred dollars to stay put," the beast interjected with a sneer. Charlotte shot him a fiery looked to which he responded with a smile and a tip of his hat. "Welcome to New York," he directed at the young couple with a snicker.

Mrs. Dunham pushed herself back into her seat, crossed her arms, and looked angrily out the window. Charlotte didn't care. After her last night at the Logan Inn, she wasn't willing to let anyone in. She should have never gone to that store, spoke to Emma Beckwith, or kissed that frightening gargoyle creature. She was certain that stench and the creature that was in her room followed her from Emma Beckwith's store. She never wanted to see that evil woman again.

Charlotte couldn't wait to get home and into her own bed. Maybe she would let Henry sleep in her bed her first night back. She wanted to make sure whatever followed her from Emma's store to her room at the Inn, didn't follow her back to New York.

The coach slipped on ice again. The rear wheels of the coach fishtailed to the left. There was a collective scream as Charlotte gripped the hanging leather strap. The coach quickly righted itself. The driver slowed the horses to a trot. Everyone took a deep breath. Charlotte closed her eyes in relief. Robert Kincaide's face floated in front of her. Her stomach fluttered from the thought of him.

"Folks we've got to hang on for one more hour, and then we'll be home free," the beast said.

"Home free..." What if that creature and its foul stench followed her home? What if there was no escaping it? What had she done? This was all Elizabeth's fault!

The horses broke into a bottom-bouncing gallop, forcing Charlotte to grip the leather strap with both hands. Her visit with Emma Beckwith and her stagecoach ride home had her holding on for dear life!

CHAPTER 31

"Fascinating. Absolutely fascinating, Mr. Dennings. I had no idea gangs in New York were so organized. They're like little companies roaming the city. I always perceived them to be more like ruffians and hooligans with no intelligence," Clara said.

"Henry, you may call me Henry. I intruded on what looked like a fun and informal gathering. I wish to play by your rules."

"Hear, hear my good man," Julius cheered, slapping the table with his hands. "You are now a part of a very elite club. You must never breathe a word of this to anyone."

"Henry, consider this our own little gang," Clara said.

"Clara, I don't think you should label us a gang," Eugenia said. "Gangs are violent."

"Oh dear, I thought Henry said the gangs were poor intellectuals."

"No, dear. Henry said that they were smart criminals."

"Oh, well we're certainly not criminals," Clara defended.

"You'll have to forgive my wife. My wealth and position has sheltered her from the realities of life."

"Don't you make apologies for me, Julius. I am not sheltered. I'm just not privy to such underhanded individuals," she reprimanded.

"You win my darling," Julius acquiesced.

"Samuel, take note. This is how you keep a happy marriage," Horace said.

"Samuel, don't you listen to your father. Patronizing your wife is not the best approach," Eugenia chimed in.

Samuel smiled at Elizabeth and then reached for her fingers to hold her hand. She felt his stocking feet rub against hers beneath the table. He gave her a sultry side glance and redirected his attention back to the conversation.

It was the most charming evening she had ever had in her life. Her father would have enjoyed relinquishing social propriety in favor of removing his boots for comfort. Her eyes went around the table. She found all her dinner guests entertaining in a peculiar way. She had no idea if this was how rich White people really behaved. Or maybe they weren't White at all. Maybe they were they all "Blue Veins" masquerading as White people.

Her eyes focused on Clara. Her skin was as white as the linen tablecloth. Her tawny brown hair was arranged in soft curls that surrounded her round face. Her nose was noticeably pointed, and her lips were thin. She barely had enough lip for a pout, if she were to be so inclined. Elizabeth wondered if all White people secretly had Negro blood in them and that's why they enslaved Negroes, so they could deflect their own truths? The tips of her ears began to burn with resentment until she looked around the table and concluded that not all White people were bad. It would be an injustice to sentence a whole race. Not all White people agreed with slavery. If they did, she wouldn't be sitting at this table right now.

"...When you really think about it, I dare say, we are all gangs," Eugenia said.

"Eugenia, how can you say that? We're not robbers and thieves," Clara defended

"No, but when you look at how we have divided ourselves into groups. We have socially defined ourselves by the color of skin, religion, money, and social standing. One could consider each group a gang."

"For that to be true, Eugenia, each group would have to be violent and unscrupulous," Clara replied.

"Eugenia, perhaps this isn't the time for this little debate," Horace chided.

"Horace this is the perfect time. What do you think Henry? You said yourself that you have had firsthand experience with the gangs of New York. Do you feel that the gangs that terrorize New York are any different than, let's say, slave masters who terrorize and enslave Negroes?"

The table grew silent. Elizabeth looked up and noticed the footman standing at attention, was red-faced. The server had disappeared from the kitchen doorway. Elizabeth saw Henry lower his eyes and rub his index finger nervously against the white tablecloth.

"I believe Eugenia has made a point that I cannot dispute," Henry responded. Elizabeth watched his eyes take a quick survey of the table.

"Thank you for your bravery Henry," Eugenia said. "Julius, I know you think my mind has sprung a leak and is flooding the table with Quaker and abolitionist rhetoric, but I must take every opportunity I find to challenge all of us to examine our own actions and consequences. We are in our own little gangs. This table here, for example, is a gang."

"She's right about that," Julius chimed in.

"But we're not hurting anyone or stealing from anyone," Clara interjected. "I would say we're a good gang."

"But the slave masters aren't," Elizabeth said. It was the first time she spoke about anything in a public forum. "They're no different than these organized gangs. They've set up the laws, so they have the upper hand. They decide who's free, who's rich, who's poor. They terrorize the enslaved and the free Negroes. I don't think you have to be a Quaker to see that," Elizabeth concluded in a soft voice.

"You'd make a wonderful politician Elizabeth. Although you'd be condemned and hung before the paint on your banner dried," Julius warned. "How wonderful it would be if there were no gangs, no color, no religion. Just a population of beings interacting without the slightest knowledge that the person next to them is different."

Elizabeth looked at Julius' eyes. They were red, but not from drinking.

"To stand by and watch others be enslaved, beaten, and suffer because of the color of their skin is unconscionable. We are human beings. Wild wolves behave better than we do," Henry argued. His fingers fumbled with his dessert spoon that rested on his empty plate. The table grew silent again.

"Henry, my dear man, you have eloquently presented a very strong argument for the abolishment of slavery," Eugenia said.

"We must all do our part," Julius confessed.

"Our part hasn't been enough," Eugenia added.

"It sounds like the cat is clawing to get out of the proverbial bag," Horace said.

"I'm sorry. I didn't mean to put a damper on tonight's fun. This was the best night I've had in a long time. Perhaps I came on a bit too strong," Henry said forcing a smile.

"Not at all," Samuel said and gave Elizabeth's hand a gentle squeeze.

"Slavery is never a good subject," Julius began. "But I think it's safe to say that everyone at this table has made a contribution, in their own way, to make a difference. Having money doesn't make us bad people. Not doing good with our money is what makes bad people," Julius asserted.

"There are times I feel guilty about my beautiful home, my beautiful wife, even the bit of laughter I find for myself. How can any human being find joy in the face of horrific inhumanity? Hatred drains life," Julius concluded and tapped the table with his fingers.

Elizabeth watched as Julius' hand reached across the table for Clara's. Clara's glistening eyes produced a tear that sat on the precipice of hers lower eyelid. Eugenia caught her tear with the end of her napkin.

"You know what I like about our little gang," Horace tossed out. "I like that our gang has fun. I think we're getting too serious," Horace warned and brought his glass of sherry to his lips and drained it.

"No, I think we're getting too real," Julius sighed heavily. "Unfortunately, the real world is not fun or fair. I fear if we continue to make gangs our topic of conversation, we will defeat the purpose of dancing about in our stocking feet," Julius concluded with a chuckle.

"I know it is not customary for the wife of the host to propose a toast, but because we have done away with all rules of social etiquette, I shall." Elizabeth stood up from her chair. The men quickly stood and joined her, raising their glasses.

"To freedom for all!"

"Freedom for all!" Everyone lifted their glasses and then took a sip.

"I would like to make one more toast," Horace announced. "To our new gang."

"Just a moment. I will toast to it as long as everyone agrees we are a good gang," Clara injected.

CHAPTER 32

When the taxi carriage came to a stop, Charlotte was never so happy to see Barclay. She was home and safe! She leaned forward to look out the window to eye Barclay's brass lion's head door knocker and sighed. The arctic January night air scraped her face as a footman opened the door to her taxi. She peered outside and saw the Mr. Twitterly. She didn't care that she had to hire a Hansom Cab to carry her home, or that Mr. Twitterly was the one who greeted her. Her frightening stay in New Hope had made her grateful for everything in her life, even the decrepit Mr. Twitterly. She was relieved to see a familiar face, even if it was his. She wished they hadn't gotten off to such an acrimonious start.

***

Mr. Twitterly was at Barclay when she married Henry. The moment she arrived and saw his shriveled face, she wanted him gone.

"Henry, Mr. Twitterly is so old he's ready to turn to dust at any moment," Charlotte complained. He reminded her of an old dried-up raisin. He was hard, stiff and void of any sweetness to mitigate her bitter life.

"I would never think of getting rid of Mr. Twitterly. If he turned to dust, I would sweep him up and put him in the finest vase. I consider him family," Henry responded without looking up from his desk

"Family? Now you have an allegiance to family?"

"This is different. You're out of place to speak on Mr. Twitterly's position," Henry fired back.

"Am I not the lady of this house? Is it not my duty and right to tend

215

to the selection of servants? Or am I now a servant who must accept your decisions about my life?"

Henry kept his eyes on his paperwork, then collected a small stack of envelopes.

"Charlotte you're in the North. Mr. Twitterly is not a servant. He is the nail that holds Barclay together. If I pull the nail out of Barclay's frame, it would collapse around us."

"You neglected to assure me that I am not a servant."

"Don't be ridiculous," Henry tossed back.

"Then why can't I have someone who is capable? Mr. Twitterly has done nothing but ruin every request I've made."

"Perhaps if you didn't refer to him as Mr. Twit, you'd find your requests to your liking," Henry scolded .

"It was just a harmless play on words."

"I suggest you find some other toy to play with." Henry He threw the handful of envelopes on the table and walked away. The following week, he hired Ava.

***

"Welcome home, Mrs. Dennings," Mr. Twitterly said. Their footman flipped the stairs down from the carriage. Charlotte waited a moment for Mr. Twitterly to look at her, acknowledge her, but his eyes remained fixed on whatever was in the distance. Their footman helped her down. She was grateful.

"Thank you..." She was embarrassed she didn't know the footman's name.

"It's Mr. Baxter, my lady."

"Thank you, Mr. Baxter."

"Welcome home, my lady," Ava said with a slight curtsey.

"Thank you, Ava."

"I hope you had a wonderful trip, my lady."

"It's good to be home."

"Mr. Baxter and Mr. Quinn, her luggage please," Mr. Twitterly ordered.

"Thank you, Mr. Twitterly, it's good to be home," Charlotte said looking him directly in his eyes.

216

"I will see that your luggage is delivered to your room immediately," he said. staring off into the darkness.

The puff of vapor from Charlotte's snort came between them and then disappeared.

"I shall take care of the driver," Mr. Twitterly said. dismissing her.

"I have paid him," Charlotte said. Mr. Twitterly raised an eyebrow. "Mr. Twitterly, do you think we can start again? I'd like to sincerely apologize for playing with your name. I realize I judged you without the benefit of knowing you."

"Is my lady well?"

"Yes, I'm well. My trip was...enlightening. It taught me to appreciate what I have. I'm so grateful to have you, Ava, and Henry," Charlotte said. "Where is my husband?"

A sudden explosion of laughter burst into the courtyard and drifted into Charlotte's ears.

"What is that?"

"Laughter, my lady."

"I know it's laughter. Where is it coming from?" Charlotte demanded.

Mr. Twitterly only smiled. Charlotte rushed inside. When she entered she was met with a deathly silence. She scurried to the drawing room, then the library. No one was there. She returned to the foyer and accosted Mr. Twitterly as he instructed the footman carrying her luggage.

"Where is Mr. Dennings?"

"He's not here, my lady."

"I can see that. Where is he?"

"Perhaps he took a evening stroll, my lady," Mr. Twitterly said with a droll smile. "Would my lady like a cup of tea brought up to her room?"

"No, your lady would not!" Charlotte shouted in his face.

"As you wish," Mr. Twitterly said, then disappeared up the steps with the footman.

"Would you like cook to prepare something for you?" Ava asked with a soft smile.

"Ava, where is my husband?"

"Your husband, my lady?"

"I don't need a parrot. I need an answer. Where is my husband?"

"I think I may have heard that he went to the carriage house..."

"My husband is at the carriage house?"

217

"Yes, my lady. He was earlier. I don't know if he's still there," Ava replied pulling her lips inward to keep from smiling. "Will you be wanting a cup of hot tea? Or shall I draw you a hot bath?"

Charlotte needed neither tea or a hot bath. She was steaming. Henry should be here comforting her.

"Unpack my bags," Charlotte ordered and stomped her way to the library. The library was quite warm from the fire that was still going strong. She felt the weight of the icy wet hem of her travelling dress. She looked out the French doors, past the small grove of cherry blossom trees that looked like a small army of weary people, to the carriage house. *Clack!*

She released the lock on the French door and bolted into the night like a dog let off its leash. She couldn't help herself. She crunched her way through the hardened snow to avoid the icy path. Her mind revved with Elizabeth's secrets. Which secret should she reveal first? Which secret would be more shocking to Henry?

As she drew nearer, she saw a carriage. The carriage was long and had two horses. Its driver was nowhere to be seen. She smiled with satisfaction at the thought of humiliating Elizabeth in front of her guests and Henry. It would make up for the horror she had to endure in New Hope. When she approached the door, she heard more laughter. She would end that.

Her hand gripped the doorknob. She formulated her words in her head.

Elizabeth Chase is a liar, a fraud, and a slave!
Not strong enough...
Elizabeth Chase is a slave's whore who bore a child out of wedlock!
Better.

The cold metal of the doorknob felt like a ball of ice in her hand. A cold hand and a cold heart were needed to ensure she'd get the job done. When she opened the door, the voices died. Whoever was sitting with Henry and Elizabeth on the other side of that door was about to be shocked to their senses.

"Who's there?" Henry's voice called out. She heard the heel of his boot thump towards the floor. As she stepped inside to make her grand appearance a footman approached her. She ignored him and closed the door.

"May I take your coat?" the footman asked.

"No, I won't be staying. I'm here to collect my husband," Charlotte declared.

"Charlotte, for God's sake what are you doing here?"

Henry's tall body eclipsed her vision of the dining room guests seated at the table, but she could see Elizabeth.

"I could ask you the same thing, Henry. I came back from my trip and you didn't have the decency to meet me at the station or be in our home to greet me."

"Charlotte, go home right now or you'll be sorry," Henry whispered as he pulled her in for an embrace and obligatory peck on the cheek.

"I will not leave," Charlotte growled under her breath.

"Henry, there's always room for one more," Julius called out.

"Yes, have her join us," Clara said.

Charlotte pushed past Henry. Two steps later, she saw who was sitting at the table. She froze. The vengeful words she had prepared to say about Elizabeth had abandoned her. Her heart jumped into her throat and rendered her mute.

What had she done?

Charlotte clutched her heaving chest and stumbled forward.

"Should we call my doctor?" Julius asked.

"Julius, give her some brandy," Clara said.

"I have hot tea," Elizabeth said.

"Mr. and Mrs. VanCleef..." Charlotte sputtered.

"Oh dear," Clara sighed.

"My dear, it looks like the jig is up," Julius said and tossed his napkin onto the table.

"Look what you've done," Henry said angrily.

The log in the fireplace popped and hissed as it broke apart. Bits of bright hot embers crumbled and fell between the grate as Charlotte dropped to the floor.

CHAPTER 33

"She knows your secret..."

Charlotte opened her eyes. A gentle breeze lifted her hair. She turned over, then closed her eyes. Another waft of breeze passed over her head. This time she heard a flapping sound. Something was flying in her room. She opened her eyes and scanned her room. She felt the breeze of its wings as it flew over her head. She ducked under the covers.

"She knows your secret..."

"Hello..." Charlotte said softly.

She lowered the covers to scan the room. The most horrific stench assaulted her senses. She quickly brought the bedding up to her nose to block the odor.

"Who's there?"

"She knows your secret..."

"Who's there?" she demanded.

In the darkness of her room, she saw the silhouette of something big as it flew past her window. She dove under her covers. All she could think of were those ugly winged gargoyles in Emma Beckwith's office.

"She knows your darkest secret...kill her...you must kill her...Kill her!"

Charlotte didn't realize it, but she was screaming. She was screaming so loud she didn't hear the pounding on her bedroom door. She struggled to free herself from the hands that held her from beneath her bedding.

"Aeeiiiiiiiiiii! Aeeeiiiiiiiiii! Help me!

"Miss Greene!"

"God help me!"

"Miss Greene! Miss Greene!"

Charlotte opened her eyes. In the glow of his oil lamp, Robert Kincaide's face loomed over hers.

"Mr. Kincaide! Mr. Kincaide!" Charlotte cried. Her arms locked around his neck.

"What's going on?" Mr. Bailey asked lighting her doorway.

"Miss Greene had a nightmare. I was minding the front desk, and I heard her screams."

"Miss Greene?"

"Yes, yes, I was having a bad dream. I'm sorry. I hope I didn't wake up the rest of your guests."

"I'm sure everyone will go right back to sleep. You, Mr. Kincaide, can get back to the front desk," Mr. Bailey ordered. Mr. Bailey and Mr. Kincaide disappeared from her doorway.

Moments later, a soft knock and the door opened again. Robert's large silhouette filled the doorway.

"If you want me to stay with you to keep you safe, I will," Robert offered. "A beautiful woman such as yourself should never be without a man to protect her."

Charlotte opened her arms and invited him into her bed. She nuzzled her face in the crook of his neck. In the darkness of the night, Robert's strong arms around her were more than comforting. He pulled her closer, tighter. The warmth of his breath floated on the top of her head. The rhythm of his heart picked up. Her heart pounded in sync with his. She pulled her head from the crook of his neck to look up at him. Before she could see his eyes, his lips were upon hers. Her arms flew upward around his neck to kiss him back and pull him down on top of her.

They fell back slowly onto her pile of pillows. She moaned from the weight of his body. In the dark, her fingers moved slowly through the thick waves of his hair. He pulled away and pecked kisses up and down her neck. The warmth of his breath excited her. It was a long time since she allowed Henry to touch her, nourish her body. She was starving for a man's touch, for love. She never allowed Henry to touch her. It was his punishment. It turned out she was the one being punished.

Robert stopped. In the darkness, she felt his eyes searing her soul. Their panting filled the space between them. She clutched a hand full of his hair. Robert slowly lifted his face from her neck to look at her. She wanted to kiss him again. She wanted to taste the passion on his lips.

When his face hovered above hers it became the snarling face of the winged gargoyle. Its eyes glowed a deep fiery orange.

"You must kill her!" *it snarled.*

"Aaaeeeiiiiiiii! Aaaaeeeeiiiiii!" Charlotte shrieked.

"Charlotte! Charlotte! Wake up!"

Charlotte opened her eyes. She was back home in her bed. Henry was holding her in his arms.

"Charlotte, what on God's earth..." Henry asked.

"I had a nightmare. Let go of me," she demanded and jerked away.

"You were screaming so loud you woke the entire house."

Charlotte looked at her door. It was empty. No one came to her aid. She pulled the blanket up to her neck to cover her partially exposed right breast.

"What was your nightmare about?"

"It was nothing..."

"Nothing? You were screaming like the devil was in your bed."

"He is," Charlotte said looking Henry in the eye.

Henry's shoulders dropped. He pushed up from her bed, and exited her bedroom closing the door behind him.

Charlotte quickly lit the oil lamps in her room. She was determined never to be in the dark again. She sat up in her bed looking at every dark corner for movement. After two hours her eyes became heavy with sleep. The moment her head dropped forward that horrible stench opened her eyes. Her head popped up with a jolt. As she looked around her lit room, she realized the hateful stench and the beast to which it belonged was real.

What had she done?

***

Elizabeth smiled when she filled her lungs with the scent of wild lavender and sweet tall grass. With each inhale, the grass bent toward her. She was standing in the field where her father's service was held. As she released her breath the grasses slowly bent away from her. It felt good to be home.

She remembered it wasn't too far of a walk home from the field. She looked up at the sun in the sky to determine which direction she should head. She needed to be facing east to head back towards town. When she looked up, the sun was high in the sky over a grove of birch and ash trees. She started walking toward the trees to find the opening to Ferry Road that would lead her home. She couldn't wait to get there.

She glided through the grasses like the night she was with Wakayeja wicahpe. At that moment, the scent of sweet pine blew across the grassy field. Wakayeja wicahpe was with her.

"What are you doing here?" Elizabeth asked.

"Do you remember me?" Wakayeja wicahpe asked.

"Why do you keep asking me the same question? I always give you the same answer, no. The first time I met you was that horrible night on Ferry Road—Am I dreaming?"

"Yes," Wakayeja wicahpe said.

Elizabeth stopped walking.

"How can you be in my dream?"

"Because you can see into my world."

"What good is seeing into your world if I can't see what I want to see? I want to see Simon and Willie," Elizabeth demanded.

"But they are not here."

Aggravated, she turned around to walk in the opposite direction. After two steps, Elizabeth came to a dead stop. Standing before her was an Asian man, his hands hidden in the cuffs of his mandarin jacket. His placid eyes and oval face invited her gaze. She couldn't take her eyes off of him. Her eyes were drawn to his thin lips that were camouflaged by a mustache that flowed into a long black silky beard. He looked like one of the men she saw in Samuel's parent's painting of the Forbidden Palace.

"Who is he?" Elizabeth asked.

"He is your father."

"No, he's not."

"Oh, but he is. Mitakuye Oyasin," Wakayeja wicahpe said.

"Why do you keep saying that? What does that mean?" Elizabeth demanded.

Wakayeja wicahpe faded.

"You're not my father," Elizabeth said angrily to the man.

"Do not let the outside distract you from the truth that lies

223

within," the man said calmly.

He removed his right hand from the cuff of his jacket and unfurled his fingers to reveal a small white ball.

"What is that?"

"Different on the outside, all the same on the inside. You must come to the city to buy more." The man popped the white ball into his mouth and smiled as he chewed.

Gazing into his eyes she saw a familiar soul staring back at her. "Poppa?"

***

Elizabeth opened her eyes and bolted up in bed. She touched her face. It was moist from tears. Samuel lifted his head from his pillow.

"Did you see your father?" He asked as his hand gently stroked her back.

"I'm not sure. Samuel, what does *Mitakuye Oyasin* mean?"

"*Wakayeja wicahpe* was there, huh?"

"Yes."

Elizabeth lowered herself onto Samuel's chest. He wrapped his arms around her and drew her in.

"I think you have a different way of meditating," Samuel suggested.

"Meditating? I was sleeping."

"You know how I sit and close my eyes to think about things?"

"Yes."

"Well, somehow you are doing that in your sleep. Meditation is a way to connect to a bigger world that we can't see here. What did you see?" he asked with a yawn.

Elizabeth shared her dream. With her head on his chest, they talked until they both returned to sleep.

***

"Aaaeeeiiiiiiiii!"

A soul-piercing scream echoed into night. Samuel bolted up in bed. "Elizabeth!"

"It wasn't me. It wasn't me," Elizabeth cried.

224

CHAPTER 34

The rhythmic clacking of the horse's shoes on the cobblestone streets of Fifth Avenue and the gentle side to side rocking of the carriage was lulling Elizabeth into a restful doze. She needed an escape from Barclay. Another shrieking scream woke them up again last night. That made three nights in a row. Samuel questioned Henry each morning, but as usual, Henry gave him no information.

Through her carriage window, Elizabeth caught a blur of white linen. A White woman roamed the streets barefooted in her nightgown. With the help of the March wind, the woman's blond hair flowed behind her. Elizabeth leaned forward and gripped the door to look out the window. A Negro woman ran to the wandering White woman and wrapped her in a cape. The vision made her think of the night Patricia wandered the yard in her nightgown trying to burn the house down.

Elizabeth yawned. She wanted to stay home and sleep, but Samuel thought getting away from Barclay for the day might do her some good. At Mr. Denning's suggestion, Samuel arranged for her to use a carriage with one of Mr. Denning's men, Franz, as her driver and bodyguard. Additionally, Samuel gave her money to do a little fun shopping— something different to take her mind off the madness encroaching on their lives. Those midnight screams and her dreams were costing her and her baby precious sleep.

According to Samuel, her pregnancy was enhancing her abilities and opening her to vivid dreams he called premonitions. She was thankful that, thus far, they were all good dreams that included her father.

As her eyes took in the city streets, she agreed it felt good to finally be away from Barclay. Her first winter in New York seemed like an eternity. Between the dreams, the screams, and being housebound by ice and cold, she had developed a severe bout of cabin fever. As beautiful and regal as Barclay was, she longed for a different view, and New York City didn't fail to deliver.

The ride from the Murray Hill section to Fifth Avenue offered a pampered view of New York City. The fine shops and Fifth Avenue's well-dressed residents were a mirror of luxury: women in elegant street gowns, clean-shaven men in tailored suits, uniformed maids, scents of French lavender soaps and floral parfums, vanilla cakes, baked breads, the arresting aroma of roasting coffee, and roasting meats if she walked near any restaurants.

But New York City was a two-sided mirror. Not too far away from all the grandeur was the reflection of poverty; the bowels of the Five Points. It was almost difficult for Elizabeth to enjoy her abundance when she knew others were forced to walk through muddy, manure loaded streets, or ride, if they had the two cents, in open-air horse drawn streetcars packed like too many peas in one pod.

Most of New York was crowded, dirty, smelled of urine, human and horse excrement, thousands of tired unwashed and cold water and lye soap washed bodies. The early spring breeze carried the protective, pungent, sulfur odor from tenements, and eye watering smoke from fires burning in street barrels. .

No matter how long she lived here, the sights and smells of the impoverished sections of New York City would forever overload her senses. But for today, Fifth Avenue and 34th Street offered her a welcomed reprieve.

Fifth Avenue was lined with markets that displayed fresh fruits and vegetables outside in wooden street carts and barrels. There was also a butcher, an apothecary, dress shops, haberdasheries, cobblers and a department store. It was a nice and safe shopping area.

However, the best shopping was not in the department stores or the shops on 34th and Fifth. Between Fifth Avenue and the East River along the curbs of some of the side streets were specialty wagons that sold ethnic foods, unique garments, books in foreign languages, religious statues, and other items she had never seen before. It was like taking a trip to different parts of the world with each cart, but Franz had orders to restrict her shopping to Fifth Avenue.

A bolt of black ran past her carriage. A Chinese man pulling a rickshaw that had stacks of bamboo containers rushed past her. Seeing him made her think of the Asian man in her dream. She tried to follow him with her eyes, but he disappeared when he cut in front of another carriage. It caused that driver to steer his horse to the left, forcing Franz to jerk their horse to the left to avoid a collision. Elizabeth bounced in her seat and gripped the strap by the door to prevent from slamming into the side of the carriage.

"Sorry Missus!" Franz called out.

She looked out the window to glimpse the Chinese man with his rickshaw as he disappeared down a side street. As they passed that side street, Elizabeth saw a colorful bounty of vendors and the wares lining the curbs. Where there was one Chinese man, there was bound to be another. She would shop there.

The carriage slowed and came to a stop in a small clearing behind a line of other carriages awaiting their owners return. She watched Franz take one big step down from the carriage and then open her door. He flipped the carriage footboard down for her to disembark.

"Thank you, Franz," Elizabeth said.

Franz was a German immigrant from The Five Points. At twenty years of age, he was big. He had a body like a bull; and chest, arms, and hands that reminded her of rising dough. In addition to his girth, he towered over everyone. Franz had to duck when entering a shop behind her. But his height permitted him to keep an eye on her in the dense crowds and see any dangerous gang activity occurring before the situation escalated to knives and guns. He reminded her of a character from a folktale; he was bigger than life.

She'd protested his presence the first time he showed up outside their hotel door, but time and the realization of how dangerous New York was, had changed her mind. Gangs were everywhere. The gangs not only controlled the Five Points, they also stalked the rich of Fifth Avenue. They were as calculating and industrious as they were vicious. Franz was familiar with their antics and anticipated their every move.

"You stay with the carriage Franz. I just want to visit the little side markets down this street," Elizabeth instructed.

"You husband said department store only. Fifth Avenue shops only."

"But I'm looking for something very specific," Elizabeth answered.

227

"Then I'm afraid I will be walking on ya heels," Franz said as he took a step behind her. Elizabeth's eyes scanned up and down Fifth Avenue. Clutching their bags, people moved quickly and deliberately through the streets, and from shop to shop as though they were trying to escape. There was something about her newfound freedom that made her question its existence. It seemed the further north she traveled, the more her sense of freedom changed. Did true freedom exist?

"Really, I'll be safe."

"Ya you will, because I will be right behind you," he added with a smile and a tip of his hat. Franz had an accent she couldn't quite place. Franz said it was Five Point brogue—part Irish, part, Russian, part German. There were so many ethnic groups that occupied and struggled to survive in the Five Points that the exchange and blending of cultural identities and language was a natural osmosis.

"Franz, you can see my every move. What harm can come to me in broad daylight?"

"Daylight is even better for a swift hand to empty your pockets."

"Why is that?"

"Better to see what they're lifting off ya," Franz answered as he swept his arm outward for her to walk.

It was times like this Elizabeth missed New Hope. She needed no bodyguard to shop or to travel to her goods store. As nice as Franz was, his tall shadow eclipsed hers and made her feel like she was back on Tobias' plantation with somebody watching her every move.

"Your hovering doesn't make me feel particularly free."

"Pardon me missus, but if you were one of the Blacks, you'd value someone watching your back."

"The Blacks?"

"The free Negroes, missus. In the Five Points, the Blacks must burrow themselves like worms into hiding at night, so no one comes in and takes them in their sleep to sell them to bounty hunters. The daytime is no better. Because of their skin, they stand out and must keep an eye trained over their shoulder. If you were a Black, you'd welcome my eyes mindin' your back. I guess it's all about the color skin you stand in," Franz concluded.

The tips of Elizabeth's ears reddened from shame. How dare she take her freedom for granted. She turned away to hide her mounting tears and faced a cart filled with carrots, cabbage, and potatoes. Her watery eyes blurred the cart's vegetables into a blob of orange, pale green, and brown. She leaned over to get a better view of the vegetables and her tears darkened the soft brown skin of a potato that was on top of a carefully built pyramid.

"You buy?" the grocer said as he quickly gathered the tear-stained potato.

"Yes, I buy. Four please."

The man gently placed each potato into a paper sack. As he did so, he looked her right in the eye.

"Twenty cents," he declared and extended his palm for payment. "I noticed you have a beautiful carriage, a driver, nice clothes, and money to buy food. It's a good day today, no?"

Elizabeth smiled at him.

His face contorted with frustration. "If Antonio Marchelli says it's a good day, then it's a good day! There is no crying on my potatoes," he scolded as he handed her paper sack with her potatoes. He then turned away from her to smooth his basket of cannellini beans. Elizabeth felt a hard glare and looked past Mr. Marchelli. An older woman sat on a wooden chair at the end of his cart.

Dressed completely in black, her ashen stone like face had a permanent scowl etched on it. Her hostile glare reflected a hard and disappointing life. Elizabeth offered the woman a smile, but her scowl remained unchanged. Elizabeth quickly scanned the row of carts and noticed the seriousness in each proprietor's eyes. It was life or death for them. Each sale contributed to their meager existence.

"If Missus tells me what's on her list, I can direct you," Franz offered.

"Thank you, but I don't have a list. Today I'd like to look around and get ideas for my husband's...birthday.".

"The department store on Fifth Avenue is just up the street," Franz added wistfully. "And you won't get your dress dirty."

"I'm content with shopping here."

"After you Missus."

Elizabeth moved away from Mr. Marchelli's wagon and headed down 34th street towards Sixth Avenue. As she waded deeper into the side street markets, the colors and ethnic food aromas ignited her senses. The banter of languages and bartering echoed off surrounding buildings. Going from wagon to cart, from cart to barrels and baskets, Elizabeth greeted eager eyes with a smile. The moment they realized she wasn't buying, their eyes locked on Elizabeth's hands because now she was a potential thief.

She came to the end of one side of the street and was about to cross when a woman's voice called out to her.

"The man you're looking for isn't here. You'll have to keep looking."

Elizabeth looked over her shoulder. Seated in the back of a wagon in an alley was a young woman, a Gypsy. Her dark olive complexion accentuated her blue eyes that seemed to glow against her skin. She had a head full of black curls that cascaded from beneath a man's hat, and a heaving bosom. While the woman didn't have the beauty of a siren, there was something spellbinding about her.

"The man you're looking for does not exist here," the woman repeated.

"Are you speaking to me?" Franz's large arm came down blocking Elizabeth's next step.

"She's Gypsy. She'll bewitch you," Franz warned under his breath.

"I'm already bewitched," Elizabeth said with a smile and moved around his arm.

"Missus..."

"I will be fine. There's no harm in talking."

"This is America, she is free to do what she chooses," the woman said. "When do American men let giant pieces of shit like you protect beautiful White women," she said angrily pointing at Franz.

The woman stood up and removed a pipe from beneath her shawl and pressed its mouthpiece on her bottom lip. Her bosom heaved upward from beneath her shawl.

"Missus talk to her from here. Don't get on her wagon."

"How do you know I'm looking for a man?"

"The answer to that question will cost you ten cents."

"Ten cents?"

"Ten cents is nothing to you. For me it's food," the Gypsy snipped and held out her hand.

Elizabeth reached into her little purse and found a nickel and counted out five pennies. As she was about to hand the Gypsy the money, she returned the coins to her purse and removed a quarter.

"Twenty-five cents and potatoes, so your family has a good meal," Elizabeth said handing over the sack of potatoes. Their eyes met.

"You are kind and generous woman. May God smile upon your family and your daughters."

A jolt of energy reddened Elizabeth's face. She thought her little shawl like cape had sufficiently covered her growing belly, which was not considered proper in public places.

"You said, daughters? I'm going to have daughters?" Elizabeth asked.

"Yes, two. I can see more if I hold your hand," the Gypsy said. "But he is right, do not come into my wagon."

"Nadya, don't touch her," Franz said coming between them.

"Franz, you know her?"

"Franz knows no one from our world now that he got his piece of American pie. The money that lines his pocket made him forget where he comes from," Nadya said with a sneer.

"Missus, we should leave this place and go back to Fifth Avenue," Franz warned. His normally easy-going countenance was gone. His face was an angry red as though he had been slapped.

"Franz, just one question and we'll leave," Elizabeth said. "I promise," Elizabeth pleaded giving him a reassuring touch on his forearm.

Franz lifted his cap, ran his sausage-sized fingers through his chestnut soft curls, brought his cap down hard over his eyes, and stepped back. Elizabeth took a few steps toward the wagon and raised her hand for Nadya to take.

Nadya reached over the wagon side and then pulled Elizabeth's hand toward her. She gave Franz one last hard look, then looked down at Elizabeth's hand.

"So much loss you've had. I see three men you have lost. Yes?"

"Yes."

"You will always be seeking men who are lost, do you understand?"

The back of Elizabeth's throat tightened as she suppressed her tears. She cleared her throat.

"Will they ever come back?"

"One cannot come back. As for the two that are together—they will each make their own decisions. I don't control life, but I think one will return."

"One will return," Elizabeth repeated with happy tears forming in her eyes.

"She answered one question. Missus, we ought to go now," Franz urged.

"What about the man I seek today? Where do I find him?"

"The wise man who came to you in your dream, yes?" Nadya asked.

"Yes. Where can I find him?"

"He will lead you," Nadya declared pointing to Franz.

"Nadya, *Baulo!*" Franz said under his breath.

Nadya leaned forward on the edge of her wagon to look up the street.

"I'm sorry. That is all I can tell you," Nadya said as she stood up. "Dadus Baulo! Go! Go!" Nadya called out and then disappeared through a makeshift curtain in the back of her wagon. The wagon jolted forward disappearing down the alleyway.

"Missus, we have to go right now," Franz ordered and ushered her away by her left forearm. They crossed the street and headed up the block towards Fifth Avenue.

"What's wrong?"

"Coppers don't like gypsies, especially fortune tellers. It's against the law," Franz said. From the other side of the street, they watched as a small group of patrons stepped back for a policeman to pass. In perfect orchestration, as he waved his bully stick at a vendor, the vendor held up a piece of paper.

"Franz, what's going on? What are they doing?"

"Showing the policeman their permit to be here. The Tammany makes them pay lots of money for a piece of paper just so they can have the privilege to stand in the filthy street and make pennies to feed their families," Franz said with disgust.

Elizabeth watched the policeman clear the sidewalk with every step.

"What happens if they don't have the permit?"

"They are beaten with his stick, if they're lucky."

"Being beaten is lucky?"

"Taking a beating is better than going to jail and losing everything in their wagon to the police and their political cronies. It's a racket for sure. Let's go back to Fifth Avenue. This is no place for you Missus especially in your condition."

Franz held her arm as they moved up 34th Street towards Fifth Avenue. Her thoughts were on Nadya's last words: *"He will lead you."* She looked up at Franz. She trusted Nadya's words. She would follow Franz and keep her eyes open for the Chinese man from her dream. They were midway up 34th Street when she saw a Chinese man running down Fifth Avenue. He was running toward them pulling a rickshaw cart filled with stacks of round baskets.

The cart slowed and made its way into a small crowd that parted to let him in. Hanging above the crowd on a rope were red lanterns with black Chinese characters written on them. Franz walked in front of Elizabeth leading her through the crowds of patrons. As they neared the cart with the lanterns, Elizabeth saw two men unloading the round baskets from the rickshaw. The two men could barely unload the baskets before they were besieged by demanding hands for the contents of the baskets.

Elizabeth slipped into the crowd and quickly disappeared into the grabbing frenzy. As people turned away with their booty, Elizabeth tried to see what was in the basket, but quick hands made the contents disappear. The two Chinese men bantered between each other as they frantically wrapped their goods in small squares of white paper.

Elizabeth approached a short White man, who wore a large red beret tilted to the right side of his head. He was dressed in pants and a smock that were covered in smudges of paint. He reeked of linseed oil, and his fingers tips were stain a deep yellow. He was dressed appropriately for the circus-like activity surrounding the rice ball vendors.

"Excuse me sir. What are they selling?"

"Rice balls. They are amazing!"

"Rice balls?"

"Yes, try the ones with black seeds. They're yummy. I come here every day to get my treat," he said waving his white cylindrical package. "Good luck!"

She watched as his red beret floated above the wave of arriving patrons for a moment and then pushed her way forward to the older Chinese man.

"How much for one?"

"Four for ten cents," the older Chinese man informed her.

He presented her with a cylindrical package and held out his hand for money.

She dug in her purse. Before she could hand her dime over to him, he snatched it and shoved the package into her hand. She quickly unraveled it. Inside she found one rice ball speckled with black seeds, one rice ball encrusted with light brown seeds, one rice ball glistening with some kind of sugary confection, and the last one looked like a smooth dough ball just like the one she saw the Chinese man eat in her dream.

"Excuse me, may I have four just like this one," she asked pointing to the smooth rice ball. "Four like this one"

"No, all the same. You eat. All the same," the older Chinese man said.

"No, this one is black, this one is brown, and this one smells sweet. I want four rice balls like this smooth one."

"All the same. You eat," the older man said. He turned his back to her, barked words in his language to his assistant who took off running down the street with his cart filled with empty baskets.

Elizabeth looked down at her culinary prize. She picked up the rice ball that looked like the one in her dream and popped it in her mouth. It was like a pillow of flavors she never tasted before. It was sweet, it was salty, it was tangy, it was savory. It had all the flavors one could consume in a five-course meal.

"Different on the outside, all the same on the inside."

The words from her dream echoed in her mind. She looked down at the remaining rice balls. They started to vibrate in her hand and became little orbs of bright light. The orbs lifted from the paper wrapping, floated before her for a moment, and then ascended into a blinding sun. She shielded her eyes and blinked to refocus. When she looked at the side street vendors, they all looked like little blurbs of white light.

"See their souls. They all carry light. They all carry love. It is fear that alters their light... "

She knew that voice. It was like she was looking at the world through a veil. Had she fainted? Was she dreaming? A stream of sunlight streaked from the sky. Within that streak of sunlight, she saw the silhouette of a man. She shielded her eyes to see the man's face. Because the man appeared to be very tall, she thought it was Franz. But the moment she heard the voice she knew who was standing before her.

"Elizabeth, do you see now? Do you understand why you

straddle four worlds, the Black and the White, the physical and the spiritual? You wanted to see this, and I am so grateful you do. You have a gift for seeing beyond the skin and into the heart."

"Poppa?"

"You have to listen Elizabeth. I can only say this once. We're all the same. No matter how we look on the outside, we're all the same on the inside. You have the power and ability to recognize yourself in others. That's why you weren't afraid to love Simon.

"We all have love, but fear disconnects us from it. Slavery is the projection of self-hatred. The things people hate about others are the things they fear within themselves. Elizabeth, keep believing in love, it will be your greatest legacy. You have been given a gift. Use it to help others who have forgotten the light and love within. You won't be able to save everyone but understand that will be their choice. They all have free will to choose love over fear.

"Show them the truth the best way you can. Allow nothing or no one to alter your beliefs about love—not even Malachai. Do not let the physical world limit the love you are capable of creating. I'm so proud of you. Daughter, you were the best part of my life. It is our love that keeps us connected." Jonathan said. His image faded into the bright sunlight.

"Missus Chase! Missus Chase!" Franz's thundering voice brought her back.

With one blink, Elizabeth was back on 34th street. The Chinese man was receiving a new delivery of rice balls. Out of nowhere, a crow swooped down and landed on the rope that held the red lanterns over the cart. Customers quickly flocked to the cart for their delectable treasures. She turned and saw Franz pushing his way through the throngs of shoppers. He looked frightened.

"Missus, where did you go? I couldn't find you."

"I was right here. I bought some rice balls."

"You couldn't have been here. I was standing right here looking for you. Where did you go? Did Nadya take you..."

"No, no... I was right here eating rice balls..." Elizabeth saw that her hands were empty. "I lost my package. I had a package of rice balls. I ate one. I swear to you Franz;, I was right here eating rice balls."

"The street devils must have lifted it right out of your hands," Franz said. "Can I take you back to Fifth Avenue now?" Franz asked with a sigh of relief.

"No, let's go home. I got what I came for."

"What about the gift for your husband?"

At that moment the policeman approached the red lantern cart and helped himself to two packages of rice balls. The younger Chinese man glared at him.

"Is there a problem?" the police officer asked, brandishing his bully club.

The young man's eyes remained locked on the policeman.

"No, no! Enjoy! Enjoy!" the older man said and handed him a third package. "For wife! Enjoy!"

"Missus, do you still need to shop?" Franz asked.

"No, I got what I came for."

The crow lifted majestically into the air from its red lantern perch. It circled once above her, then swooped over the street. When Elizabeth looked up the street, she saw little flags of white permits salute the policeman as he strolled towards Fifth Avenue eating his rice balls.

As the policeman approached another food cart, Elizabeth heard the cawing of the crow as it dove downward at the policeman's head. On its first pass, it knocked the policeman's hat off into a muddy puddle. When the policeman bent to pick it up, the bird returned and took a swipe at his head. The policeman swung at the bird with his billy club. The laughter of the street vendors followed the policeman as the crow made several more passes at the policeman's head, forcing him into a sprint towards Fifth Avenue.

"Franz, did you see the crow attack that policeman?"

"Missus, that was no crow, that was one of Duvvell's angels," Franz said with a smile as he lifted his cap to comb his fingers through his hair. He reached for a leather cord hung around his neck and pulled forth a medal from beneath his shirt and kissed it.

"Who is Duvvell?"

"The greatest judge of justice, God."

"Mrs. Samuel Chase...?"

"Yes?" Elizabeth replied and turned.

She came face to face with a man who smelled like horse and beer. Her hand immediately covered her nose. His yellow and bloodshot eyes looked her over.

"I never forget a pretty face," he grumbled. Elizabeth felt her stomach churn. There was something horribly familiar about the man. Before Elizabeth had a chance to place his face, Franz's fist connected with it. The man careened backward into the street.

"Stinkin' bounty hunter. Worse than the police. Let's go!"

As they made their way back to their carriage, Elizabeth saw a bubble of light which revealed the man's identity. He was the same bounty hunter Samuel put down on their first night in New York. He knew their name. If he recognized her, he would recognize Samuel.

"Oh my goodness! Did you kill him?"

"Don't worry Missus, I only tapped him. Your husband will kill him."

Those were the last words she wanted to hear because she knew it was the truth.

CHAPTER 35

Benny Gaines was far from home. Paducah, Kentucky was nice, but not profitable unless you owned a plantation. His taste for whiskey, wild women, and money brought him to New York. Profitable tales of bounty hunting made the more logical choice for work. Bounty hunting was far more reliable than farming and required no special place to call home. Wandering was preferable over stability, and freedom was more acceptable than familial responsibility. He liked his life just the way it was; all the whiskey he could drink, and promiscuous women who satisfied his carnal urges.

He turned over and looked at Red Claire, who was snoring louder than a ranch hand. Her mountain of red curls was now a landslide across her face. He saw the outline of her right breast and resisted another round. He didn't want to pay for more. He stood up and slipped his pants on, and the door to their room opened.

"Time's up, not unless you want to pay for another hour," Bess said. Bess was a wide-bodied woman with dark hair, rouged jowly cheeks, and a dark hairy mole over the right side of her upper lip.

"No, I'm good," Benny said.

"You sure?"

Benny looked down at Red Claire's breast one more time, to make sure he didn't harden with excitement.

"I'm spent."

"Be downstairs in sixty seconds or Big Jim will help you down," Bess warned.

"Let me put my boots on."

Bess closed the door with a bang. Benny dropped down on the bed and collected his right boot.

"Where you going baby?" Red Claire murmured beneath her curls.

"Work," Benny replied coldly.

Claire turned over on her back to expose her breasts.

"Are you sure I can't convince you to stay another hour?" Red Claire asked fingering her left breast.

"Nope. My cock and pocket are spent," he grumbled and shoved on his other boot.

Red Claire bolted up onto her knees and reached out for him. He swatted her hands away.

"Get off. I ain't paying more for you."

"Cheap bastard!" Red Claire yelled.

"Whore be thankful for us cheap bastards. We're the only men you whores will ever have," he shot back.

Benny walked out, slammed door, then bounded down the stairs, past Big Jim, and out into the street. Once outside, he reached inside his jacket for his flask. There was one good swallow of whiskey left. He would need more. The pain under his right eye and jaw was still present. The blow from Mrs. Chase's bodyguard earlier had landed solidly on his right cheek, just missing his nose. He drained his flask.

His index finger pushed its way into a split of fabric in his vest, where he created a small secret breast pocket, and rubbed two silver dollars. Red Claire didn't clean him out. He grinned, then winced from the pain radiating from his jaw. He had enough to get two fingers worth of whiskey to numb the inside of his mouth, and breakfast in the morning. He needed to make more money. It was time for another roundup. He needed to find his partner, Jake—after he numbed his pain.

When he turned to head back to Bess' for whiskey, the caw of a crow made him look up to a rooftop distracting him from a blur of black that dropped down on the ground behind him. The last and only thing Benny saw was the flash of a knife blade as it sliced through the air to move across his throat. His hands slapped over his throat. His scream was muffled by the gushing of blood that filled his mouth and sprayed the air. As he fell back gripping his throat, his eyes searched for his assailant, who had vanished like a ghost.

***

"Is it over?"

"Yes," Samuel replied removing a black hooded mask from his head.

"You did it? You really did it?" Elizabeth asked getting out of bed. Samuel stripped out of his darkness. He pulled his black shirt over his head returning his creamy body to the light of the room. He quickly pulled off his black pants and slipper-like shoes and dropped them in a pile on the floor.

"We promised each other there would be no secrets between us. This is the other part of me that I didn't want you or anyone to ever see, but I'm glad you know. There's no telling what I'll have to do to keep us safe."

"No, I've caused enough death...Those bounty hunters..."

"Don't go back to Amos' field, Elizabeth. Your father did what he had to do to save you, as I did what I had to do tonight."

"Samuel, let's move. Let's move to...Philadelphia. We can start clean with no blood on our hands," Elizabeth pleaded.

"Elizabeth, our life is here," Samuel said grabbing the pile of clothes. "We're going to have to burn these."

"Why?"

"No part of him should be left alive."

"I think I'm going to be sick."

"You are stronger than you think," Samuel said and headed for the stairs.

Elizabeth padded after him.

"What kind of life will I and your children have if they arrest and hang you for killing that bounty hunter?" Elizabeth said in a hushed whisper bounding down the stairs behind him.

"Once he touched you...It was him or you, and I chose you...I chose us..." Samuel threw his clothing into the fire. The fire erupted and jumped out towards the room. "Don't worry. No one saw me, and no one will ever know it was me. I was completely covered." He gripped her tightly around her shoulders and pulled her in. "I promised your father I would protect you. I will not lie to him."

"Samuel, won't the police look for his killer?"

"He was in the Five Points. I'm sure he had plenty of enemies there. No one will care about a dead bounty hunter."

"God is watching, doesn't that mean something?"

"What if I killed him while he was trying to take you or me to the south to sell us into slavery? Would you still have remorse?"

"No, of course not."

"This is the world we live in, Elizabeth. We must protect the sheep from the wolves. Your father had to make similar choices. Fighting for human decency is war. Your father fought a war. We are fighting a war."

"When you put it that way..."

"There is no other way to put it. It's the truth."

"Samuel, what are we going to do? How can we help free Negroes and slaves without killing people?"

"Let everyone think we're White."

"But if our own people think we're White, they won't trust us."

"Then we have to earn their trust. It's what the Quakers did with us. Not all White people are bad. "

"What if our own people hate us the way my mother hated me?" Elizabeth asked wiping a tear.

"Those who accept our love, we can help. And those who refuse our love will have to find their own way. Imagine what would have become of us if we pushed away the love our parents gave us?" Samuel countered.

"We would have become...like Patricia Beeson."

"What do you mean 'like Patricia Beeson'?"

"Patricia Beeson was just like us."

Samuel stared into the fire for a moment, then adjusted the burning logs. The fire smacked its lips as the flames devoured a sleeve of his shirt.

"All that time I thought she was just bitter. Her double identity was ripping her apart and driving her to madness," Samuel said remorsefully. The pungent smoke from the burning clothing scratched at their eyes. "Elizabeth, we can't let what happened to Patricia happen to us, or to our children. We have to create a safe place to live. Even if it means never revealing who we are."

"Never?"

"Maybe not never, but certainly not now. Maybe this is the legacy your father said you were destined to create. We'll have to find the right people to help us. Let's take Cassandra's lead and find other 'Blue Vein' Negroes and create a community."

"With who? We don't know anyone. Where do we start?" Elizabeth said.

Samuel's only response was to grab the oil lamp and Elizabeth by the hand. Elizabeth felt like she was in a cave about to uncover a treasure. Samuel led her upstairs to their bedroom and handed her the oil lamp. Without a word, he removed a foot chest from beneath their bed. Elizabeth held the light over the chest as he removed a few belongings, they were items she had seen before until he retrieved a small plaid sack.

"What is that?"

"I was waiting for the right moment to give these to you." He laid the small drawstring sack on their bed in front of her. "These are for you, from your father," Samuel said softly. He took the lamp from her.

Without waiting Elizabeth seized the sack, pulled it open, and dumped the contents onto the bed. Three small black leather journals spilled out.

"What are these?"

"Your father said these journals have the names of people who help free slaves, and lists of safe houses from the south all the way to Canada. The VanCleefs are in one of those journals," Samuel added.

"The VanCleefs?"

"I don't understand. They don't seem like the kind of people who would want to help free slaves."

"Julius would. He knows what it feels like to have people hate you because of your religion."

"What does his being Jewish have to do with freeing slaves?"

"You saw that he was Jewish?

"Yes, but it doesn't matter to me. Nor, should it matter to you."

"You didn't tell me you knew that he was Jewish."

"I saw the night he danced with. I didn't think it should matter."

"It doesn't to us, but others it does. Why do you think Julius changed his name? His real name is in the journal."

"I still don't understand. Why would my father give these to me?"

"For safekeeping, and in case you wanted to carry on his legacy or use them to create your own."

"Why didn't you tell me?"

"I was following your father's strict instructions. I was only to give them to you if you showed interest in saving slaves. He didn't want to burden you with a responsibility if you didn't choose to take it on yourself. Elizabeth, we can go to the VanCleefs. They adore you."

"How do you know that?" Elizabeth said clutching the journals to her chest.

"My father told me. He and Julius have known each other a very long time."

"Adoration doesn't guarantee help." She noticed a black shape on his right forearm that was not there before. "Samuel, what is that?" She grabbed his arm to get a better look. "Why do you have the same tattoo Mr. Dennings and Franz have?"

"It keeps me safe."

"Safe?"

"Mr. Dennings has his own gang."

"You're part of a New York gang?"

"I think I used the wrong word. The Blackbirds aren't quite a gang the way that you think."

"Then tell me what I should be thinking," Elizabeth demanded.

"The Blackbirds are here to provide a little justice for when things get out of balance."

"I don't understand."

"The support and guidance from Tammany is corrupt. It's leaders and laws are inconsistent. The only consistency it offers are for those in power. Forgive my horrible pun, when it comes to the law, I'm afraid our world isn't as black and white as we would think. There are people who you think you can trust, but you quickly find out you can't. And then there are people who you would never think of trusting but are forced to trust so you can stay alive. The Blackbirds try to provide assurance that justice will be granted...we try to even out the score and restore what was taken."

"You steal?"

"No, I restore."

"Does your restoration require that you steal?" Elizabeth asked.

"I call it taking something back that was stolen and returning it to its rightful owner."

"Samuel...killing and stealing...we're having a baby. How can we bring a child into this kind of life? How can we ever be safe?"

Samuel moved swiftly to wrap his arms around her before she could blink.

"I promise you. We are very careful..."

"Who's we? Who else is in your Blackbird gang?"

"That you don't need to know," Samuel said.

"If you want me to trust you, you have to trust me," Elizabeth countered. "What if I need help and can't get to you or Franz, or Mr. Dennings for that matter. I need to know who I can trust out in the street."

"Telling you would make you part of this."

"I'm already a part of this. Whatever you know, I know. We said there are no secrets between us. Who are the others?"

"If I tell you, you must never let them know that you know unless it's an absolute emergency," Samuel warned.

"I promise."

"And you must not judge them."

"I promise."

"...You already know a few of them," Samuel began.

"Other than Mr. Dennings and Franz I don't know anyone...the VanCleefs!..." Elizabeth gasped and covered her mouth.

"Yes, the VanCleefs."

"Is that why they were here for dinner? To induct you into their little gang? Your parents are going to be devastated."

"No, they won't..." Samuel scratched his head sheepishly. "...My parents are...Blackbirds too. Actually, my father is the official member and that's only because my mother's father brought him into the group after they were married."

"Your mother knows? You're acting like the Blackbirds are some kind of prestigious social club."

"We're here to do good, Elizabeth."

"Anyone else I know?" Elizabeth demanded.

"Yes."

"Who is it?"

"Your father," Samuel said softly.

"Poppa? —The crow..." The image of the crow on the red lantern cart flashed in her mind. "But why wouldn't he tell me—All these secrets make me want to scream! We promised each other there would be no secrets between us.

"From what we just shared, It seems like we're keeping our promise."

"Aaaeeeeiiiiiiiiii!" A woman's shriek filled the courtyard.

They rushed to the bedroom window to look at the rear of Barclay.

"Look to see if a light comes on," Samuel instructed.

"There is no light." Elizabeth said and exhaled. "Fire and brimstone, fire and brimstone."

CHAPTER 36

The VanCleefs' townhome on Fifth Avenue stood two floors taller than the others that were lined up on either side of it. As Elizabeth stepped down from the carriage, she realized the additional two floors were intentional. She could see a defined line across the face of the townhome that conveyed where the roof used to be. The VanCleefs' life wasn't as seamless as they would want her to believe. She stared at the line for a moment. It looked like a stoic smile drawn on a painting designed to keep the viewer guessing if the subject was happy or not.

"Ready?" Samuel said under his breath.

"Yes," Elizabeth said with a forced smile.

On her approach to the front door, she tried to recall the vision of Julius VanCleef and the men with the black yarmulkes. While she had the utmost compassion for him and his fear of persecution, she would use that information if she had to. She was not only there to get assistance to help others, but also to secure their own safety. Being seen under the VanCleefs' protective social umbrella meant access to other wealthy doors. Money was needed to establish better housing and opportunities for Negroes, free and enslaved.

"Remember, start small and don't get greedy," Samuel warned her.

"The reason why we are here has nothing to do with greed. I'm here for justice," Elizabeth replied through her plastered smile. She felt eyes upon her and looked up. Julius VanCleef was standing in one of his floor to ceiling windows looking down on them.

"Samuel we've got company. Upstairs window on the right," Elizabeth said through her teeth.

Samuel's eyes rolled upward and caught Julius disappearing from the window.

"En garde my darling," Samuel warned, patting the top of her hand. "En garde."

The large bright red door opened.

"Welcome to the Vanguard," a well-dressed butler greeted them. He took her shawl and Samuel's gloves and hat. They were dressed to conduct business. Samuel wore a coat, a double-breasted vest, shirt, and silk tie. Elizabeth bought a sateen navy blue dress. She had it deftly altered by removing a few of the stays to make room for her swollen belly.

She wanted the VanCleefs to view her as a serious businesswoman. Navy was a good color to do business, and the sheen of the sateen was dressy enough for a day visit at Vanguard.

She wanted to be taken seriously, but she wished she hadn't relinquished her shawl. It offered her obvious condition a modicum of privacy and decency. The wonderment of carrying a child was always a welcome sight on a married woman if she kept her condition at home and away from young impressionable eyes.

The foyer at Vanguard was like a ballroom. A crystal chandelier the size of their carriage hung high in the two-story entrance. As hard as she tried not to appear like a country bumpkin, she couldn't stop herself from looking up and gawking at every nook and cranny as the butler led them to the drawing room.

Vanguard was grander than Elysian, which she never thought would be possible. The artwork, the walls, the floors, the carpets, the furnishings, even the bric-a-brac reflected monetary significance.

"Obviously we're underdressed. We forgot my tiara and your scepter," Elizabeth quipped with a smile.

"Chin up darling, this is only their city home," Samuel whispered back.

Elizabeth's emotions bubbled up inside her, pushing tears to the corner of her eyes. She had no right to be here or to demand anything. She was completely out of her league. Samuel gently squeezed her hand as they approached a set of double doors. On either side stood a footman who promptly opened the doors to the drawing room. When Elizabeth saw Julius and Clara sitting regally in their chairs, she felt like a peasant approaching royalty. Their chairs were positioned on a raised platform. A beautiful oriental rug cascaded over the front of the platform onto a matching rug below. The gilded chairs in which the VanCleefs sat were as intimidating as the VanCleefs' stern faces.

"Mr. and Mrs. Samuel Chase," the butler announced.

"Thank you, Stewart. That will be all," Julius said.

Julius VanCleef was dressed in formal attire. The light-hearted man that danced in his stocking feet in her carriage house was nowhere in sight. Elizabeth looked to Clara VanCleef for a smile of recognition but received only a rolling eye that examined her from head to toe. Samuel squeezed her hand as they approached. Julius didn't speak. Instead, he gestured for them to sit on chairs that were at least ten feet from the base of the platform, making the VanCleefs appear unreachable. Without a word, the VanCleefs had already put them in their place.

Samuel bent his knees but popped back up the moment he saw Elizabeth was still standing. The VanCleefs' deliberate slight infuriated Elizabeth. When the VanCleefs came to their little carriage house, everyone was on equal standing. Elizabeth dug her heels into the oriental rug and refused to sit or lower herself. The VanCleefs looked at each other.

"Please sit," Clara ordered.

"I prefer to stand, thank you," Elizabeth eyed them. Samuel gently touched her elbow to help her down onto the divan and she pulled her elbow away.

"You have the fire of a good boiler, Mrs. Chase," Julius replied with a jovial smirk.

"Thank you, but I am here to take a stand," Elizabeth replied lifting her chin.

Julius' eyes squinted. Samuel cleared his throat to get Elizabeth's attention. Elizabeth kept her eyes on the VanCleefs. The only sound in the room was the clock on a far wall.

"Oh, for God's sake Julius, she's like an impetuous child. She has already seen you dancing in your stocking feet. Do you think she'll take all this ridiculous pomp and circumstance seriously? Honestly, can we please get out of these silly chairs and sit on our comfortable divan? I can't breathe and my back is killing me. Sarah strung my corset too tight again," Clara complained.

After a slight pause, a smile stretched across Julius' face.

"You wield a very pointy saber, my dear Elizabeth. I dare say many men in my position would not be able to match your tenacity," Julius concluded as he stood up. "Let's reconvene at the more comfortable divan as Clara requested."

"I can only hope that the day will arrive when women are no longer strapped into their bodices like sausages in their casings. Maybe, my dear Elizabeth, you can do something about corsets," Clara said as Julius helped her down the two side steps of the platform.

Elizabeth immediately linked her arm through Clara's and escorted her to the other sitting area. Clearly, Clara was the power source in this couple.

"May I call you Clara?" Elizabeth asked.

"Yes, do. We are way past any sense of social duty and formality. I feel as though I have known you all of my life. You are the daughter I wish I had," Clara said and patted Elizabeth's forearm.

"And if I could dream a mother, she would appear in your image."

"My dear Elizabeth, you are quite the charmer. Julius, we are most fortunate she is on our side. You are on our side?"

"Yes, and I hope you are on mine," Elizabeth replied.

"Well here we are walking side by side," Clara said and then lowered herself onto her plump pillowed divan. "Elizabeth you sit here next to me. We shall talk nose to nose. Now tell us truthfully why you are here."

"I know that Julius is Jewish," Elizabeth declared without hesitation. Grief washed over Clara's face. "As you know, I am the child of a slave."

"Young woman, you've entered our home with such accusations without so much as a lead-in or introduction. How immobilizing...and refreshing–I like that," Julius responded. "However, the true gift to having power, is finding a way to keep it. I also know that you have special abilities to access people's secrets, which you have so aptly demonstrated."

"Touché, Julius," Elizabeth said.

"Touché?" Julius chuckled. "Samuel, you have married quite the negotiator. I would be afraid to be in competition with her in business or in war. With the proper training, I bet she can talk a miserable miser out of his wallet."

"Julius, she has proven she can be trusted, let's get on with it," Clara said plainly.

"I don't understand?" Elizabeth looked into Clara's eyes.

"Elizabeth, dear, we came to dinner to test you. We wanted to see if you would find out about Julius' Jewish heritage, and what you'd do with the information. You saw exactly what we hoped you would see and didn't try to use it for personal gain. You passed our test," Clara said with a smile of relief.

"You deliberately wanted me to see your secret?"

"I'm afraid so," Julius said.

"But Samuel said you were there to initiate him...Samuel, did you know?"

"Of course Samuel knew. He brought you to New York to help us," Julius admitted.

"Elizabeth, darling, I had to let you decide if you wanted to be a part of this..."

Elizabeth looked in Samuel's eyes. She was far from the heat of the fire on the other side of the room, but her face was searing with rage.

"Is this how people conduct their business in New York with tests and deception?"

"Actually, Elizabeth, it's a bit more overtly cutthroat and cold-hearted. I'm afraid I know of no one else with your special...capabilities," Julius replied.

"Which is why we would like you to join forces with us," Clara said.

"My dear, you have proven without a doubt that you can be trusted," Julius said. He stood up and removed his coat, and then quickly rolled up his right sleeve. On his right forearm, Elizabeth saw the same black bird tattoo Samuel had.

"She knows about the Blackbirds," Samuel offered.

"We're a good gang," Clara interjected.

"We need you Elizabeth," Julius pleaded. "We need your ability to help us help others and protect us from those who want to keep their feet on the throats of the downtrodden. A few of us have talents, like your husband, but nothing like the caliber of your talents, or shall I say gifts.

"We have a plan," Clara said. "You would be perfect to help us."

"Here I thought we were coming to ask you for your help."

"I guess it's a blessing that we need you and not the other way around."

"I don't want to use my gifts to manipulate or steal from anyone," Elizabeth said firmly.

Julius and Clara looked at each other.

"Elizabeth, ultimately only you can decide how best to use your gifts. Please believe me when I say our silence was in no way designed to deceive you. Our silence was a respectful way to let you make the decision that is right for you," Clara said trying to comfort her.

"Clara, let's leave and let the newlyweds talk."

"For the record my dear, we don't steal. We restore. We are a good gang," Clara patted Elizabeth's hand and then reached for Julius' hand to assist her rise from the divan.

Elizabeth watched them leave closing the door behind them. She hoped her silence warned Samuel to choose his words carefully.

"I suppose you have a lot of questions?" Samuel began.

"How could you? You knew all along and said nothing to me. We promised we'd never keep secrets from each other."

"I had no idea as to how you'd handle yourself here today. You had to be the one to decide your fate; not me, or the VanCleefs."

"You knew when you married me. You had it all planned out, all of you. Is that why your mother begged me to talk you out of moving to New York?"

"Yes. But this is where we thought you could do the most good."

"Why did you marry me?"

"Because I loved you the moment I saw you."

"Are you sure it was me that you loved, or was it the things I could do for you that you loved?"

"Elizabeth..."

"Why are you acting hurt? I was the one who was lied to, manipulated, used."

"No one used you, Elizabeth. Your father thought long and hard about your future..."

"My father....my father was part of this?"

"It was his idea," Samuel said softly.

Hot tears raced down Elizabeth's face. She covered her mouth to contain the scream lurking in her throat.

"In all fairness, he didn't deceive you. If he told you to come to New York and help the VanCleefs, would you have made that choice for

251

yourself, or would you have done it because he asked you? Elizabeth, the work we do has to be of our free will otherwise it won't succeed. Telling someone what to do with their life and letting them decide what they do with their life creates two entirely different beings. This work is hard and thankless, but it's necessary.

"Throughout every step, you have displayed the utmost regard for human decency and compassion. Your father saw it and knew that we would need it. Without it, our little so-called *gang* would become a pack of wild wolves feeding off each other. There was never any intention of manipulating you. All we could do was show you that you and your gifts were needed, and let you decide for yourself. Your gifts are yours to do with as you will. Your father was certain you'd want to use them for good."

Elizabeth's mind was drowning from the wave of betrayal that knocked her off her feet. She looked at her husband through watery eyes, his image and his love now appeared distorted.

"That night you saved Cassandra and Bethany, was that staged for my benefit?"

"No, absolutely not. That was real."

"Your job with Mr. Dennings?"

"That was real too. He was never a part of any of this. We were supposed to meet only the VanCleefs. Meeting Mr. Dennings was a fluke. I didn't know he was a Blackbird until I met him for the first time at his house and saw his gold ring with a black bird stamped on it. I quickly put two and two together. For the record, Mr. Dennings didn't know the VanCleefs were Blackbirds either...You must believe me," Samuel pleaded. He took a step toward her and Elizabeth took two steps back.

"You were right when you said, that there are people who you think you should trust, but you quickly find out you can't. And then there are people who you would never think of trusting but are forced to trust so you can stay alive. At least you spoke the truth about that. As far as I can see, I can't trust any of you. Least of all my father. I'm still a slave in all of your eyes."

"If you're a slave, I'm a slave," he cried and tried to reach for her hands.

"Don't touch me! How dare you let them treat me like a slave? How dare you let them manipulate me to get me to use my gifts for their personal gains. Simon would have never allowed anyone to use me!"

Her words knocked Samuel back a few steps.

"Elizabeth, you have to understand that I couldn't tell you because it had to be your choice," Samuel said through tears. "No one was treating you like a slave...I love you Elizabeth."

"If you loved me, truly loved me, you would have protected me from this moment. Simon would have never allowed anyone..."

"Simon's not standing here with you Elizabeth. I am!"

Samuel's booming voice rattled her heart and the crystal bric-a brac on the nearby tables. She had no response except to run. Elizabeth heard the clicking of her heels echoing in the two-story foyer as she made her way to the front door. Once outside, she scurried down the street holding her stomach. Within a short distance, she came to a section of fine shops and ducked inside a lady's dressmaker's shop. When she entered, she banged the door closed. Everyone stopped to look at her.

"Oh dear..." an older woman blurted.

Three of the patrons covered their mouths, another simply turned away. Elizabeth's eyes focused on a dress to her right. It was a wedding dress. She was in a dress shop for wedding dresses. Given her visible condition, she couldn't have picked a more socially inappropriate asylum. The few women that glared at her, stared at her stomach.

"Miss Banner, quickly cover her." the older woman instructed.

The seamstress approached Elizabeth with an awkward smile and a swath of fabric. She quickly and deftly draped the wedding dress fabric over Elizabeth's shoulders like a shawl to cover her stomach. Elizabeth scanned the women who were protesting the vision of her pregnancy and burst into tears.

CHAPTER 37

Crossing Canal street meant Elizabeth was heading into dangerous territory, but there was only one other person Elizabeth felt could relate to her predicament. The Five Points was not a place Franz would ever allow her to go even if she had three bodyguards, but she was desperate.

She hoped she could quickly and quietly enter their world undetected. Elizabeth backed into a doorway to tear her dress and rub soot from a pile of ashes from a fire barrel she had passed. Walking down Chapel Street the quality of air became heavy, dank, and foul with the odors of unwashed bodies, stale cigars, beer, urine, decay, and excrement.

Her eyes looked ahead. Nadya's wagon wouldn't be hard to spot. Elizabeth distinctly remembered the patchwork quilt stretched across the top of the back of her wagon. And the dirty red velvet curtain with the two halves of a dingy yellow full moon sewn on either side of its opening. Nor would she forget Nadya, who was the one person Elizabeth believed was like her.

A mangy brown and white emaciated dog approached her. She stopped on the sidewalk, and the dog stopped in the street. Its head dropped down low, locked its eyes on her, and then a ridge of hair along its back lifted. She was only fifteen feet into the Five Points and their guard dog had already detected her intrusion. Her thoughts went to Genghis Khan. The dog was no different except it had teeth instead of spurs.

She looked around for a rock, a stick, anything to protect herself. From a pile of burnt lumber, she picked the longest piece she could find. It was only three feet long and half of it was charred. No doubt it would break in half after her first swing. She found a piece of brick and threw it at the dog.

"Go on, git!' She yelled. The brick landed within a foot of the dog. It didn't move. A man sitting on the top step to a hovel stood up. His dirty hands gripped a pipe.

"That's a good throw for a lady."

"Is that your dog?" Elizabeth called out.

"Nope, it's everybody's dog," he called back. The whites of his eyes were yellow and obscured his blue pupils.

"Can you help me?"

"Nope! This here is the Points. People help themselves or perish. It's dog eat dog. It looks like that dog is about ready to eat you." He returned the pipe to his lips.

Elizabeth found another piece of brick and gripped it in her right hand while holding onto the piece of charred lumber in her left. She moved slowly against the buildings to pass the dog.

"Easy boy. I'm not here to hurt you. I just want to find my friend. Easy...easy..." The closer she got, the louder its growl grew. When she got within five feet of passing it, the dog lunged at her. Elizabeth threw the piece of brick striking it on the head. It released a whelp and fell to the ground panting and growling. Elizabeth gasped and covered her mouth in horror. She had never intentionally caused an animal pain in her life. She slowly approached the animal with her stick extending outward for protection in case it lunged at her.

"I wouldn't go near it," the man warned.

"It's hurt."

"It's rabid. Can't you recognize a rabid dog?" He said and then descended the steps. He walked right passed Elizabeth over to the panting growling dog, pulled out a revolver and shot it. Elizabeth jumped.

"I hated to waste a bullet. I was saving that one for myself. I didn't want to see the dang animal suffer, unnecessarily," the man said and slipped his revolver back into his leg holster.

"Gal, who are you looking for in these parts?" he asked, eyeing her earrings. Elizabeth forgot she was wearing jewelry. "It easy to see you ain't from here"

"I'm looking for Nadya. She's a Gypsy. She has a wagon..."

"I know Nadya. What is it worth to ya? You got any money?"

"No, but you can have my earrings."

"Them earrings look nice, but don't look like they'll get me much around here. What else you got?"

"Maybe you can sell them at a street market. I'm sure you can get at least two dollars for them," Elizabeth urged. She quickly laid the piece of lumber against her dress to free her hands to remove her right earring and handed it to him to examine.

"You say these earrings could fetch two dollars."

"I believe so, yes."

"Hand them over."

"No. You take me to Nadya, and you'll get the second one."

"You realize I could just take it off you and throw you in the mud with the dead dog."

Elizabeth gripped her piece of lumber. "I supposed you could try. As you saw I was a good shot with the brick. I'm a better shot up close with this piece of wood."

He cocked his head to one side, sucked on his pipe and gave her a hard smile.

"You strike a hard deal, little lady. I like you."

"It would be a harder deal if you try to double-cross me," Elizabeth added, gripping her piece of charred wood.

"I'm the one with the gun," he countered.

"A gun with no bullets. I know what it takes to fill one of those guns. You've got one chamber for one bullet. It's a dueling pistol."

His eyes popped and his lips clamped down on his pipe. Elizabeth heard the one front tooth he had clacking against its bit.

"If you deliver me to Nadya straight away, I'll throw in some pipe tobacco for you."

His eyes widened at her offer and then narrowed to scrutinize her face.

"I'm a woman of my word. Are you a man of yours?"

"Why would you *give* me something for nothing?"

"Because I would appreciate your assistance. Do we have a deal Mr..."

"Mr. James Earlston of Defiance County Ohio," he replied. He wiped his hands on his jacket, then extended it to her. "Deals in the Points are usually done with spit. I'd like to do it the way we do it in Defiance County, a good clean handshake. I'll take you to that Gypsy woman. She's the one that got that moon on her back curtain?"

"Yes."

"One earring now," he said and slipped it into his pocket. "And one earring when I put you face to face with the Gypsy woman," Mr. Earlston concluded. Elizabeth cautiously held out her hand to shake his. The moment their hands touched, he yanked her inward and wrapped his arm around her neck. "I think I take both earrings now, Missy!"

The stench of his unwashed body and the pungent smell of burnt coal shocked her senses. Her eyes widened from desperation to breathe fresh air. They struggled in the middle of the road. Her eyes caught a small audience, who looked on as though her struggle was entertainment.

Thwack!

She quickly swung the piece of charred lumber upward, striking Mr. Earlston on the right side of the head.

"Oww...give me my earring you little heifer!" he growled in her ear. *Thwack! Thwack!*

His grip on her neck loosened. The piece of lumber was now splintered. Her arms flailed in the air behind her trying to grab at his face. She gouged his eyes to free herself. But his grip tightened around her throat again. She heard a screech and glimpsed a shadow overhead just before she heard his scream.

"Aaaaaaaaahhh!" He fell to the ground writhing, gripping his bloody face.

When Elizabeth stumbled back, she turned and caught the wind of a large black wing as it swooped down in front of her to claw at Mr. Earlston's face again. Elizabeth looked up and saw a young girl, whose tattered pale blue dress had a splatter of red across it. When Elizabeth looked back at Mr. Earlston again, she saw the round bulbous handle of an ice pick sticking out of his leg. His blood began to pool into the street. The young girl looked at her bloody dress, and then at Elizabeth.

Mr. Earlston's hand blindly slapped the ground trying to find his assailant.

"I'll kill you, damn Gypsy!" he threatened, as he rolled about in agony on the street.

"This way!" the girl said and took off running.

Elizabeth lifted the hoop of her dress as she followed the young girl through the street. People stepped outside onto their grimy, rickety doorsteps and poked the heads out of their windows. Many waved Mr.

Earlston's scream away and retreated into their hovels; others just stared.

The young girl dragged Elizabeth through a maze of alleyways dotted with people, garbage, and a stench that rivaled Malachai's.

"Wait!" Elizabeth held her stomach and came to a stop.

"No, don't stop. They will come after you. We run a little more to Nadya, and then I get the earring, yes?"

"Yes," Elizabeth replied with a burst of breath. Her lungs were burning, her feet were throbbing. Elizabeth went to place her hand on a building for support.

"Don't touch anything! You'll get sick! Disease is everywhere," the young girl said, pointing to the street, the buildings and the sky.

"Look at what your selfishness has wrought!" Patricia words rang in Elizabeth's ears.

Elizabeth looked at the young girl, whose round, brown eyes and chestnut hair showed promise of beauty. What that young girl did to save her life may have cost the young girl her own. Guilt of the dead bounty hunters brought tears to her eyes. Elizabeth was sorry she came to The Five Points. Not only did she endanger herself and her baby, she also endangered the life of someone's daughter.

"There are no tears in The Points!" the young girl scolded and stomped her foot. "Now cover your nose. We have to run and get through the Bend. Don't stop or they'll rob you and leave you for dead. Now come on!"

"Run you fool!" A woman's voice bounced between the tenement walls.

Elizabeth looked up and saw a woman's head. "Yer best get going! It's not safe here for man or woman! Go!"

Above the woman's head, Elizabeth saw a large black bird flying between the buildings. She hoped her father was leading her. Elizabeth scurried after the young girl who led her through a maze of tenements and dilapidated row houses. With the hoops of her dress up and pressed against her body, they squeezed through a narrow alley. She held her breath the best she could and tried not to touch the walls of the building. When she turned her head to the right, she saw an expanse of daylight ahead that held plumes of white smoke.

They emerged from the narrow alley to a spit of grass and a lonely tree. Elizabeth's eyes adjusted and saw a small cluster of wagons, carts, tents, and makeshift housing. A violin played a melancholy melody. The eerie stillness of the site offered a sense of peace after the heinous labyrinth. The glint of a mirror, hanging from a stick embedded in the ground, caught her eye. When she surveyed the small area, she noticed more sticks with mirrors surrounded the little Gypsy camp.

"This way," the young girl said, waving Elizabeth forward.

Elizabeth approached the campsite. The pungent odor of sulfur strangled her senses. She quickly covered her nose.

"No," the young girl pulled Elizabeth's arm down. "This smell is a good one. It makes the air safer to breathe," she instructed. "There. Nadya is there."

Elizabeth's eyes followed the end of the young girl's finger and saw the familiar quilt stretched across the back of a small wagon. The young girl crossed the mirror boundary. Elizabeth followed without hesitation. When they passed the first wagon, the music stopped. A man stood up holding a violin.

"Dika, who is this?" The man asked as he gently rested his violin on his chair.

"She looks for Nadya. She is a good woman. She saved me from a gaujo and helped me get home," the young girl said eyeing Elizabeth.

The man pulled at Dika's blood splattered dress and raised an eyebrow.

"Whose blood is this?"

"It belongs to the man who tried to kill us. If she hadn't saved me, it would be my body in the street," Dika said with big sorrowful eyes.

"Dika can you remember this man?"

"Yes."

"Then you will point him out later," he demanded.

"Yes."

"Good!" he said tousling her head of hair affectionately. *"Dika, si tut bocklo?"* He asked.

"Yes."

"Then go eat while there is still food," he ordered. He put his hand on Dika's head and pushed her forward into the camp.

"Wait. Lady, you owe me an earring," Dika demanded with an open palm.

Elizabeth removed her left earring and placed it in Dika's hand.

259

"Thank you, Dika."

Dika looked down at the earring, quickly closed her hand, and pressed it to her heart. She crossed to the other side of the camp where she was greeted by two other children, to whom she quickly showed her jeweled prize.

"Are you hungry?" the man asked Elizabeth.

"No, but thank you. I came for..."

"Yes, Nadya. You've come a long and hard way to see Nadya. Must be important?"

"Yes."

Even though Elizabeth was a complete stranger in their camp, she felt safe and welcomed. Like her, they belong nowhere but in their own world. Elizabeth felt a flap of wind. Something brushed the top of her head. She ducked. When she stood up, a large black bird sat on the man's shoulder.

"Oh my, is that your bird?"

"Yes. I'm Andrej, and this is Mihai," he said and offered a piece of something to the bird. "He is my eyes and ears in the sky." The bird squawked on cue.

"That is the biggest crow I have ever seen," Elizabeth said.

"Crow," Andrej snorted. "Mihai is a raven, a majestic and magical bird of the skies!" His hand dipped into his pocket and offered Mihai another treat. Mihai took off. The wind from his wings lifted Elizabeth's fallen tendrils of hair from her face.

"He has important work to do. He watches over us. Come," Andrej instructed as he led her across the small campfire area. Elizabeth shopkeeper's eye immediately took inventory: five wagons, two carts, five children— three boys, two girls, five women, eight men including Andrej. All eyes watched her every move.

"Andrej, may I ask why you have mirrors hanging from sticks?"

"You may ask."

"Why do you have mirrors hanging from sticks all around your camp?"

"Mirrors protect us."

"From what?"

He stopped and turned to face her with a peaceful smile.

"Look around you. What do you see?" He asked her.

"I see people—people who deserve a chance at life," Elizabeth responded.

"Humph—not everybody sees what you see. We are all human. The mirrors are there to send away the people who don't see what you see. We welcome everyone who can see us, and not just themselves."

"I don't understand."

"The mirrors are a test. If someone approaches and sees only our mirrors, they will think, 'Oh no, these gypsies are trying to curse me. I must run.' But if someone approaches with love in their heart for all people, and include gypsies in all people, then we know they will embrace us and help us. Our mirrors teach people how to look past themselves. Hurray for you, you passed the test. You walked without hesitation into our little circle like the mirrors weren't there. So we like you, we help you, and you help us—no?"

"Yes, I'll help you."

"Good. Then we will help each other."

"I didn't know mirrors could do that."

"But it's not the mirror. Because you will help us, I will share our little secret that you must promise never to share with anyone else unless you believe with all of your heart that they love gypsies, or you will bring us great harm."

"I promise."

Andrej closed his eyes and took a deep breath and exhaled. Elizabeth watched his lashes flutter against his skin as he nodded his head. His eyes popped open. A small smile scrolled across his face.

"The spirit of my mother tells me your promise is worth a great deal, so I will tell you. It is not the mirror that possesses the magic, but our intention that we give the mirror. Gypsies believe thoughts to be powerful. Every thought can be brought to life with our intention. So, we put our thought with each mirror that if you approach us with love and acceptance, you may enter our circle. But if you come with hatred for us, you will see your own hateful reflection in the mirror that will make you stop and run away."

"I would have never believed we could do that with our thoughts."

"Our thoughts are more alive than we are. Think only what you want to bring to life, and then bless the mirror with it," Andrej instructed. "Now you are a Gypsy like us. I must feed you now, and when you return you will bring food to feed us. Yes?"

"Of course," Elizabeth replied.

A woman approached Elizabeth. She was shorter than Elizabeth and older. Elizabeth stopped and let the woman look her over. After a moment, the woman touched Elizabeth's dress.

"How much?"

"What?"

"I buy. How much?" the older woman said.

"I can't sell my dress, I won't have anything to wear," Elizabeth explained.

"No sell. Trade," the woman said with a hard grin. She lifted her chin. "My clothes just as good."

"Simza leave her alone," Nadya's voice called out. Nadya stood in the back of her wagon. She clutched her shawl around her shoulders, sat down on the back ledge of her wagon, then pushed herself off to jump down. "Simza will talk you out of your body if you bargain with her," Nadya said with a smirk. "You come for the rest of your reading?"

"Yes."

"You found each other—good," Andrej said and returned to his stool. He picked up his violin and resumed playing.

Elizabeth and Nadya stood silently looking at each other. All eyes were on them.

"You look like you have paid enough to get here," Nadya said lifting her chin to acknowledge the dirt and tear in Elizabeth's dress.

"Yes."

"That's a good thing. It means you will appreciate and value what I have to say. No charge. Come sit with me."

"My dress...I don't think I can get into your wagon," Elizabeth warned.

"Not my wagon, you are carrying a child. It would bring bad spirits to my wagon and sleep if you were to go inside. We will talk beneath that tree over there."

Elizabeth saw two small stools that were low to the ground positioned beneath the tree. "I don't think I can sit on a stool in this dress."

"We're gypsies, we'll find a way."

CHAPTER 38

"Don't touch!" Simza scolded and smacked Kizzy's hand away from her. "Your hands are chikly!"

"Just one touch. I'll use one finger," Kizzy said.

"Fine, only one finger," Simza said.

Kizzy extended her right index finger and slid it down the sateen on Elizabeth's dress.

"That's enough," Simza said, pulling the dress fabric away.

"Your dress is made of wood," Kizzy said as she fingered the first hoop. "Pretty, but not practical. Who wears a dress made with parts of a tree?"

"I do," Simza said and flounced away from Kizzy.

Sitting beneath the tree in Simza's dress was a lot more comfortable than Elizabeth imagined. Simza's clothing had no restrictive whale bones or corsets of any kind. The fabric of Simza's bodice flowed comfortably across her swollen stomach. Likewise, the skirt moved easily around her legs despite the fact it had no hoops. It certainly was a lot lighter than her hoop dress. Elizabeth was completely at ease with her inner Gypsy. It felt natural to be sitting on stools beneath the lone tree.

"What do you think of what I've told you?" Elizabeth asked.

"Your husband and father have not betrayed you. It may look that way, but it would not be the truth."

"You're taking their side?"

"Side? Nadya takes no one's side but her own. When I see a man, who loves you as much as your husband does, there should be nothing but happiness in your heart. Any woman would give everything to have your gifts and a husband who deeply loves her. He would kill for you, and has," Nadya said. "Stop thinking the gifts you have are bad. You are

263

altering your vision of the good in your life."

"I am cursed."

"Self-pity is a cheap parlor trick to make you look pitiful and weak instead of the strong and powerful woman you are. You and I are not evil. We possess a deeper form of love. Now give me your hand," Nadya demanded without taking a breath.

Elizabeth presented her right hand. As Nadya read her palm, images from Nadya's life began to flash in Elizabeth's mind. After the third painful flash, Nadya withdrew her hand.

"I'm sorry...I didn't mean to intrude. I don't know how to control it," Elizabeth explained.

"You control it by not fearing it," Nadya scolded.

"But it scares people."

"No, it doesn't scare people, it scares you. It is your own fear that scares people."

"My fear?"

"Don't be afraid of what you see, because you were meant to see it. Duvvell gave you the vision to see, so why not look at what is shown you, learn from it, and help people with what you can see. Apologizing is an admission of wrongdoing. Do you apologize because you feel Duvvell was wrong to give you the gift of sight?"

"No, of course not."

"Everybody has secrets. If Duvvell gave you the ability to see secrets, then Duvvell also trusts that you will do what is right."

"I get to see for others and not myself. That hardly seems fair."

"Humph—Your gift is for others, your faith is for you," Nadya explained.

"You are so wise."

"Wisdom is pain's gift," Nadya said solemnly.

"I promise I won't say anything to Franz about the baby," Elizabeth said softly and then reached for Nadya's hand.

"The baby is gone, so there is nothing to say. But if you keep my secret, I'll keep yours." Nadya turned Elizabeth's hand over to examine her lifelines.

"You remember I told you about always looking for lost men, that is still true."

"Will any of the lost men come back?"

"My answer is still the same, there is the possibility of one returning, but it will be of his free will." Nadya pressed two fingers in Elizabeth's palm and followed a line across her hand. "Still two daughters..." Nadya's eyes squinted. "You have lots of *káulochírilos* around you. It feels like a good omen."

"What's káulochírilo?"

"Black birds. They fly around. Some protect you, some will turn into vultures and try to pick your flesh down to the bone. You'll have to pay attention to how they fly around you. Understand?"

"How will I know?"

"They will change into vultures right before your eyes. Do this thing that has been asked of you, and you will weed out the vultures from the flock and gain respect by the káulochírilos. Your purpose is good and your intention is pure. No one or nothing can turn you into a vulture because you have help from beyond the veil."

"My father?"

"Yes, and others are coming," Nadya added. "Humph..." The calm in Nadya's face vanished.

"What is it?" Elizabeth's heart jumped in her chest.

Nadya lowered her face to scrutinize Elizabeth's hand.

"...There is a woman who will try to stand in your way. It is her jealousy that consumes her, but something else consumes her..." Nadya dropped Elizabeth's hand.

"What is it?

"It's a...*muló*," Nadya said. "I'm sorry."

"Nadya, what's a moo...low?"

"It is a spirit that has had ties to you for many, many times you've lived. This *muló* lives alongside of you."

"I don't understand. What do you mean many times?"

"Gypsies believe we reincarnate and can come back to live again and again. I don't know why, but this *muló* that chases after you, refuses to be born again. Instead, it likes to take from your life. It wants something you have or took from it, so it will use others when it can't get to you. But something was done to stop him—for now."

"Yes, my husband stopped him." She didn't dare say his name out loud.

"Then you already know this *muló*?" Nadya released Elizabeth's hand

265

and stood up. "Franz..."

"Franz?" Elizabeth twisted on her stool and saw Franz towering over her. "How on earth did you find me?"

"I followed the bird," Franz said. His eyes remained locked on Nadya. "Missus where are your clothes? We have to go."

Elizabeth pointed to Simza who gripped the hoop to keep its hem from dragging on the ground. With men's boots on her feet, Simza clomped over to Elizabeth.

"My clothes are better. We trade again, yes?"

***

The moment Elizabeth saw Samuel standing by their carriage, she ran to him. Onlookers from across the road gawked at their display of emotion as Samuel embraced Elizabeth and smothered her face with kisses.

"Oh, my darling! Did anyone hurt you? Is the baby safe?" His breath felt warm against her cheek.

"We're both fine."

Samuel squeezed her tighter and dotted her face with more kisses. His tears blended with hers.

"I was wrong not to trust you. I'm so sorry Samuel. I was afraid," Elizabeth cried between kisses.

"What are you sorry for?" Samuel said in her ear.

"I embarrassed you in front of the VanCleefs."

"You did no such thing."

"I ran out of their home, without a word like a crazy woman. What they must think of me."

"Ssssh ssssh ssssh ssssh ssssh...Remember they are the ones who danced in our home in their stocking feet."

"I have so much to tell you."

"Perhaps, we should talk in the carriage," Samuel suggested. "We are attracting an audience."

"I think that would be a good idea. I'm absolutely filthy, and I tore my dress."

Elizabeth looked around. Nothing looked familiar. Their carriage was next to a small cluster of trees on a gentle slope of land.

"Samuel, where are we?"

"I'd like you to see something and you don't have to get out of the carriage. It's not far."

"I've seen enough of the Five Points. I'd like to go home," Elizabeth said wearily.

"I'd like to show you a bit of hope. Trust me."

Franz slapped the reins across the horse's back. Their carriage rolled forward. Samuel covered Elizabeth with a blanket up to her chin, then gripped her hand so tight that it was almost painful. After a few minutes, Elizabeth noticed an area of the city that was void of townhomes, tenements, and row houses.

"I still don't know where we are."

"We're almost there."

Like a child, Elizabeth moved to peer out of her carriage window. A wide expanse of trees and grass. Small homes dotted the landscape.

"Are we still in New York?"

"Yes."

"There's grass and trees! My goodness, I miss seeing open fields," Elizabeth said wistfully.

"I thought this would give you inspiration."

"What is this place?"

"It's called Seneca Village."

The carriage went over a large rock, bouncing them in their seats.

"Sorry boss!" Franz called out from the front.

Elizabeth gripped the carriage door. Her eyes roamed the open field. The houses, while not pretty, were in better condition than homes in the Five Points. Franz guided the horse down the main dirt road littered with rocks. She saw a couple of buildings that looked like churches; the rest were homes. A few of the homes were constructed with lumber that offered a front porch, two front windows and a little fenced in yard; but most of the homes were very rudimentary and provided a doorstep and a wood door. If she wasn't in New York, she would have thought them to be slave cabins. With that thought, her heart quickened.

"Who lives here?"

"Free Negroes. There are also some Irish families as well. Now typically the Irish and Negroes don't get along, but here they found a way to live side by side without tormenting each other."

"Maybe the churches help to keep the peace," Elizabeth suggested.

"The most important thing is that there are free Negroes establishing a community. I was thinking we could start here."

"I don't understand."

"We talked about finding other free Negroes like us to start a community. I thought if we had enough money, we could buy land, build housing and businesses—imagine freeing slaves and giving them a home of their own, and an opportunity to start a business. Slaves run the plantation; they know how to farm, how to harvest, how to tan hide, carpentry, just about everything needed to build and run a community. It was slaves who built the White House. If we can build the house for the President of the United States, why can't we build a community for ourselves? I believe if we work together with all the immigrants, there will be no limit to what we can do."

Samuel's words brought tears to her eyes. Elizabeth looked out onto the field. A little Negro boy happily pushed the inside rim of a wagon wheel down the road. Even though the shanty homes reminded her of slave cabins, Samuel's words offered a brighter future. If she had the money, she would buy the lumber and give it to each family so they could start fresh with dignity. Maybe Nadya and her family could set down roots. There was plenty of room for the gypsies to have a section.

Elizabeth turned to him. Flecks of amber twinkled in his eyes, reflecting the passion in his heart. She looked back out onto the field one last time before they exited back onto the main road. Seneca Village was big enough to make a difference, yet small enough to accomplish a goal. Her head snapped back around to Samuel.

"Let's do it!"

Samuel's hug lifted Elizabeth off her seat.

"My darling, I love you!" He kissed her, but her mind was already busy planning. "Samuel, we're going to need money, lots of money," Elizabeth declared as she pulled away. "Probably more money than the VanCleefs have."

"The VanCleefs probably wouldn't put their money into this idea."

"If the VanCleefs want to use my abilities, to dig up people's secrets, I want something in return. Poppa always said a good business deal is about an even exchange. 'Give a little, get a little'."

"I love when you dig your heels in," Samuel said and kissed the back of her hand.

"Let me talk to Clara," Elizabeth said.

"Being with the gypsies today has certainly ignited your fire."

"Did Franz tell you I was at the Gypsy camp?"

"No. I followed you."

Elizabeth bolted forward. The blanket fell to the floor of the carriage.

"You couldn't have possibly followed me. I would have seen you."

"You saw me. You looked me right in the eye. You gave that little girl your earring." He leaned in and kissed her gently on her neck and whispered, "I was the bird."

CHAPTER 39

Two weeks later, and the month of April brought more rain to New York than Elizabeth ever saw in New Hope. Back home she appreciated the rain. It played a major role for farmer's crops and green fields for livestock. Here in New York, it turned the city's streets in some areas into one big mud puddle.

Elizabeth and Samuel giggled and tried to dodge large raindrops as they raced to the open doors of Vanguard. They rushed to the door trying their best to shield their papers and Samuel's artwork beneath their cloaks. Not even an umbrella provided much protection from the rain that was falling horizontally. Their futile attempt to keep dry in the driving rain sent them into a burst of laughter when they arrived at the threshold looking like two wet cats.

The last time Elizabeth was at the Vanguard, she ran out. This time the weather forced her to run in. She was excited about their plan to develop Seneca Village into a more upscale community for free Negroes and immigrants. With the VanCleef name at the top of her list of potential investors, Elizabeth was certain they would attract others with money and compassion. She had been so busy with their dream, she forgot she was carrying a child. She was grateful she was too busy to care about her widening girth.

"Samuel, we look absolutely dreadful," Elizabeth said, swiping wet strands of hair from her face. "We look like we went swimming in Honey Hollow." She took off her soaked cloak and smoothed her damp smock over her belly.

"Wait a minute, I think I caught a fish on the way in," Samuel added with a laugh as he removed a black canvas-type case from beneath his cloak.

Stewart, the VanCleef's butler, greeted their frivolity with a stern face. Without a smile or a word, Stewart nodded at a footman, who stepped forward and presented them with tea towels to dry their face and hands. The moment the last tea towel touched the footman's tray, he briskly walked away with his nose in the air.

"This way," Stewart said dryly and escorted them to the library.

Damp but excited, they anxiously awaited their benefactors in Vanguard's impressive library. Elizabeth had never seen so many books in one place. They were all beautifully leather bound, some with gold lettering on their spines. The library was divided into two sections. Near the entry, there were oak bookcases that climbed the walls to the ceiling. A long ladder hung from a brass rail that stretched across the top of the shelves. Marble pedestals with priceless vases were positioned about the room. The dark oak floors gleamed beneath an oversized brass chandelier. Elizabeth stood with her mouth open, gawking at the library's opulence.

"We'll have a library like this one day," Samuel said as he grabbed her hand and pulled her towards a long table at the other end of the room. They weaved their way through a grouping of four leather chairs that were arranged on the largest oriental rug she had ever seen. A twinge of fear stabbed at her gut as she passed through. The group of high back leather chairs was designed to hide their occupants from view.

What was Julius hiding?

The ominous feeling made her come to a dead stop. She looked at the large mouth of the fireplace that roared with fire hoping it would share the secret discussed in those chairs. Her eyes looked around the room and noticed the drapes drawn on the windows that faced the street.

"What's wrong?"

"I'm not sure," she replied, holding her stomach. "Samuel, why are the curtains drawn?"

Samuel's smile disappeared.

"I don't know, but know that I trust you." He reached for her hand. "Let's set up."

As Elizabeth moved to the table, she couldn't help but feel intimidated. There was something about the library that was oppressive. Perhaps it was the grandeur. It could easily make anyone feel small and insignificant. But Elizabeth believed their plan and the reason they were there was greater than all the leather-bound books and expensive vases the library held. She pushed away any intimidation lurking within the library's walls and focused on arranging her notes on the table.

A week ago, when they received a message from Julius requesting a meeting, she couldn't sleep. She felt like a bona fide businesswoman. Her experience running the store with her father prepared her for their presentation. She and Samuel decided that, she would speak about investments, costs, and profits, and Samuel would present their vision and how their program would work. Samuel had prepared an impressive discussion on the merits of what he called *The Seneca Village Revitalization Program.*

When Samuel wasn't working for Mr. Dennings, he spent his free time drafting notes, practicing his presentation on her, and creating art renderings of the future Seneca Village. She had no idea he was such a great orator and artist. His devotion to their project only deepened her love for him.

Samuel opened his folder and placed four renderings on the library table for Julius to review. She watched him fuss with the placement of his artistry on the large library table like a museum curator hanging a famous masterpiece.

"Samuel, they are beautiful!"

"Let's hope that Julius and Clara feel the same way," he replied, then stepped back to view the table.

The plan was for Samuel to verbally present his vision of Seneca Village, then escort the VanCleefs over to the table and unveil his art renderings. Elizabeth would then present all the financial information, so they would know there would be a return on their investment. Elizabeth had worked hard calculating the financial costs for their project. She used all of the accounting lessons her father taught her when they operated the store together. When she was forced to take over the running the family store by herself, she was able to make record profits, which in turn attracted a wealthy buyer who offered her a good price.

She had a proven record that she could make money and that she was bankable. She would make it abundantly clear to Julius and Clara that the monies she was requesting was a loan. She didn't want any handouts. Both she and Samuel decided that it was better for all recipients to work and earn the money to pay for their homes.

She also created a way to employ people. Poppa always said people want a decent place to live, and New York had plenty of places that needed repair. She and Samuel would use her dowry to create a little construction company to buy properties at a low cost. They would then employ the free Negroes to fix up the property, so they could sell it and make a profit. The money from the sale would replace her dowry and pay the workers money, so the workers could pay back Julius and the other investors, with interest. It was a win-win plan for everyone involved.

Elizabeth heard Julius' voice on the other side of the library door. She smoothed her bodice smock over her stomach, pressed her fingers over the sides of her hair, pinched her cheeks, and smiled. The door handle clicked. Julius entered without Clara. Elizabeth's smile left her face. He was dressed in a simple shirt, pants, and boots. Something was horribly wrong. He didn't look like the Julius she knew.

"Hello to my two-favorite people," he said with a wavering smile. "I'm sorry I'm late, but I had urgent business to tend to at the last minute. Oh, I guess I'm a bit underdressed for our meeting."

"Julius, it's so wonderful to see you," Elizabeth said. She moved in to greet him and he politely waved her back.

"Elizabeth, you should be off your feet. Please, sit, sit." He sat in one of the high back leather chairs without offering Samuel the greeting of a handshake. "Samuel, Elizabeth, please sit," Julius ordered, pointing to two chairs across from him.

He was distant. Elizabeth wished she could give him a hug to see what was going on.

"Julius, if this isn't a good time, we can come back..."

"No. Actually Samuel, this is perfect timing. Elizabeth, I am grateful you agreed to help us. Let me get right to the point. I'm hosting a small formal dinner with some men from Wall Street. Can the two of you attend? It's next Saturday. I told our guests to arrive at seven, but I'd like the two of you to arrive at six thirty. Now the two men I need you to focus on, Elizabeth, are..."

"Julius," Elizabeth interjected. "We thought you wanted to hear our plan to revitalize Seneca Village."

"Seneca Village? That little shanty town in the middle of nowhere?"

"Julius, you said you wanted to use my abilities to help the...the downtrodden."

"Yes, yes, the downtrodden..."

"Samuel and I believe that area has a nice parcel of land, and if developed properly, we could build a beautiful little village of small houses for free Negroes and..."

"No," Julius said firmly.

Elizabeth looked at Samuel confused.

"But I thought you wanted me to use my ability to help the less fortunate..."

"Yes, yes, yes— help the less fortunate," Julius repeated.

"Julius, are you not well?" Samuel asked.

"Yes, yes I am fine...I..."

"Where's Clara? I thought she would be joining us," Elizabeth said softly.

"Clara? Yes, Clara is resting."

"Is she not well?" Elizabeth asked.

"Julius, what is wrong?" Samuel asked.

Julius blotted his brow.

"They have Clara," Julius blurted, and then blotted his upper lip with his handkerchief.

"Who?" Samuel asked.

"The *Roach Guards.*" He covered his mouth with his handkerchief to contain his grief. "They're an Irish gang. A violent one. They want control..." Julius said wearily and fell back in his seat.

"Clara's been kidnapped. When?" Samuel asked leaping from his chair.

"Yesterday afternoon, when she was shopping on Fifth Avenue. She ventured down a side street to buy cookies from an Italian cart...and they snatched her like she was a sack of potatoes," Julius lowered his head. "I don't know what else to do."

"We'll get everyone together," Samuel announced.

"No, no. It's no use. It's that damn Tammany. They run this city and control all the political power. I can't go to the police because the Irish control the Tammany and the Tammany control the police. No doubt the Roach Guards were ordered by the Tammany to take my Clara..." Julius' voice cracked.

"Julius let me..." Samuel began

274

"No, no. If I do anything, try to enlist your help–they'll kill her," he whimpered.

"Kill her?" Elizabeth gasped.

"Yes, if I don't do what they want, they'll kill her," Julius covered his eyes and released a sob.

"What do they want?" Samuel pleaded.

Elizabeth stared at Julius. She felt absolutely nothing for him, but an unexplained rage.

"The Tammany wants to take control of Wall Street. Money is the true power in this city, and they want it. They're trying to take over New York completely. I warned everyone that this day would come. You've got to help me, or they will kill her," Julius cried, dabbing at his tears with a handkerchief.

"What can we do to help?" When Samuel moved in, Julius jumped up and moved behind his chair.

"I'm afraid there is only one thing you can do to help me...Elizabeth, if you can help us get the information they want about Wall Street Trustees, they said they would release Clara."

"What kind of information?" Elizabeth asked coldly. Elizabeth knew her tone was insensitive, but she couldn't help herself. Something inside her was taking over. Samuel's eyes were on her. His face contorted with confusion.

"Elizabeth?"

"No offense taken. I understand her suspicion."

"Elizabeth, if you could see your way to access the information they want, they promised they would release Clara unharmed."

A blip of light flashed in her mind. She saw Julius with three wealthy men sitting in the four high back leather chairs in his library. They raised their brandy snifters.

"To controlling Wall Street," they toasted.

The vision was gone. She focused on Julius, who stood before them as an alleged broken man. She heard Samuel's voice.

"Julius of course she will," Samuel assured.

"I will not," Elizabeth shot back. "Samuel, he's lying." Julius' face flash a bright red.

"On Clara's life, I am telling the truth," Julius countered.

"Samuel, he's lying."

"Elizabeth!" Samuel scolded

"I saw them. They were sitting in those chairs toasting Wall Street."

"How dare you!" Julius admonished and threw his handkerchief onto the floor like a gauntlet to declare war.

"...you will weed out the vultures from the flock and gain respect."

"Elizabeth you're accusing Julius VanCleef of lying about the kidnapping of his wife," Samuel countered.

"Samuel, he wants to use the information for himself. He's the one who wants to gain control of Wall Street," Elizabeth said, pointing a condemning finger. "Julius, how could you? I trusted you," Elizabeth said through tears.

She went to Samuel, grabbed his hands, and placed them on her stomach. "Samuel, I swear on the life of Willie and our unborn child, he's lying."

Samuel's eyes moved back and forth between them.

"You have to believe me," Elizabeth begged. He released her hands. "Samuel..."

Samuel approached Julius.

"Julius, I need you to look me in the eye and tell me Elizabeth has misperceived this situation," Samuel demanded.

They were almost nose to nose. Julius' chest heaved with each breath.

"Help us, and I will make you very rich," Julius offered.

Samuel's eyes widened. He slowly stepped back from Julius and reached out for Elizabeth's hand.

"Let's go," Samuel told her.

Elizabeth moved to get their work from the library table.

"Leave it," Samuel ordered.

"But you worked so hard..."

"Elizabeth leave all of it! It's tainted."

"Samuel don't let him take our dream," Elizabeth urged.

"We'll have more dreams."

"Your plans will make a good fire," Julius threatened.

Elizabeth looked into her husband's eyes that were red as though he had cried a good cry. She took a last look at Samuel's drawings and her neat pile of financial wizardry and bade farewell to another dream. She joined hands with her husband. They were almost through the library door to the foyer.

"Neophyte fools!"

They stopped.

"Do you think the world wants to deal with uppity Negroes like you? They'll smell your slave stench the moment you say hello. Stand amongst real White people in the sun and your white skin will melt like cheap candle wax and expose your darkie heritage the moment you draw a bead of perspiration.

"Without me, you're nothing and will be nothing. You know nothing about this city, its people, or its power. This city will eat you alive and leave your bones for the mangy dogs to polish off. Money is the true power in this world. Elizabeth, your gift is nothing more than a cheap parlor trick. I sent you those images. Yes, that's right, I have powers, too. I can get Wall Street without you. When I do, I will see to it that people lock their doors when they see you coming. You'll get nowhere without my say so!" Julius threatened.

"The limitation you set for us will be your own jail," Samuel volleyed back and then turned and swiped his hands in the air.

"Samuel, no!"

Crash!

One of the vases toppled from its marble pedestal and shattered as it hit the floor.

"You can do that to a vase that is standing still, but you cannot stop a moving bullet," Julius threatened.

"Come after me, my wife, my children, or anyone I love, and I will level your house with you in it," Samuel growled.

"I will have you arrested for destruction of property, and then call the bounty hunter to take you back to the South where you belong!"

Elizabeth found herself moving towards Julius. Her right hand cradled her swollen stomach to protect her baby.

"Abraham Adelman, you are a liar and a hateful fraud! Your name, and everything about you I have written down. Should anything happen to me, my husband or my children, I have given strict instruction to the one person we do trust to deliver your true identity to every newspaper in New York, Philadelphia, and Washington. If I were you, I wouldn't say another word."

"You can never be better than me." Julius rebutted menacingly.

"Is that what all of this is about? You enslaved my people because

277

you believe white skin is better dark skin. Look in a mirror. You are the fools!"

Elizabeth's words slapped his senses. Julius stumbled back.

"It is your inadequacies that created slavery. You needed to feel superior. You lack the skills and ability to succeed on your own. You need us to build you up." Elizabeth charged at Julius with her words, backing him up against his bookcase.

"We built your plantations and raised your bratty children. We built the White House as you stood by and observed and claimed our handiwork. You could never run a plantation on your own. You can't make a nickel without us." With nowhere to go, Julius hunched his shoulders and cowered as the truth of Elizabeth's words beat him down to the floor.

"All this time, you made us feel like nothing when you were the ones who felt like nothing. You projected your insecurities and inadequacies onto our backs and injected your self-hatred into our blood to make us believe you are superior. You are nothing without us." A tear slid down her face and slipped into her mouth. "My father trusted you with my life!"

Julius slumped to floor with his arms shielding his head. Elizabeth raised her hand to strike the top of his head, but Samuel pulled her away.

"You have already beaten him. Let's go," Samuel said softly. With his hand against the small of her back, he moved her toward the library door. She looked over her shoulder and saw Julius scrambled to his feet.

"I am Julius VanCleef," he mumbled. Elizabeth turned around ready for another round. She saw a pitiful and disheveled old man wavering on his feet, declaring his final battle cry.

"I am Julius VanCleef," he announced combing, his fingers through his slivery pompadour of hair. "I am Julius VanCleef," he declared with a raised fist.

His arrogance enraged her. She took a step towards him for her final blow.

"Take away your prestigious VanCleef name, and you'd become a neighbor knocking on our door for a cup of acceptance," Elizabeth said flatly. "Vanguard is nothing but a cheap illusion of your arrogance."

"I am Julius VanCleef!" Julius grabbed a vase and raised it above his head and hurled it to the floor. Samuel stepped in front her to shield her.

Crash!

"I am Julius VanCleef!" He grabbed the fire poker and swung at another vase.

Smash!

"Goddammit! I'm Julius VanCleef!"

Samuel shielded Elizabeth as they scurried out of the library. Once out of the library, they walked briskly through the foyer, right through the front door Stewart held open and then closed promptly behind them.

The rain had miraculously stopped. The blinding April sun forced her hands up to shield her eyes. The sound of more smashing glass seeped over the threshold and spilled onto the city street. Passersby stopped to listen. Elizabeth turned and saw that the oversized red door was closed. Did her righteousness close a door of opportunity for freedom for others? Elizabeth wasn't sure if they had escaped, or if they were booted out of Julius' cutthroat world.

Samuel grabbed her beneath her elbow and ushered her towards their carriage. Franz jumped off the coach and raced towards them. He guarded their backs as they climbed inside their carriage.

"Boss?"

"Eyes wide open, Franz," Samuel said and slid in next to Elizabeth. Samuel took her hand in his and held it close to his heart. Just before Franz climbed up onto the driver's bench, Elizabeth saw him remove a revolver from behind his back, place it on his seat, and then climb up. Their carriage pulled smoothly away from the curb.

"Don't look back," Samuel instructed.

"Samuel, I..."

"You did the right thing."

"I said too much."

"No, you were perfect. For the record, I would never want to go to war with you," he said offering a soft smile. His tears moistened the back of her hand as he kissed it. "We have to let that dream go."

"Do not let the physical world limit the love you are capable of creating." Her father's words whispered in her mind.

"Samuel, we don't have to let go of our dream, we just have to stay away from the vultures who want to devour it."

"There will always be more vultures."

"Then we will have to create more dreams."

279

CHAPTER 40

Immediately after the VanCleef debacle, Elizabeth posted a letter to Horace and Eugenia about their horrifying incident. Mindful of Horace and Eugenia's long-term friendship with Julius and Clara, Elizabeth did her best to keep the contents of her letter factual and a tad apologetic. More than three weeks had passed, and they had not heard one threatening word from the VanCleefs. No doubt Horace took swift action upon receiving her letter. Although appearing jovial and socially pleasing Elizabeth knew Horace, if provoked, could draw a hard line in the dirt if he had to.

Elizabeth was grateful for the arrival of spring. It allowed her to open windows and doors and air out her little carriage house, and her mind. For some reason the cherry blossom trees bloomed late. Thirteen of the trees bloomed mid-April and provided Barclay's landscape with a scintillating sight of precious pink petals.

By the first week of May there was still one cherry blossom tree in bloom. It was the tree Elizabeth had watered. Its late blooming plush pink petals beckoned the attention of everyone who saw it–Henry, the cook, the maids, the stable hand, the postman, even the stoic Mr. Twitterly. Everyone stood in front of it, at least once, to marvel at the botany miracle; everyone, except Charlotte.

The pink petals beckoned her to come outside, sit beneath it, and enjoy her recently installed terrace. Elizabeth happily accepted nature's invitation before wispy fingers of clouds flicked the morning sun away. With the May sun high in the sky warming the top of her head and shoulders, Elizabeth reached into her apron pocket to retrieve Eugenia's letter which was in between the pages of one of her father's journals.

Eugenia's letter offered a heartwarming lesson of acceptance and compassion that she admired. It gave Elizabeth hope, that perhaps one day, she could cultivate the same compassion for her birth mother.

She opened the letter and went immediately to the second page. Rereading her favorite part of Eugenia's letter offered her solace, inspiration, and the courage needed to keep their dream alive. Her eyes immediately dropped to the third paragraph. Its first sentence was marred by the crease from the fold of the letter.

"To have such a wretched betrayal in one's life is like being crushed by an immeasurable mountain. I see no way to recover. Your father is so beyond grief that he has paid a mason to create a grave marker for Julius. While I find the idea appalling, it has provided consolation for your father's insurmountable rage and grief at the loss of his dear friend, even though he is still alive.

As for me, I am working hard to harbor no ill will toward Julius and Clara. Nor do I wish to speak ill of them. It is moments like this that I am grateful for my Quaker principals of peace and tolerance. It is my suggestion that you and Samuel follow suit. Focus on loving each other and relish the anticipation of the arrival of your new baby.

We cannot undo what has happened, but we can learn from it and build a stronger future. Release all anger and disappointment like they were reckless children in need of freedom and let love flow into your hearts where it can be embraced and cherished for the soul saving commodity that it is.

Sincerely yours,

Mrs. Horace Chase

Elizabeth wiped an errant tear, refolded the letter and pressed it against her heart. Leaving all their plans and visions of an improved Seneca Village in the VanCleef's library was like leaving Simon and Willie all over again. She desperately wanted to let go. She certainly didn't need to add more disappointment to her life.

Their plans for Seneca Village had offered her another opportunity to love a part of herself she couldn't acknowledge. More importantly, it was a chance to help and love the Simons and the Willies of the world. If she couldn't have them physically in her life, she would find a way to love them vicariously through others. Her throat constricted with emotion. She closed her eyes and took a deep breath like Samuel taught her. She imagined herself a balloon filled with an unpleasant memory and then let go.

"Puuuuuuhhhh!"

She felt so blessed that Samuel wasn't jealous of her distant love affair with Simon and Willie. He understood the impact of her loss and trusted the love they shared. His trust opened her even more. The more she opened to him, the more he opened to her. Their bed was the one place they were free and shared every part of themselves. They renewed their promise to never keep secrets from each other. That promise united them into a single force of love that made their isolation bearable.

She slipped the letter back into her apron pocket, removed the black journal, and flipped through it until she found the page whose corner she had folded down. Her finger moved down the list of names until she came to the VanCleefs. She crossed their names off with her pencil and wrote next to their name, "Neophyte fools!"

Since receiving the journals, she made it her duty to study them, and familiarize herself with the names and places her father had so dutifully recorded. She had a responsibility to maintain the journals and remove anyone who no longer belonged. She returned the journal to her pocket, and then lifted her feet to examine them.

Both her feet and ankles were swollen. Four and a half months into her pregnancy and it was getting harder to put on her shoes. Her puffy feet forced her into wearing her slippers most of the time. Samuel offered to buy her a larger pair of shoes to accommodate the change, but vanity won out. It was enough she had to get new smocks to cover her increasing mid-section. The last thing she wanted to do was admit her feet were getting bigger.

When Samuel wasn't home, she slipped on a pair of his boots to wander outside. Thankfully the morning sun afforded her the freedom of bare feet. She looked around to make sure no one was looking and released her feet from Samuel's boots. She peeled off her stockings and placed her feet on the cool blue flagstone terrace hoping it would reduce her swelling.

After the fiasco at the VanCleefs', she became mindful and appreciative for the freedom her father gifted her. She relished the freedom of sitting, taking off her shoes and stockings, and letting her feet bask in the sun. Had she remained a slave this comfort would have been a dream. She wiggled her toes in the sun and sighed as she took in the view of her new terrace and its little garden.

Samuel channeled his disappointment and frustration with the VanCleefs into his new hobby, landscaping. His artistry on paper was transferred to Barclay's parcel of land. During his spare time, and with Henry's permission, Samuel created three visually pleasing gardens. With the assistance of Barclay's grounds men, Samuel transferred pieces of his art renderings for Seneca Village to Barclay's grounds. Her terrace garden was the final project.

She was happy and relieved Samuel found a way to bring a part of his dream to life. It was a sign that Julius had failed to kill Samuel's hope for humanity. Although Samuel wouldn't talk about Seneca, the landscape was proof that Seneca Village was still dear to his heart. She had faith that together they would find a way to create a thriving community for the less fortunate.

Elizabeth turned to her right to view the lilac bush he planted on the right side of the house. She didn't expect the bush to flower until its second or third year, but Samuel's love cultivated dark lavender buds that were starting to open. She couldn't wait to have its floral scent take over their carriage house.

The blue flagstone terrace that cooled her swelling feet was installed next to a row of privet bushes, which would bloom after her lilac. The small herb garden, included with her terrace, was filled with lemon balm, rosemary, French lavender, mint, parsley, oregano, and basil. Samuel completed her garden with a beautiful white wrought iron garden table set he purchased from the Marquis DeMontier, who insisted on overseeing its delivery.

She couldn't help but giggle the day the table set arrived. It brought Henry out of the house and turned them all into schoolboys. The Marquis DeMontier was in pure form.

"This eeze an original. The only one like it in zee world. Jules Hardouin-Mansart, Louis XIV's chief architect, responsible for many magnificent structures in France, and zee stunning gates to Versailles, is the creator of this very, very, unique garden seating. So sit with care. Treat it like you would treat your newborn baby. Oh, it eeze so hard to part with great works of art," DeMontier exclaimed with a flamboyant wave of his handkerchief. "But for you Cherie, I will endure this hardship," DeMontier said and then kissed her on both cheeks.

With DeMontier breathing down Samuel and Henry's necks, DeMontier orchestrated the unloading of the garden set. She then watched and listened as Samuel, DeMontier, and Henry bickered about its placement.

"It should go on zee grass right next to zee bushes, so zee greenery of your little bushes can be a lush little backdrop. Once they mature, you can turn them into topiaries of whimsical garden creatures, *Oiu?*"

"No. When I look out my library window it will look better to the right of the bushes on the blue terrace for a nice visual contrast. Besides, the stone terrace will keep her feet dry when the grass is wet," Henry asserted.

"That stone is not blue. You Americans are color blind. My peacock, he is blue. That stone is black and too harsh for the delicate white of Hardouin-Mansart."

"Monty, it's two chairs and a table," Henry said plainly.

"These are not chairs. Chairs are wood."

"But she's my wife, and I paid for the seating, and created the garden. It's my design, and my wife, so I should decide. I know exactly where she would want it-right next to her lilac bush. Lilacs are her favorite.""Monsieur Chase, I love it when you're testy, even when you're wrong. Zee set belongs on zee soft green grass."

"It can't go on the grass because that's going to be an herb garden," Samuel defended.

"You're both wrong. You've got ornamental trees, herb gardens, bushes, blue flagstone, and furniture. Visually, it's too crowded. You want the furniture to make a statement wherever you put it. If you put the garden set over there, the statement will be that it's too crowded."

It had been a while since she had seen Henry. He looked a lot thinner than his normal robust physique, his face seemed more drawn, and his normal strong brown eyes were bloodshot from either too much drinking or not enough sleep. The little banter with Samuel and DeMontier brought back the old "know it all" Henry. He looked happy.

"I say we ask Elizabeth. She's the one who's going to be using the garden chairs the most," Henry said.

"Elizabeth, what do you say? Whose idea do you like more?" Samuel asked with a smile and a raised eyebrow.

Elizabeth had two roosters and a peacock squawking before her. Biscuits were not going to work.

"I like all of your ideas," Elizabeth said.

"That eeze impossible. You can't like all of zee ideas when my idea is zee best. I'm zee artist in this group."

"Gentlemen, how about we place it beneath that cherry tree on the stone terrace. When it's sunny, I'll have shade, and with the bushes behind me, they will help to cut down the wind that blows across the courtyard. I'll still be able to enjoy the site and scent of my lilac bush, which will bloom before the privets, and have easy access to my lovely herb garden."

"Makes sense to me," Henry said.

"See, she wanted to be near her lilac bush," Samuel declared with a satisfied grin.

"It eeze exactly where I said zee Hardouin-Mansart should be placed, so it can take in all zee beauty of the landscape. I will have my gardener deliver you some of my French lavender and your garden will be complete. My work here is done, *Cherie. Au revoir!*"

DeMontier held her gently by the shoulders, kissed both of her cheeks, did a half twirl on his heels, flipped his cascading wig over the collar of his brocade jacket, and returned to his ornate carriage. His two white horses pranced down the lane back to the main road. He was in an eccentric category of his own.

The thought of that day made Elizabeth smile. While she lost three men, God had blessed her with three more, who loved and cared for her in their own special ways. Each taught her that there were different forms of love. She lifted her face to the sun and closed her eyes. She was grateful DeMontier considered her a friend and not an enemy. She couldn't afford any more enemies. While distance and death may have miraculously freed her from Emma and Patricia, she knew Mal... She stopped herself. She didn't want to give him breath with her thoughts.

A slight breeze showered her with pink petals from the cherry blossom and lifted the scent of DeMontier's French lavender to her nose. For the moment, she was in her own little heaven and was happy and grateful. The moment her eyes landed on the drawn library drapes on Barclay, guilt demanded her attention. She wished she could share her peace with Henry, but he had shut her and Samuel out. With the exception of his viewing of the Cherry Blossom tree and that day when DeMontier and Hardouin-Mansart drew him out of the Barclay, they had not seen him. Something had forced him into hiding, but what?

Everything seemed normal until Charlotte's surprise appearance during their "no rules" dinner in February. It was shortly after that they heard the first scream. After that scream, Elizabeth had not seen Charlotte enter or leave the house by foot or by carriage. She thought the screams she and Samuel heard at night, and sometimes during the day, belonged to Charlotte, but the screams ceased. Perhaps they left with Charlotte? Perhaps Henry's gloom was due to Charlotte's hasty departure and a pending scandalous divorce?

To Elizabeth's surprise, the rear door to Barclay opened. A female figure emerged and was headed her way. Elizabeth jumped up from her seat to cover her bare feet with the hem of her dress. The sun blinded her view.

"It's good to see you out and about!" Cassandra called across the courtyard as she approached. The moment Elizabeth waved back. Cassandra broke into a run. Their bodies bumped each other as Cassandra pulled Elizabeth in for a quick hug and a kiss on the cheek. Cassandra's hug revealed a bubble of light containing an image of Cassandra's life. It was the same vision Elizabeth saw before when they had tea at the Astor House Hotel. Elizabeth's cheeks heated with embarrassment. Cassandra was in love and Elizabeth hated intruding into Cassandra's private affair.

"Elizabeth, you are simply growing and glowing with motherhood!" Cassandra announced between panted breaths and a smile. "Your cheeks are as pink as the petals on this miraculous cherry blossom. My goodness, father's grounds men have outdone themselves. This new terrace and its garden are simply heavenly! I'm so glad you're home," Cassandra added gripping Elizabeth's hand.

A field of clouds passed overhead providing Elizabeth a respite from the glaring sun. She was able to see that Cassandra's eyes were brimming with tears.

"Cassandra, what has happened?"

Cassandra sucked in a mouth full of air and burst into tears.

"I... I... just wish my father could be happy..." Cassandra's voice trailed off. "My father...my father...doesn't deserve this..."

"Deserve what?" Elizabeth asked. Her eyes did a quick scan of the library windows to see if they were being watched. The drapes were still drawn.

"Can we talk inside?"

"Yes, of course."

Elizabeth ushered Cassandra inside to the kitchen where she had set up a little breakfast nook for her and Samuel. It was intimate and away from the sitting area with its cavernous window and prying eyes.

"I just heard the most distressing news," Cassandra began.

"Is it your father?"

"I don't know how to help him."

"Perhaps Samuel and I can help him if we know what it is."

"It's Charlotte."

"Charlotte? Is she sick?"

"Yes, very. Please, talk to him. He'll listen to you. For some reason he trusts you more than anyone else; even more than me. I don't mind that he favors you. I know I have disappointed him..."

"Your father loves you so much. I am certain you could never disappoint him."

"But I have. There is no disputing it," Cassandra blotted the corners of her eyes with a damp handkerchief.

"Cassandra, I know deep in my heart that your father loves you and he will always be there for you. You have to believe that."

"I have violated his senses. There's no changing that. I know he loves me; we just see love differently."

"Don't we all?" Elizabeth knew Cassandra's secret was much deeper than the skin of slaves and wasn't sure how she could help.

"I was in love with a free Negro name Simon Calhoun. I bore him a son, who I will probably never see again because of the differences in the color of our skin." Elizabeth began.

"You have a son that you'll never see again? How awful!," Cassandra burst into tears.

Elizabeth was ready to strip down to her skin and expose every detail of her past to help Cassandra feel comfortable with her predicament.

"Yes, it is awful, but I chose to give Simon and our son Willie a freedom they would never be able to have if I stayed in their lives. The world seems to have decided there is only one version of love to which everyone must conform. The truth is, there are so many forms of love. Who we love, or why we love, should never carry a penalty. I'm sure your father is happy you found love, even if it's not conventional. There's no denying the love between you and Bethany."

Cassandra's mouth dropped open, her eyes widened, and then her chest heaved upwards as she stole the air between them.

"I know. That's why the two of you were running away to Boston, isn't it? It's also the reason the servants in your father's house dislike Charlotte because she told him that she caught the two of you together."

Cassandra jumped up from the table and backed into a freestanding cupboard. The dishes and glassware rattled and clanked from her impact. New tears quickly formed. Her face reddened with anger.

"Did Charlotte tell you? The moment I try to be kind and show her a modicum of compassion, Charlotte places a dagger in my heart. If she told you, I hope the flying gargoyles carry her straight to hell!"

"It wasn't her," Elizabeth said. Her mind rushed to find the right words to explain. "I saw you."

"What? What do you mean you saw me?"

"I saw the two of you, together. You shared a kiss after she tied your corset...in your bedroom. Your bedroom is the room that has a crystal vase of yellow roses on a table in front of your window."

"That's impossible. You weren't there. I didn't know you. You hadn't arrived in New York. How could you have seen? There are only four people who knew...Witch!" Cassandra blurted under her breath with a condemning finger.

"I'm not a witch. I can see people's secrets. I was hoping we could continue to be close friends, perhaps confidants. I need a friend, a sister, I can trust with my secret the same way you can trust me to keep yours."

Cassandra's eyes widened with bewilderment. Her face shifted from distrust to an empathetic frown as she burst into tears and moved towards Elizabeth. They stood in the cozy carriage house kitchen, sobbing and holding each other.

"I shall always remain your most trusted, truest friend and confidant," Cassandra declared through sobs.

"What is going on?" a male's voice interjected slicing them apart.

Elizabeth and Cassandra quickly separated and blotted their tears. Samuel stood in the kitchen doorway stone-faced and solemn.

"It's not what you think," Cassandra quickly defended. Cassandra looked to Elizabeth. Cassandra's puffy eyes pleaded for confidentiality.

"It's Charlotte. She's not well," Elizabeth explained dabbing at her tears.

"Did Cassandra tell you everything?"

Elizabeth stared at Samuel. His eyes were red.

"Just that Charlotte is not well. Samuel, what is wrong?"

"He has seen Charlotte," Cassandra said flatly and left them.

Elizabeth felt Samuel's grip tighten around her. His tears moistened her cheek.

"Samuel?"

"It's Malachai," he whispered.

His name paralyzed her. Their kitchen began to spin. Her legs went numb. Samuel gripped her by the small of her back and as he relayed what happened. Each word pulled her down deeper into a whirlpool of fear that only Malachai could create. When he was done, she and Charlotte were now neighbors in the worst way.

CHAPTER 41

"I really appreciate your expertise," Henry said, holding the oil lamp out in front of him. As Henry led the way through the attic, Samuel did not have a good feeling. Over the last few weeks, whenever he entered the house to meet with Henry, he heard rumors about a demon, a possession. However, as soon as he got close enough to hear, the servants became silent. He had no idea what Henry wanted him to witness or examine, but his gut told him it had to do with Charlotte.

Henry's request was as ominous as their long walk through the windowless attic. Samuel was certain he saw two windows from the main drive below, but where they were walking was completely dark except for the light of their oil lamp. His eyes did a quick inventory. To the left, was a wide-open space filled with furniture including the dining table and chairs from the carriage house. On the right, were trunks, luggage, and crates. Where were the two windows? When they arrived at a door, Henry came to a dead stop.

"I am prevailing upon you for the utmost secrecy. I've not told a soul except for my daughter...and Mr. Twitterly."

The door and its walls looked relatively new. The scent of fresh plaster, paint, and new lumber lingered in the musty air.

"Of course," Samuel replied.

Henry gripped Samuel's shoulder with a weak smile. A woman's moan slipped from beneath the door. Henry finagled the key into the hole, closed his eyes, took a deep breath, twisted the key, then eased the door open. The space was eerily silent. Henry stepped inside and then waved Samuel to follow him. From the first glimpse of furniture, Samuel knew it was a bedroom. Samuel found the two windows, but they were boarded up. No light allowed in or out.

"This is Nurse Gerta," Henry said nervously.

nurse promptly stood up. She was barrel shaped with a permanent scowl etched on her face.

"Mr. Denninks, *guten tag*," the nurse said with a heavy German accent. She quickly stood next to her chair with her chin lifted like a soldier on duty. Her blue eyes locked on Samuel.

In the shadows of the darkness, Samuel saw a narrow poster bed. It's canopy and its curtains were not the usual elegant light sheers. The material was plain and heavy, designed to conceal its occupant.

"Mr. Chase is kind of a specialist. He's here to see if he can find the problem. Please draw the bed curtains."

"But if he is not a doctor, how can he help?"

"Nurse Gerta, you work for me. Draw the curtains!" Henry ordered.

Nurse Gerta's nose flared like an angry horse. She yanked open the curtain panels on the side of the bed, then secured them to the posts. Samuel felt his breath leave his body when his eyes locked on the woman sitting in a catatonic trance on a bed.

"Is that Mrs. Dennings?"

Charlotte's face held a deranged countenance. Her normal coiffed mound of tight curls looked like a tangled mane around her face.

"Mr. Denninks, if I knew you were bringing company, I would have battled with her to do her hair," Gerta said flatly.

"What happened to her?"

"Whatever is wrong with her is tied to these drawings she did. I thought with your export background in foreign art, you might know if the drawings have any meaning."

Samuel took Henry's lamp and lifted it to see the drawings. The walls nearest the bed were covered in crude charcoal drawings. They all looked like dragons, bats, or cats with wings. He put the lamp on Charlotte and noticed the palms of her hands and fingertips were black from charcoal. Her ashen face and parts of her body and dress bore smudges of charcoal. She looked like a crazed beggar woman.

"Charlotte did these drawings?" Samuel asked Gerta.

"Ja. Every day when she is awake, she does these pictures on the walls. It is the only thing that quiets her, so I let her draw on the walls. I tell Mr. Denninks he will have to whitewash this wall many times. This will never wash off," Gerta defended.

"Gerta, I told you I don't care about the damn walls!. Samuel, I'm sorry. This has been very difficult. Before I was forced to move her up here, I had several doctors, and a specialist in psychiatry, examine her. That was before all the artwork on the walls. All of them took one look at her and wanted to send her down to the Philadelphia Hospital for the insane but..." The rest of Henry's words lodged in the back of his throat. "...but I couldn't bear to do that to her. This is all my fault."

"You're not responsible for this."

"Of course, I am. I'm sure it won't surprise you that Charlotte and I haven't been very compatible for a while. Once upon a time, there was a wonderful woman inside her...I should have never separated them...Maybe I'm selfish for wanting to hold onto her, and maybe she's already left me, but I can't be heartless. It is not in me to be cold, unfeeling and heartless. I know I shouldn't have separated them."

"Separated Charlotte from who?"

Henry moved away to stroke Charlottes beehive of tangled curls.

"She didn't want to leave..."

"Leave who? Henry, I can't help you unless you tell me."

"Charlotte has family she wanted me to bring with us. We were newly married. I didn't think it appropriate to bring...her family when we were trying to begin a new life together. I should have listened, but it was the right thing to do. It was the only thing to do. You do understand, don't you? Am I being punished for what I did? Has Charlotte been cursed, or has she just gone mad from being separated?" His cheeks glistened from his tears.

"Henry, if it will help Charlotte to feel better, bring her family here..."

"No! You don't understand. Please give me another solution."

"Henry, I'm not a physician or a psychiatrist."

Henry pulled Samuel out of earshot of the nurse.

"Your father mentioned at your dinner party that you received special training in the far east," Henry said in a husky whisper.

"Yes, and I am using it to train your men to protect your businesses," Samuel defended.

"Samuel, your father wasn't referring to your fighting skills. He specifically said you had received training to be in control of the body, the mind...and spirits..." Henry countered.

"Henry, I assure you my father had too much to drink for his thoughts to be clear and his words reliable."

"Your father's mind was crystal clear to me, and I trust his words to be very reliable. Samuel, I beg of you. I have no one else to turn to. Use what you've learned abroad to determine if I should have my wife sent away, or if there is a way for you to reach her and bring her back to me. She shouldn't be punished for what I did. It wasn't her fault," Henry pleaded and then marched over to stand next to Charlotte.

Samuel looked at them. Henry looked like a soldier and Charlotte, a fallen comrade. She sat on the bed with her legs outstretched and her blackened hands lying limp in her lap like a rag doll.

His teachers warned him about using his abilities to help others, who may not understand. The consequences of misunderstanding his special gift could result in a witch hunt. He and Elizabeth had seven months before there would be plenty of money for them to buy their own home, and the baby was due to arrive in five. He couldn't move Elizabeth now. The painful desperation on Henry's face tugged hard on his heart. He couldn't continue working for Henry and not help him. That would be callous and inhumane.

"I can't promise you anything, but I will try my best," Samuel replied.

Samuel approached Charlotte and gently turned her face to look into her listless eyes. Charlotte's rich emerald green eyes that were once bright and sparkled with self-serving determination were gone.

"I can't examine her like this. I'd like to put her in a chair. Can she sit up?"

"Ja," Gerta said.

Samuel lifted Gerta's chair and moved it closer to the bed. He then slipped his arms under Charlotte's knees and back to lift her. Charlotte's stale breath made him turn his head to the foot of her bed. What he saw on the inside of her curtains made him freeze, and quickly withdraw.

"What? What is it?" Henry asked.

"When did Mrs. Dennings start to...change?" Samuel asked.

"The night she came back from her trip."

"Trip?"

"Yes. It was a while ago. The night she barged in on your dinner party, she had just returned from a shopping trip."

"Where?"

"Philadelphia. Do you think something happened in Philadelphia?"

Samuel leaned inside of the canopy of curtains to look at the crude painting on the inside curtain at the foot of the bed. It wasn't a bat or winged creature like the others. Samuel's eyes followed the black lines of the half human, half lion, figure on the curtain. His heart began to race. When he saw the spear, he knew it was Malachai! His stomach did a somersault. Blood scorched his face and the tips of his ears. Without much detail, Charlotte had captured Malachai's malicious essence. Samuel went to the foot of the bed and ripped the painted curtain down, pulling the crossbar down with it.

"Burn this," Samuel instructed, thrusting the panel of curtains into Henry's hands.

Henry opened the curtain to examine it.

"My God, what the hell is this?" Henry demanded.

"Pure evil. Whatever Charlotte went to Philadelphia to buy, she bought more than she bargained for."

CHAPTER 42

"Malachai is in that house across the courtyard from us and our child!" Elizabeth yelled.

Her fear was replaced by rage. Her arms embraced her extending stomach to protect their baby from the news Samuel just shared. She wanted to pack her trunks and run, but she didn't know where she could go. There was no escaping Malachai. It would be a matter of time before he would find her again.

"I didn't want to tell you, but we promised each other we would never keep secrets," Samuel said.

"I wished to God this was one secret you hadn't shared. You said you stopped him," Elizabeth shot back.

"He's found another way to reach you. I won't let him near you or our baby."

"Please, don't make promises you can't keep. Malachai can come through anyone."

"Why would he want Charlotte?"

"Or maybe Charlotte wanted him to hurt me because I know about her twin sister."

"Charlotte has a twin sister?"

"Yes," Elizabeth answered and pressed her lips together.

She didn't dare say more. Malachai's constant threat to her own peace was a good reminder of what it feels like to have someone have power over your life. No matter how many secrets she was able to see about others, meddling and controlling them was not what she wanted. She desperately wanted to be in control of her own life.

"If I had known that bit of information, I could have handled today's incident differently," Samuel remarked.

"I'm sorry. I wasn't trying to keep a secret from you. I said nothing because I didn't want to meddle."

"You mustn't be sorry. It's not your fault. You didn't send Charlotte to Philadelphia."

"I hope you didn't tell Henry that you knew Malachai. He'll blame you for Charlotte's state, and fire you for bringing Malachai to his home," Elizabeth cried.

"No, of course not. I merely said the painting she did was of an evil nature and that he should burn it. Henry believes his separating Charlotte from her twin sister is the cause of her delirium. He has no idea who Malachai is."

"Samuel..." Elizabeth whimpered. Samuel opened his arms to embrace her. She fell against him.

"Elizabeth, you didn't send Charlotte to Philadelphia. She went on her own volition. She went with the intention of hurting you. Whatever Charlotte was planning, obviously backfired."

"Samuel, our baby...No. I won't allow it!" Elizabeth declared as she pushed away from Samuel. "I won't allow Malachai back into our lives. Samuel, we have to fight. We have to find a way to fight all this hatred so that we can live in peace. I can't bring our child into this. I can't live another day like this," Elizabeth declared with a stomp of her foot and a raised fist.

"Nadya said Malachai was a *Muló*, the living dead. She said he wanted something I had or something he believed I took from him."

"Did she say how you could stop him?"

"No. Franz showed up and brought me back to you. If I knew what I took, I'd happily give it back," Elizabeth offered. She paced in a small circle and then turned to go to the kitchen. The reflection of the outside sun in the small wall mirror sent a flash of light into her eyes, blinding her. At that moment she saw all the mirrors hanging on sticks surrounding the Gypsy camp. Her eyes met Samuel's.

"Mirrors!" She exclaimed. "Samuel, when I was at the Gypsy camp, they had mirrors hanging from sticks on the edge of their little camp. Andrej said the mirrors were used to..."

"Block evil forces."

"How do you know about the mirrors?"

"When I was in Peking I was taught that mirrors can be used to reflect, deflect, and create an illusion. It's all about what the mind thinks it's seeing. You said your father told you that racism is a projection of self-hatred. Then that's what we have to do; reflect Malachai's projection of hatred back him using a mirror."

"Andrej said we can put the intention of our thoughts into the mirrors."

"Yes, it's called transference."

"Yes, but how can we use mirrors? We can't put mirrors around the carriage house."

"We'll put the mirrors around his house,"

"What?"

"I'll go back to his camp."

"No. You're not leaving me. Teach me what you know, so I can go with you," Elizabeth demanded.

"It took me years to learn how to do what I do. I can't teach you how to leave your body, especially since you are carrying our child."

"Leave your body? Leave your body and go where? Into Malachai's hellish lair? I won't allow it!"

"I've gone there before."

"You went when he didn't expect you. You had the upper hand. If he has found Charlotte, he has something planned. If you go alone, you'll walk right into his trap."

"He won't be alone."

Before Elizabeth could turn around, the familiar sweet scent of pine found Elizabeth's nose. Samuel's mouth hung open. Elizabeth could feel the heat of a good fire against her back, except their fireplace was cold. Elizabeth turned around and saw Wakayeja wicahpe and two other Native Americans standing with her. Their presence was more than an eyeful.

"Puuuhhhhhhhhhhh!"

297

CHAPTER 43

Elizabeth didn't know which one to look at first. The tallest one was wide like a grizzly bear. On top of his head was a bear's head. Around his massive chest was a necklace of what looked like a ring of bear claws. Just above his heart was the large tattoo of a bear's paw. Elizabeth's eyes scrolled down to his feet. He was bigger than Franz. But when she looked into his eyes, underneath his painted face, she saw the soul of a child staring back at her.

The other Native American was incredibly handsome and wore no face paint. His hair popped up in the center of his head like the quills of a porcupine, while the rest of his jet-black hair rested on his shoulders. He released a small grunt and lifted his chin. The larger Native American approached them. The house shook with his every step. His broad shoulders swayed side to side. In two giant strides, he was towering over them.

"Don't move," Samuel warned Elizabeth.

He sniffed the tops of their heads and then stepped back.

"*Black bird,*" he said to Samuel. His deep growling voice rumbled across their wood floors.

"Yes, black bird," Samuel responded with a nervous smile.

"*Black bird good, but eagle better,*" he grumbled and then offered them a childlike smile.

Wakayeja wicahpe's face popped out from behind the large bear of a man.

"*I bring you help. This is Standing Bear,*" she said with a smile.

"*Bear bigger than black bird,*" Standing Bear said smacking his chest with the palm of his large hand. He then stepped aside and pointed to the other Native American. "*Wanbli Luta!*" he announced.

298

Wanbli Luta approached. A little pouch around his neck swayed with each step. His bronze chest was taut, muscular, and bore a distinct wound over his heart. A bright red streak of red paint ran the length of each of his arms. As he came closer, Elizabeth saw how peaceful his face was. He offered them no smile or grimace. Wanbli Luta came to a halt in front of her. His eyes locked on hers and then entered her soul. He was viewing her secrets like she had done to others.

"This is Wanbli Luta. Chief Red Eagle in your language," **Wakayeja wicahpe explained.**

"Red Eagle–bigger bird," Standing Bear declared as he gave them a hard nod and crossed his large arms.

"Mitakuye Oyasin," Red Eagle said. He gestured an invisible circle around them. *"Mitakuye Oyasin."*

"Mitakuye Oyasin," Samuel said, repeating Red Eagle's circular gesture.

Red Eagle held up one finger.

"One?" Samuel asked.

Red Eagle grunted in agreement,

"Mitakuye Oyasin," Red Eagle said creating a circle around them.

"We are one?" Samuel asked.

Red Eagle nodded.

***

Despite the language barrier, Elizabeth and Samuel were able to communicate perfectly with the Chief, the warrior, and Wakayeja wicahpe, their Shaman. Standing Bear used sign language, Red Eagle spoke only Lakota and Wakayeja wicahpe was the interpreter for both. From the tenor of their conversation, Elizabeth believed all three to be patient teachers of the workings of the human soul and life's tribulations in the physical world. They all sat together in front of the fireplace taking turns talking, explaining, and listening to each other. It was an effortless meeting of the minds.

Before they realized it, their house was completely dark except for the glow of the fire. The day had ended. Elizabeth had no idea of what time it was, nor did she care. She didn't want to move. She wanted to stay in this new place they found themselves: a place where the spirit world collided with the physical world. It was a place where she and Simon

299

were immediately welcomed. It was home.

Elizabeth wondered what their little ghostly pow wow looked like to the outside world. Did the view from outside of their cavernous window show her in a chair and Samuel on the floor appearing to talk to each other? Or had they vanished into Wakayeja wicahpe's world without realizing. She didn't dare turn around to look outside. She was part of a beautiful synergy of minds and cultures from the physical world and beyond. This moment, these people, this fire was all that mattered.

Elizabeth studied the glow of the fire on her husband's face. He was far more handsome in this moment than any moment she could remember. The charisma he exuded was not because of his physical looks, it was Samuel's profound wisdom. Samuel shared his perspective on life, his life in a place he called the Shaolin Monastery, and in the remote mountains of a place called Dharamshala, India.

It was the first time Samuel ever spoke at great length about his life. Red Eagle and Standing Bear listened intently. Samuel's stories of Monks walking on water, and people he called Yogis who could levitate their bodies and make objects appear out of thin air, made the Monastery and Dharamshala sound like magical places she hoped he would take her to one day. Samuel was not limited by any religion. She would have believed Samuel to be a spirit had she not been able to touch him. Despite Malachai rearing his ugly evil head, she was strangely happy.

Red Eagle cleared his throat to announce he was prepared to talk again. His Lakota language was rhythmical and soft to the ear, and his presence was peaceful yet majestic. Elizabeth saw why he was a chief when he was in the physical world. There was something about him that made her want to grab and cherish his every word.

"Before the White man, it was tribe against tribe..," *Wakayeja wicahpe translated.* Red Eagle waited politely for Wakayeja wicahpe to finish and then spoke more. The softness in his voice emoted the pain in his heart. *"We fought the Pawnee, the Chippewa, the Ponca, and shamefully too many more to keep in my mind and in my heart. That's where the real hatred began,"* Wakayeja wicahpe said. Red Eagle shook his head solemnly.

Standing Bear made gestures with his hands. His right fist came down into the palm of his left hand to emphasize his point.

"So much waste killing each other," Wakayeja wicahpe translated.

300

"We have wars too. White man against White man and White man against Negroes, White man against Indian," Samuel added. Wakayeja wicahpe quickly translated.

Red Eagle, Standing Bear, and Wakayeja wicahpe nodded in agreement. Red Eagle raised a finger to announce he was prepared to speak again.

"So, when we fought ourselves...our own people...and fired our hateful arrows at each other..." Wakayeja wicahpe translated.

Red Eagle stopped. Wakayeja wicahpe looked away to allow him privacy. His chest heaved with emotion. His finger lifted again.

"....we made way for White soldiers to come and make more anger between us...Soon White soldiers used Pawnee to track my people...The White soldiers used the hatred each tribe had for the other to the White soldier advantage... We failed to see ourselves in each other. Our own hatred of each other did us in. This is what I have learned."

The truth of Red Eagle's words felt like rocks pelting her body. Elizabeth gained a deeper understanding of racism, and it was a painful one. Self-hatred was at the root of it. Red Eagle began speaking again without warning. Wakayeja wicahpe translated as quickly as he spoke.

"Just like our tribes fought amongst each other...so did the dark man's...They enslaved each other tribes and sold them into slavery to White men in big boats...soon the White men realized they didn't need another dark tribe to get them slaves...they could make slaves of everyone with skin like the night...All this self-hatred is like running buffalo...If we don't stop and recognize each other as...as...another part of ourselves, we won't be able to get out of the way...we will be underfoot, we will be trampled...deep into the ground as though we never existed."

Red Eagle punctuated the end of his speech with an angry grunt and a snort of air, which pushed the flames of the fires against the back of the fireplace wall. Everyone sat in solemn silence, nodding their heads in agreement.

"Red Eagle, Samuel want to help our people. They are slaves to White men who consider themselves the master of all men. How can we help them when we appear, in their eyes, like the very people who enslave them? They will not trust the color of our skin. Is there another way?"

301

Wakayeja wicahpe quickly translated. Red Eagle gazed into the fire as he listened intently. When Wakayeja wicahpe was done, they sat in silence waiting for his response. Elizabeth felt a familiar stillness as they sat and stared into the fire. It was as though she had done this before.

"Hmmm," Red Eagle grunted with a nod of his head. "Forgiveness is all that is left."

The bear head on Standing Bear's moved with his nod. Wakayeja wicahpe, wiped a tear.

"Forgiveness is harder than love, and you will need both. You must look to Great Spirit to grant you a big...supply," Red Eagle concluded.

"You speak English?" Samuel asked.

Red Eagle nodded yes and kept his eyes on the fire.

"Why didn't you just speak English to us?" Elizabeth asked.

"Why don't you speak Lakota?" Red Eagle replied with a smile and then stood up.

"Please, don't leave. I'm sorry if my question offended you."

"Questions do not chase me away," Red Eagle snorted.

"But you're leaving. I thought you came to help us stop Malachai."

"We were hoping you and Standing Bear would help us," Samuel added.

"You don't need warriors, you need a Shaman. I will go with you," Wakayeja wicahpe said.

Red Eagle's head recoiled as though he had been slapped. He erupted into Lakota, directing his words at Wakayeja wicahpe. They argued in Lakota briefly. Red Eagle's hand sliced horizontally across the air as his eyes widened from anger. He was adamant that Wakayeja wicahpe not go.

Elizabeth saw a flash of light pop between the two. In the bubble of light Wakayeja wicahpe and Red Eagle were standing by a lake. Their bodies were entwined beneath a buffalo hide. They were husband and wife. When the bubble of light popped, Elizabeth saw Wakayeja wicahpe's hands were curled into fists. She stomped her foot with her last words to him. Standing Bear's eyes widened from shock.

"He doesn't want me to go with you Samuel because he knows the history between Malachai and me, but he also knows that is why I must go."

"You know Malachai?" Samuel asked.

"Yes."

"Is that why you were able to get Malachai to chase after you that night in the Amos' cornfield?" Elizabeth asked.

"He looks for me.".

The last Lakota words Red Eagle spoke left Wakayeja wicahpe teary-eyed. He then faded before them.

"Go with him. You're too big and would be easily seen where we have to go," Wakayeja wicahpe instructed Standing Bear. As he turned to leave, he disappeared mid-step. *"Samuel, before we do this, you must eat. Your body must be as strong as your mind,"* Wakayeja wicahpe instructed. *"In Malachai's world, we must use our thoughts to battle his hatred. Know that what we think, we create. Our thoughts and intentions are powerful weapons there."*

"What if Malachai has a destructive thought. Won't it harm you and my husband?" Elizabeth asked, grabbing Samuel's hand.

"No, he cannot harm us. He does not know about this power yet. Samuel, you will be able to hear and know my thoughts. Focus on only what I share with you in thought and we will defeat him. Now eat, and I will return."

"Wait! Wakayeja wicahpe, a long time ago you asked me if I remembered you. Is that because we shared a life together?" Elizabeth asked.

"We shared many lifetimes together," Wakayeja wicahpe explained.

"Many lifetimes? I don't understand. When? How?" Elizabeth asked.

"Not now," Wakayeja wicahpe said as she walked into the fire and disappeared.

"Aaaaeeeeeiiiiii!" Charlotte's shriek filled the courtyard. A blast of wind came down the flue and parted the fire's flames. Elizabeth looked at Samuel.

"Samuel, what is a Shaman?"

"In this case, a woman who communicates with the spirit world to provide healing and guidance. She is a holy person."

"Is that why she can come back and forth like she does?"

"Elizabeth, is she really going back and forth as you say, or is there another level of life that you can see and others cannot?"

"Samuel, I don't believe that's possible."

303

"You see, but don't believe; that can be a problem. But, she's right. Now is not the time for this discussion. I must prepare. I promise I will explain it to you when I return."

"But what if you don't return?" Elizabeth asked with tears in her eyes.

Samuel held her face in his hands.

"Think only of what you want and not what you fear. I shall return before sunrise," he said and kissed her lips. The heat of the fire melded their bodies and she felt his heart pounding against hers. It was the first time she felt his fear.

CHAPTER 44

Scrreeep! Scrreeep! Scrreeep!

Malachai was closer to him than ever before. Thanks to that green-eyed woman he would be able to enter his life undetected and kill him, so he can bring his family and people back home and never worry again about them being stolen by the pale people across the water. There was no hiding behind skin. The thief could not hide in a woman's body or disguise his cowardice with female frailty. Malachai would never forget the eyes of the soul of the man who stole his sister.

"Now he will know what it feels like to look into the eyes of death. Now he will know what it feels like to be enslaved!" Malachai spoke with the rhythm of his movement.

With the spirit of Jatoo Jinoo and the spirit of the panther, he named Kori, Malachai believed he was an unbeatable force. He chose the name Kori because he believed the spirit of the panther would provide him and his people new hope for regeneration. Killing the panther gave him the power to populate his village again.

Malachai insured the panther's procreation power by carefully removing its scrotum and placing it in a small pouch made of the panther's pelt. He tied the pouch to a cord around his waist that held a flap of water buffalo hide used to shield his manhood from curses and evil eyes. He felt complete. He had the fierceness of a warrior and the powerful loin of Kori. With his seed, he would replenish his barren village with great warriors that would go across the waters and bring his family and people home!

305

Scrreeep! Scrreeep! Scrreeep!

The pale green-eyed woman was weakening nicely. His nightly visits to her world were breaking down her mind. Soon he could control her fragile mind and use her pale hands to kill his enemy. Once the metal chest warrior was gone, he would be safe to free his sister.

Scrreeep! Scrreeep! Scrreeep!

One final pass across the edge of his spear and he was ready. Malachai lifted his spear into a throwing stance. He bounced the spear in his hand a few times to check its balance, and then turned and launched it at a tree. The spear went through the tree without a sound.

"I am the greatest Mandinka warrior and the father of my people!" His words echoed into the jungle for a moment and then disappeared. He listened patiently for a voice to acknowledge his declaration, but only the wind responded as it lifted his water buffalo flap. He was alone.

CHAPTER 45

Wakayeja wicahpe stood before Elizabeth and Samuel. Her normal smiling face was solemn and serious. Even the glow of her skin was softer. The stillness in the air was ominous. Elizabeth didn't want Samuel to go.

"You must keep the fire going. Do not let it go out. Understand?" Wakayeja wicahpe instructed Elizabeth.

"The fire will be our light back," she told Samuel. "Look for fire there and fire here."

Samuel approached Elizabeth and pulled her in for a tight hug. Shirtless, his heart pounded against hers.

"You come back to me, Samuel Chase," Elizabeth said. One tear escaped from her eye and Samuel kissed her cheek to capture it.

"No matter what, don't touch me. No matter what I say or look like, you mustn't touch me," Samuel urged.

"You must listen to him."

"Why can't you go, and leave Samuel here? Why can't you take that monster away from us? You're the only one that seems to know him," Elizabeth said.

"I'm not the only who knows him. You know him, too. You just don't remember—yet"

"Then tell me so we can finish this madness."

"That is not how it works. Telling you would be cheating. Your free will must release the information, the memory. I cannot."

"I'll be back. I promise," Samuel said and pressed his lips on Elizabeth's one last time. He sat on the floor in front of the fireplace and looked up to Wakayeja wicahpe and nodded.

Wakayeja wicahpe's thumb pulled on the gold cord that was around her neck and lifted her large pink heart-shaped stone from beneath her dress.

"We live in three worlds: the physical, love, and fear. Only love can enter all realms," Wakayeja wicahpe declared.

A burst of light emitted from the pink heart, lighting up the face of their fireplace. Inside the light, Elizabeth saw an iridescent looking darkness.

"Come when you are ready. Remember to focus only on love." Wakayeja wicahpe stepped into the darkness.

Samuel reached for Elizabeth's hand one last time. She looked into his eyes. He nodded, then released her hand.

"Keep the fire going for me," he said and closed his eyes.

"Om ma ni pad me hum..." Samuel began. His voice was like a deep growl. He took three deep breaths and released a gut growling chant,

"Ommanipademehumommanipademehum
Ommanipademehumommanipademehum
Ommanipademehumommanipademehum
Ommanipademehumommanipademehum
Ommanipademehumommanipademehum..."

As Samuel chanted, Elizabeth's body began to tremble. The small glass bric-a-brac on the side table in the seating area began to vibrate and dance across the table. The fire's flames leapt upward. Elizabeth sat in the chair next to Samuel and gripped its arms to avoid touching him. The vibrations emanating from his words rumbled across the floor tickling her stocking feet.

Samuel said his words faster and the growl of his chant deepened until she couldn't recognize what he was saying. A small gust of wind blew past her sucking the flames of the fire upward into the chimney. She saw a ghostly image of Samuel as he looked over his shoulder, smiled at her, and then step into the fireplace.

A thin white silvery line extended from Samuel's ghostly image back to his body. The silvery line looked like the long finger of a cloud. One end of the silvery rope disappeared up the chimney. The other end was still connected to Samuel. She lifted her hand to touch it, but Samuel stopped chanting. The silvery rope between Samuel's essence and his physical body undulated in the air like a wave of water.

Elizabeth looked down at Samuel's chest, it wasn't moving. She wanted to touch him to make sure he was alive but heeded his earlier warning. Her eyes looked at the fire in the fireplace. Its flame was dying. She quickly tossed a piece of wood onto the fire and got the bellows. Kneeling on the stone hearth, she fanned the flames. Samuel and Wakayeja wicahpe warned had her not to let the fire go out.

As she pumped the bellows, her eye monitored the silvery white rope that remained connected to Samuel. She wondered if the silvery vaporous rope is what Samuel would use to find his way home. Would he grab hold and tug on it until it brought him back to his body? She didn't dare touch it or pass through it. She added another log to the fire and pumped the bellows until the fire grew hot enough to roast her face.

CHAPTER 46

The hot glow from their fireplace could be seen through a tunnel-like corridor. When Samuel looked back, he saw Elizabeth's small shadow move up and down as she fanned the flames of the fire.

He moved through the jungle quickly. The dense brush made it difficult to move undetected. He slowed his steps and crouched down. Malachai knew who he was now. He had no doubt Malachai would try to launch his spear right through his heart.

Samuel's eyes shifted left and then right. He tried to find the outline of Wakayeja wicahpe's body amidst the foliage. He hoped they were in the same vicinity. He had never traveled with another being before. Astral travel was all about thought. Thought created placement. If he and Wakayeja wicahpe didn't share the same thought or vision, they could end up in different spectrums of Malachai's world.

Wakayeja wicahpe instructed him to focus on Malachai's campfire. He hunched down, closed his eyes, and immediately smelled Malachai's familiar stench. When he opened his eyes, he was at Malachai's campfire. A gentle touch on his shoulder announced Wakayeja wicahpe's presence. She brought a finger to her lips to silence him. She shared a vision of their plan telepathically.

Samuel's eyes widened. There was more to Wakayeja wicahpe than he realized.

Wakayeja wicahpe stood up and moved away from him. As she moved through the brush into Malachai's camp clearing, he

310

watched the first part of her plan unfold.

"Malachai," Wakayeja wicahpe said.

Malachai's mouth dropped open. Tears filled his eyes.

"Nyima? Nyima, is it really you?"

"Yes," she opened her arms and he ran into them.

"I cannot believe my eyes," Malachai murmured. "You look the same. As though there has been no passing of time. Am I dreaming?"

"No," she responded.

"It is so good to see you," Malachai whimpered through tears as he embraced her. "I thought I should never see you again. You're free."

"Yes," she said softly.

"Thanks be to the heavens! I was so afraid the soldier stole you and carried you across the water with the others," Malachai said. "The whole village of our people is gone. I am the only one left. I killed Jatoo Jinoo!" He declared pulling on his cape of lion hide. And I killed Kori, the big black cat. Now our family will be rich with warriors who command the best women everywhere! Together, you and I can fight to bring back our people, find our mother, find our father..."

She moved away from him. Seeing her brother was harder than she thought. Even with all the love she had to offer, his sadness, pain, and despair were overwhelming.

"...Nyima...what is wrong? Are our parents still alive?" Malachai asked.

When she turned to face him, he was leaning on his spear for support.

"Our parents are in a better place," she responded.

Malachai's eyes filled with tears.

"And the rest of village, are they all gone too?" Malachai asked, wiping a tear.

"Yes."

"How is that so? How can a whole village of people disappear like it never existed? How can people come into our world and take us?" His tearful face suddenly became serious. "How did you get free from the metal chest soldier? I saw him take you. I killed the

Jatoo Jinoo, and then I saw the metal chest soldier pull you through the bush. That was the last time I saw you. How did you get free and everybody else in our village did not?"

"Malachai, I am your sister, and I would never lie to you. Yes, you saw me leave the village with Adao because the soldiers were after us..."

"Who's Adao?"

"The name of the soldier who was helping me escape."

"No, I saw with my own eyes. He pulled you away...he was stealing you...why would he help you?" Malachai's eyes turned dark and unwelcoming.

"The soldiers found out about us."

"Tell me what you mean."

"Adao and I were lovers."

"That is not possible. Those metal-chest men steal our people," Malachai protested.

"The others yes, but not this one. He came to warn me, to warn our people that the soldiers were coming so we could get away, hide in the jungle until the boat left, but the soldiers found us together and chased us. That is when you saw us. We were running..."

"No!"

"I wanted to tell you I was safe, but I was afraid that you would kill Adao. He was only trying to help me. Not all the soldiers were bad."

"No! You allow the pale skins to try to kill your brother? I am your blood!"

The jungle shook with his voice. The shock wave of Malachai's anger cracked the dry earth between them. She tried to go to him.

"Malachai..."

Malachai drew his spear and pointed it at her.

"Did you bring this Adao back to take me?"

"No, Adao's gone. Everyone's gone. There are no more metal-chest soldiers."

"Did our people kill them?"

"No," Nyima answered.

"Then what happened to everyone? Where are our people?

Where are my parents?" Malachai cried.

"They are in a new home now. I have come to take you to them. It's time you come home now," Nyima said nervously.

"No, this is home!" Malachai declared thumping the butt of his spear into the ground. "This is home. Nowhere else!" He stomped his foot. "Graaawwwww!"

"This is not home!" She took a deep breath. She wanted to maintain control. Conveying anger in Malachai's world would only weaken her and taint her own energy. "Malachai, this is not home. Don't you see you are here alone?"

"I am not alone. I have Jatoo Jinoo and Kori. You are here," he added.

"But I cannot stay here. Neither should you. Let me take you home. Our parents miss you." She took two steps toward him and he angled his spear at her, pushing her back.

"How can I believe you? You betrayed me, your own brother, to hold hands with Adao. I think you want to give me to your precious Adao for kodicoroosoos! You'd trade your own blood for gold kodicoroosoos!"

"Malachai, no... I could never hurt you. I never meant to hurt you. Adao and I, through a miracle from the heavens found love even though our people were at war. The difference in the color of their skin did not make them all bad. We had tribes with the same color skin as us, who were equally treacherous. It is not the color of one's skin that makes someone bad, evil, or unworthy. It is the content of one's heart that determines their true nature and value. Brother, hear my heart. Not everything we don't know is bad. Just like not everything we do know is good..."

"Buwaa!" Malachai roared at her across his fire. "Adao has made you a Buwaa! Only a Buwaa would come to Malachai and trick him into surrendering. I will continue to fight for my people. I will fight every Adao until my people have been returned."

"Malachai, I'm not a witch. There is no one here left to fight. I've come with love to ask you to stop this war," Nyima pleaded.

"This war will never end until everything is put back. I want to see my father, my mother, and my friends. I want my village where I was born alive with laughter again. Until then, I will make war on

313

all metal chest soldiers and all pale skin. I will not let the pale skin take our people to treat them worse than a goat! Pale skin and dark hands will never join. I will fight them until they no longer breathe! I am Malachai, Mandinka warrior and now chief of our village!" He proclaimed raising his spear. "Graaawwwww!"

"I am so sorry my brother." A flash of light blinded him. When he regained his sight, Wakayeja wicahpe and Samuel stood before him.

"Buwaa what have you done with Nyima!"

"I am Nyima," Wakayeja wicahpe said.

Wakayeja wicahpe's morphed back into Nyima and then back to Wakayeja wicahpe.

"You are Buwaa!" Malachai yelled. "You worship this devil and bring him to my home!" Malachai launched his spear at Samuel.

Samuel hands went up in front of him and directed the spear into a nearby tree.

"Listen to your sister," Samuel warned.

"Buwaa! I will fight you all until you draw no breath!"

"Malachai, you must listen. Come with me now. Leave this place, leave this hatred behind," Wakayeja wicahpe pleaded.

"My hatred for you and your pale skin devil will never die."

"You have to tell him, or I will," Samuel said.

"You cannot tell me what I can already see. You hold hands with this pale devil that steals your people..."

"Malachai our village still exists...There are still people in our village..."

"You lie buwaa! I would see people like I see you."

"No, you won't. You won't see them here, but I can take you to a new home so you can live again."

"I am already living."

Samuel looked at Wakayeja wicahpe.

"That day you killed the lion...I saw a soldier kill you..." Wakayeja wicahpe said. "The soldier shot you once in the chest. Look at your chest where your heart is, you'll find a wound that has not healed and cannot heal here. You must come with me. Let me take you home."

Malachai lifted his lion's cape and examined his chest. He put

314

his finger in a hole just above his left nipple and stumbled back. His eyes widened with shock and fear. He looked at Wakayeja wicahpe and then to Samuel.

"You shot me..." Malachai declared, pointing to Samuel.

"I didn't shoot you. You died a very long time ago, but you just didn't know it," Samuel said.

"Malachai, you're dead. That's why there's no one here. There's only you. Please brother, come with me. Let me take you home. Leave this hatred." Wakayeja wicahpe extended an opened hand.

Malachai opened his mouth and released a silent cry. The trees and vegetation rustled, echoing his pain. He dropped to his knees clutching his wound.

"Graaww, graawww, graaawwwww!" He jumped to his feet.

"I am Malachai—Mandinka warrior and Chief! I will fight you until you draw your last breath!"

"Is fighting all that you wish?" Wakayeja wicahpe shot back.

"Fighting is all that I know," Malachai growled.

"Then we will leave you to your fight," Wakayeja wicahpe said.

"Graaawwwww!" Malachai released an earth-shaking battle cry. He quickly turned and withdrew his spear from the tree, but Samuel and Wakayeja wicahpe were gone. He was surrounded by a frightening image of a scrawny thirteen-year-old boy weighed down by the weight of a lion's hide.

"Buwaa!" Malachai yelled. He chucked his spear at one of the images of himself. The spear bounced off the mirror, pierced his stomach, and then fell to the ground. He felt the pain of his own anger.

Holding his stomach, he picked up his spear again. Everywhere he turned he saw his scrawny child-like self. He launched his spear again. His spear struck the image of his leg in another mirror. He howled and grabbed his left leg.

With a hobbling run, he slammed his body against a mirror hoping to break through. The force propelled him backward, knocking him down. He got up, gripped his spear.

"Graaawwwwww!"

Malachai moved in a circle looking at his pitiful image.

"Graaww...graaww...graa..."

315

"Graaawwwww!"

His chest heaved from Nyima's betrayal. He dropped, crossed legged, onto his bottom, buried his face in the well of his knees, and bawled like a little boy.

CHAPTER 47

Running down Ferry Road Elizabeth saw the wagon just ahead. The silhouette of Simon, Belinda and Willie's bodies bounced about as the wagon careened down the hill. All of sudden she was flying above Ferry Road. She lifted herself into the air just above the trees. Looking down she could see Belinda holding Willie. She was getting closer. She opened her mouth to call out to Simon.

"Qua qua! Qua qua qua."

She was crowing. Elizabeth looked at her arms which were now large black wings. Her bird form shocked her and sent her into a downward spiral. The bough of a pine tree broke her fall. Her feet quickly clamped on to a branch to steady herself, which bobbed from her weight.

"Qua qua! Qua qua!" she squawked.

"Elizabeth, would you come down from that tree. I'd like to talk to you."

Elizabeth looked down and her eyes blinked several times before she was able to focus and see her father.

"Qua qua qua!" she crowed. Her wings flapped and she felt herself dropping downward. She landed on his shoulder. She squawked excitedly in his ear gripping his shoulder with her feet.

"It's time to move on Elizabeth. You can't stay on this road for the rest of your life wondering if you did the right thing or not. Simon and Willie will make the best of their lives and so will you, but you've got to let go.

"Qua qua qua qua!"

"I'm sorry I had to make you a bird, but this is my dream, so

317

you can be whatever I perceive you to be. I thought it would be helpful if you saw life from a different perspective. You've been so focused on what you lost that you can't see all the love you have. Time changes us. If you were to meet Simon today, tomorrow, next week, or next year, he will be different and so will you."

Her father's words were ruffling her feathers. She squawked and pushed out her wings in protest. She continued squawking, sidestepping down her father's right arm to balance on his hand. She couldn't envision letting go of Simon and Willie. Her guilt would not allow her. She flapped her wings and continued squawking.

"For some, seeing is believing. Time to fly," her father said and then swung his hand upward launching her into the air.

"Make her whole," her father called out to her. "Make her whole!"

Instinctively her wings opened, and she began flapping. Within moments she was flying over a place she had never seen before. There was an open field and a dot of a house surrounded by trees. As she soared over the field, she noticed a horse driving a plow into the earth and a man behind it. It was Simon! She dove downward and landed on the horse's back.

"Qua qua! Qua qua!" Elizabeth tried to get his attention.

Simon stopped and looked up at her. She flapped her wings excitedly and danced on the rear of the horse forcing it to do a side-to-side dance to shake her off. She flapped her wings and moved to the horse's harness.

"Bird, what are you doing out here trying to ride my horse?" Simon asked.

He pulled a rag from his pocket and blotted the sweat from his brow.

"Go on now, I got to plow my field. Go find a field mouse or something," Simon said, flapping his rag at her.

Elizabeth launched off the harness and tried to land on Simon's shoulder. He ducked and flailed his arms at her. Elizabeth landed back on the harness.

"Qua, qua, qua!"

"Simon!" a woman's voice called out. "Simon!" A woman made

318

her way across the field. She was carrying a glass filled with lemonade.

"Belinda!" Simon waved back.

Elizabeth watched as Belinda approached Simon, gave him a peck on the cheek, and then handed him a glass of lemonade.

"Thought you could use something to drink."

"Sure could," Simon said and downed his glass of lemonade.

"Looks like you got yourself a big ol' black bird," Belinda said. "Maybe you can train it to drop seed for you," Belinda said with a smile.

"Don't know why it's here, but it sure looks like it's trying to tell us something," Simon said.

"That there is a magic bird they call a raven," Belinda said. "A raven showing up in your field means a good crop. He'll keep all the crows from scavenging your seed, and rabbits from eating your vegetables. "I think we got ourselves a lucky charm."

Simon slipped his arm around her waist and then drew her in for a kiss.

"I want to thank you," Simon said to her.

"No, I should be the one doing the thanking. I'm very happy."

"I know this isn't how we envisioned our lives turning out..."

"No, it isn't, but I'm happy. I only hope you are."

"I am," he said.

"I'm very happy to be your wife...and Willie's mother. I couldn't be more happy or proud."

Elizabeth watched them in their intimate embrace. They were happy. Simon was happy. He managed to find happiness after she sent him away. Initially, she wished Belinda brought Willie to the field, but realized seeing Willie would have made it too hard for her. Her father was right. It was time to let go. Simon had managed to carve out a life for himself, Willie, and....Belinda. She didn't belong in the picture anymore.

While Belinda's presence in Simon and Willie's life was a surprise to her, it was serendipitous. Belinda couldn't have children, which was why her husband had left her and moved somewhere in Boston. Their initial plan was to deliver her to Boston so she could find him, but fate selected Belinda a new husband. Elizabeth had no doubt Belinda loved and cherished both Simon and Willie. And from the way Simon embraced Belinda, it looked like the feelings were mutual.

All the time she wasted feeling guilty about abandoning Simon and Willie was for naught. God had another plan for them, as he had for her. She was ready to let them go to live their lives and live hers.

Elizabeth watched Simon playfully pull Belinda in for another kiss and some gentle fondling, the same way he used to do with her. Instead of feeling jealousy, she felt relieved. Her head darted around to survey the field. It was nice, but it wasn't the life she wanted for herself. Her little carriage house in the big city in her new "Blue Vein" world was her true home. Samuel's touch, Samuel's kiss is what made her happy. Together they were building a life and a family. Her purpose with Simon and Belinda was complete. She gave them Willie. She gave them a chance at love and freedom. If that was her purpose, she was happy and at peace.

"Simon, stop..." Belinda said coyly as she escaped Simon's grasp. "I got to get back before Willie wakes up from his nap." Belinda took his empty glass.

"I hope you got dinner on the stove because I sho am hungry."

"Oh, I made your dinner, and my special pie." Her right index finger slid down his muscular right arm. She dabbed the sweat from his arm on either side of her neck like perfume.

"Awww shucks woman. You better hurry up and get up out of this dirt, before we're both covered in it," Simon said as he slipped the reins to the plow harness behind his back.

"I'm going to make you a bath. Don't be too long. We don't want your water to get cold." Belinda sashayed down the hill to the house.

Elizabeth hopped down the horse's back and cocked her head to one side to take one last look at Samuel.

"Bird, you're looking at a happy man, a very happy man!"

"Qua, qua, qua..." Elizabeth crowed and then lifted into the air. She felt Simon's eyes on her as she circled once above his head. She was grateful her father showed her Simon's life, but it was time for her to get back to hers. With that thought, Elizabeth heard a

320

familiar shriek that struck her wings like a shotgun blast. She felt herself freefall to the ground below.

***

Charlotte's shriek filled Elizabeth's ears forcing her eyes open. She jumped up from her chair. Her heart thumped hard against her chest. She had fallen asleep. Her eyes immediately looked at Samuel. His body was as it was earlier, sitting upright and deathly still. She got down on her knees and slowly moved the palm of her right hand beneath his nose. Her palm felt a few shallow breaths. He was still breathing.

The fire! She was supposed to keep the fire burning bright for them to return home. The two logs on the grate glowed brightly, but there was no flame. She quickly arranged two more logs on top and pumped the bellows furiously to build fire's flames to guide Samuel home. She ignored the pain of the new calluses and blisters on her hands. Samuel had to be her only thought.

She turned her head to look out the cavernous window. The sun was making its way up into a lavender and coral streaked sky. Their small grandfather clock chimed five times. Samuel left his body hours ago. They should have been back by now. Maybe they couldn't find their way back because she let the fire die down too low.

She frantically pumped the bellows until orange flamed tongues licked and ignited the new wood giving her permission to stop and catch her breath. A sudden downdraft of wind pushed the flames downward and blew bits of ash and embers out into the room. Elizabeth jumped back to avoid the hot embers from landing on her dress. A sudden high pitch whistle of air drew the flames upward and into a swirl. A tickling type humming vibrated her body. Light sliced through the stone of the fireplace illuminating the cottage. They were coming home!

Within the swirl of fiery embers, Elizabeth saw the outline of a luminescent body. It moved quickly past her. It was Samuel. Elizabeth saw a glint of his eyes before his essence used the slivery rope to funnel into his physical body. Samuel's body jolted once, and then it was still. Elizabeth rushed to him.

"Do not touch him."

Elizabeth turned and saw Wakayeja wicahpe. Her face was solemn.

321

"I have to go find Charlotte now. Call his name, but do not touch him until he tells you to," she instructed and then faded.

"Samuel...Samuel..."

Elizabeth saw Samuel's chest lift with breath and then drop down.

"Samuel...Samuel..."

Samuel's chest began to lift and drop, lift and drop. He was breathing.

"Samuel...Samuel...Sam..."

"I'm here...I'm here..." Samuel muttered. His eyes flickered, and then slowly opened. "Give me a moment," he said and closed his eyes. He took a few more deep breaths and opened his eyes again.

"Samuel, are you alright?"

"We got him. Malachai can't bother you anymore," Samuel said with a weak smile.

"Thank you. Thank you. Can I touch you now?"

"Yes, I ..."

Elizabeth leapt at him wrapping her arms around his neck. They fell backward onto a nest of pillows she had placed behind him. She smothered his face with kisses. She had her new life, a man who loved her, and a baby on the way. She had her own family, and Simon had his. Most importantly, Malachai was gone! She didn't need to know the details; she could feel that the even the air had changed.

"I'm so grateful to have you back!" Elizabeth exclaimed. "We shall never speak of him again because we're free; free to live our lives," Elizabeth said and kissed him. When she pulled away, a dust of light flashed between them. Her body trembled and then something interrupted her breath. A searing heat began at her toes, coursed up through her spine, and then her ears popped. Her breath returned.

"What's wrong? Is it the baby?"

Afraid to move, she sat still.

"Elizabeth?" Samuel scrambled to his knees. "Don't move. I'll send for the doctor..."

"Samuel, no—wait." Elizabeth looked at Samuel. A shimmering wavy light surrounded his body. She blinked. The light didn't go away. Something had changed. "You're surrounded by light."

"What?"

"I see light all around you," Elizabeth said. A smile embraced her face. Samuel took a step towards her. "No, wait, don't move." With her next breath, the light vanished. "It's gone," Elizabeth announced with disappointment. "What was that?"

"I'm not sure."

Samuel lifted her from the floor. The dawn of a warm May sun flooded the cavernous window of their carriage house.

"Samuel, look at that sunrise. Our new beginning."

The dawning sun sprayed a coral wash of light across the sky filling their main floor with peace. In the stillness of the morning air, Elizabeth heard the bend and creak of the cherry blossom trees branches and the flitter of their leaves. Was it the dream with her father, or her kiss from Samuel that heightened her senses? A slight buzz cycled through her arms and legs, and then tingled the top of her head. She examined her hands. She wanted to see the wavy light.

"Are you sure I shouldn't get the doctor?"

"Samuel, I feel fine."

"Darling, you must rest. Let's go to bed."

With his arm draped around her shoulder, Elizabeth led her husband to the stairs. He was right that they should rest, but she felt wide awake in a different way. Her head was still buzzing! Her eyes locked on a small arrangement of cherry blossom branches in a vase on the dining table. One branch had unopened flowers. Three unopened flowers blossomed right before her eyes.

"Did you see that?"

"See what?" Samuel asked.

"The flowers on that branch just opened," Elizabeth exclaimed.

"That's what flowers are supposed to do," Samuel replied wearily as they climbed the steps to their cozy bedroom.

Like the cherry blossom flowers, she was opening. With Malachai's threat gone, the range of her powers was blossoming. Her newfound energy animated her. She was ready to start their day but forced herself to lay with Samuel for the sake of their baby.

With Samuel's arm wrapped around her and the baby, Elizabeth rambled on about Charlotte's twin until the hum of her body lulled her to sleep, but not for long.

CHAPTER 48

Three hours of sleep was more than enough. Elizabeth awakened refreshed, clean, with her body buzzing ready to live and fight for love! She wasn't sure if the energy came from kissing Samuel's loving spirit, or if it was already in her and freed by the knowledge of Malachai's containment. All that she knew was she felt alive. The strange buzzing she experienced last night, and the powers that came with it, seemed to have vanished while she slept. She had to rely on her visions and conviction for truth to complete her plan.

After laying awake in bed for an hour watching Samuel
sleep, his eyelashes finally fluttered open. All she needed was to see the whites of his eyes so she could jump out of bed and begin battle for love and unity. Samuel barely had time to dress before he was forced to run after her.

"Elizabeth! We can't just barge in," Samuel called out, trailing behind her as he hopped and struggled to put on his other boot.

"We're not barging in, we're knocking," she replied over her shoulder.

The wrought iron knocker banged against the lion's face. Samuel placed his hands on Elizabeth's hands to stop her from barging in.

"Elizabeth, we should talk about this. You don't know what condition Henry is in."

"Yes, I do. He's miserable."

"He's my employer. He won't take kindly to our meddling."

"He's our dear friend, and you yourself said he already asked you for your expertise. Now I will give him mine," Elizabeth said firmly.

Mr. Twitterly opened the door and glared at Samuel's partially dressed body.

"Is there a fire?"

"Good morning Mr. Twitterly. We're here to see Henry," Elizabeth announced and then pushed past Mr. Twitterly.

"Mrs. Chase. Mrs. Chase!" Mr. Twitterly called out as he scurried after her. "Mr. Chase, may I help you and your wife?"

"There's no time to stand on ceremony. Where is Henry?" Elizabeth demanded.

Mr. Twitterly pressed his lips together.

"We're here to help Mrs. Dennings," Elizabeth explained. "Mr. Twitterly, please. Let's us help."

Mr. Twitterly's eyes watered. He puffed his chest outward and lifted his chin to assume his formal stature.

"I'm sorry, but Mr. Dennings asked not to be disturbed."

"Mr. Twitterly, I can help Mrs. Dennings, but I have to speak with Henry. Where is he? If you don't want to be responsible for me having my baby in your grand foyer, then lead us to him, or I promise I will get so excited my child will be forced to jump from my body. I prevail upon your compassion for Mrs. Dennings and my unborn child," Elizabeth pleaded.

"Mr. Dennings asked not to be disturbed...while he was in the east salon," Mr. Twitterly said without looking at them. "But I don't think you'll find it...I daresay no one has ventured *down the hall past* the library because it is strictly off limits," Mr. Twitterly concluded and then walked away.

"Samuel, I need you to trust me and take me there," Elizabeth pleaded.

Samuel took Elizabeth's hand. They took off down the wide corridor. It was Elizabeth's first time in Barclay. It was as massive on the inside as it appeared on the outside. The clacking of her heels on the marble floors slapped the walls and rang in her ears. As Samuel pulled Elizabeth past Barclay's lavishly decorated rooms, she felt a heaviness pushing down her shoulders. As beautifully appointed as the rooms were, they lacked any kind of life or joy. She wondered if rich people's houses were so big because they needed a place to house all their sadness.

They made their way to the east side of the house. The hall was a tunnel of closed doors. Grief hung in the cool musty air.

"Which door?"

"There's only one way to find out." Samuel pulled her into the darkness. He began opening each door along the way. Behind each door was only more dust and darkness.

"Samuel, look," Elizabeth spotted a pair of brass doorknobs at the end of the hall.

Without knocking, Elizabeth opened the doors. After her eyes adjusted to the darkness, she saw an outline of a body sitting in a chair next to a fireplace.

"Samuel, pull back those drapes," Elizabeth instructed with a pointed finger. She made her way around the ghostly furniture to Henry.

Henry raised his left hand to shield his eyes. The sunlight struck the crystal whiskey glass in his hand shooting prisms around the room. Particles of dust danced about in the light. Over the fireplace was a large painting of Elise Dennings. Dressed in an elegant royal blue velvet ball gown, Elise sat regally in a chair with a young Cassandra standing dutifully next to her.

Elise was a stunning raven-haired beauty. Although obviously older than Elizabeth, Elise conveyed a youthful spirit. Her oval face possessed a joyful glow for life. Elise's crystal blue eyes brought Elizabeth's hand to her heart. They reminded her of Wakayeja wicahpe's eyes, peaceful and full of an indefatigable love.

Elizabeth scanned the room. Henry had turned the east wing into a mausoleum for Elise's life: Elise's royal blue ball gown from the painting was displayed on life-size bodice enclosed in a glass case; another curio case displayed Elise's jewelry; a standing needlepoint lap frame, positioned to the right of a divan, still held an unfinished needlepoint project; and next to a window that over looked the cheery blossom trees was a table with four chairs. Playing cards were arranged on table as though the card game was in progress and frozen in time. She empathized with Charlotte. It would be hard for any woman to compete with Elise's memory.

"Don't you touch her cards. She had a winning hand," Henry grumbled.

Elizabeth went to Henry. the musky scent from his unwashed body greeted her. A week's growth of a beard covered his face making him appear older than his actual age. She stood before him waiting for acknowledgment. He kept his eyes downward, staring into his half-empty glass of liquor. A burp made his head do a slight bob, but he wouldn't look up at her. He lifted his eyes from the floor to stare at the waist of her dress.

"Henry, we're here to help you and Charlotte. We know what we need to do to heal her. Charlotte needs that part of herself that is missing. We need to make her whole."

Henry slowly lifted his hand and reached outward. Elizabeth took his hand. It was clammy and trembled in hers. His shoulders began to shake as he broke into a silent cry.

"We know about Charlotte's twin...and that she is Negro," Elizabeth added softly. When Elizabeth saw his bloodshot eyes, it was clear he had not slept in days. Unshaven and disheveled, Henry looked like he had been locked up in a prison. His right hand pressed against his mouth to contain his cry.

"Henry...we also know that you are Negro," Elizabeth said softly.

"I have feared this very moment since Elise bought me," Henry said with a sigh.

Elizabeth covered her mouth.

"I'm judging from your reaction you didn't have that piece of information...Elise bought me from a plantation in Virginia. She schooled me, taught me how to read and write. Gave me lessons on how to be a gentleman of wealth and prestige, and then married me. I did what I was told because I believed I was still her slave," Henry lamented.

"She loved you."

"Love? I was a slave for seventeen years before she found me. Love was never an option. I have heard stories of Negroes losing their minds once they become free. Slavery forbids love and human decency. I can't relate to any of this. I feel obligation and not love. My soul is torn in two. Do I dare love a woman who bought me like I was a horse, a farm animal, or do I kill her in her sleep and flee. My mind is still trying to answer that question...No one tells us what to do with our rage and hatred. I'm not free. I am not free. I am bound by self-loathing and constant fear of losing my freedom. Can't you understand the madness I am in?"

Thoughts of Patricia bubbled in her mind. Guilt massaged her heart.

"My marriage did not bring me happiness. I have only guilt and shame that my marriage was a betrayal to my own kind," he said, through tears and a messy nose. He dragged the cuff of his sleeve beneath his nose. "How can I reconcile that?"

"Henry, that's not true," Elizabeth uttered between tears. "You are using your position to make a difference, to help free others. Look at what your marriage created: a beautiful, loving, and devoted daughter. Look at all the work that Cassandra is doing. She wouldn't care about helping slaves and free Negroes if it weren't for you. She knows she has the blood of a slave coursing through her body, and she owns every drop of it. You instilled that pride in her. You instilled that fight in her to make things better for slaves and free Negroes."

"Cassandra...she's so beautiful..." Henry broke into a sob.

"Yes, she is and she is a reason why you must forgive yourself and not give up hope. She is hope. You and Elise brought hope into the world", Elizabeth added with a bright smile.

"Charlotte..." Henry whimpered. "Charlotte."

"Yes Henry, we have to help Charlotte."

"I drove her to that madness," Henry blurted.

"No, you did no such thing," Elizabeth pleaded.

"I did. I did the exact thing to Charlotte that Elise did to me." Henry confessed. "The day I ripped Charlotte away from her twin sister was the day I handed her a gun. Can't you see? The grandest house and all the money in the world can't make up for the pain I've caused her. All of this grandeur has done nothing but made me a selfish whore of a man. A bullet can be a welcome alternative." Henry removed a gun from beneath his jacket and placed it at his right temple. "Tell Cassandra I love her..."

"Henry, no!" Elizabeth screamed.

Samuel pounced on Henry to grab the gun knocking him back in his chair. They landed on the floor together, shattering the chair. Samuel quickly thrust his hand outward sending the gun sliding across the carpet beneath a divan and out of reach. Henry scrambled to get the gun. Samuel put Henry in a choke hold.

"Let me die...let me die..."

"Stop with your selfishness! Henry Dennings, you're not the man I thought you were. Cassandra would die of shame to see you wallowing in self-pity and cowardice! Elise risked her life to save yours, to give you a family and the means to take care of them, and you have the audacity to squander it by trying to kill yourself!"

Henry stopped struggling. His body went limp. Samuel released him. On his knees, Henry brought his hands to his face and sobbed.

"Slavery has taken enough. Don't give it your soul. Get up and fight back!" Elizabeth demanded.

Henry looked up at Elizabeth. A strand of saliva connected his lips.

"I think you better do as she says," Samuel said.

Henry's chin and bottom lip quiver. Elizabeth lifted her chin to contain her tears.

"Mr. Dennings, the road of self-pity is a rocky one. You'll find no comfort there. Get up," Elizabeth said firmly.

Henry took Samuel's hand and allowed himself to be pulled up off the floor.

"Now tuck in your shirt and be the gentleman I know you are."

Henry turned to tuck in his shirt.

"That's better. I'll have Mr. Twitterly bring you a pot of hot coffee and a good razor."

"Why are you helping me?"

"Because a White man once helped me. 'You may not find comfort out in the world, but you can find comfort in family.' My father owns those words, and he saved me like Elise saved you. They saved us for a reason. Our journeys have united us and have given us purpose. I consider us family now. As your newly adopted sister and brother, we have come to help you save Charlotte."

"Hannah...Charlotte's sister's name is Hannah Stevens of Lancaster Pennsylvania." Henry exhaled.

CHAPTER 49

Their muddy hands clawed at her white flesh. Charlotte slapped and kicked at them to free herself. They clawed at her ankles, her feet, her arms, and body. She was tired of fighting. She was ready to give up and be swallowed up by the muddy dank cloud that was enveloping her. A muddy hand tugged on her arm; another wrapped around her throat. She couldn't breathe. Her body writhed beneath the sea of hands that were taking her under.

A blast of blinding light suddenly engulfed her. The light had a high-pitched humming sound that made her ears and teeth tickle from its vibration. She saw a woman standing in a tunnel. The woman was glowing.

"Charlotte!" the woman yelled.

Another blast of light hit her body jolting the hands that clawed her. After the third blast of light, the hands retreated into the mud. Charlotte scrambled up from the dank muddy earth and ran towards the woman. Even though the woman stood directly in front of her, all that Charlotte could see was a pink heart that hung from around her neck.

"You are free now. Follow me." The woman took off. Charlotte followed the steps of the woman's moccasins. The woman led Charlotte through what felt like a brick tunnel back to a world she recognized. She tried to catch up to the woman to thank her, but she had disappeared.

When Charlotte looked around, she was standing in front of Independence Hall in Philadelphia. Charlotte saw a familiar mound or soft brown ringlets of hair. It was her sister.

"Hannah? Hannah!" Charlotte called out.

Everyone looked at her. She didn't care. "Hannah!" Charlotte called out. She picked up her pace. People were getting in her way. "Move out of my way! That's my sister. Hannah!"

Charlotte scurried through the street. Hannah turned a corner. Charlotte rushed to catch up with her. Just as Charlotte neared the corner, she slammed into Robert Kincaide.

"Miss Greene, will you be needing my help?" he asked.

"Yes...my sister. I saw my sister. Can you help me reach my sister?" Charlotte asked.

"Where is she?" Robert asked scanning the crowd.

"She's there," Charlotte pointed.

"That Negro woman?"

"Yes, she's my sister," Charlotte declared.

Robert held her shoulders.

"Let no one dictate the love in your heart." He kissed her. "That should keep ya goin' till we meet again. Now, go for it, me lass. Run!"

"Hannah!" Charlotte could still see Hannah's signature mane of dark tight curls as she moved through the crowds. "Hannah! "Hannah!"

Hannah stopped and turned. The surrounding crowds stopped to watch them with disapproving faces. Charlotte's heart pounded against her rib cage.

"If you truly love yourself, you will embrace me and care not what the rest of the world thinks," Hannah said loudly.

Charlotte took her first step, and then bolted into a run. She pushed her way through the disapproving crowds of people and ran into Hannah's arms.

"I love you. I never stopped loving you!" they said together.

***

Charlotte opened her eyes. It was the first time in a long time she dreamt about her sister. Her face was damp from the tears she cried in her dream. She used the edge of her bedding to blot her face. She looked down at the bedding and realized it wasn't hers, neither was the bed. It was small. She was enclosed in a canopy bed surrounded by the drabbest curtain fabric. Had she been kidnapped? Was she being held for ransom? Or worse, had she been sold back into slavery? The last thing she could remember was being at the Logan Inn and having tea with that evil Emma Beckwith... and Robert Kincaide...Robert Kincaide passionately kissed her in her dream. When she went to touch her lips, she noticed her charcoal colored fingers and hands.

What had she done?

A deep snore from outside of her canopy curtain redirected her attention. Her charcoal stained finger slipped between the curtain and post on the right side of her bed. She saw a broad chest woman asleep in a chair next to her bed. Charlotte tried to look at the woman's face, but the woman's head dropped and fell to the right. Her double chin rested on her ample breasts. The woman snorted a few times and then adjusted in her seat. Her hand opened and released a wooden dowel about a yard long that fell against her dress.

Charlotte released the curtain, eased herself up to a sitting position, peeked out the left side of the bed and saw two windows against the far-left wall. She immediately recognized they were attic windows to Barclay. But how did she get up here and why were the windows boarded up? She noticed the crude drawings on the walls and looked at her charcoal stained hands and blackened nails. Gargoyles!

She was the artist, but when? She had no recollection of drawing gargoyles on the walls. The only time in her life she saw gargoyles was in Emma Beckwith's office. When did she get home? How long had she been in the attic? What day was it? Except for her dream of Hannah, and the dream in which she kissed Robert Kincaide, Charlotte couldn't remember anything after her tea with Emma Beckwith.

She had to get answers. She eased her legs over the left side of the bed and then froze. The woman stopped snoring. Charlotte waited and then pushed herself into a standing position and froze. She took her first step, froze, and then three more steps on her tiptoes that delivered her to the foot of her little canopy prison. A coil of rope at the foot of the bed caught her eye.

Had she been tied up? Was she a prisoner in her own home?

"Mrs. Denninks, you're awake." Gerta stood holding the wooden dowel.

"If you touch me, I'll scream."

"Ja, we are used to you screaming. Get back into bed," Gerta ordered extending her stick. Gerta waved the stick at Charlotte like a shepherd herding his sheep. "Back to bed, like a good girl and I won't have to help you. Ja?"

"Keep away from me," Charlotte demanded, trying to move to the door.

"You are a very sick woman."

"I'm feeling just fine. I want my husband. I want a bath," Charlotte demanded. Charlotte tried to run past Gerta, but Gerta's stick caught Charlotte around her midsection and pulled her back, pinning Charlotte against her. "You're hurting me!" Charlotte cried.

"We must call the doctor first," Gerta growled back.

"I don't want to see a doctor!" Charlotte yelled and then bit down hard on Gerta's right hand, forcing Gerta to release the stick. Charlotte began to run, but Gerta snatched a handful of Charlotte's hair and dragged her back to the bed.

"A rich woman who bites like a rabid dog must be caged!" Gerta warned. "Now back into your cage," Gerta yelled and flung Charlotte face first onto the bed.

"I will have you fired!" Charlotte scramble passed Gerta and grabbed the wooden dowel.

"You can't fire me. I work for Mr. Denninks," Gerta replied with a sneer.

"I am Mrs. Denninks!" Charlotte scream mocking her and swung with all of her might.

CHAPTER 50

The ride back from Lancaster was uncomfortably silent. Hannah had no intention of saying a word to them. Hannah's husband, Kenneth Stevens, said very little as well. He refused to allow Hannah to be alone with them. Even after Elizabeth explained they were there to take Hannah to her twin sister, Mr. Stevens still refused to let Hannah out of his sight.

The seven-hour trip was a long and bumpy ride of white knuckles and grim faces. Elizabeth was amazed that although Charlotte and Hannah had different skin colors, they were identical. With the exception of Charlotte's green eyes and Hannah's brown eyes, they mirrored each other physically. Their height, their svelte bodies, their delicate noses, almond-shaped faces and even the ringlet curls of their hair–although Charlotte's hair was black, and Hannah's was soft brown. Elizabeth couldn't help but stare.

Her baby's first kicked made her redirect her attention. She jolted in her seat.

"What's wrong?" Samuel asked.

"Our baby just kicked," Elizabeth announced with a smile. She grabbed his hand and placed it on her stomach. Hannah and her husband stared at their affectionate spectacle and were torn between envy and a necessary stoicism.

Samuel jumped when he felt the baby kicked. His eyes softened with tears. Unable to contain his joy, he promptly kissed Elizabeth hard on her cheek and then grabbed her hand and held it tight and exhaled. The coach remained silent as their bodies swayed with the horses' gallop and the bounce of the carriage.

Elizabeth was about to rest her eyes when she saw Hannah reached for Mr. Stevens' hand. He hesitated to respond, but then cautiously placed his hand over Hannah's. When he thought no one was watching, Mr. Stevens pecked the back of Hannah's hand with a kiss. Elizabeth offered a smile of approval, but they ignored her and focused their attention to the scenery outside the coach with their fingers interlocked and their lips pressed together. There was going to be no polite conversation between the two couples. The small gun in a holster under the right breast pocket of Mr. Stevens' street coat was a strong reminder.

Samuel noticed the gun as Mr. Stevens boarded the carriage. Samuel's trained eye could spot the slightest arsenal bulge beneath a gentleman's clothing. Elizabeth surmised Mr. Stevens probably believed them to be bounty hunters disguised as a couple. Sadly, she would have done the same. Her first day in New York taught her that bounty hunters were ruthless and could be anyone, and anywhere.

The carriage slowed as it made a right turn on Madison Avenue at 36th street in the Murray Hill Section of New York. Elizabeth was grateful they made it back before dark. She wanted the Stevens to see Barclay and how impressive it was. As they made their approach, the horses clacked their way down the private drive. Hannah adjusted cape and gripped her husband's hand. Franz brought the carriage to a halt; a footman opened the door.

"Mr. and Mrs. Chase, Mr. and Mrs. Stevens, welcome," Mr. Twitterly greeted them.

"Mr. Twitterly, we've had a long trip. I'm sure Mr. and Mrs. Stevens would like to freshen up," Samuel said.

"I want to see my sister," Hannah said plainly.

"Mr. Twitterly is Mr. Dennings ready for us?"

"Mr. Dennings is waiting for you in the library. Right this way."

The moment they stepped into the foyer, a clean-shaven Henry was waiting like a dutiful dog. His face was red and his chest was lifted high as though he was holding his breath.

"Hannah!" Henry rushed to greet her.

Hannah stood like a rock in Barclay's foyer and raised her hand to stop him. "Hannah, this is your brother in-law Henry."

"I know who he is," Hannah replied coldly.

"Hannah, thank you for coming all this way," Henry offered with a nervous smile.

"Where is my sister?"

"Mr. Stevens, thank you for accompanying her. My home is your home," Henry stepped forward to greet Mr. Stevens with an open hand. Without warning, Mr. Stevens' right fist landed on Henry's left jaw. Henry went sailing backward. He landed, bottom first, slid, and then came to a stop. His body laid sprawled on the marble floor. Mr. Stevens drew his gun and aimed it at Henry. Franz drew his gun and pressed it against the back of Mr. Steven's head.

"Franz! No! Don't! I deserved it," Henry said sitting up.

"Husband, did you come all this way with me to make me a widow?" Hannah quickly intervened. "If you fire that gun, who will be there to protect me and our child? Please, put the gun away, Both of you!"

"You aren't worth a good bullet," Mr. Stevens said and slid his gun back in its holster.

"I know..."

"You deserve more of a pounding for what you did! When you took Charlotte away, you ripped the love they had for each other right from their hearts. You almost killed Hannah!"

"Gentlemen, control yourselves." Samuel warned.

Henry stood up, holding his jaw. "Hannah, if you'd let me explain,"

"You have nothing to explain to me. I want to see my sister," Hannah demanded.

"Let her see her sister and spare her your nauseating excuses. You owe them that much," Mr. Stevens said snidely.

"I could only save one. Don't you understand? I could only save one! If I had bought them both, I would have killed us all. People would have seen Charlotte was Negro. There would have been no way I could have married Charlotte and given her this kind of life," Henry contested.

"Coward! I married Hannah without a care to the law."

"Does she bare your name in public? Henry volleyed back.

"We have to make the necessary adjustments, but I am not afraid or ashamed to be with her or have her by my side."

"Gentlemen, please. We must not turn against each other. A very wise Indian chief, by the name of Red Eagle, came to me and gave me the most valuable wisdom. He said if we fight amongst ourselves, we will only aid slavery not end it. We must work together.

Focus on what we are doing today, right now, and not the past. We can't change the past. I beseech you, you Mr. Stevens..."

"He's guilty, too," Mr. Stevens whined, pointing a finger at Henry.

"I was told Hannah would be safe. He told me he'd find a husband for Hannah. After what he did for me, I had faith she would be safe," Henry explained. "I received word months later, that Hannah was married and safe. I didn't know to whom, but I knew Charlotte and I could go forth with our life, but she didn't want one without Hannah. Can't you understand the risk involved."

"All I understand is if it wasn't for Jonathan Beeson, Hannah would be lost in some overseer's field,. You'll get no sympathy from me."

"Did you say Jonathan Beeson?" Elizabeth exclaimed.

"Yes. Mr. Beeson stole me away in the middle of the night," Hannah said. "I was about to be delivered to my new master in payment of a gambling loss. Do you know of Mr. Beeson?"

"Who doesn't know of Jonathan Beeson? He was a daring man who stared down the face of slavery when others were too afraid to speak up. He was a true abolitionist!" Mr. Stevens proclaimed. "He swooped down, in the dead of night, to snatch slaves and carry them to freedom. They called him the Black Bird. Quaker or Christian, that was a man I respected, which is more than what I can say for the likes of you Mr. Dennings. Even a wolf knows not to separate its young..."

"Jonathan Beeson was my father," Elizabeth announced.

"What? You're Elizabeth Beeson I thought your surname was Chase?" Mr. Stevens asked bewildered.

"It is. Beeson is my maiden name before I married Samuel. We're Quakers."

"And we're also Blackbirds," Samuel interjected.

Samuel stepped forward, removed his coat, rolled up his sleeve and revealed his tattoo. Samuel gave Henry and Franz a nod to reveal their tattoos.

"What is this?"

"We're continuing my father's legacy."

"Not him! He's not fit to stand next to Jonathan Beeson," Mr. Stevens growled aiming an angry finger at Henry. "I am a Christian and will not judge a man lest ye be judge; but, you, Mr. Dennings are not a man!"

"It was Jonathan Beeson who told me Hannah would be safe. He was the one who told me he would find Hannah a husband. I listened and took orders from the lips of Jonathan Beeson."

"Mr. Stevens, would you continue to condemn Mr. Dennings for honoring my father's words? As a Christian, you know that forgiveness is a mandatory component. None of us are perfect. We have all made mistakes when we thought we were doing the right thing. I beg of you to forgive Mr. Dennings. Please trust me when I say, there is no suffering or punishment you could administer to him that he has not already taken on," Elizabeth countered.

Mr. Stevens hung his head for a moment.

"How can I ever trust him? Or any of you for that matter? Blackbirds or not, with the exception of my wife and her sister, we are all White Americans. We're above reproach. Our freedom is guaranteed. How do I know Mr. Dennings, or anyone of you, won't endeavor to profit from the lives of the Negro, free or enslaved?"

"Mr. Stevens, truthfully you're the only White man present," Elizabeth responded.

"What do you mean?" Mr. Stevens exclaimed. His eyes roamed their faces.

"We're all descendants of slaves," Elizabeth confessed.

"I don't believe you. Are all of you Negroes?" Mr. Stevens asked bewildered. He searched their faces and hands for evidence.

"Except for me; I'm Gypsy." Franz announced.

"Because of people like my father, we're free. Unless you decide to expose us," Elizabeth said.

"It would be a blaspheme against my soul," Mr. Stevens declared.

"Hannah?... Am I dreaming again?"

Gasps filled the foyer. Charlotte emerged from behind Franz. She was in her nightgown, dirty, barefoot, hair askew but alert. The vibrancy of her green eyes had returned, and quickly filled with tears.

"Charlotte? What have they done to you?" Hannah blurted.

Hannah unbuttoned her cape and immediately wrapped it around her sister to cover her. The vision of the barefoot woman in her nightgown running up Fifth Avenue came to Elizabeth's mind; it was a premonition about the miracle of love before her.

Hannah and Charlotte clung to each other weeping. There were no words. Their muffled cries reverberated in the grand foyer of Barclay reminding Elizabeth of her purpose, and as she would quickly learn, her challenges...

***

The men were standing for Hannah to leave the table. Elizabeth wanted to take advantage of Charlotte's gratuitous absence. She was relieved that the removal of charcoal required a lengthy bath, because Charlotte would never allow Elizabeth to be alone with her sister. A tandem visit to the water closet was the perfect opportunity to enlist Hannah's support for unity.

Before the men could sit, Elizabeth popped up out of her chair with a smile, laid her napkin next to her plate, and followed Hannah as quickly as she could—without appearing that she was chasing her. Samuel's eyes followed her until she gave him a slight nod that all was well.

Once outside of the dining room, their heels clicked and clacked against the marble hallway floor in unison. As Elizabeth tried to catch up with Hannah, she decided she would begin her conversation about their pending motherhood. It was the logical and least threatening subject.

Elizabeth wanted to catch Hannah before Hannah reached the water closet, which was located near the hub of the kitchen. She wanted their conversation to be private and avoid the eyes and ears of the Barclay staff. However, Hannah continued down the hall without looking back.

"Mrs. Stevens, may I walk with you?" Elizabeth called out hoping to slow Hannah down.

"You are walking with me," Hannah said without looking back, and then turned the corner and disappeared into the water closet. Elizabeth stood away from its door, waiting for it to open.

"Are you in need of something, mum?" Ava asked standing in an opened kitchen door. She held a crystal decanter of wine on a silver tray. The clanging of pots and pans and rustling of silverware and busy bodies in the kitchen spilled into the hallway.

"No, thank you. I am waiting," Elizabeth pointed to the water closet door.

"Begging your pardon, mum, but if it is urgent, you can use the staff's. It's nothing fancy, but it will serve you just the same."

"Thank you, but I will wait."

"Suit yourself." Ava disappeared through a servant's door to the dining room.

The kitchen activity filled the awkward silence as she waited for Hannah to emerge. Two more servants appeared and disappeared before Elizabeth heard the gush of water as it coursed through the plumbing in the walls. Hannah opened the door, shared a faint smile, and tried to walk past her.

"Mrs. Stevens, congratulations on your bundle of joy. You and I have that in common," Elizabeth offered with a smile. Hannah continued walking away. "Mrs. Stevens, may I have a word?" Hannah spun around with an angry glare that was reminiscent of her encounters with Patricia. "I know you don't wish to speak with me…"

"Yet, Mrs. Chase, you still insist on trying to do so."

"I understand you believe there are differences between us," Elizabeth began with a shaky voice.

"Do you?"

"Well… I can't truly imagine what you've had to endure…"

"On that you are correct," Hannah quipped.

"Please, I only want to help."

"Please? Please? You think because you have escaped slavery, that you can please me? That you can make a difference in the lives of those who are still chained and suffering?"

"Mrs. Stevens, I truly believe if we all work together…"

"My people are enraged!" Hannah growled. When you beat a dog with one hand, don't try to pet it with the other. You will get bitten. The White hand is one we've been taught not to trust, so you will forgive me if I feel the need to bark and bite to protect me and mine."

"But I am Negro, like you."

"No, you are not like me. When you walk outside that door, you are a White woman. Your appearance does not draw looks of contempt. You are not denied the simplest civility. You are free to breathe as you wish; free to move about without blue eyes riding your back like a tick on a dog. You, Mrs. Chase, are not tracked like a wild animal because of the bounty on your head, while at the same time you are made to feel absolutely worthless…"

THE ORACLE FILES: ESCAPE

"Mrs. Stevens, please, I..."

"There's that word again, please. You do not please me. Your presence brings me discomfort and erupts fear that I must mind my words; watch my breath, and my back. In my eyes, you are White and are responsible for the theft of millions of my people, whose bodies you have pounded into your soil. You have used the dust of their bones to fertilize the fields of your plantations.

"But you're married to Mr. Stevens, a White man..."

"And he is the only White man I am forced to trust if I am going to breathe this air."

"Can you not see I am like your sister?"

"You are not my sister."

"What about your baby?"

"I will love my baby, Negro or White, because my baby will be from my blood—just like Charlotte. The White slave traders may have removed us from our homeland, stripped us of our family and freedom, but we own the blood that is in our body."

"Mrs. Stevens, if we allow our anger to blind us, we will never be able to see a solution."

Hannah grabbed Elizabeth's hand and pulled her into the water closet. Once inside, Hannah turned her back to her.

"Unbutton me," Hannah ordered. She scooped and lifted a mound of her soft brown ringlets into her hand for Elizabeth to access the buttons at the base of her neck. Elizabeth's eye scanned the row of small buttons that trailed down Hannah's spine.

"I...I don't understand."

"Undo my bodice!"

With both the hoops of their dresses pushing and fighting against the other to gain space, they were forced to reposition themselves. Elizabeth's fingers fumbled as she unbuttoned five buttons and stopped.

"Keep going," Hannah ordered.

Elizabeth continued extricating buttons from their holes until she reached the middle of Hannah's back.

"Stop," Hannah said.

When Elizabeth lifted her head, she saw scarred skin peeking out from between Hannah's shoulder blades.

"Open it."

341

"I'm so sorry..."

"Open it..."

Elizabeth peeled opened the back of her bodice. Hannah's skin had the scored stamp of a whip. The scars crossed each other. In one area, the skin on her back was a pile of scars. Hannah's wound was deeper than Elizabeth could ever understand.

Hannah spun around and looked Elizabeth directly in the eye.

"You still want to talk to me about forgiveness?" Hannah's full lips were pressed together in angry solidarity.

Hannah's scars had assaulted her senses. There was no place to run. Elizabeth's body tightened from horror, squeezing tears from her eyes that created dark spots on her linen smock.

"Forgive me. Please, forgive me."

Without another word, Hannah turn her back on Elizabeth, and hoisted a mound full of ringlets above her neck. Elizabeth quickly went to work. Her fingers trembled and stumbled over the fifteen buttons as she forced them back into their holes to cover Hannah's pain. Water trickling through the bathroom plumbing filled the silence between them. Once Elizabeth was done, Hannah faced her. Elizabeth's shoulders hunched upwards in preparation of another emotional blow.

"Anger is the only other thing White masters can't take away from us. Mr. Stevens told me that millions of my people have been stolen, taken from our homeland. He said our lost souls can fill the night sky like stars. I don't know how to count to a million, do you?

"The deed has been done, and we will never forget. If you have a drop of Negro blood, as you claim, you should never forget either," Hannah declared. The water closet door released a soft squeak as Hannah opened it. She paused in its doorway. Elizabeth kept her eye on Hannah's soft mound of brown ringlets. She held her breath and waited for Hannah to speak, but she would not turn around.

"Mrs. Chase, if you think you can change the minds of White masters, end slavery, and the slaughter of my people you are insane...insanely courageous. Just remember one thing. Your tears will be a useless commodity," Hannah warned. Without looking back, Hannah's mound of ringlets disappeared through the door, which then closed, sealing the memory of their exchange.

"Puuuuuuhhhh!"

Hannah's brutal vision of reality severely wounded Elizabeth's heart and confidence. She had to accept that slavery would remain a hateful stain on the cloth of humanity. The sight of the gruesome scars on Hannah's back flashed before her. Her stomach twisted into a nauseous knot. She spun around and lowered her face down into the copper sink. A few dry heaves, released throat stinging bile.

She twisted the tap on the faucet. The faucet sputtered and cool water came out in a thin stream carrying her bile down into the drain. This was her first attempt at unity, and she was already sick to her stomach. She splashed her mouth and then turn off the tap. She lifted her face from the sink to reach for a hand towel, that was part of a small pyramid of towels on a narrow wall shelf.

As she dried her hands and blotted her wet mouth, she wondered why she didn't intuitively see Hannah's vicious beating? She should have been able to see it when she first laid eyes on Hannah in Lancaster. Why was it unveiled to her in the most horrifying manner? Had she known, she would have never approached Hannah in such an insensitive manner.

The vision of Hannah's brutal scars popped into her mind again and forced Elizabeth's face back to the sink to release her disgust. Her throat was now raw from the bitterness of her bile. She frantically twisted the tap back on, and her fingers slapped at the stream sending splashes of water around the sink's bowl to cleanse it.

She then cupped handfuls of water to rinse her mouth and twisted the tap off to stop the noxious sulfur odor from filling the water closet. The water's sulfur odor coupled with its metallic taste only accentuated the bitterness of slavery. She spat in the sink to get rid of the taste. She had tasted this hatred before-Malachai! Her head popped up.

The image of a White woman was staring back at her in a small oval gilded mirror that hung over the sink. Her hand reached up to touch the woman's face. It was hers. There was no denying it, her skin held the

343

slightest hue of butter when it was freshly made. She was White and a threat in the eyes of her people.

Her attempt to escape with Simon, Belinda, and her baby must have appeared as another kidnapping of Negroes. She thought she was playing a role, but to Malachai, she was a 'real' White woman abducting his people.

Chief Red Eagle warned her about the consequences of fighting within one's race. If Malachai and Hannah saw her as a threat, so would others. She angrily swiped at her damp mouth with the hand towel and tossed it into the sink. Circling in front of the sink, she tried to collect her thoughts. The hem of her skirt *swished* against the floor with every turn. She didn't know where to go, what to feel, or what to do.

Swish thwack. The hem of her skirt knocked against the wall's baseboard. She twisted her body just enough to make her skirt's hem hit the baseboard again. *Swish thwack*. Her truth was still there. .

No matter how she appeared to the world, and how her own people treated her, she knew she was Negro. She had physical evidence that no one could ever alter or get her to deny. She lifted the hem of her skirt and moved her fingers along its stitching until she reached its side seam. Two fingers rubbed a little bulge that was secured inside the hem. Her owl eye marble was safe.

The house fire taught her the importance of keeping her only possession in a safe place—with her. Using the hem and the side seam of all her dresses and skirts, she created a little secret pocket to house her marble, so she would never lose it.

No one knew of her secret, not even Samuel. While she knew Samuel loved her dearly and would have been very understanding, she didn't want him to view her as foolish for caring so much about an inanimate object. Only she, and the mouse that rolled the marble to her that night, understood the marble's significance.

It was her first possession, and now it was evidence of her life as a slave. It represented her bondage and her freedom; her losses and triumphs; her love for Samuel; and her last emotional bridge to Simon and Willie. She marveled how such a small insignificant piece of glass could hold such power. The moment she claimed that marble, was the moment she dared to claim a life for herself and her future children.

She used two fingers to press on both sides of the fabric to squeeze the marble out of its hiding place. It sat in the palm of her hand with the pair of owl eyes looking up at her. Her right index finger rolled it back and forth in her palm to make it blink. It's simple entertainment still fascinated her. A few more blinks and she was ready to return it to its secret compartment.

Her moment of childlike play brought a bit of clarity about her life. As she pushed the marble back into its hole, she realized God gave her the blood of a slave and the skin of a White woman to create unity—within herself. If she couldn't do it for herself, how could she lead others. She lowered the hem of her skirt to the floor, looked in the mirror, and sighed. She looked the same but felt different—tired.

Her father's wisdom echoed in her mind.

"The fiercest warrior, man will ever meet, is a mother bear. Nothing can stop her from protecting her cubs. If she catches you, she'll tear your limbs off and gut your bowels, and she does that just to make a point. Man can only hope he has one impeccable shot, or he has the feet of Hermes to outrun the mother bear—which is not likely."

"Cheek se ya," Elizabeth said without thinking. Her brow furrowed. *"Cheek se ya?"*

"Cheek se ya," Wakayeja wicahpe echoed.

"Oh!" Elizabeth jumped, spun around, and saw Wakayeja wicahpe sitting on top of the wooden commode cover. Elizabeth covered her heart with her left hand and the swell of her belly with her right."This is a private place. You're supposed to knock," Elizabeth admonished.

"I have no doors."

"Then you're supposed to clear your throat to announce your arrival.

Wakayeja wicahpe, stood, cleared her throat and smiled.

"It's too late, I know you're here, but I *don't* know what those words mean."

"You spoke words of the Lakota people. 'Cheek se ya' means, 'I remember you'."

"I spoke your language?"

"Yes, and very good."

"But I am not Indian."

"You are more than this moment. Your soul can be many things. I was a mouse once." Wakayeja wicahpe began. **"I gave you the marble you hide inside your dress. If I can be an**

345

Itukala, you can be Indian."

"You were the mouse?"

"A very smart one. Your mother's hatred was so dark. Only the eyes of waksica could guide you through the darkness that surrounded you. That is why Malachai was able to find you. You were the light in his darkness."

'No, I was a soldier. That's why he came after me? How do I know this?"

"You are remembering."

"So I was a soldier—a White soldier?

"You were a White soldier, and I was Malachai's sister. You tried to protect me from being captured by soldiers."

"Did I succeed?"

"No, the other soldiers killed us all."

"Malachai blamed me for his death?"

"Yes, but now he blames me, too."

"How am I able to remember that? It's so strange."

"Your mind is opening? You must be careful. It can be very dangerous to know too much about a life lived before. It can make you... witko tko ke– make your mind not right.

"You mean, crazy?"

"Yes.

"So I was a White soldier and an Indian."

"And more."

"Did you and Red Eagle have a life together?"

"Yes."

"Was he your husband?"

"No, I was not allowed to take a husband. I was a healer, but I was not liked...because I was a woman. In my village, there was one man who thought he should be the only holy man."

"But Red Eagle decided against that, didn't he? I saw the way he looked at you when he was here."

"His decision was not a good one. His heart still battles with his choice."

"I'm so sorry." Elizabeth felt the heaviness in Wakayeja wicahpe's words. Evidently, spirits can have issues too. Elizabeth felt like the intruder now. She had barged into Wakayeja wicahpe and Red Eagle's

346

past with her questions and observations. She needed to make a quick escape. "When I was an Indian, was I healer like you?"

"That is for you to remember."

"Why are you not allowed to tell me who I am?"

"Because that would be cheating. A little help is allowed, but free will is the true way. If you want to remember you will."

"Did I choose to be who I am?"

"Free will gives us choice. You chose a life with great purpose."

"I did?"

"Tunkasila, Great Spirit, does not give such gifts to be tossed like seeds to the wind. All that you do has great purpose."

Elizabeth grew silent.

"What good am I if the very people I'm supposed to help hate me?"

"Oh ya hey he. You need a bigger marble. There! I will make that your new marble," Wakayeja wicahpe announced pointing to the mirror hanging over the sink.

Wakayeja wicahpe closed her eyes, raised her right hand, palm out, as though she was trying to stop something. Her left hand gripped her pink heart. Light began to flow from her palm toward the mirror. It looked like the wavy silvery rope that connected Samuel to his physical body.

Elizabeth felt a surge of energy entered her feet. It moved quickly through her body as it vibrated its way up to the top of her head tickling her teeth. A high pitch sound filled her ears.

"Iiiiiiiiiiiiiiing…"

It reminded her of the vibrational sound of Mr. Harrison's desk bell at The Astor House Hotel. The bell still continued to ring in her ear long after his finger tapped it. Or maybe it was more like the high pitch buzz of a mosquito.

When Wakayeja wicahpe dropped her hand, Elizabeth's ears popped. The light and the tingling sensation ended. Everything looked hazy, like she was standing in a mist after a summer rain. Her right hand immediately cradle her stomach to check on her baby, who quickly responded with a heel against the palm of her hand.

Wakayeja wicahpe moved to the mirror to examine it. Her right

347

hand passed over its glass surface a few times..

"It feels good."

"What did you do?"

"I blessed it with the truth. Only your eyes will see the truth it offers. But, the truth is a very sharp arrow in your world. Be careful how you load your bow. If you load it with vengeance, you can pierce your own skin before you have a chance to release it. You will do well. Oh ya hey he."

"Oh ya...hey he? Elizabeth repeated.

"You can do it." Wakayeja wicahpe faded.

Elizabeth stood staring at the mirror for a full minute before she made her approached. Instinctively, she knew she shouldn't do what she was about to do, but she was still a shopkeeper's daughter.

She cautiously raised a finger to touch the mirror. The glass was neither hot nor cold. It felt and looked like a regular mirror. She leaned over the sink to examine it up close. She found several fine surface scratches on its glass and a few tiny nicks on its gold frame. Her right index finger lifted for the final test. With her fingernail, she gently scraped at the mirror's gold paint. It flaked.

The mirror responded to her touch with a flash of light forcing Elizabeth to jump back. The flash was followed by a small stream of light that projected out into the water closet. It produced hundreds of tiny dancing prisms that covered every surface of the space. Elizabeth's eyes scanned the walls, the ceiling, and the floor delighting in the magic of Wakayeja wicahpe's love. It made her giddy.

"Give everyone a mirror. Help them to see..."

"Poppa?"

"Give everyone a mirror, so they can see..."

Her thoughts went to the mirrors that surrounded Andrej's camp. *"Think only what you want to bring to life, and then bless the mirror with it."*

They used Andrej's secret to stop Malachai. Why not use Andrej's secret to abolish slavery? Her fight with Julius VanCleef popped into her mind. They could sell beautiful gilded mirrors to slave owners that will reflect their hateful truth back at them.

"Be careful how you load your bow." Wakayeja wicahpe's warning echoed in her thoughts. She needed to come up with the perfect thought, one that is not filled with anger or vengeance. Otherwise, her intention will

348

backfire. She would pray for the right words. Once she found the words, she would bless the every mirror with it—just like Wakayeja wicahpe did!

"Iiiiiiiiiiiiiing..." The mirror responded to her thoughts.

The little dancing prisms were now pulsating and emitting a humming vibration that tickled her teeth. She pressed her hands against her lips to contain her squeals of excitement and to keep her teeth from falling out of her mouth.

"Iiiiiiiiiiiiiing..."

She felt the pulse of the light as it moved through her body to the top of her head. Her teeth began to chatter.

"Iiiiiiiiiiiiiing..."

She believed the light was beckoning her to touch it. She placed her right hand into the stream of light. It died. Her new marble had rejected her.

"No no no no no!" She rushed to the mirror. "Come back. Please come back." She was about to touch the glass, when a small bubble-like orb appeared. She stepped back. This time she would not interfere. Her eyes followed the orb as it floated and bobbed inside the mirror. Moments later, another orb appeared. Elizabeth covered her mouth.

She watched the two orbs float and bob inside the mirror. Five more appeared and they did a bobbing dance inside the mirror. She joined their dance with a side to side waltz of her own—until the first orb popped revealing a letter. The other orbs quickly followed spelling a name that would change her world forever:

L ... I ... N ... C ... O ... L ... N .

"Oh wa key he!" Elizabeth exclaimed and slapped her hand over her mouth. She had no idea what she said, but it felt right.

MASHERI CHAPPELLE

Visit www.myportalstar.com to learn more about the author other stories.

CPSIA information can be obtained
at www.ICGtesting.com
Printed in the USA
LVHW041001290919
632606LV00001B/92